Bonny Kate

Bonny Kate

Pioneer Lady

Many Blessings !
Mark Strength

Mark Strength

To order additional copies of this book, contact:
Xlibris Corporation
1-888-795-4274
www.Xlibris.com
Orders@Xlibris.com
38983

Contents

Chapter 1:   Over the Mountains 7

Chapter 2:   Watauga Bound 16

Chapter 3:   In a Far Country 26

Chapter 4:   Panic on the Frontier 31

Chapter 5:   One Fateful Day 38

Chapter 6:   The Hero's Reward 48

Chapter 7:   Sweet Lips 55

Chapter 8:   The Captive Community 60

Chapter 9:   Washday 69

Chapter 10:   The Birthday Party 78

Chapter 11:   The Sherrills Find a Home 83

Chapter 12:   Mrs. Sevier's Homecoming 93

Chapter 13:   The Housewarming 99

Chapter 14:   Confessions 105

Chapter 15:   The Beauty and the Beast 111

Chapter 16:   The Snow Baby 120

Chapter 17:   Trouble with Tories 129

Chapter 18:   The Beloved Woman 139

Chapter 19:   The Words of the Beloved Woman 153

Chapter 20:   The Spring Gathering 166

Chapter 21:   Plum Grove 176

Chapter 22:   Daisy Fields 188

Chapter 23:   Liberty and Justice for All 201

Chapter 24:   Never a Dull Moment 211

Chapter 25:   Game Day 225

Chapter 26:   The Dreaded Pox 238

Chapter 27:   The Attack at Sherrill's Station 252

Chapter 28:   An Angel Flies Home 263

Chapter 29:   The Night of Lamentations 268

Chapter 30:   The Days of Mourning 273

Chapter 31:   The Childcare Problem 278

Chapter 32:   A State of Emergency 288

Chapter 33:   Something Needs to be Done 293

Chapter 34:   The Horse Traders 300

Chapter 35:   The Hunted Man 309

Chapter 36:   Colonel Shelby Calls 316

Chapter 37:   Virginia Sends an Army 322

Chapter 38:   An Important Conversation Interrupted 331

Chapter 39:   The Triumph of the Matchmakers 337

Chapter 40:   Courting Bonny Kate 345

Epilogue 353

Chapter 1

Over the Mountains

A solitary Conestoga wagon rumbled along the narrow forest trail behind the plodding team of four oxen. Sam Sherrill, the driver, walking beside the oxen, directing their progress, looked ahead through the dark green forest beneath majestic trees standing as they had since creation. Sam, the experienced hunter, saw a vast range for every kind of useful game animal. A rider appeared in a glade some distance ahead. Sam breathed a sigh of relief and turned to his fair companion, his wife of twenty-nine years, riding on the front board of the big wagon.

"Mary, I told her not to ride so far ahead. She's going to stumble into an ambush of Indians or highwaymen or worse!"

"Sam, who is going to tangle with as tough a customer as that one?"

The rider, straight and tall on a powerful horse, did not appear vulnerable and gave no hint of femininity. Dressed in her father's hunting shirt and deerskin breeches with a rifle resting across her lap, she looked for all, the world, like a fit and well-seasoned long hunter. Her sharp blue eyes peered from beneath a broad-brimmed black felt hat. Only closer examination could reveal a feminine brow, graceful nose, high cheekbones, and thin lips. Her raven hair, tied back under the hat, cascaded down her back. A young woman of remarkable beauty was thus cleverly disguised. In addition to her healthful, athletic constitution, she possessed a beautiful smile, a sense of humor, an intelligent curiosity, and a love of song and dance.

Mary continued, "Don't forget, she is your most enthusiastic supporter in this enterprise."

"Aye, she's that!" Sam replied.

"She's so much like her Granny Sherrill," Mary observed.

"She's one to watch out for," he agreed.

The wagon rolled into the glade where the buckskin-clad girl waited, and Sam stopped the oxen.

"Papa, this glade would make a pleasant camp if you want to make an early stop."

"No, Katie, I want to push on," Sam replied.

"Well, sir," she said, pointing down the trail with the muzzle of her long rifle, "a mile farther are some men setting up a camp."

"What sort of men? Did they see you?"

"No, sir. They are gentlemen, finely dressed. Not like the shirt men we have seen before, but still, well armed." She watched her father's face, reading the subtle lines. She was good at discerning what he was thinking. She admired his honest expression and dearly loved the features of his kind face.

"Find Adam and the two of you ride up there and ask if the gentlemen would let us camp nearby. Use good judgment now. Make sure the men are respectable."

"Yes, sir. Are the boys close?" She looked in the direction they had come.

"Close enough for me to hear the cowbells," Sam replied.

Kate Sherrill turned her horse and galloped back along the trace.

"Mary, this may be an interesting night. If these men are from the Watauga settlement, we can learn much about what lies ahead." Sam started the team again, and the wagon lurched forward.

"How far is Watauga, Sam?" Mary asked.

"I can't tell. It seems as though these mountains go on forever," her husband replied.

Moments later two riders raced up behind them. Kate's horse was clearly leading when they passed the wagon in the glade.

"Slow down, children!" Sam shouted after them.

Katie and her brother Adam raced along the forest trail. Eighteen-year-old Adam never liked being bested by his sister, but her four years of seniority always gave her the edge. A small creek crossed the trail, and Katie stopped to let her horse drink. Adam joined her a moment later.

"Are we close to the camp?" Adam asked.

"Yes, they are set up on the next creek." She looked all around, listening like a wary hunter. When the horses had finished drinking, they rode on cautiously.

Adam was blue eyed and black haired like his sister and quite handsome. He was broad shouldered and well suited for a day's work on the farm. He was a practical young man, polite, and serious, patiently enduring the whims of romantic imagination that often swept over his sister. Adam saw things as they were, while she dreamed of big possibilities. Nine children in all, six boys and three girls made up the Sherrill clan, but only six of the children had made the journey. Twenty-eight-year-old Samuel Junior was the eldest and managed the herd of cattle on the trail behind the wagon. Katie's married sister, Susan, had stayed behind at Sherrill's Ford, North Carolina, with two of her brothers—John, age twenty, and Uriah, nineteen—to keep safe the family's herd of horses until the Sherrills could find a suitable farm in the west. The other children employed by Sam Junior in various herding activities were William, age seventeen; Mary Jane, sixteen; and George, who was fourteen.

"I wonder who they are," she mused. "They could be Indian traders returning with valuable furs or surveyors looking at new lands. Maybe they are commissioners appointed by the governor to make a peace treaty with the Indians."

"Or Tory spies sent to infuriate the Indians against the settlers," Adam answered, "so you better let me do the talking. They'll think you're a man if you keep your mouth shut and your rifle at the ready."

"Don't worry about me. I'll conduct myself as I see fit," she retorted.

Four men worked at setting up camp in the forest clearing. The late-afternoon sun illuminated the young riders as they entered the clearing. A tall portly man with graying temples looked up at their approach.

"We've got company," he said, and his men moved instinctively to pick up their hunting rifles. When the riders were close, he addressed them. "Good evening! Where're you fellows headed?"

"Good evening, sir," Adam responded politely. "We are bound for Watauga settlement. Can you tell us how far that is?"

"I'd make that three or four days at an easy pace. Mighty fine-looking horses you have there."

"Thank you, sir. Maryland bloodlines but North Carolina bred. My name is Adam Sherrill, and we're looking for a likely place to camp for the night."

"Adam Sherrill is a name I know," the leader said. "There was a man of that name in Augusta County, Virginia. His wife's name was Betsy. But that was almost thirty years ago."

"You knew our grandparents!" Katie exclaimed. The men all looked at her as she spoke with a voice that betrayed her disguise. "Adam and Betsy Sherrill were our grandparents. Sam Sherrill is our father."

"Well, I'm pleased to know you; but, ma'am, you surprised me. I didn't know you were a lady," said the stranger, removing his hat. The other men did likewise.

"This is my sister, Kate," Adam said. "Our parents are close behind and looking for a place to camp." Adam was always one to remember his business.

"Then, by all means, join us. I should like to catch up on how the Sherrills have fared in the years since I knew them." The stranger and his companions seemed to be the right sort of men and less tense after seeing that Kate and her brother posed no apparent threat.

"Sir, could we be privileged to know your name?" Kate inquired.

"Oh, excuse me, miss. I'm Colonel John Carter, of the Watauga district; and this is Mr. John Haile, Mr. George Russell, and Mr. Charles Robertson."

"Thank you, sir! We'll be back directly." She wheeled about her high-spirited horse and dashed back the way they had come, with Adam close behind.

"So you know them?" Mr. Haile asked.

"I know something of the family," Carter replied, watching the way they had gone.

"Could they threaten our mission? Many lives depend on our success." Charles Robertson wanted to know.

"The Sherrills I knew were sensible people," replied the colonel. "I sure hope they are not Tories, but we'll keep an eye on them just the same."

"I thought for sure that girl was a feller." Mr. Haile laughed.

"She sure surprised me," replied Colonel Carter.

It wasn't long before the big Conestoga rolled into the clearing behind the four oxen. The Sherrill family went right to work, hobbling the horses, feeding, and securing the livestock. Sam walked across the clearing to greet Colonel Carter. Kate accompanied her father. She always liked watching the men conduct themselves. It was an education for a girl interested in the events of the world around her.

"Colonel Carter, I'm Sam Sherrill," he began. "Thank you for letting us share your camp." The men shook hands warmly but each with eyes that studied the other for signs of danger.

"It's my pleasure, Mr. Sherrill. I was hoping you could tell me all the news from the east." Colonel Carter seemed sincere to Kate when he smiled at her. She was reassured by his remembrance of her grandparents.

Sam paused then answered carefully, "I'm afraid, sir, my news is not very current. We have been on the trace through the mountains for over a month. But I can tell you about the condition of our community of Sherrill's Ford on the Catawba at the time we left, if you and your men would join us for dinner."

"Mr. Sherrill, your hospitality is most generous. We accept your kind offer." Colonel Carter smiled again, and Kate decided she liked the man. Her judgments about the quality of men were usually accurate. The two men each returned to their camp tasks leaving her standing in the middle of the clearing to study the four men from Watauga.

"Katie!" Mrs. Sherrill called to her daughter. Kate turned toward her. "Come, help me with the dinner. Your father has invited the men to join us."

"Yes, Mama," Kate replied, and she moved quickly to comply. She was always quick at her tasks and moved to each one, in turn, with purpose and energy. When the dinner was, at last, nearly ready, buckskin-clad Kate climbed into the wagon and opened a trunk. She pulled out a linen dress and quickly changed into it. She pulled out the ribbon that tied back her silken hair and let it fall loosely around her shoulders. Tonight she would be resplendent in the fullness of her beauty. It had been many weeks since she had seen gentlemen such as these. These were good men, perhaps great men, and powerful, no doubt landed men of great influence. The thought crossed her mind that the men were somewhat older than she, but older men have sons, don't they? Of course they do!

"Katie, where are you? It's time to call the gentlemen to dinner."

"Here I am, Mother." Kate emerged from the wagon and gracefully climbed down to the ground. She joined her mother at the cook fires. "So everything is ready for our guests?"

"I'm taking up the biscuits now. Call the gentlemen," her mother replied.

"Yes, ma'am." Kate crossed the clearing to Colonel Carter's camp. She loved summer evenings. A verdant coolness settled over the forest, with hours of daylight still to enjoy. Kate found Colonel Carter sitting on the ground leaning against his saddle, writing in a journal. "Colonel Carter, sir, dinner is ready."

Colonel Carter looked up at the beautiful girl and quickly put away his writing; and standing, he replied, "Yes, ma'am, have we met?"

"Yes, sir, we met this afternoon. I'm Kate Sherrill."

"Miss Sherrill, you have surprised me again! You were not so nicely made up when we met earlier." Colonel Carter looked at her admiringly as his companions joined him.

"Oh, I thought I'd dress for dinner to honor our distinguished guests." Her blue eyes communicated the humor of her miraculous transformation. She enjoyed the attention she always drew when she dressed like a lady.

"I thought you were a feller when you rode in, but my, oh my, you are no feller," exclaimed Mr. Haile.

"May I escort you to dinner, my dear?" Colonel Carter asked, gallantly offering his arm.

"Yes, sir," she replied, taking his arm and smiling at the others. They proceeded across the clearing to a long table the Sherrill boys had rigged up from some boards that were carried on the wagon. They also had made benches for seating. The table was laid out with a fine dinner of fresh venison, biscuits, carrots, onions, and boiled potatoes.

Sam stepped forward and greeted the guests. "Colonel Carter, I'd like to present my wife, Mary."

"It's a pleasure to meet you, Mrs. Sherrill," Colonel Carter said. "I never expected anything so fine as this, out here on the trail. This is quite a feast!"

"Thank you, Colonel Carter," Mary replied. "My girls are good cooks, and my boys are good hunters, and the Lord provides for us all."

"Let us bless this food. Thank you, Lord. Amen." Sam was an honest man, direct, and efficient with words. "Now it's been blessed, let's eat. Please have a seat, gentlemen. Ask for anything you can't reach, and the girls will serve you. Kate, if you can untangle yourself from our guests, long enough for them to try this venison, I think they will be pleased."

"Yes, sir. Please be seated, gentlemen." Kate went to work, making sure the men had enough to eat and drink.

"Mr. Sherrill, I see you are laden with household goods and family possessions. Are you removing permanently to the western waters?" asked Colonel Carter.

"Yes, sir, I hunted this area some years back; and it seemed to be a land of opportunity," Sam responded. "My brother, William, inherited my papa's place at Sherrill's Ford, so Mary and I need a place of our own."

"So your father passed on?" asked Colonel Carter.

"Yes, sir, Mama too."

"I knew Adam Sherrill back in Augusta County, and I knew he had several sons," Colonel Carter mused.

"There were eight of us," Sam said. "I was twenty-two when we left Virginia to settle at the Yadkin Valley, and newly married. Those were happy times. Sam Junior and Susan were our little darlings. Then along came Katie, and the French and Indian War started."

"Sam, those two events have no connection," Mary interrupted. Everyone laughed as Katie became indignant.

"Thank you, Mother, I want it understood. I had nothing to do with the French and Indian War; I was nothing but a babe."

"I didn't mean to say you did, my dear," Sam continued. "But I had to go fight, and fight we did. I served with Colonel Hugh Waddell's rangers, the most successful unit on the continent. Waddell was a military genius!"

"We sure need experienced men like you out at Watauga, Mr. Sherrill," Colonel Carter said. "Do you have a farm waiting for you?"

"No, I don't. I need to see what is available."

"You know, Mr. Sherrill, His Majesty's government does not allow settlement in the Overmountain Country."

"I would like to see His Majesty try to stop me!" Sam replied. "The upland counties speak of nothing but independence from England. You'll see when you reach the Yadkin Valley."

"And how do you feel about independence, Mr. Sherrill?" Carter asked.

"Most folks I know are for it, so I guess I'm for it too," Sam said. "The men of the liberty party say they favor validation of land transactions in the west. I'm counting on that promise to get my place established."

"I am pleased to hear you support the cause," Colonel Carter said. "I am chairman of the Committee of Safety for Watauga District. The British are stirring up the Indians against us, and while there has been no hostile activity to date, we are very anxious to secure the protection of the North Carolina General Assembly."

"So trouble is brewing out here; the same as it is back home," Sam remarked to Mary.

"What trouble do you speak of, Mr. Sherrill?" asked Mr. Russell.

"The question of independence has split the province entirely. The Tory party is very strong everywhere, especially among the rich eastern merchants and the big landed planters."

"What's happening in the General Assembly?" asked Colonel Carter.

"Can't say," Sam replied. "We get no reliable news in the western counties."

Long into the night, the men talked politics, business, farming, hunting, and land buying as the Sherrill children finished their dinners and left the table. Mary and the children cleared the table and washed the dishes and cook pots as they listened to the men talk. Soon the men brought out their tobacco and smoking pipes. The Sherrill boys bedded down around the wagon, and sixteen-year-old Mary Jane Sherrill made a bed beneath the wagon for herself and Kate. Having walked far and worked hard that day, the boys and Mary Jane fell asleep to the drone of the men's voices. There was laughter at times. Sam Sherrill was good humored, and so seemed Colonel Carter. Mary Sherrill and Kate lit more candles on the table and brought out their mending.

Colonel Carter shared much useful information about the Watauga settlement, the principal families of the community, the fort that had recently been built, the farms, and the trading station operated by James and Charlotte Robertson. Colonel Carter described other settlements beyond the Watauga—places the Sherrills had never heard about—Carter's Valley, Brown's purchase on the Nolichucky, and the Long Island in the Holston where the Indian treaty had been made the year before. He talked about the Indians, their main towns, their chiefs, and Nancy Ward, the Beloved Woman of the Cherokees. Kate listened, fascinated with Colonel Carter's stories. She could envision the places and people he described, and her imagination filled in the gaps.

"Colonel Carter, tell us about the Cherokee woman that is called the Beloved," Kate requested.

"Katie! Mind your manners," Mary exclaimed. "Do not interrupt your elders. The men are discussing important business."

"Please forgive me, Colonel Carter," Kate apologized. "I forgot myself, but there is so much to learn about the land that will be our new home."

"I understand, Miss Sherrill," replied Colonel Carter. "It is good to know what lies ahead. I will tell you the story of Nancy Ward. She is the daughter of Tame Doe, the sister of Attacullacula, peace chief of the Cherokees. This important family lives in Chota, the capital city of the Cherokee nation. Nancy married a young warrior named King Fisher and had two children. The Cherokees and the Creeks went to war, and Nancy took the warpath with her husband. In a great battle, King Fisher was killed, and Nancy picked up his gun and fought on as a warrior. Her courage and skill inspired the other Cherokees to turn the tide of battle and win a convincing victory. She was given the title Ghigan, which means Beloved Woman. She is the principal woman of the female councils and is endowed with the power to speak in the councils of the chiefs. She carries a swan's wing as her badge of authority."

"I think it is a fine thing for a woman to be so honored among her people," Kate exclaimed.

"There is no better friend to the white settlers than Nancy Ward. She promotes peace and prosperity between us and the Cherokees, whenever she can, but there is more to her story. Back during the French and Indian War, the Indians captured a white merchant, named Brian Ward. Convinced he was a spy, they condemned him to run the gauntlet where the braves would club him and tomahawk him to death. Nancy intervened on the white captive's behalf and persuaded the braves to give Ward a sporting chance. She proposed a twenty-mile footrace from the village where he was held to the town of Chota. She also negotiated a half-mile head start, so if he could outrun the fastest warriors, his life would be spared. Nancy and her uncle, Chief Attacullaculla, traveled to Chota to await the outcome. The deadly race began, and Brian Ward gave it his best effort. Mile after mile those howling savages gained on him. He set a furious pace, and many of his pursuers had to drop out and rest, but a handful of braves were greater in stature and fitter to run the race than poor Brian. They were the ones intent on a grim finish to a brave man's life. At last, Brian stumbled into view of Chota where Nancy and the chief waited. A couple of warriors were hot on his heels. An exhausted Brian Ward collapsed a few feet from the circle of safety, completely done in. The nearest warrior drew his scalping knife and prepared to take his prize, but Nancy was there first. She lifted Brian and carried him into the boundaries of Chota, the city of sanctuary."

"Oh, a truly noble woman!" Kate marveled. "I should so wish to be as great as she. Please tell us how it ended."

Colonel Carter relit his pipe and drew a few puffs before continuing. "Well, Miss Sherrill, Brian Ward nearly died of exhaustion; but Nancy nursed him back to health and married him."

"How splendidly romantic!" Kate sighed. "And they lived happily ever after?"

Colonel Carter smiled wryly. "That is only half true, my dear."

"What do you mean?" she persisted.

"Every other year, Mr. Ward comes to trade among the Indians and live with Nancy," Colonel Carter replied. "Then he returns to South Carolina to live with his white wife and family."

Sam and his boys laughed at the strange ending to the story, but Kate and her mother expressed disapproval.

"Why would he do such a thing?" Kate reacted.

"The man is a scoundrel!" Mary exclaimed.

"Do not rush to judgment, Mrs. Sherrill," continued the colonel. "Brian Ward had little choice in the matter when having just escaped condemnation and certain death, the chief offered him the honor of a marriage to his beautiful niece. Under the circumstances, not of his own making, Brian probably made the wisest choice."

"But that is against the law," Kate insisted.

"Things are different out here, Miss Sherrill," Colonel Carter replied. "Obeying the law depends on whose law you choose. You can have your Cherokee law, the king's law, North Carolina law, Virginia law, or the law of survival. Until we can get our Watauga Association recognized and our own courts set up, the situation remains much confused."

"God's law is universal and unchanging," Mary said quietly. No one else spoke for a few moments. The crickets, tree frogs, and night birds played their familiar, comforting music. Moths circled the candles on the table.

"Colonel Carter, is there a church in Watauga?" Kate asked.

"No, miss," he answered. "Whenever a preacher comes, we gather beneath the Sycamores. That's our church, and it's a rare thing when we even see a preacher. We need a good church to help civilize this country, and that's not all. We need every kind of improvement to make this wilderness livable. First we need government and courts. Most of the families are from Virginia. But Virginia turned down our bid to organize a new county. James Robertson insisted we give North Carolina a try. That is the purpose of our journey." Colonel Carter again allowed the sounds of the forest to be all they heard.

Mary laid down her mending and turned to Kate. "It's time to settle in for the night, Katie. Let us be going." The women stood, and the men rose too. "Colonel Carter, thank you for sharing your camp with us. We have enjoyed the conversation immensely."

"The pleasure was all mine, Mrs. Sherrill. Thank you for the delicious dinner."

"You are welcome, sir. Good night, gentlemen."

"Good night, Mrs. Sherrill, Goodnight, Miss Kate."

"Good night, Colonel Carter." Kate and Mary retired to the wagon and climbed up inside to dress for bed. In minutes, Kate repacked her good dress and took her place in bed on the ground, beneath the wagon.

Katie considered the family's good fortune and offered a prayer of thanksgiving. She and her sister, Mary Jane, soon slept serenely, virgin girls in a virgin wilderness, ripe with the promises of fruitfulness.

Chapter 2

Watauga Bound

Morning dawned gloriously cool for mid-July, and the camp was astir with activity. The Sherrill family prepared for their western progress while Colonel Carter's party made ready for their rapid dash to the east. The colonel had refused the offer of a good breakfast with the Sherrills because of the urgency of his business at the General Assembly. So it surprised Katie when he walked across the clearing to speak with her father. He carried a parchment, which he handled with extraordinary care.

"Mr. Sherrill," Colonel Carter began, "we appreciate your willingness to speak freely your political ideas with us last night. Many of the western settlers think the same way you do." Colonel Carter laid out the parchment paper on the Sherrill table and continued. "We would be honored, sir, if you would add your name to our Watauga Petition."

"You honor me, sir," replied Sam. "So this is it."

"Yes," Colonel Carter affirmed, "our petition to become a new county in the state of North Carolina. It promises our allegiance and support to the people of North Carolina in the cause of securing our rights, even if it goes so far as independency and the armed conflict that will certainly follow."

Sam studied the document, paying special attention to the names already affixed to it. "I see some names I know, Virginia names and a like number of good Carolina men."

"Your new neighbors and friends you can depend upon," Colonel Carter promised.

"You can count me in." Sam Sherrill was cautious and willing to consider all sides of an issue when formulating an opinion but decisive and resolute once he arrived at a conviction.

Colonel Carter produced a bottle of ink and a sharpened quill. "Mr. Sherrill, I'd like to invite your boys, if any be of age, to sign it as well."

"Sam Junior and Adam are of age, and they can handle a rifle if need be," Sam declared. The boys stepped forward and signed the document after their father.

"I wish I could sign it," Kate spoke up. "I'm just as committed to independence as my brothers, and I'm a better shot."

Colonel Carter laughed until he realized he was the only one laughing. Sam looked embarrassed, Mary shocked, and Kate serious. Her brothers knew better than to laugh at their sister.

"Miss Sherrill," Colonel Carter began slowly but kindly, "I admire your commitment to the cause, but the petition shall only contain the names of those men who will shoulder the responsibilities of citizenship and soldiering."

"What about the women who must run the farm, raise the children, make a living, and take up arms to defend their homes from the Indian, Tory, and thief while their husbands are away soldiering? I say that's a heavy responsibility!"

"True enough, but it's still only the men who sign," Colonel Carter replied.

Kate bristled at the rebuff and walked away to saddle and pack her horse.

"Mr. Sherrill," Colonel Carter began, "I meant no offense to your daughter."

"Don't worry about her," Sam explained. "I raised her to think the way I think, and sometimes strange ideas are the result. I'm afraid all this talk of liberty has got her thinking the whole world is about to change."

When Sam, Adam, and Sam Junior had signed the petition, Colonel Carter carefully folded it and placed it in a leather pouch.

"Mr. Sherrill, thank you for your hospitality last night and your support for the cause," Colonel Carter said. "I look forward to seeing you and your family happily settled in your new home at Watauga." The men shook hands. Once the Carolina-bound men had mounted, Colonel Carter led them out of the clearing on the road east.

High noon of the day following their parting with Colonel Carter's group, the Sherrills crested a bald ridge that afforded them a view of a wide valley blanketed with lush green trees extending miles ahead into the summer haze.

"This is it!" Sam exclaimed. "The valley of the Watauga!" He took a deep breath of the pine-scented mountain air. "It is a good land, Mary, as far as the eye can see, and practically unsettled. We should be able to find a sizable spread for our herds and a much better future for our children out here."

"Yes, Sam, it is beautiful country," Mary agreed, "but it will take a long time and a lot of work to clear the garden plot and pastureland for the horses, sheep, and cattle."

"That's why we had so many children, my dear." He grinned.

"Oh, Sam." She laughed. "And I thought it was for the love of me!"

The children came up behind them and marveled at the view. It was like standing on top of the world and being in the presence of the Almighty. They spent some time resting in the meadow and grazing the livestock as the Sherrill ladies fixed lunch.

Sam had noticed Kate leading her horse instead of riding him up that last long slope. "Katie," he asked, "why are you walking that horse?"

"He throwed a shoe, Papa," she replied. "I reckon I'll walk the rest of the way to Watauga."

"I reckon you will," he agreed.

"Papa, why can't we stay here to enjoy the view and camp here tonight?" Kate asked. "It is so lovely!"

"That it is, my dear, but we find a lesson from nature here," he replied. "You see we are above the tree line, and trees don't live here for a very good reason. It gets cold and windy up here at night, even in July, and the storms are especially violent. There's no firewood, no water, no safe place to pen the livestock; and nothing would keep the wolves, lions, and bears from feasting on our herds. So a place that looks good in the light of noonday can be evil and full of devils in the dark of night. That's why our country needs to take a long hard look at this thing called independence before we unleash it. What will it look like in the dark of night?"

"I've heard this lesson before." She laughed. "It's the one you tell when a young man takes a fancy to me."

"It holds true with men too," Sam told her. "What looks good in the light of day may have a very different look in the dark of night. So watch out, I say!"

"Papa, how did you ever get so much wisdom?" she asked.

Sam laughed. "I've lived through some dark nights, I reckon." His thoughts returned to the horses. "The mountain trail has been rocky and rough on horse's hooves. Both horses will need some care as soon as we can find a blacksmith."

After lunch, the family continued their journey down the mountain, below the tree line, through the mountain evergreens, and back into the shady forest of mixed oak, hickory, sweet gum, poplar, and maple. The trail led down into a valley and followed a fast rushing river as they descended from the heights. Hour after hour, the oxen plodded along easily pulling the wagon downhill, making good time.

Late in the afternoon, the road led into a wider valley with a good-sized clearing beside the river containing a recently established farmstead with some outbuildings, one of which looked as though it might be a simple forge. A good stand of corn and a productive garden indicated prosperity. Sam brought the oxen to a stop in front of the cabin and greeted the man and woman who came out.

"Good evening, sir. My name is Sam Sherrill, and this is my wife, Mary. We are on our way to Watauga."

"Howdy, my name is John Miller, and this is my wife, Eliza."

"It's good to meet you, Mr. Miller," Sam said. "How far is it to Sycamore Shoals?"

"Twenty miles," Mr. Miller replied.

"Does this river road take you there?" Sam asked.

"No, sir," Mr. Miller informed him. "This river eventually flows into the Watauga, but when it cuts through Iron Mountain, there was no place to put a road. You'll find the road turns west at the next gap in the mountains. You follow that branch about two miles upstream until you come to a trace leading off due west. Follow the trace to the head of Gap Creek and follow that stream to the Watauga. It's a much easier way, and it comes out just below the gathering place at Sycamore Shoals."

"Much obliged," Sam said. "So I figure it is two more days to Watauga."

"Unless you ride those fine horses you have there. They could get you there in half a day," Mr. Miller observed.

"Not in their present condition," Sam lamented. "They need reshoeing and rest after those rough mountain trails."

"Mind if I take a look?" Mr. Miller asked.

"Help yourself," Sam allowed.

John Miller was a large man, strong, and obviously used to hard work. He walked over to the black stallion, Kate's favorite, and examined his hoof.

"I see cracks in the hoof wall," Miller observed. "No shoes for at least a month. Why not let me pasture them here and I'll shoe them when they are ready?"

Sam looked back at his children herding the livestock. "Boys!" Sam shouted. "Keep the cattle moving! Don't let them get into Mr. Miller's corn!" Sam returned to the conversation. "I'm sorry, Mr. Miller, I don't want them destroying your corn. So you sound like you may be a blacksmith."

"The best blacksmith west of the mountains!" he boasted. "I'll keep your horses and do the work as soon as the horses are ready."

"Do you have room?" Sam asked.

"I sure do," Miller replied. "Not far from the house is the prettiest hidden cove with a meadow of sweet grass where your horses can be kept safely until I can shoe them."

"Well, we need to keep moving," Sam stalled. "But thanks just the same."

Sam was not going to rush into any decision, especially one concerning his horses. The horses were his livelihood, his inheritance from his father, and his hope for the future. He always loved horse breeding better than farming and even better than hunting, but he had enjoyed success at all frontier enterprises and was known as a good provider.

"It's getting late. Why not camp in the cove I told you about?" Mr. Miller offered. "Eliza would love a visit with you, folks."

Eliza smiled and insisted, "Yes, please stay the night."

"Much obliged, ma'am," Sam decided.

"I'll show you the way." Mr. Miller led the Sherrills and their entire caravan off the well-traveled road onto a trail that ran behind his forge. The trail led into a deeply wooded narrow defile. The big Conestoga wagon brushed the trees as the oxen pulled it through. On the right-hand side, the rapid stream coursed over the rocks; and on the left, a steep tree-covered slope rose higher than they could see. Ahead there was light filtering through the forest; and in a moment, a beautiful meadow came into view as the way widened into a pristine grassy cove, more than a musket-shot long and about one hundred yards wide. The stream kept to the western side of the cove, so they pitched their camp on the eastern side and freed the livestock to graze wherever they chose. The entrance to the cove could be closed off with a brush barrier. Mr. Miller pointed out a rock cliff boxing off the upper end of the valley, so thus was formed a natural corral of about thirty acres. Mr. Miller returned to his cabin leaving a very satisfied family, thrilled at the natural beauty of the place.

The Sherrills set up camp quickly; and Mrs. Sherrill, Katie, and Mary Jane began to plan the dinner. The younger children explored the cove. Adam and George went to the far end and discovered a beautiful waterfall tumbling into the cove from the cliff above. They called to the others to come and see the swimming hole. The excitement lured Mary Jane away immediately to see the grand sight. Katie, however, asked permission of her mother to go and supervise the children's swim.

"Yes, dear, go and have fun," she allowed. "The dinner may be a little delayed, but there's time enough for a good swim. Watch out for snakes."

"Yes, ma'am," Kate said, running to overtake the others.

At the waterfall, the two daughters and four sons of Samuel and Mary Sherrill undressed and swam in the cold, refreshing water, which paused to form a pool before rushing down the valley toward the Doe River. Kate loved to swim. Having grown up at Sherrill's Ford along the Catawba River, she had plenty of opportunity to enjoy the exercise on hot summer days. The adolescent Sherrills had developed a sense of modesty that required both boys and girls to wear underclothes when swimming together. Kate's shift covered her athletic, slender, and well-developed body. Her muscles were firm from the constant activity of farm life. Her father had always encouraged her to work with the horses, tend the cattle, and herd the sheep. And she was as fond of the hunt as she was the hearth, with great enthusiasm for all arenas of life. The swimming hole reminded her so much of her childhood; she reflected a long time on her past and the past of her family. She considered herself fortunate indeed to have grown up under the watchful eye and excellent example of her granny, Betsy Sherrill. Now there was a real pioneer woman!

Betsy Sherrill, born Elizabeth Corzine, in Cecil County, Maryland, married Adam Sherrill of the prominent Conestoga-trading Sherrills. She learned to manage home and family while her young husband transported valuable goods to settlers on the frontier with his father and brothers. Business was very good, and Adam and his brother William became well known as reliable suppliers to merchants all down through the big valley of Virginia in the early 1700s. Betsy even traveled with Adam on some of his trips and saw for herself the beautiful country that beckoned to Scots-Irish immigrants arriving by boatloads at the port of Philadelphia in those days. As Betsy bore sons to carry on the Sherrill name, she stayed home and persuaded Adam to move into other businesses related to the freight-moving enterprise for which the Sherrills were best known. Adam moved the family to the Falls of the Potomac and operated a ferry, bred and sold horses, and built freight wagons. Later the growing family moved to Augusta County, Virginia, and continued to prosper. Adam and Betsy Sherrill had eight sons in all working in the family business. Adam Sherrill, the pioneer, was always looking for new opportunities; and in 1747, he heard about rich new lands opening up for settlement in the Yadkin Valley of North Carolina. The Sherrills, in their fifties, moved to the Yadkin with their eight sons and settled on the Catawba River, at a place they called Sherrill's Ford, where once again the family prospered.

Sherrill's Ford became an important way station for North Carolina settlers going west. Adam and Betsy Sherrill came to know hundreds of families as they provided horses, wagons, furniture, trade goods, and supplies. They also hosted parties with barefoot and moccasin dancing every week for the families passing through. That was the big life that Katie was born into and learned to love as a child. It was her father's world.

Kate's mother's story was quite different. Mary Preston was born into a prominent merchant-class family of Northern Ireland, educated in the Presbyterian faith, encouraged to read the Bible, and allowed to think and speak freely. Unfortunately, her father lost everything by choosing the wrong side in a royal political squabble in the early 1740s, leaving his two daughters orphaned, displaced, and entirely dispossessed. Mary and her young sister Polly shipped out to Virginia to live under the care of their father's brother, John. Shortly after their arrival in Augusta County, Virginia, Uncle John died; and his distressed widow could ill afford to care for her own children, let alone the poor cousins. The Preston girls in their poverty, without dowry, and nearing marriageable age had to do for themselves the best they could. Mary was equal to the challenge, finding her comfort and salvation in the Presbyterian Church. She insisted on regular church attendance, pious living, and honest work. Mary had the gift of teaching younger children to read and write in the church school and subsisted long enough to see Polly make a good marriage. By then, Mary's grace and beauty had attracted the attention of young Samuel Sherrill, second son of Adam and Betsy Sherrill. She married him and that same year moved, with all his family, to the Yadkin Valley of North Carolina to begin a new life.

Mary Preston Sherrill, having suffered the loss of parents, uncle, country, and fortune in her first fifteen years of life, proved her family's claim to nobility, facing adversity as a true highland princess. She had kept her faith and never lost her Scots-Irish accent, a manner of speaking that charmed all who listened.

Mary prepared the evening dinner with the help of her husband as the children joyfully played at the refreshing waterfall. John and Eliza Miller came into camp with fresh vegetables from their garden.

"Oh, thank you!" Mary exclaimed. "Fresh garden produce is what we have missed the most on this journey."

Mrs. Eliza Miller was a young woman, a few months pregnant with her first child, and just beginning to show. She was talkative and very interested in news from the east.

Mary invited the Millers to dinner, and Mrs. Miller went right to work helping prepare it. Sam and Mr. Miller took another look at the horses and then set up the long boards the Sherrills used as a dinner table. Presently the young Sherrills returned from their swim, and the camp became lively with the joyful sounds of youthful enthusiasm.

At dinner that evening, the Millers made fine company; and Mr. Miller entertained with stories of the various families who had settled at the Watauga Valley. He spoke about the Beans, the Boones, the Robertsons, the Shelbys, the Carters, the Isbells, the Lucases, the Seviers, and numerous others who were the first and foremost leaders of the growing overmountain community.

"We met Colonel Carter on the trail a few nights ago and shared a camp," Sam told Mr. Miller.

"Colonel John Carter came out from Virginia about six years ago, and he is the elected leader of the Watauga Association," Mr. Miller explained. "He is also the military leader in charge of defense. But I'll tell you, my friends, James Robertson is the one who makes things happen down there."

"James Robertson would be a good man to know," Sam remarked to Mary.

"You know, after the Virginia House of Burgesses turned down our bid to become a part of that state, Robertson went right to work and contacted his North Carolina friends, Governor Caswell and Judge Henderson. Now it seems likely we will become part of their state."

"Why the rush to be part of the state we left behind?" Sam inquired.

"Indians!" Mr. Miller exclaimed. "We need protection. Only a provincial government can afford the cost of organizing a militia and paying for a campaign against the Indians. The other reasons are less obvious; we need courts to settle disputes and punish wrongdoers, but most important, we need a government to validate our land claims."

"We signed the petition that Colonel Carter had with him," Adam Sherrill declared.

"Well now, you are already citizens of Watauga!" Mr. Miller responded.

"For the time being," Sam observed. "The British are not finished with this business. When the royal governor comes back to North Carolina, with the king's army and navy, there will be plenty of trouble."

"Mr. Sherrill, I am a forthright man," Mr. Miller declared. "I say what I think. I hope I do not offend, but I am for independence!"

"No offense taken," Sam replied. "I too believe that independence is the better way, but as an older man, speaking from experience, I know the cost will be great, and many of our loved ones will pay with their lives."

There was silence at the table. The night sounds of the forest blended with the rushing waters of the nearby brook to fill the human silence. Mr. Miller, deep in thought, brought out his pipe and tobacco pouch. Sam did likewise, and the men reflected on the consequences of armed conflict.

"It's mighty peaceful here, Mrs. Miller," Mary observed. "You have found the ideal place to raise your family."

Eliza shifted uncomfortably. "I wish I had some neighbors, especially when the baby comes." Her fears were suddenly evident; and Mary understood her isolation, her vulnerability, and her dread of the inevitable blessed event. Mary knew the perils of childbirth when things sometimes go terribly wrong, even for robust young women like Eliza Miller.

"Don't you have family nearby?" Mary inquired.

"We both came from Wake County."

"My goodness, what a long way," Mary exclaimed. "Why did you settle here?"

"There is a coal seam in this hill to fire my forge," John Miller explained, rousing himself from his reflections. "And Yellow Mountain, the next ridge to the northwest is full of iron. Someday I'm going to build the biggest ironworks in the country!"

Sam was impressed with Miller's ambition and enthusiasm. "I certainly wish you well with that, Mr. Miller."

"When is the baby due?" Mary asked, refocusing on the important.

"January, I think," Eliza replied. "We may be snowbound."

"I will be here," Mary declared. "Katie and one of the boys will come with me, and we will make sure your baby gets a proper welcome into the world!"

Eliza was surprised that Mary Sherrill, a stranger before that afternoon, would make such an offer. "You would do that for me?"

"Of course we will, won't we, Katie?"

"Yes, ma'am," Katie agreed, proud that her mother was such a good Christian.

"But I am a stranger to you," Eliza marveled.

"No pregnant woman is a stranger to me, she's a sister," Mary assured her. "I've borne nine children, so I know what you will need."

Eliza smiled at her husband. "That would be wonderful! Oh, John, we have found some good neighbors! I cannot believe our good fortune and Mrs. Sherrill's great kindness."

"It is no less than a new mother deserves," Mary affirmed. "Listen, we plan to settle near Watauga. Is there a station or trading post where you could send word to us when your time is near?"

"Robertson's place, on the north side of Sycamore Shoals," suggested Mr. Miller. "Charlotte, his wife, can pass the word. If you settle anywhere in the valley, Charlotte will know your place."

"Eliza, I promise I will be here," Mary assured her.

"Thank you, Mrs. Sherrill, and you too, Katie." Eliza was a different woman the rest of that evening. With the relief of a great burden lifted, or at least shared with some understanding new neighbors, she was free to be herself. She was talkative, witty, and charmingly funny. John Miller changed also—more relaxed, more engaging, and more loving toward his relieved wife.

When the conversation began to wind down, Sam stood up and put down his pipe. "Katie, the fiddles," he announced. "It is time for the fiddles."

"Yes, sir," she replied and ran to the dark wagon. She climbed inside and groped among the baggage for the requested treasures, knowing where she had last seen them.

"I was wondering when you would get around to that," Mary said approvingly. "Mr. Sherrill does not often favor us with such a treat, but tonight he is in a festive mood, I think." Sam winked at her. Kate soon returned with two fiddles and placed them before the master. Sam picked up one and bowed the strings to test the tuning.

"Who will play the harmony?" Sam asked.

"Adam will," Katie answered.

"I want to dance," Adam protested. "Let Junior play."

"You are too short, Adam," she explained. "Junior is a better partner for me."

"Then I'll dance with Mary Jane!" Adam declared.

"Now, children, we must take turns," Mary admonished, picking up the other fiddle and tuning it. "But I'll play first."

Sam began playing, Mary joined in, and the children danced to the lively music that filled the moonlit cove. Never before had such sounds been heard in that wild place. Sam Junior took Kate's hand, and Adam paired up with his fair sister Mary Jane. Mr. and Mrs. Miller danced with such obvious enjoyment that it was apparent to all that this was a rare event in their lonely lives.

Sam Junior—tall, dark, and handsome—had grown up dancing with his sister Susan; but since she married Mr. Taylor and stayed behind in Rowan County, Katie had claimed him for her dancing partner. Junior contemplated his younger sister's prospects. Indeed, she was beautiful like Susan, capable of so many accomplishments like their Granny Sherrill, but willful and headstrong like nobody they knew. What man would tolerate such a woman as a life partner? He would have to be a bull of a man, stubborn enough to balance her willfulness, powerful enough to remain master of his own household, yet gentle enough to overlook her shortcomings without thrashing her for bad behavior. If any of the Sherrill sisters were to become an old maid, it would be the beautiful Catharine. To make matters worse, she was completely unaware of her obvious faults and already twenty-one years into this life. The great paradox was her effect on children. They loved her unconventional behavior. They laughed with her at the humorous situations her outspoken opinions produced and felt safe and loved in her capable presence. They often felt the kindness and charity that lay concealed behind the wild freedom she cherished as a frontier farm girl. Everyone loved Kate except the string of potential suitors that well-meaning matchmakers had tried to present over the years. Kate had been as disinterested in them, as they had been in her. *What a pity,* Sam Junior thought.

Papa Sherrill, playing the fiddle magnificently for nearly an hour, had arrived at a decision to leave his two good breeding horses in Mr. Miller's care. It was a decision that would smile on the fortunes of his family in the weeks to come.

Chapter 3

In a Far Country

At the junction where Big Limestone Creek runs into the Nolichucky River, Lieutenant John Sevier was felling trees and dressing them for the palisade walls of a stockade that he had decided to call Fort Lee. Thirteen militiamen helped him, but they were all Watauga men, Sevier's men, his close friends, relatives, and neighbors. The men of the Nolichucky had packed up and gone north or east on rumors that the Cherokees might soon take the War Road to drive the settlers all the way up country to the valleys of Virginia. There were suspicions that many of the Nolichucky settlers were Tories and had been warned to clear out by British agents who worked among the Cherokees planning attacks on the frontiers and pushing the Indians into war.

John Sevier, a tall, well-built, blue-eyed blond, was a natural leader among men. His leadership talents had been recognized in the Virginia colonial militia, where he had been a captain, and again by the self-government experiment called the Watauga Association, where he was appointed a lieutenant. He was intensely interested in westward settlement and left his home in the big valley of Virginia, moving by stages, farther and farther into the wilderness. The Nolichucky Valley, at the edge of civilization, was the most beautiful landscape he had ever seen. He located a tract of land along the Nolichucky, offered by a man named Jacob Brown, and purchased it. Jacob Brown lived nearby and held title to a vast region from an agreement he had made with friendly Cherokee chiefs. Brown's purchase, as it was called, was illegal under British Colonial law; but in 1776 with political changes sweeping the continent, the states in rebellion were willing to legalize western land claims. Men like Jacob Brown and John Sevier supported the patriotic cause, not only for the freedom from British taxes and oppressions but for the opportunity that enterprise and hard work might afford a considerable gain.

Sevier's lookout, young Landon Carter, announced the arrival of a single rider entering the clearing from upstream. The man was dressed in the manner of the long hunter and packed for a journey. He pulled up, remained on his horse, and spat out a wad of tobacco.

"Hello, Jacob," Sevier greeted the man.

"Howdy, Jack," Jacob Brown replied. "You sure are going to a lot of trouble here," he observed, looking around at the construction project. "It may be all for nothing."

"Have you heard any news?" asked John pausing from his work to lean on the handle of his broad ax.

"I'll tell you what I know," Jacob responded. "All the families along the Nolichucky have cleared out and gone to Watauga Fort. I took Mrs. Brown and the children up there and had a talk with James Robertson. He just got back from talks with the Cherokees."

"What did he have to say?" John asked.

"The young chiefs of the war faction are going to have their way, Jack. All out, total war!"

"The chiefs told this to Robertson?" John questioned.

"Naw, but Robertson knows how to read what Indians are thinking. The message lies in what they don't say," Jacob replied.

"How soon does he think they will attack?" John asked. John's men were the exposed vanguard and information like this was of vital interest to him.

"Nobody knows," Jacob continued. "But everybody I know is heading into Watauga Fort. You'd best do the same. There is no good reason to build a fort here with the valley empty of settlers."

John looked over the unfinished defenses of Fort Lee. "If they would wait until after the corn harvest, we could be ready to stand off the whole Cherokee nation, right here!" John exclaimed.

"The Indians ain't gonna wait until you are ready. The surprise attack is their style, just like the ambush is their favorite tactic. I think they will be here within the week and at the gates of Watauga, two days after that. You better get out of the way!" Jacob was as serious as John had ever seen him.

"Does Robertson have Watauga Fort ready?" John asked.

"Hell no." Jacob laughed. "You know him better than that! He needs you, Jack, and all these men too. He's only got thirty men up there, fit to be called soldiers."

"Riders, across river!" called out young Landon Carter.

Four men rode rapidly down to the opposite bank of the river and forded it. The soldiers instinctively picked up their rifles, which they always kept within easy reach anywhere they worked. John recognized Isaac Thomas, a seasoned long hunter who traded Virginia goods among the Indians whenever conditions allowed. His companions were Jarret Williams, William Falling, and Andrew Greer, all independent merchants who made regular trading expeditions to the frontier. The fact that all these men were traveling together, in great haste, told

John that something of great import was about to happen. John stepped forward to meet the riders.

"Good day, gentlemen," John greeted them.

"Same to you, Jack," Isaac Thomas replied.

"What's the news?" John asked.

"The whole nation is turned out for war. Six hundred braves are headed this way," Isaac told him gravely.

John turned to his men and gave the order. "Men, get ready to move! Pack up everything! We won't be coming back anytime soon." The men scrambled to saddle their horses and pack for the move.

"How did you manage to get out of Indian country without them stopping you?" John asked.

"Nancy Ward came to us by night and warned us to leave immediately. She even had our horses saddled and waiting," Isaac explained.

"God bless her!" John exclaimed. "The settlers never had a better friend. Well, it's up to us to warn every station on the frontier. I will write a short report to James Robertson, John Shelby, and Evan Shelby. That covers the main forts. Then I'll take my men to Bean's Valley and gather those people into Watauga." John got out his pen, ink, and paper and began scrawling messages. When he finished the first one, he gave it to Isaac Thomas. "Isaac, this is to James Robertson at Watauga. Jacob Brown is going there to join his family. You two can travel together." Isaac was in the saddle a moment later, and he and Mr. Brown rode away immediately.

Next, John completed a letter to Major Evan Shelby, an experienced Indian fighter from the French and Indian War, who commanded several militia companies assembled the month before at Eaton's Station on the Long Island of the Holston. John felt confident that Shelby's rangers would give a good account of themselves in battle and perhaps send relief to other forts where settlers would be under siege. Jarret Williams and William Falling rode out to deliver that message.

The last message John wrote was to John Shelby's fort twenty-five miles beyond Watauga to the north. This he gave to Andrew Greer, and he called over another man from his detachment, Val Sevier, his brother.

"Val, you travel with Mr. Greer to John Shelby's fort," John ordered.

"What and miss all the action?" Val protested.

"There will be plenty of action everywhere with six hundred warriors out lifting hair," John told him. "I want our families protected properly. Get them over to John Shelby's fort, and do your best to keep our folks safe."

"John, what about you?" Val expressed concern for his elder brother in a hushed voice so the other men would not hear.

"I'll take my stand at Watauga Fort," John answered quietly. "If we can weaken them before they reach the Holston, you can conduct a successful defense if Shelby's rangers are able to reinforce you."

"John, you'll only have forty men at Watauga," Val whispered.

"That's a fact," John agreed. "Tell Sarah and the children I was alive and well and happy with my work when last you saw me. Tell them all how much I love them. God bless you and all the family." John embraced his brother who then mounted and turned sadly, but rapidly, north.

"Lieutenant Sevier, the men are ready," young Carter reported.

John reviewed his brave men, standing ready beside their horses. Smiling, he casually said, "Well, my good fellows, let us ride up and have a good visit with Lydia and William Bean. Perhaps they have a sweet watermelon ripening on the vine they might share with us." The men smiled at his nonchalance, mounted, and rode away from their unfinished fort.

Late that afternoon, John and his troops arrived at the junction of Boone's Creek and the Watauga River. On high ground nearby, hidden from view to travelers along the river, was the cabin of William and Lydia Bean, the first white settlers to move to the Watauga Valley and stay. John led his company up the steep path to the cabin, and they dismounted. Lydia Bean greeted them from the doorway of her cabin.

"Hello, Jackie boy," she said. "What brings you this way?"

"Howdy, Mrs. Bean," John replied. "My men have ridden all day to sample one of your fine watermelons."

"Help yourselves, boys," she offered.

"Thank you, ma'am!" The men made tracks for the melon patch.

"Lydia," John began seriously, "we have received word that the Indians have taken the War Road, and all settlers are being ordered into Watauga Fort. Is Captain Bean here?"

"No, he's gone to muster at Eaton's Station," she answered.

"Why didn't you go with him?" John asked.

"I figure I'm safer here than in the fort," she answered. "We have an agreement of eternal friendship with Chief Oconostota. He will not allow any harm to come to us."

William and Lydia Bean lived simply, like the Cherokees, and had gone to the trouble of learning their language and understood their customs. They often fed entire hunting parties and gave generously of whatever they had. Yet Lydia Bean was resourceful enough to always produce more. Among her assets were her family connections. She was born a Russell, and both her father and her brother held high rank in the southwest Virginia militia. Even in the current crisis, Russell's rangers were known to be playing an active role.

"Chief Oconostota has lost control of the younger warriors," John continued. "Anything is likely to happen. I'm going down the Watauga, collecting all the families so we can escort them into the fort."

"So you are taking me down the Watauga as you collect the other families?" she asked. "Why not pick me up on your way back upriver?"

"Because I'm not returning this way," he explained. "I'm going to make a circuit to the north, collect some other folks there, and make it back to the fort by tomorrow night."

"It would be easier for me to stay here the night, pack a few things, and leave for the fort in the morning by the most direct route. I could be there by noon." Lydia had better sense and a more thorough knowledge of the country than anyone else John knew.

"I guess that would make better sense," John agreed. "But don't waste any time in the morning. Set out early," he warned.

"I will," she promised. "Can I fix your boys some supper?"

"No, ma'am, we need to travel on while we still have some daylight," John said, looking at the position of the sun.

The men had finished with the watermelon and returned to their horses to continue their journey. Landon Carter brought a piece of the sweet fruit to John. He took a bite.

"Mmm, that's mighty good. I'll see you tomorrow, Liddy," John said as he swung back into the saddle.

"Be careful, Jackie Boy," she replied.

"Same to you," he answered. John tipped his hat to her, and the next moment the soldiers were gone.

Chapter 4

Panic on the Frontier

The Sherrills had an uneventful day descending Gap Creek to the Watauga River. They passed one deserted farm after another, where settlers had left everything. Well-tended fields and livestock were abandoned as though the family would return that very day. Sam thought perhaps they were attending some kind of gathering down at the Watauga. But every farm was the same, completely equipped, but no people. At last in the late afternoon, Gap Creek led them to the Watauga River. To their right, into the distance, acres of open fields spread out before them, some planted in crops and some in open grasslands. Stumps from recently cut trees dotted the landscape; and on a hill overlooking the fields, but not far from the river, stood a sizable stockade that Sam identified as Watauga Fort. Across the river a long, low log cabin stood, that Sam guessed might be Robertson's Station. They made their way toward the stockade.

The Sycamore Shoals of the Watauga River provided a natural crossing place for animals and people traveling through the valley. Open meadows, along the banks of the river, known as the Old Fields, had long been a meeting place for the Cherokee clans. As the men hunted, the women tilled and planted, weeded and watered, cultivated and harvested abundant produce in those fields until the wars with the Creeks began. The hostilities caused the nation to relocate to the southwest where the warriors could more easily strike at the Creek towns on the southern waters. Shawnee hunting parties from the north took advantage of the Cherokee absence and hunted the area but did not settle there. The fields lay idle until discovered by the white long hunters from North Carolina and Virginia.

James Robertson, a North Carolina hunter, trader, and land speculator came out in '69 with Boone's hunting party. He saw the Old Fields and decided to plant a crop of corn there that spring and return with his family for the harvest. Things did not go as he planned. Setting out alone, he got lost in the mountains on his return trip home. In the heat of summer, amidst lush green vegetation, he became hopelessly disoriented in the winding valleys and towering ridges of the Yellow Mountains. He released his horse when the terrain became too steep for riding. He abandoned his rifle when he ran out of ammunition. The gun had become too much of a burden for the weakened man. Robertson nearly perished before another hunting party heading west discovered him and gave him the supplies and directions to get safely home. Undaunted, he came out the next year, stayed, and built a trading station and promoted the establishment of a pioneer community.

James Robertson formed the self-governing Watauga Association with Colonel John Carter, Evan Shelby, brothers Valentine and John Sevier, and other settlers who thought a community ought to have laws, courts, and civic structure for the safety and progress of all. As the political situation with Great Britain worsened, the Watauga settlers commissioned James Robertson and Nathaniel Hart to go and make a treaty of peace with the Cherokee Indians to counteract the influence of British agents. In the wisdom that comes with experience, the commissioners also authorized Lieutenant John Sevier to construct a fort on the crest of a hill overlooking the Watauga Old Fields, just in case of trouble. John Sevier had finished Watauga Fort in May and named it for the governor of North Carolina, Richard Caswell, as a rather obvious attempt to curry favor and gain support for the Wataugans to become a North Carolina county. The name Fort Caswell never caught on, and the settlers always called it Watauga Fort.

On July 5, 1776, the Watauga settlers gathered at their new fort to sign their Watauga Petition describing why they thought they should be recognized as a North Carolina county. They also pledged their support for the new state governor and General Assembly that had been set up to replace the royal governor and colonial legislature promising that "nothing would be withheld" in support of the cause. Colonel John Carter, the commander at Watauga Fort, took a party of the leading men of the community and headed to North Carolina to deliver their Watauga Petition and persuade the General Assembly then meeting in Halifax to accept their bid to join North Carolina. James Robertson left for the Cherokee capital of Chota for more peace talks while Lieutenant John Sevier left Watauga to continue work on the construction of another fort on the Nolichucky River to defend settlers who lived in that neighborhood.

In less than a week, Robertson had returned to Watauga after friendly Indians had intercepted his mission and warned him not to proceed to their capital city. He knew from their behavior that mischief was planned. He called for all settlers to gather to the forts and prepare for the worst.

As the Sherrill family wagon came into view, Luke Bowyer—the lookout at Watauga Fort—called Captain James Robertson to come take a look.

"Hey, James, have you ever seen a Conestoga freight wagon in this part of the country?" Mr. Bowyer asked.

"Never seen one south of the Holston," Captain Robertson admitted. "It must be the Virginia supplies."

"Why would a Virginia supply wagon come down Gap Creek?" asked Bowyer.

"Gap Creek? That's impossible!" exclaimed Captain Robertson. "No wagon like that could cross those Carolina Mountains!"

"I watched it, and it came down Gap Creek," Mr. Bowyer insisted. He was a young trial lawyer, so when Captain Robertson challenged his testimony, he was just a little annoyed.

"Maybe they took a wrong turn somewhere and ended up on Gap Creek," Captain Robertson suggested. "I hope they brought plenty of lead and powder."

Word soon circulated among the people in the fort that the approaching wagon was the long-awaited Virginia supply wagon bringing much-needed powder and shot for the defense of Watauga Fort. Thirty militiamen along the walls waved their hats and cheered the supposed instrument of their salvation. Only Mr. Bowyer, the attorney-at-law, stopped to wonder why the wagon was approaching from the wrong direction. Some two hundred women and children soon joined in the jubilation. If ammunition were being delivered, the Virginia troops could not be far behind to reinforce the tiny garrison. A joyous reception awaited the bewildered Sherrill family.

"Wataugans are the friendliest people in the world," marveled Kate as she walked beside her father. Today she wore a fine linen go-to-meeting dress and matching bonnet that she knew would impress the young men they might meet. She wanted to make a good impression and waved to the crowds waiting at the gate of the fort.

"It ain't natural," Sam grumbled. "What's all the fuss about?"

"Sam, they have mistaken us for somebody else," Mary decided. "Somebody important."

"This is great!" Adam exclaimed as he caught up with Kate and Sam.

"Get back there and stop the cattle!" Sam ordered. "This noise will stampede them!"

No sooner had he said it, it happened. The cattle bolted and ran, but they did not go far. The rich green grass of the Old Fields soon interested them more than escaping the commotion coming from the people in the fort.

Captain Robertson came out to meet them, and the people crowded around the wagon. "I'm Captain James Robertson," he shouted above the crowd noise. "Do you have the supplies from Virginia?"

"Nope," replied Sam. "We come from Carolina. I'm Sam Sherrill, and this is my wife, Mary." The crowd got quieter.

"Well, what's in the wagon?" Captain Robertson wanted to know. He realized his mistake and knew the Sherrills were just another family of refugees he would have to shelter, protect, and feed. He was hoping a wagon that big might have brought supplies enough to sustain the whole community.

"Household goods, farm implements, seed stocks, just what I need to start my farm," Sam replied.

"We need powder and shot and food enough for all these people," Captain Robertson declared.

Sam looked around at the disappointed faces, mostly women and children, and felt sickened by the situation. He wondered how the community could have gotten itself into such a mess. Where were the men that belonged to all these women? He intended to have a talk with Robertson and get the answers as soon as opportunity allowed. "Are you expecting trouble?" he innocently inquired.

"Good Lord, man, the whole Cherokee tribe has taken the war path! Everybody has been ordered into this fort without delay, and that includes you!" Captain Robertson exclaimed. The crowd returned to the fort, but the mood was not a pretty one.

The Sherrills guided the big Conestoga into the fort to the center of the common ground, and Sam unhitched the team of oxen. Katie felt a cool reception from the icy stares and the biting remarks overheard from the frustrated, disappointed women who kept their distance and watched the Sherrills unpack. She suddenly felt ridiculously overdressed. Where were the men she had dressed that way to impress? She dispensed with her good bonnet first and went to work beside her mother, unpacking the kitchen equipment. William and George were sent out to find firewood. Adam and Sam Junior were somewhere in the fields trying their best to manage the family livestock.

Sam led the oxen toward the fort gate and paused to speak to his wife. "Mary, I want our new neighbors to eat well tonight, so I'm going to offer Captain Robertson some beef. Maybe you could cook up the vegetables the Millers gave us and make some of your wonderful corn cakes?"

"Mr. Sherrill," Mary replied. "You are a wonder. I was just going to suggest the same idea." Sam smiled and continued on to the gate where he was able to speak with Captain Robertson and prevail upon the commander to accept the Sherrill family offer.

A man named Jacob Brown was sent to help Sam and his sons slaughter the cattle for the dinner. Jacob was not as old as Sam Sherrill but seemed to have a lot of hunting experience and great knowledge about the overmountain communities. Working together with Mr. Brown was a good opportunity for Sam to learn about the latest news.

"I wonder why Robertson thinks the Indians are coming here," Sam asked Mr. Brown.

"I was at the Nolichucky yesterday morning when Isaac Thomas and three other Indian traders came tearing into the camp where Jack Sevier was building another fort," Jacob explained. "They delivered the news that eight hundred braves were on the war path. Then Lieutenant Sevier sent dispatches to all the stations on the frontier to be on the lookout for trouble."

"When will the Indians be here?" Sam asked.

"Nobody knows," Jacob replied. "But Robertson and Evan Shelby, the commander up at Eaton's Station, have it figured this way. Near Eaton's Station lies the Long Island of the Holston, sacred ground to the Cherokee. If the Indians attack there first, and the Great Spirit gives them victory, then their success is assured. So Evan Shelby gathered all the companies of militia there to meet the main attack."

"That explains where all the fighting men went," Sam observed. "What if the Indians attack here first?"

"Then James Robertson and Evan Shelby guessed wrong," Jacob said quietly.

"And Watauga Fort becomes another Fort Loudon," Sam concluded. He referred to an English frontier fort on the Tennessee River in the heart of Cherokee country during the French and Indian War. The Cherokees turned against the English garrison and starved them out. Under the terms of surrender, the men, their women, and their children were allowed to abandon the fort and return to Carolina in safety. But for reasons that remained a mystery, warriors attacked the refugees and massacred over two hundred.

"Keep that quiet, Mr. Sherrill," Jacob warned him. "The last thing Robertson needs is two hundred hysterical women and children. We live, day to day, in the hope that those Virginia troops arrive with the supplies we need."

"The powder and shot supply . . ." Sam began. "How bad is it?"

"Each man has ten rounds," Jacob replied. "I wouldn't think there's more than three pounds of lead in the entire company."

"Thunderation!" Sam exclaimed. "That's a poorly contrived plan."

"You could pack that big wagon and go back to North Carolina," Jacob suggested.

"Mr. Brown," Sam began. "I promised beef for dinner tonight. I'm sacrificing the oxen that pull that big wagon. The Sherrills have arrived, citizens of Watauga. Live or die, we are with you!"

The dinner, despite the sacrifice and skill of the hands that prepared it, did little to dispel the gloom that gripped the community that night. The thirty men ate at their posts along the palisade walls, watching for any movement or signs of danger. The women, strangely silent, sat lost in their thoughts of farm and family. *Would life, if continued beyond the dark of this night, ever return to normal?* That was a question pondered silently in many a feminine heart through the dark hours.

Katie thought the after dinner hours would afford the Sherrills the opportunity to engage their new neighbors in interesting conversation, getting to know their names and their relationships to one another. She tried to strike up several conversations with some of the women, but her efforts were rewarded with stony silence. When she resorted to engaging the children, the women would silence their children and quietly admonish them. Captain James Robertson soon solved the mystery of the silent women, when he approached her and explained.

"You are one of the new refugees, aren't you?" he addressed her. She had never thought of herself as a refugee; but since they had arrived in the fort and the gates were solidly closed, trapping her family with all the others, she admitted to herself that she might be called a refugee.

"I am Catharine Sherrill," she said, using a dramatic air that might have made her seem important in another place and time.

"Well, Miss Sherrill, the community is under the order of strict silence, so the men on watch can hear the approach of danger," Captain Robertson explained. "So I'll thank you to obey the same orders as everyone else."

Katie felt the humiliation at being so publicly reprimanded, in front of two hundred women and children. Her quick temper caused a reaction that she could not contain.

"I suppose there's nothing more to be said than to let you know I'm going to bed!" She came to attention and saluted smartly. "With your permission, Captain?"

"Permission granted." James smiled. "But quietly."

She wheeled an about-face and marched away to the big wagon.

"And that means no snoring!" Robertson called after her. The large audience laughed at his joke, at her expense.

The captain's humor did not disarm her anger, which she displayed in her movements throughout the bedtime rituals of undressing, washing, and brushing her long silky hair. Finally, in the act of kneeling for her prayers, she let go of the anger and the shame and silently asked the Lord's forgiveness. Then the tears came. She had tried so hard to make a good impression, and it had been so important to her. Instead, she had made a scene causing embarrassment to her mama and papa and her sister and brothers. Bounder, the Sherrill sheepdog, came over to her and nuzzled her hand.

"Oh, Bounder, we are in such a terrible mess!" she whispered. "All my hopes for Watauga have turned to nightmares." She could not begin to understand the size of the mess they were in, because Sam had not shared what he learned from Mr. Brown. Neither could she know the magnitude of the nightmares that awaited her in the hours ahead. She crawled under the wagon to her customary place beneath the rear axle, and Mary Jane soon joined her.

"Hush, Mary Jane," Katie said.

"I didn't say anything," she answered.

"You were going to."

"Katie, anybody could have made that mistake," Mary Jane tried to console her.

"But it was me. It's always me," Katie despaired.

Sleep did not come to Katie Sherrill. She replayed in her mind the embarrassing scenes of the day, the strange reception, the expensive dinner given by her family that produced no pleasure, the coldness of these worried women, the oppression of their children, and her personal encounter with Captain Robertson.

After midnight, Katie was still awake when the night watch opened the gate and admitted a number of exhausted refugees. They were quickly bedded down in the open commons and found sleep easily. Katie watched as the soldiers who accompanied them filed in, carrying their saddles and equipment, and likewise bedded down. At the gate, Captain Robertson was having a disagreement with the leader of the horse soldiers.

"Lieutenant, you are not bringing those horses in here. I order you to release them to pasture," Captain Robertson insisted, raising his voice.

The lieutenant did as he was told, but Katie could tell that he was angered by his encounter with the captain, just as she had been earlier. She felt empathy for the angry lieutenant as she noted the location he chose to make his bed. She resolved to find him in the morning and have a closer look. Captain Robertson and Mr. Brown walked by her wagon on the way to the blockhouse, and she could hear them.

"Think you ought to go ahead and tell Jack he's going to be in charge of the night watch?" Mr. Brown asked.

"Not tonight," answered the captain. "Let him rest. He needs to cool off about those horses. By Jove, the man loves his horses!"

Katie looked over again at the resting, angry Lieutenant Jack—horse lover and officer of the night watch. She had just spent the last evening of her life unacquainted with the man who would rise to become her savior and awaken such desires as she had never known.

Chapter 5

One Fateful Day

July 21, 1776, dawned hazy and hot at the Sycamore Shoals. Kate Sherrill awoke to the hushed voices, cook-fire activities, and clanging of cast-iron pots and skillets all around the commons of the fort. Her nightclothes were damp from humid air and sweat, for the night had not cooled down the land, and another hot day was in store. She rose up and peered out between the spokes of the wheel viewing the soldiers still sleeping in the same places they had taken last night. Lieutenant Jack wore the beige breeches and white shirt of a Virginia militia officer's uniform. His blue coat and his waistcoat were thrown over his saddle, which served as a pillow under his long blond hair. He had removed his knee-high riding boots and placed them neatly beside the saddle. His rifle, powder horn, and shot bag lay beside him on his blanket. He had nice things compared to the homespun hunting-shirt men who rode with him.

She crawled out from under the wagon rousing both Mary Jane and Bounder who slept close to her. The girls prepared themselves for the day in work clothes and took great care in washing their faces, hands, and arms for the morning activities. Katie brushed her hair in front of a small mirror they had hung on the side of the wagon. Shortly they heard their mother stirring around, dressing for the day, in the privacy of the bed of the covered wagon. Sam too was waking inside the wagon beside his wife.

"Sam, we're going out to milk," Mary roused him gently.

"Be careful to stay near the fort, Mary," Sam warned.

"We will be with all the other ladies," Mary assured him.

Sam never was a man to stay in bed after his wife got up. He dressed also and climbed down from the wagon so he could help Mary climb down. He did this out of a sense chivalry only, because Mary was completely fit and capable of doing everything herself. Sam enjoyed helping her, touching her, being close to her, and sensing all her qualities.

"We'll cook breakfast when the milking is done. If the children get hungry, they can have some of the corn cakes left over from last night." She kissed him and turned to her daughters who waited beside the wagon. She noticed Katie gazing at the militiamen still sleeping on the open commons of the fort.

"Let's go, Katie," Mary interrupted her thoughts. "Good morning, Mary Jane, darling. Ah, good morning, Bounder, there's a good dog!"

The barefoot girls had their milk buckets and stools in hand, ready to follow their mother into the meadows. On the way to the gate, Katie steered off course, carelessly looking up at the morning sky, watching the birds, looking up to the hills, completely self-absorbed with the beauty all around her when her foot struck the leg of one of the sleeping soldiers, and she tripped over him. She tumbled to the ground dropping her bucket and stool and sat on the ground looking at him. The handsome, blond, muscular, natural leader of men, she knew only as Lieutenant Jack, sat up sleepily.

"Excuse me, sir, I wasn't watching where I was going. Forgive me for waking you!" Kate apologized. The officer looked at the girl and grinned, good naturedly.

"That's all right, miss," he spoke politely. "Forgive me for getting in your way."

She smiled and got up collecting her things. "Good day, sir." She curtsied and rushed away toward the gate where she joined her mother and the other women.

"What did you do?" her mother asked, having missed seeing the fall of her daughter.

"I wanted a better look," Kate said in a hushed voice. "He has the most beautiful blue eyes." The men opened the gate slowly, and the women filed out with their milking equipment.

Back at the wagon, Sam Sherrill had watched his daughter's stunt and called over to the young officer. "You have to watch out for that girl. She tripped over you to get your attention."

"A girl such as that would not have to work so hard for a man's attention," the lieutenant responded. He stood up and shook out his blanket and folded it neatly. Sam walked over to him.

"You don't know her like I do," Sam told him.

"Who is she?" inquired the lieutenant, tying back his hair in a queue.

"My darling daughter, Kate Sherrill." Sam held out his hand in friendship. "I'm Sam Sherrill." The soldier took his hand in a hearty handshake.

"Lieutenant John Sevier."

"You led the troops that came in last night?" Sam inquired.

"Yes, sir," John answered. "We abandoned Fort Lee, down on the Nolichucky. We didn't have time to finish building it. I only have fourteen men. I wish it were a hundred." John pulled on his riding boots and reached for his waistcoat.

"See any signs of Indians?"

"Everywhere!" John exclaimed. "We've been dodging them for two days. I told Captain Robertson to expect an attack any day. I'm surprised he let those women go out this morning." John put on his uniform coat and picked up his hat.

Sam looked anxiously toward the open gate. "I warned my wife, Mary, to stay close."

"I reckon they'll be safe enough if they stay within rifle range of the lookouts at the walls," John reassured him. "Let's find some breakfast. Robertson usually has something good."

In the fields, down the hill from the fort, the women had made some progress toward the milk cows. That troop of worthy women included some of the most prominent names in the country. Susan Carter was the wife of John Carter, leader of the Watauga Association and the queen of perhaps the wealthiest family in the west. Charlotte Robertson was the no-nonsense wife of Captain James Robertson, and Ruth Brown was the wife of Jacob Brown, owner of most of the Nolichucky Valley. Young, red-haired, and vivacious Ann Robertson Johnston was the beloved schoolmarm, sister to Captain James Robertson and wife of Lieutenant Johnston, then serving heroically at the defense of Charleston, South Carolina. Kesiah Robertson, a cousin of Ann the schoolmarm, was the daughter of Captain Charles Robertson, the leaseholder and land broker of the entire territory subject to the Watauga Indian Agreement of 1775. Then there were the unknown Sherrills, Mary and her two barefoot daughters.

"Katie, I don't see Flowerbell." Mary was a little concerned about their favorite cow.

"I'll find her, Mama," Kate volunteered. She walked through the open meadows beside the rushing waters of the Watauga, farther and farther from the fort looking for the missing cow.

"How old is your girl, Mrs. Sherrill?" asked Charlotte Robertson.

"Katie's twenty-one, and Mary Jane is sixteen. I have another daughter Susan, who is married and living back in Sherrill's Ford. Then I have the six boys . . ."

"Tell us more about Katie! Does she have a husband?" Ruth Brown inquired.

"No, she has never married," Mary answered.

"She sure doesn't look like one to become an old maid," Charlotte observed.

"She's not going to be an old maid," Mary declared. "She just hasn't found the right man. I'm sure the prospects will improve when we find a farm and settle down."

"Mrs. Sherrill, we have land to sell, beautiful land, down on the Nolichucky," Ruth offered. "Jacob and I would be delighted to have you as neighbors."

"Thank you, Mrs. Brown. I'll tell Sam about it." Mary liked Mrs. Brown's warmness of personality, her friendly smile, and welcoming overtures. She thought she would like to have the Browns as neighbors too.

The women separated and began milking the cows nearest the fort.

James Robertson's family occupied one of the four cabins in Watauga Fort. Outside was a cook fire, where Sallie, the Robertson's serving woman worked preparing the family breakfast. John Sevier followed by Sam Sherrill approached and greeted her.

"What's for breakfast, Sallie? I rode half the night thinking about your delicious biscuits and the way you cook those eggs and bacon!" John exclaimed.

"Mr. Jack, you always know how to make a gal feel appreciated. I got biscuits, grits, and everything you like best," she answered. "Sit down the both of you, and I'll serve it up, right now."

"Watch this lady cook, Sam, it's a true art."

"Talk about art. You oughta see this man work his charms on the ladies!" she responded. John laughed along with Sallie.

"Pay no attention to that, Mr. Sherrill," John reacted. "I am a happily married man these fifteen years."

"And many a gal wishes he wasn't," Sallie teased.

On a rough bench outside Robertson's cabin, John Sevier and Sam Sherrill enjoyed a truly artful breakfast, served with cups of hot spice wood tea. Sevier's soldiers joined them and were fed the magnificent breakfast that Sallie prepared and generously dished out.

"I couldn't help but notice your wagon. It's the first one I've seen this far into the wilderness. Where are you from, Mr. Sherrill?" John inquired.

"We came from Sherrill's Ford on the Catawba, Rowan County. We are looking for a farm where Mary and I can provide a good future for the children."

"This is sure the right place for a great future!" John agreed. "I'm just sorry you moved your family right into the path of an Indian War. How many of your family can shoot, and how many rifles have you got?"

"Six rifles, and we all know how to use them. My Kate is the best shot in the family," he boasted.

"That's the girl who doesn't watch where she's going?"

"That's Kate! She can hit the mark at any range, almost every time."

"When the fighting starts, the women will stay off the wall and reload rifles. There's no need to expose the ladies to danger."

James Robertson stepped out of his cabin into the early morning sun.

"Well, good morning, Lieutenant Sevier," Robertson greeted his best friend. "Raiding my kitchen again, are you?"

"Good morning, Captain Robertson," John said with a smile. "Say, what's the idea of letting those women out this morning?"

"Fresh milk, butter, cheese . . ." James returned with a smile.

"What about the Indians?"

"Life must go on as normally as possible," James explained. "Besides, a rider came in last night after you bedded down. He said five companies of militia surprised the Indians yesterday on the Long Island of the Holston and really gave them a fight. He also reported that Chief Dragging Canoe was wounded, and the war party is in full retreat."

"It was a great day's work in the woods!" John exclaimed. "I knew the Shelbys would handle the crisis with characteristic zeal."

"I'd say so," James agreed. "That's why I let the women go out this morning."

"It just sounds too easy though," John said cautiously. "We heard the whole Cherokee nation was out for war. What if they split their forces? I think they could still cause us trouble here at Watauga."

"I am the captain, let me do the thinking," James asserted.

"In the Virginia militia, I held a captain's commission from the governor himself," boasted John.

"This ain't Virginia, John," James reminded him. "Virginia has done nothing to help us. That's why we drafted our petition to be recognized as a county of North Carolina. Then we'll get the protection we need against the Indians. Besides, one North Carolina lieutenant is worth any dozen Virginia captains." John's men laughed to see how Robertson's provincial pride effectively countered John's affection for his good old Virginia.

"Where's Colonel Carter?" John demanded.

"Didn't you know?" James informed him. "He's gone to Halifax to carry our petition to the North Carolina General Assembly. I am completely in charge now."

"His timing couldn't have been worse," John declared. "James, we need to ride out, hunt down the enemy, and strike hard. That's the best defense!" Sam Sherrill was taking in all this information, and liked the way John Sevier handled himself.

"No, John," Robertson spoke gravely. "We have been undermanned ever since our riflemen went down to defend Charleston from the British invasion. When the boys come back, we will fight more aggressively. But now we owe it to our families to stay close to the forts and be ready for anything." Then Robertson's mischievous grin returned. "John, had you finished your own fort on the Nolichucky, you too could have been a captain."

John smiled and shot back at Robertson, "I could have finished Fort Lee if I hadn't spent so much time building this fort for you, and just so you could go down to Chota and talk peace with the chiefs. By the way, how did those treaty talks go?"

Captain Robertson laughed. "Why don't you ask the war chiefs yourself. You seem to think they'll be along any day now."

Now it was John's turn to be serious. "They are close, James. I can feel it! By the way, where is Lydia Bean?"

"The Beans aren't here," replied James.

"She was supposed to be here by noon yesterday," John stated. "She promised she would be here."

"The only people that came in yesterday were the Sherrills," Robertson added. "And what a show that was!"

"Something's wrong, James." John concluded. "I'm riding down to Beans right after breakfast to find out why she's overdue. I should have insisted she travel with us."

"Maybe she went to Eaton's station," the captain suggested.

"Then she would have been right in the middle of yesterday's battle at Long Island," John lamented. "That would be even worse!"

"Very well then," Robertson directed. "Take a couple of men with you, but leave the rest of them here. We have to get organized for whatever happens next. By the way, you will be in charge of the night watch."

John sprang to his feet. "The night watch! Why me?"

"The rest of us have families here," Robertson explained. "We can't stay up all night and neglect our families the way you can."

"I don't neglect my family," he protested. "I make sacrifices in the service of my country! They understand it's my duty."

"Good man," Robertson praised him. "I knew I could depend on you to do your duty, Lieutenant Sevier. You also get to choose your men for the night watch. That should help your popularity!"

"Now wait a minute, James."

Robertson had himself a good laugh. "Carry on, Lieutenant. I'm busy with my own responsibilities." Robertson walked toward the blockhouse.

John turned to Sam. "There you are, Mr. Sherrill. You have witnessed for yourself the marvelous workings of the Watauga Association. Now you know how things get done around here." Sam smiled at the good-humored banter he had just enjoyed as breakfast entertainment.

Kate Sherrill, walking briskly, enjoyed the warmth of the early morning sun as it dried away the last of the night's dampness clinging to her shift. When working in the fields, she wore no gown over her petticoat or bodice over her shift to give her the most freedom of movement possible. The shift came down to her elbows, leaving bare her tanned lower arms. The one adornment she would not leave behind was her fine linen lace cap, which she wore like a crown, perched atop the cascading raven hair. The wet dew on the grass was cool to her bare feet, but it soaked the hem of her ankle-length linen petticoat.

Bounder had accompanied her from the fort, but about half a mile out, he stopped short and growled.

"What is it, Bounder?" Kate said, looking at the alert dog. The hair on his back was up, and he continued growling. "Do you smell a bear? Or is it a skunk?" Bounder turned and ran back a few yards and turned again in the direction of her progress, repeating his warning. "Come on, boy! Go with me just a little farther. Flowerbell is just at the end of the clearing. I can hear her calling." The brave sheepdog could not be induced to proceed another step. She had seen this behavior before over insignificant things and decided to go ahead anyway, but much more cautiously. She would just retrieve the cow and get back before whatever Bounder was worried about could do any harm.

At the edge of the cleared fields, thick underbrush took advantage of the sunlight and grew in profusion. There, Kate found Flowerbell with her head in the brush grazing.

"Oh, you naughty cow, you better not be eating that bitter weed!" The boys must have left a lead rope on her yesterday, and it seemed to be all tangled up in the brush. "Here we go, Flowerbell. Come with me. How did you get all tangled up here?"

Kate dropped her milking stool and reached for the lead rope, but suddenly a strong hand grabbed her wrist from the underbrush below. A frightful war-painted Indian stood up. Other Indians emerged from the bushes all along the edge of the clearing. Kate pulled her body back trying to free her wrist from the iron grip of the savage.

"Oh no! Let go of me!" she resisted. Her free hand still held the heavy oak milk bucket. She swung it at the face of her attacker as hard as she could. As he reeled from the force of the blow, her smooth skin slid free of his sweaty palm, and she stumbled back a few steps. She turned, regained her balance, lifted her petticoat, and accelerated as fast as her legs could move toward the fort. The bushes behind her exploded with howling warriors, and the death race began.

Mrs. Sherrill milked a cow close enough to Charlotte Robertson's to continue the conversation about Katie's prospects for marriage.

"You know, Mrs. Robertson, it is not as though my Katie does not attract men. She certainly does; in fact, she's constantly being pursued . . ."

The distant screams of the terrified young woman, at that moment, reached the ears of the working women. "Mama! Run for the fort! Indians! Run, Mama, run!" The screams issued by her daughter, accompanied by a chorus of Indian war whoops, were like nothing Mary Sherrill had ever heard before, a sort of shouting and mournful crying mixed together, between gasps for precious air. The women stood up from their work and saw brave Kate at a great distance running toward them with over two dozen Indians in pursuit.

"I see what you mean," Charlotte said dryly. "I'll say she's being pursued."

"Oh, my dear Katie! What has she gotten herself into now?" Mary fretted.

"Looks like big trouble!" Charlotte shouted. "To the fort, ladies, quickly! Come, now, Mrs. Sherrill!" She grabbed Mary's arm and pulled her toward the gate. The ladies ran as they realized the rapidly developing danger. Mary Jane joined her mother and helped her stay focused on saving her own life.

Kate set an early pace the Indians could not overtake. She focused on her breathing, deep, full, and rhythmic. She took no notice of the pounding her bare feet were taking in the wet stubble of recently cleared fields. Rocks, sticks, and brushy debris were no obstacles to a girl trying to survive. She felt the wind in her hair pulling at her lacy cap and snatched it from her head. She clenched it in her hand tightly so she wouldn't lose it and looked ahead at the fort on the hill. Men appeared along the top of the wall taking defensive positions. She could hear the sounds of men shouting orders, alarmed into action. She saw the other women make it inside the gate. Her mother stopped and turned to shout encouragement in the forlorn hope that Kate, still a couple of hundred yards away, might make it.

Crying hysterically, her heart breaking, Mary shouted, "Run! Oh, Katie! Run!" Captain Robertson himself stepped out and roughly pulled Mrs. Sherrill inside the gate. The heavy wooden gate swung shut, sealing the doom of the brave girl still running for her life. Kate saw clearly why she had been sacrificed. Waves of Indians appeared along the river and rushed the gate, cutting off her escape. Shots rang from the palisades, and a sharp engagement began. Kate was not giving up.

Inside the fort the men barred the heavy gates. Mary Sherrill pleaded frantically. "My bonny daughter's out there. Oh, please, don't lock her out! Save my Bonny Kate!"

James Robertson, with rifle in hand, stood blocking the gate, unmoved by the cries of the women. John Sevier and Sam Sherrill, armed with their rifles, made their way through the flock of panicked women to reach the gate. Sam embraced Mary, trying to console her.

John Sevier stepped forward. "I'll save your Bonny Kate. Open the gate, James."

"No!" the captain shouted. "You can't save her! Open that gate and we'll all be killed." Musket shot and arrows peppered the gate like hail.

John turned to the men on the wall. "Aim for the ones chasing the girl! Don't let them lay a hand on her!" he ordered. The men complied with great precision.

"She's heading for the back wall . . . Go, you girl, go!" shouted young Landon Carter. John Sevier ran across the commons with Captain Robertson on his heels. John flew to the catwalk along the back wall, and Robertson joined him in time to see the exhausted Kate round the corner of the blockhouse. She was looking up for a way over the high wall.

A man named Tipton, on the ground beside the catwalk, had an idea. He shoved a long stick through a gap in the palisade wall and anchored it with the heel of his boot. "Step on the stick, and climb up!" he shouted to the desperate girl.

Kate threw her cap over the wall and jumped to get a foot on the protruding stick, but her weight rolled the stick from under the man's boot, and the stick flew up between his legs with a sickening thud. She fell equally hard in a heap outside the wall gasping for breath. She looked up again and reached out to touch the solid log wall only a few inches away from safety. Her heart was pounding so hard she never heard the one warrior who finally reached the wall beneath the shelter of the overhanging blockhouse. He grabbed her by the hair and roughly dragged her away from the wall, and she knew she was once again in the clutches of Satan. She tried to resist, but the pain inflicted on her scalp was too much, and she gave ground several feet from the wall to relieve that pain. She reached up and grabbed the man's hand to counteract the influence he exerted on her long dark hair and fell to a sitting position. She wasn't going any farther. The death race would have to end there. The Indian standing over his prize now raised his tomahawk.

John Sevier had primed his pan, leveled his rifle, cocked, and aimed. All the other men on that wall were reloading. He spoke to his rifle, as a man speaks to his woman, "Don't fail me, Sweet Lips . . ."

Crack! The rifle shot sent the warrior falling away from the struggling Kate. She untangled herself from the loosening grip of the dying man and struggled to her feet. More Indians approached the back wall to complete their encirclement of all sides of the fort.

"Ohhh!" she exclaimed at the sight of more Indians.

John handed his rifle to James and leaned over the top of the wall, with both hands reaching down.

"Jump for me, Kate!" he shouted. "You can make it!"

Kate saw her salvation and with a running start, through a hail of arrows and bullets, made a mighty leap for John's outstretched hands. Their hands met, and she held tight, but there was a tremor of exhaustion or terror or something in that desperate powerful grip.

John knew he had to pull her up quickly as an arrow glanced off his cheek. The athletic girl kicked her right leg toward the top of the wall with her last ounce of energy, and James Robertson was there to grab it and help pull her up. She rolled over the top of the wall into John's arms, and he eased her down to the catwalk. She clung to him with powerful hands, gasping for breath and sobbing with relief. Her eyes, tightly closed, shut out the horror of what might have been. She allowed her other senses to slowly awaken to the fact that she had found safety in the arms of a strong man—her savior, who risked his life leaning over the wall to bring her back from the dead.

"Good shot, John! You saved the girl's life!" James exclaimed.

John wanted so much to linger and comfort this hot, sweat-drenched little thing, who a little while earlier had tried to get his attention. Well, now she had it.

Seeking to relieve the emotional tension surrounding them, John imitated the Scots-Irish accent of Mrs. Sherrill that he had noted at the gate. "A bonny lass for a footrace you are, my Bonny Kate! There's a brave girl!"

Bonny Kate raised her head and looked into the beautiful blue eyes of her savior. It was Lieutenant Jack. All happened so fast, she didn't know who had saved her; but her hero was the same man she watched bedding down in the wee hours, and the same man she had awakened that morning. *Oh, Providence, how perfect are thy gifts!*

The women and children shouted for joy when they saw her move. Strong arms picked her up, removing her from the embrace of the lieutenant, and carefully lifted her down to the ground setting her on her poor tortured bleeding feet.

Mary Sherrill, weeping for joy, rushed to embrace her daughter. "Oh, sweetheart. Praise the Lord!" she cried breathlessly. She raised her eyes to John sitting on the catwalk. "Thank you, good sir. God bless you!"

John acknowledged her gratitude with a smile and a salute. As the women led the dazed young heroine away, James bent down and picked up the girl's cap from where it had landed on the catwalk. He handed it to John. "I believe the pleasure of returning this to its owner goes to you, good sir." As John received the cap, a drop of blood from his arrow wound fell on it and stained it. He stuffed it in his waistcoat and returned to the rifle work. A life was taken, a life was spared, but the war wasn't over.

Chapter 6

The Hero's Reward

The women praised much the virtues of Catharine Sherrill as they escorted her to a blanket Mary Jane spread out beside the Sherrill wagon. Charlotte Robertson and her sister-in-law Ann were particularly concerned about her well-being and took charge. Ruth Brown and Mary Sherrill stood by for emotional support. The subject of their collective concern collapsed on the blanket; her chest heaving for want of air.

Charlotte wanted to treat the wounds, assuming there were many. "Now catch your breath, we'll get you some water. What an ordeal! Ann, my dear, fetch some water, and clean linen for bandages. Also bring me that pair of moccasins I was stitching." Ann ran to the Robertson's cabin for the requested items. "Now, Miss Kate, where are your wounds?"

"My feet and legs," she moaned.

Charlotte pulled up her petticoat well above her knees looking for injuries. Kate sat up for a look too. "I see nothing but scrapes and cuts!" Charlotte exclaimed. "I would have thought all that shooting would have produced serious wounds. It's a miracle for sure!"

"Praise the Lord!" Mary Sherrill rejoiced. "Oh, sweetheart, when they barred the gate, I was so afraid you were lost!" She burst into tears again as the women laid hands on her to comfort her. Mary Jane brought a dipper of water to her sister. Kate never tasted better.

"Don't cry, Mama. I was more worried for you," Kate said between draughts of the cool sweet water. "I'm so glad everyone got in safely!" Mrs. Sherrill regained her composure. Ann returned with the items for cleaning and dressing the injuries, and she brought a pair of moccasins. Charlotte and Ann washed Kate's feet and wrapped them in the cloth bandages.

"Who was that brave soldier that pulled me over the wall?"

"Lieutenant John Sevier," Charlotte answered. "I owe my life to that courageous man! He called me . . . Bonny Kate . . ." As soon as Charlotte tied the last bandage in place, she picked up the moccasins. "All right, Bonny Kate, I want you to wear these moccasins until your cuts heal. They'll keep out the dirt."

"Whose moccasins are they?" Bonny Kate asked.

"I was restitching them for Lieutenant Sevier," Charlotte answered. "I'm sure he won't mind."

The battle at the walls was raging. Jacob Brown came running over to the gathering of women. "More help to the wall! The captain needs everyone who can tote, load, or shoot to come on the run!"

"All right, girls, let's go to work!" Charlotte ordered. They all got up and headed toward the wall. Bonny Kate paused long enough to slip the lieutenant's moccasins on her sore feet and ran to the wall where her father and brothers were posted. Sam Sherrill was on the catwalk with his sons Adam and Sam Junior. They needed reloaders; and that's where Bonny Kate, Mary Jane, and their mother went to work. Her younger brothers William and George were distributing gunpowder and filling powder horns from kegs the Sherrills had brought for hunting game in the new land.

Ann Johnston worked nearby and watched Bonny Kate reload the rifles very rapidly. Her skill amazed Ann.

"You are pretty handy with a gun," Ann observed. "Where did you learn to load that fast?"

"Hunting rabbits," Bonny Kate joked. "How else could I get a second shot?" Ann laughed. Bonny Kate handed up another loaded rifle to her father. "Primed and ready!" she called. Sam took it and passed down another to reload. "Watch this," Bonny Kate said to Ann. She put a handful of shot in her mouth and loaded the next five rifles in rapid succession, dispensing shot from her mouth and powder from the horn in her hand. "Now let's have some fun," she called to Ann. In the next rifle, she added a little extra powder and handed it up to her favorite brother Adam. He fired the rifle with a bigger-than-normal kick.

"Ow!" Adam exclaimed. Father Sam looked over at Adam and saw him rubbing his shoulder.

"Are you hit?" Sam asked with great concern.

"Katie overcharged that one," he complained.

Sam looked sternly at his grinning daughter. "Ease up on that powder, girl. We may run out before this thing is over."

"Yes, sir," she said respectfully. Bonny Kate looked over at Ann. "They ought to let me do the shooting. I don't waste any powder with missed shots." Ann was both amused with and amazed at the abilities of this rare girl. She resolved to know her better if time allowed.

After about an hour from the first war whoop, the firing died down. James Robertson shouted the command, "Hold your fire, men. They're well out of range." The leading men gathered for a conference near the front gate.

"Well, that was a hot contest!" Lieutenant Sevier exclaimed.

"Yes," Captain Robertson agreed. "I'd say Miss Sherrill got the best of them this round. They wore themselves out trying to catch her."

The men laughed heartily. Sam Sherrill left his post and walked into the leader's circle. He looked John in the eye and held out his hand.

"Sir, I want to thank you properly for what you did," Sam said in all seriousness. John took his hand, but Sam pulled him into a bear hug. "Katie is our most precious treasure, and you saved her!"

"I did my duty, sir," John replied modestly. Sam released him and looked him in the eye again.

"It was Divine Providence!" he declared. "The spirit of greatness shines in you, sir. You are one to watch out for!" The plain-speaking men of the frontier, who surrounded them, stood in silent awe of Sam Sherrill's words until the silence became a little too uncomfortable for James Robertson.

"Yes, I agree with Mr. Sherrill," James spoke up. "I believe Divine Providence is with us. But the good Lord helps those who help themselves. Gentlemen, keep a sharp lookout for any activity that looks like another attack. We could be holed up here for a long time. John, how many men do we have?"

"Forty good men at arms," John replied.

"Forty men to protect two hundred women and children is a mighty big job," James said. "We need an inventory of the supplies and a plan to ration the food and ammunition."

"For how long?" John asked.

"Maybe two weeks," James guessed. "Help should arrive from the Holston by then. Lieutenant Sevier, would you get that inventory done?"

"Yes, sir," John agreed.

The Indians chose not to renew their attack that day. Several that had been wounded and left in the fields either crawled or walked away. Captain Robertson gave strict orders not to shoot the enemy wounded. Jacob Brown told the captain that the wounded would return to the Indian camp, discourage their fellows, and eat up the supplies. Jacob Brown usually knew what he was talking about when it came to the Indians.

That afternoon John was in the blockhouse at the corner of the fort, taking inventory of the supplies and trying to figure out how long those supplies would last. Bonny Kate, washed and redressed, entered the open door quietly.

"Captain Sevier?" she addressed him. A man like him ought to be at least a captain, she reasoned; and so in her own mind, she had promoted him.

John looked up from his work. "Well, Miss Bonny Kate, it's a pleasure to see you in less dangerous circumstances."

She smiled and stepped closer to him. "I want to thank you for risking your life to save me this morning."

"You're a brave girl, and that was an amazing jump."

"It was leap or die for I would not have lived a captive!" She stepped closer again. "I'm sorry you were wounded."

"It's just a scratch," he replied. "Oh, I have something that belongs to you." He pulled out her cap and handed it to her. "We found it near the wall."

She noticed the bloodstain. "Oh, there's blood!"

"I'm sorry," he said. "It's probably mine. I should clean that up for you."

"No," she said rather abruptly, clutching the lace cap to her bosom. She had the blood of her savior, shed for her, on the cap she wore as her crown of glory. It was hers to treasure; and no one, not even him, would clean it up. She looked at the scratch on his cheek and stepped closer again. "I feel bad to think you'll always wear that scar on my account."

John laughed. "I'm sure it will heal without a scar. You did the smart thing running around to the back wall."

"I never saw anything so good as you, leaning over that wall with your hands reaching down for me." Her feelings were causing her to say things she could not predict and think of things she should never do. It was all coming at her like a pot boiling over. "Run, Katie, run!" she could remember her mother shouting.

The man smiled at her and said, "I'm sure glad it turned out the way it did."

"Thank you, with all my heart." She took one final step and quickly kissed him on his wounded cheek. She paused to look at his surprised face and immediately left the blockhouse.

Lieutenant Sevier could not have been more surprised at her action than she was. What had possessed her to do that? She knew almost nothing about the man except that he saved her life; he was strong, polite, good humored, loved his horses, and was assigned to command the night watch. In his dress and appearance, he was, without exception, the handsomest man she had ever seen. Everyone seemed to be his friend, but he appeared not to have any family connections at Watauga Fort. She had to know more.

Storm clouds rose high over the valley west of Watauga Fort. The thunder rumbled, and the cooling winds came down. Bonny Kate ran to the wall where her father was posted, watching the gathering storm. She stood beside him and felt the cool wind caress her face. One hundred women had watched her go into the blockhouse and knew who she was with and how long she had been there.

"Where have you been daughter?" Sam asked.

"I wanted to thank Captain Sevier," she replied.

Sam smiled. "He's quite a character."

"You know him?" she asked.

"Had breakfast with him," Sam replied. "He was very entertaining. Now I'm much beholden to him." Sam took his little girl into his arms and hugged her. His heart was full of gratitude for the opportunity to enjoy such a moment again. A tear came to the man's eye. "They had given you up for dead when they closed that gate. They completely discounted your life to save everyone else. There's a hard lesson there. Your mother took a terrible shock by that. She told me she was the one who sent you out to find Flowerbell."

"But because I found the Indians first and warned everyone, these people regard me as someone special," she pointed out.

"No one is special or any better than anyone else, without the gifts of Divine Providence," Sam reminded his daughter.

"I always trust to Providence," she professed. She immediately thought of Lieutenant Sevier and ached to ask the one question she wanted answered. Her father might know, but she did not want to be obvious. Runaway feelings in a daughter are a father's great fear. She did not want to display these feelings to her father, not now.

There was insufficient shelter from the elements at Watauga Fort. When the sudden cloudburst came, women and children crowded into the blockhouse, the cabins, and under the flimsy canvas tents. Bonny Kate and Mary Jane, along with William and George took shelter under the big Conestoga while mother Mary Sherrill rested in the bed above them.

Ann Robertson Johnston and her two small daughters ran to the Sherrill wagon to seek shelter.

"Do you have room for three more?" Ann asked.

"We will make room!" Bonny Kate invited her. "Come in." Ann and her children settled in and the two women considered each other thoughtfully.

"Thank you," Ann said, "Bonny Kate, isn't it?"

"That's what folks are calling me now. Bonny Kate . . . I think I like it better than plain old Kate."

"It's a name folks are going to remember," Ann predicted.

"I reckon so. What's your name?"

"Ann Robertson Johnston."

"Are you Captain Robertson's daughter?"

"No, his sister," Ann replied.

"Are these your children?" Bonny Kate inquired.

"Yes, this is Mary, and that's Elizabeth. My husband, David, went with the volunteers to defend Charleston."

Bonny Kate could wait no longer for the information she longed to have. "What do you know about the lieutenant? Is he married?" Bonny Kate inquired.

"John Sevier? Oh Lord, yes, and with eight children," Ann responded.

The answer crushed Bonny Kate. It was all she could do to hide her disappointment. Maybe there was some mistake. "Oh . . . but he looks so young!"

"He's only thirty, but he married his childhood sweetheart at sixteen and loves her dearly."

"Is she here in the fort?" Bonny Kate asked.

"No, his family lives in the Holston settlement." Ann's daughter, Elizabeth, crawled into her mother's lap; and her thumb went into her mouth for a nap. Ann laughed gently. "It looks like we are going to be here awhile, Bonny Kate. Why not tell me the story of your life and loves?"

Bonny Kate smiled wistfully. "There's not much to tell . . ." The thunder rumbled, the rain poured, and a friendship began.

The rain stopped in time for the women of the fort to cook the night dinner. Bonny Kate wondered what the night would bring. Would it be the same as last night with its dreadful silence? Or would things change after the successful defense of Watauga Fort, and the command of the night watch transferring to Lieutenant Sevier? She just didn't know.

After dinner, Bonny Kate strolled around the inside walls of the fort. The clouds still obscured the sky so there was no moon. People were talking tonight but in low hushed voices. She was hoping to encounter Lieutenant Sevier, just for one last look, because she knew she had to stay away from him, now that she knew he was married. That made her blue as blue as his eyes. "Stop it," she told herself. "Don't think about him that way, Kate. No, Bonny Kate. I'm keeping the name. I like it. It's proper for a lady of quality to have a double name." There he was, walking toward her after stepping down from the wall.

"How's our Bonny Kate this evening?" John greeted her.

"Still alive, thanks to you!" she answered.

John put his hand to his cheek. "Please, don't thank me again."

She laughed in spite of herself. He was funny, engaging, and charming.

"Are we allowed to speak?" she asked. "Last night, I got in trouble for disobeying the order of strict silence."

"Oh, forget about Robertson's foolishness." He laughed. "I'm in charge of the night watch now. Besides how is anybody going to keep a hundred women quiet? That's unnatural." She laughed again.

"I understand your wife and family are back in Virginia." She wanted him to know she knew he was married.

"Well, our farm is on the Holston. If the Indian attacks go that far north, Sarah and the children will go to John Shelby's fort."

She now knew his wife's name was Sarah, a name she always liked. She felt a sudden impulse to care for this man, out of charity, gratitude, or some such feeling.

"I was thinking you probably need the help and support of a family here like the other men have. I can cook for you, wash, and mend your clothes and do anything else you require." She felt her feelings running away with her again, but it had been that kind of a day.

"I appreciate the kind offer, ma'am, but I'm used to going it alone. We're riding out soon to chase the Indians all the way back to their villages."

"I don't understand how, in as much as the Indians stole your horses," she pointed out.

"So you know about that, do you?" John was impressed she was so knowledgeable about the situation. Usually the men didn't worry the women with such dire details.

"Your horses are missing; so is my dog, and they probably got my cow too," she complained. "Please, Captain, let me help you until we get out of this mess," she insisted.

"Well, for just a few days, but you'll find I do not require much maintenance."

"Thank you, Captain!"

Sam Sherrill joined them as she turned to leave.

"Good night, Miss Bonny Kate," John said.

"Good night, sir. Good night, Father, dear," she said sweetly.

"Sleep well, my darling."

Bonny Kate kissed her father and walked away as John watched her go.

"Quite some girl you have there, Mr. Sherrill."

"Aye, she's one to watch out for!"

"I imagine she's ready to find a husband and settle down."

"She spins, weaves, sews, cooks, gardens, herds, hunts, and fights better than any woman I've ever seen," Sam boasted. "And her mother has even taught her to read the Bible and write."

"I reckon she is one to watch out for!" John marveled.

"Lieutenant Sevier, I want to join your outfit."

"It's the night watch, Sam, not the best place for a family man," John cautioned.

"Listen, Lieutenant, I was a ranger with Colonel Hugh Waddell in the last war, so I've seen good officers. You have the same qualities. I trust you and would prefer to serve on your watch."

"You honor me, sir. I would be delighted to have a man with your experience!" John exclaimed.

"The Sherrills stick together, so Sam Junior and Adam will also serve," Sam volunteered.

"Very well, Mr. Sherrill," John replied. "Get your boys with their rifles, and join us on the walls."

"Thank you, sir." Sam saluted and turned toward his wagon to round up his sons.

Chapter 7

Sweet Lips

John Sevier and James Robertson conferred quietly as the sun peeked over the eastern horizon. John was showing the captain some activity the night watch had been observing during the misty gray predawn. Several Indians had been seen moving about in the fields slightly beyond rifle range.

"We located their camp last night by the glow of their fires," John told the captain. "They are downriver beyond Gap Creek. We could sally out this morning and give them a surprise attack."

"Absolutely not!" James reacted. "I saw no fewer than three hundred warriors yesterday, and we were very lucky to not lose a single life. Can you imagine the panic and despair that would have accompanied the cruel murder of that Sherrill girl? Had the women and children witnessed that, and the scene of a scalping, we would be in a hell of a fix. I'm taking no risks."

John accepted the captain's assessment of the situation. His thoughts turned to the fortunate Miss Sherrill. No ordinary woman would have survived that ordeal. John was amazed at Bonny Kate Sherrill's display of stamina, courage, and physical strength that enabled her to cling so ferociously to life. He remembered her intelligent, confident way of speaking from their two conversations and her father's boasting about her abilities. He wondered how Sam had managed to raise up such qualities in a child. He wondered how old she was. If she was so accomplished, why wasn't she married?

"We will keep an eye on them," James promised. "If they try to close in for harassing fire, I'll have my sharpshooters drive them back. Why don't you and your men get some sleep?"

Sleep sounded mighty good to John. None of his men had slept since the previous dawn. They had successfully defended Watauga Fort, stayed at their posts all day, even through the thunderstorm, and stayed on watch all night.

Robertson's men replaced them at the walls, and John dismissed his tired men for breakfast and bed.

"I need a place that's dark and quiet," he told James Robertson.

"The loft in my cabin would be good in the cool of the morning," Robertson offered. John thanked him and walked to Robertson's. He leaned his rifle, Sweet Lips, beside the door of the cabin, accepted one of Sallie's biscuits and a cup of water on his way to bed, and was the first of the night watch to find repose. Nothing short of a shooting war would wake him today.

The Sherrill men came from the night watch tired and hungry. As Bonny Kate served them their breakfast, Adam told her about the Indians sneaking around outside the fort.

"Why didn't you shoot them?" she asked.

"Lieutenant Sevier didn't want to wake the ladies," Adam explained.

Bonny Kate looked around the fort and saw almost everyone awake and working at their breakfasts. "There are no sleeping ladies to worry about now. I'm going to see what's out there for myself." She picked up her own rifle, a small caliber fowling piece, and walked toward the wall.

"There she goes again, Sam," Mary observed. "Aren't you going to stop her?"

"Nope," Sam replied wearily. "The sooner she wins this war, the sooner we can get some sleep."

James Robertson, having posted his men at the walls, returned to the cooking area and enjoyed a hot steaming drink.

"Good morning, Miss Sherrill. Where are you going with that rifle?" he asked.

"My brother Adam said he saw some Indians creeping around out there. I'm going to even the score for the discomfort they caused me yesterday."

"Let me see your rifle," he requested. She stopped and presented the rifle to him for inspection.

"It was my Granny Sherrill's," she declared proudly.

"A bird gun won't do much good," he judged. "Wait, I've got just the rifle for the job." He walked over to the door of the cabin and picked up John's rifle Sweet Lips, leaving Bonny Kate's bird gun in its place. "I think you can handle this," he said, giving her the long rifle, and a shot pouch to go with it.

"Is it yours?" she hesitated.

"Belongs to a friend," he answered. "He won't mind."

"It's a fine-looking rifle!"

"Go up to the wall and give it a try," he urged. Bonny Kate carried Sweet Lips to the palisade wall.

Jacob Brown had become something of an admirer of the athletic and talented girl who stole so many hearts the day before with her death-defying exploits. He welcomed her pleasant company and showed her where the Indians were last seen lurking around, just out of rifle range.

"You see, Miss Sherrill," Mr. Brown explained, "these fellows are trying to move in close enough to pick off our men on the wall. That way they can harass us all day." She listened attentively to Mr. Brown as she loaded the rifle. "You are overcharging that rifle, miss."

"Not for this range," she replied.

"You mean to tell me, you are going to try to reach them from here?" he challenged.

"If this rifle here can stand the heavy use, and I believe it can," she reasoned as she rammed the ball down the barrel.

Jacob Brown moved behind her as she aimed at the distant Indian. "You sure are aiming high."

"The ball's going to drop," she explained. "Now, sir, watch his powder horn."

"Boom!" went the rifle. The smoke had cleared the muzzle before the Indian jumped like he had been stung by a bee. He discovered his shattered powder horn and looked all around trying to find the source of that shot.

"Incredible luck!" Jacob Brown exclaimed.

"Ooo! I love this rifle," she purred.

"I wouldn't have believed it if I hadn't seen it with my own two eyes. I'd give anything to see that again," Mr. Brown exclaimed.

"Give me a moment to reload, and we'll try it again!" she replied.

The rifle shot attracted the attention of the entire fort including the sleeping lieutenant, who was rudely jolted awake. He sleepily struggled to pull on his boots and gear and tumbled out of Robertson's loft. At the cabin door, he reached for Sweet Lips but instead found a small bird gun. Robertson stood nearby, amused with John's frantic scramble.

"Anybody seen my rifle?" he called out.

"What's wrong?" answered the captain.

"I can't find Sweet Lips!" John shouted.

James Robertson pointed to the catwalk on the wall where Bonny Kate aimed the rifle and fired a second round. "She's up there," Robertson announced to John and to a large audience of onlookers.

"No, I mean my rifle!" John insisted.

James smiled and called over to the girl on the wall, "Hey, Bonny Kate, Lieutenant Sevier wants to know if you've got Sweet Lips!"

Bewildered why anyone would ask such a question of a lady, and innocent to the joke being played on Lieutenant Sevier, she responded with a good-natured smile. "Let the lieutenant come up here and find out!"

Almost everyone in the fort burst out laughing at her reply, enjoying John's embarrassment. John walked to the wall and climbed up on the catwalk. She was confused and completely unsure what he was about to do. Had he told the captain about her kiss? Was he now going to take liberties with her, in front of all these people, that her careless answer had invited? How would her wildly running feelings respond? As he stepped close to her, she tried to read his intentions in his eyes, but to no avail. Smiling, he reached over and took the rifle from her.

"I reckon the joke is on me," John explained. "You see, Miss Sherrill, I call my rifle Sweet Lips because when she speaks, the whole valley listens!"

With a sigh of relief and the confusion cleared up, she again felt the thrill of being close to him and spoke, "Then I reckon the joke is on both of us!"

"Jack, you ought to see this girl shoot!" Jacob Brown exclaimed. "She just ran off two braves who were trying to get close enough for a shot." John peered over the wall. "See them running there? She busted that feller's powder horn with her first shot; and to prove it wasn't luck, she did the same thing to the other feller. I ain't never seen shooting like that!"

"That's out of range!" John marveled.

"I'll make the Indians run out of powder," she explained. "Then they'll leave us alone."

"Well, we need to save our ammunition," John concluded. "This could be a long siege." He climbed off the catwalk and helped Bonny Kate down. They walked toward the cook fires.

Bonny Kate still felt uncomfortable about the embarrassing moment they had just experienced. She thought if she could just keep talking, the issue might be resolved. John was ready to go back to bed and wanted peace and quiet. His natural politeness was about to be overcome by his state of exhaustion.

"Papa says my shooting makes men feel uncomfortable. Do I make you uncomfortable?"

"No, ma'am," he replied angrily in a low voice so as not to alarm the women and children nearby. "About a thousand angry Cherokee warriors make me uncomfortable. I have only forty riflemen protecting over two hundred women and children, with only two pounds of shot and three weeks of rations. And I'm haunted by nightmares of the Fort Loudon massacre! Now why do you think that you could make me feel uncomfortable?"

"I'm glad, I don't," she answered so wishing she could change the subject. "By the way, thank you for the use of your moccasins."

John looked down at her feet and saw his moccasins as they arrived before the door of the Robertson cabin. "How did you get my moccasins?"

"I gave them to her to wear while her feet heal," Charlotte answered. "How do you feel this morning Bonny Kate, any aches or pains?"

"My feet and legs are still sore, but the moccasins have really helped." She turned again to John. "I hope you don't mind me wearing them."

"No, help yourself to anything I own; but don't ever take a man's rifle without asking, especially in the middle of a war!" John scolded. He turned abruptly, entered the cabin, and slammed the door.

"But the captain said—" she began her defense to the closed door, feeling her own anger beginning to rise.

The door to the cabin opened again, and John spoke one last time. "Keep it quiet out here so the night watch can get some sleep. I'm going back to bed." The door closed again.

Bonny Kate was not finished. She stepped up to James Robertson with her unresolved anger. "You made me look foolish, and now Captain Sevier is angry with me!"

"Lieutenant Sevier will get over it," he countered. "Besides, the men needed a good laugh this morning, and they sure got it!"

"I'm glad somebody was amused at my expense!" Bonny Kate grabbed her bird rifle and abruptly walked away toward the Sherrill wagon.

James turned to Charlotte. "Some temper!"

"Mr. Robertson," Charlotte warned, "you better leave her alone until you know more about her family."

"Why?" James asked.

"I think it's odd she's not married, as old as she is," Charlotte pointed out. "Why is she so handy with a gun? And why did her family come over the mountains in the middle of an Indian uprising?"

"I haven't thought about that," James replied.

"You have always said the outlaws and Tories are overrunning this country," Charlotte reminded him. "We have a right to be suspicious of newcomers. You be careful of those people, James."

At the Indian Camp, Chief Abram listened to his warriors describe how the Spirit Warrior of the Wataugans had broken their powder horns. They insisted that they were out of range of the fort, and no mere mortal man could have performed such a feat, twice. The Spirit Warrior was assisting the whites they declared. Chief Abram kept his warriors in camp that day while his medicine man worked on a counter measure that might induce the Spirit Warrior to leave the whites and help the Cherokees.

Chapter 8

The Captive Community

All morning, the men of the night watch slept. Bonny Kate set up her mother's spinning wheel and worked at spinning some linen thread. As she produced yard after yard of thread, she had time to reflect on the events of the previous day and the early morning encounter with Lieutenant Sevier. She had to admit, Captain Robertson's elaborate amusement designed to give the people of the fort a good laugh had worked perfectly. Her own innocent, but carelessly suggestive, reaction to the Sweet Lips question truly embarrassed Lieutenant Sevier; but the way he handled it before the large audience, with such easy grace and politeness toward her, was truly masterful. The public man was well polished, gracious, and popular. In the next instant, she had been privileged to view the private man, worried, exhausted, irritated, and angry at her. At both extremes of his personality, he was honest, expressive, never profane, and without the vanity of pride. This Lieutenant John Sevier was the model of a great man, which made Bonny Kate wonder about his wife. What skills and attributes did Sarah possess to deserve being his dearly beloved child bride and mother of his eight children?

Ann Robertson came over to help Bonny Kate change her bandages. As Ann washed her feet, Bonny Kate examined the lieutenant's moccasins. Perhaps the neat stitching had been done lovingly by Sarah Sevier herself.

"These wounds are healing nicely," Ann observed. "Charlotte was smart to give you those moccasins."

"Yes, I've had the best of care," agreed Bonny Kate. "I appreciate your kindness."

"Nothing slows you down, does it?" Ann asked.

"What do you mean?" Bonny Kate responded.

"That was quite a demonstration you put on this morning," Ann declared.

"Oh, that!" she said. "Well, it really embarrassed Captain Sevier, and I shouldn't have said what I said, but I had no idea that he named his rifle

Sweet Lips. Your brother really played a good joke on me and on poor Captain Sevier."

"No, I mean the shooting," Ann said seriously. "Jacob Brown can't stop talking about it. How do you do it?"

"The shooting?" Bonny Kate repeated. "I don't know. It just comes kind of natural. I've been doing it all my life. One of my uncles had a powder mill, so we always had plenty of powder for practice."

"It was amazing!" Ann marveled. "And almost nobody noticed the real show because of the comedy that followed."

"Thank you, Ann," Bonny Kate said. "It is nice to be able to appreciate each other for who we really are, instead of how we are cast in certain situations in which we never wanted to find ourselves in the first place."

Ann laughed. "That's deep, Bonny Kate, too deep for me!"

Bonny Kate laughed with her. "Forgive me, Ann, sometimes I say things like that without realizing myself what they mean."

"Yes, you're really good at that too." Ann laughed. The conversation that followed was warm, and their friendship deepened, and much thread was spun that morning. After about two hours, Kesiah Robertson came looking for Ann. "Bonny Kate, I want you to meet my cousin Kesiah Robertson. She's the daughter of my Uncle Charles; and her sister Susannah married Captain Felix Walker, the leader of the Watauga men who went to defend Charleston. That's where my husband is."

"Kesiah, I'm pleased to meet you," Bonny Kate greeted her.

"Likewise," Kesiah responded. "I thank you for discovering the Indians yesterday. We all came back safely, thanks to you."

"I'm glad I could help." Bonny Kate smiled.

"Lucky for you, Lieutenant Sevier was there to help you over the wall."

"I know," she agreed. "It was leap or die, for I would not have lived a captive!"

"You made a spectacle of yourself this morning too," Kesiah observed.

"I was so embarrassed by that!" Bonny Kate exclaimed. "I couldn't imagine what Captain Robertson meant by asking if I had sweet lips."

There were too many things Kesiah didn't like about the new girl. She was a show-off, too beautiful, too lucky, and too easily the center of attention. She was the same age as Kesiah, and like her still unmarried. Therefore, Kesiah viewed her as a rival for the attentions of the few available men left in the Watauga community.

"That's what you get for being such a big show-off," Kesiah criticized. "If you had half the ability you pretend to have, maybe you could use some of that to stay out of trouble."

Not knowing how to take such a withering attack from such a new acquaintance, Bonny Kate laughed. "Trouble has ever been my constant companion. It goes against my nature to turn my back on an old friend."

"Well, then," Kesiah continued. "We can expect you will provide another such entertainment every morning."

"We never know," Bonny Kate replied.

"Dear cousin, Ann, you promised to help me with my bath," Kesiah continued. "Well, nevermind. You brother informs me that the community is running low on water. No more baths for anybody, not even the children."

"Oh, that is bad news," Ann fretted. "That will make my dear brother James such a popular hero with the ladies of Watauga Fort." Kesiah turned and left without another word.

"What did I do to her that she would speak to me like that?" Bonny Kate wondered aloud.

Ann laughed. "Give her a chance, Bonny Kate. It takes time for Kesiah to warm up to strangers. When you get to know her, you'll find that my cousin is delightfully funny, caring, gay, and witty. She can even read and write!" Ann and Bonny Kate laughed. That last attribute was important to Ann, the schoolmarm. Bonny Kate was glad that she could read and write too.

The quiet that day could not be easily explained by the leaders at Watauga Fort. The defenders at the walls, accustomed to complete independence of action and thought, grew restless and more willing to take greater chances than the cautious Captain Robertson would allow. The active Lieutenant Sevier might be willing to lead them in an expedition had he not been catching up on his sleep. Some of the more enterprising frontiersmen resolved to press Sevier to lead some sort of action when he awoke. There were needs. Firewood was running low, the water barrels were emptying, and there was a great need for more shelter before the next thunder shower.

Lieutenant Sevier made his appearance at lunch. Robertson's loft had become oppressively hot at midday, and he couldn't sleep any longer. There was much to do before the Indians renewed their attacks. Bonny Kate was disappointed that Lieutenant Sevier had yet to avail himself of the invitation she had extended the night before. He continued in the hospitality offered by the Robertson's. Perhaps he had misunderstood her so she decided to repeat the offer.

After lunch, she observed him shaving at a small mirror hanging on the outside wall of Robertson's cabin. She strolled over.

"Now, Captain Sevier," she began. "Why don't you let me help? I could give you a close shave."

"I think, Miss Sherrill, that you and I have already had our close shave. I wouldn't care to have one any closer," he replied. She laughed and watched him as he continued to work at his personal care. He was extremely clean and well groomed every time she had seen him and always well dressed.

"Would you care to have dinner with the Sherrill family before you go on watch?" she offered.

"I would be delighted," he responded, and it surprised her. "What are you cooking?"

"Chickens," she replied. "That's about all we have left. We have plenty of livestock out in the fields, but it's a little hard to get to right now."

"Chicken is just fine," he said as he washed his razor in a bowl of water and rinsed with a face wash. She stayed and just watched. After finishing, he noticed she was still standing next to him. "Is there something else to discuss, Miss Sherrill?"

"Well, sir, about this morning," she began. "I am so sorry for what I said."

"I am the one who was out of sorts," he replied. "Please accept my apology. I was much too harsh with you."

"Oh, but I provoked you," she admitted.

"If that's the way you see it, then all is forgiven!" he declared. He tied on his shirt lace, put on his waistcoat, uniform coat, and placed his cocked hat upon his head. He was an imposing officer, indeed, and the courageous girl felt strangely weak in the knees. "But I must beg your forgiveness for my boorish behavior, and have it quickly, so I can attend to the defense of Watauga Fort."

"You have it," was all she could manage to say. Bonny Kate would have given him anything he asked for at that moment. He tipped his hat, smiled, and strode away to the wall where men waited anxiously to talk to him.

The rest of the afternoon was quiet on the military front but very active on the home front. Never was a chicken dinner so important nor prepared with any greater care than the one Lieutenant Sevier had promised to attend.

The soldiers of the night watch had been called to an hour-long meeting in the early afternoon in the blockhouse to discuss what they referred to as operations. When they were dismissed, they had been instructed to take an afternoon nap, get a good supper, and assemble at sundown.

Sam Sherrill's afternoon nap was made impossible by the activity of the women engaged in the preparation of the chicken dinner. He tossed and turned and never did get to sleep in the bed of his wagon. He rose and climbed down from the wagon. He discovered his womenfolk were preparing to host Lieutenant Sevier for dinner and instructed them to make enough for the rest of the night watch as well since several of them had no families at Watauga Fort either. Bonny Kate and her mother looked at each other for a moment. "Three more chickens?" Bonny Kate asked.

"Better make it four," Mary recommended. "There is no telling who Mr. Sherrill might invite next, the good Christian man that he is!"

The chicken dinner was served right on schedule despite the expanded guest list. The party was much different than Bonny Kate imagined it would be. The extra guests kept the ladies moving constantly, filling cups, serving out extra helpings, and cleaning up afterward. Bonny Kate was disappointed that she was unable to converse with the lieutenant and observe his manners more closely, but the men of the night watch were excited and animated about the duty that night and dominated the conversation. Lieutenant Sevier was jovial and spoke often but not so loud that she could make out what he was saying. The dinner was soon over, and the men took their positions at the wall for the first part of the night, but great adventures were planned for later. None of the women knew any of the details.

After midnight as the moon was rising, six men went out the gate including Sam Sherrill and his son Junior. Lieutenant Sevier led the party, and they were all carrying water buckets. Minutes later, they returned with water from the river and poured twelve buckets into the water barrels. The process went on until all the water barrels were replenished. After that, a detail went out for firewood. Finally some of the Sherrill sheep and cattle were herded up to the fort for food. In one night, Lieutenant Sevier had solved the supply problem for at least three more days. During the operations of the night, two great discoveries were made: a horse was found among Mr. Sherrill's cattle that had escaped the notice of the Indians and Bonny Kate's sheep dog was found in the fields, tending the sheep. The horse was brought up to the fort, saddled, and young Landon Carter, one of John's most reliable men, was dispatched to Eaton's Station on the Holston with another request for help. At dawn, Bonny Kate had a joyful reunion with her dog, Bounder. The night watch was relieved, and the tired soldiers went to breakfast. They had taken risks, but important supplies were replenished.

The success of the night watch had led James Cooper to believe he could make a quick trip down to Robertson's store just across the Watauga to find some boards to build a shelter to protect his family from the storms. He took with him an orphan boy, Samuel Moore, and they slipped out the gate as the guard changed. They ran down to the Watauga and waded across.

Bonny Kate and her mother had cooked a breakfast for the night watch and were cleaning up when a rifle shot down by the river announced the return of trouble. Lieutenant Sevier was among the first to the wall to find out what was going on. Robertson's men were able to tell him that Cooper and Moore had slipped out without permission. Indian War whoops followed the rifle shot and the screams of the Moore boy could be heard. Lieutenant Sevier quickly assembled his twelve men with the intention of leading the rescue party.

"Where do you think you are going?" Captain Robertson asked his lieutenant.

"We are going to rescue those poor souls," Lieutenant Sevier answered. "That boy is calling for help!"

"Go cautiously," Robertson warned. "Watch out for an ambush. We can't afford to lose any men."

Little Samuel Moore's cries for help moved Lieutenant Sevier and his men out the gate. Jacob Brown watched from the top of the wall as the rescue party started down the hill, but he saw Indians along the riverbank and called out a warning.

"Indians!" shouted Jacob Brown. "Hundreds of them!"

Robertson climbed to the catwalk and saw what Jacob Brown had seen. Sevier stopped his men and turned to see Robertson waving him back in. "Call it off, Jack! We are surrounded again!" Sevier and his men returned to the fort in good order, without incident, and the lieutenant soon could see for himself the impossibility of rescuing the unfortunates.

Bonny Kate could see clearly the anguish in his demeanor. The man cared deeply and would have risked the lives of many to save the two. The women and children had gathered to see what was going on and heard the pitiful cries of the boy taken captive. Bonny Kate quickly realized what such terror would do to the children so she found Ann Robertson. "Ann, we have to do something for these children. They shouldn't be exposed to this terror."

"What can we do?" Ann asked.

"Get them all into the blockhouse and I'll provide a noisy diversion," Bonny Kate directed. Ann went right to work, and the mothers seemed relieved to let their children go with her to the blockhouse. Bonny Kate ran to the wagon, and once inside, dropped her petticoat and pulled on her buckskin hunting breeches. She jumped down from the wagon looking for the right costume for what she had in mind. Lieutenant Sevier, in his haste, had left his impressive cocked hat on the breakfast table. *Perfect,* she thought. She placed the hat on her head to hold the hair out of her eyes and pulled her long tresses over her shoulders and tied the locks under her chin with a thin black ribbon. The effect produced what looked like a long black beard.

Mary Sherrill saw her preparations. "What's the meaning of this?" she asked her creative daughter.

"Blackbeard the Pirate," she growled, already in character. "I could use a good wench like you to come play the fiddle for me crew. Please, Mama?" Mary nodded. Then Bonny Kate took two broomsticks to use as swords and ran to the blockhouse.

Mary shook her head disapprovingly, but she went to fetch her fiddle from the wagon anyway.

Ann had gathered the children and seated them on the floor of the blockhouse. Then the fierce pirate walked in and greeted her crew.

"Good day, mates, I'm Blackbeard the Pirate. Welcome aboard me ship, are ye ready to have some fun?" The children stared in awe and didn't respond, at first. "If you are ready to have some fun, say argh!" Some caught on and responded. Then she said, "Let me hear everybody say argh!"

"Argh!" the children shouted, and the show began. For hours, Bonny Kate entertained with stories and songs as her mother played the fiddle. She introduced Ann as Anne Bonny, the queen of the good pirates. The children laughed as Blackbeard stole a kiss from Anne Bonny leading to a dramatic sword fight. Anne Bonny won the fight, scolded Blackbeard for being naughty, and made him apologize. The highlight of the morning was when Blackbeard arranged the barrels in the blockhouse into the shape of two ships, one for the boys and one for the girls, and started a cannonade between the two ships with some rolled up socks serving as cannon balls. All of the children had fun, and none of the children heard what went on outside.

For two hours, the screams of the tortured victims assailed the captive community. The women suffered especially as every plea for help tore at their tender heartstrings. The men strained at every plaintive wail desiring so desperately to rush down upon the enemy and relieve the suffering. Robertson walked around trying to convince everyone the screams were coming from Indian decoys trying to trick them into attempting a rescue. Any party venturing forth would easily be cut off and destroyed. Lieutenant Sevier quietly discussed with Mr. Brown what the Indians might do next if the garrison resisted the temptation to sally forth. They agreed the Indians would probably conduct another full-scale attack. They would exhaust the garrison's shot supply and then breech the walls to engage them with the tomahawk. Sevier knew that the walled fortress was an advantage only while the shot supply lasted. At tomahawk time, the protective wall would become nothing better than a slaughter pen.

There was another factor that neither Sevier, nor Brown, nor Robertson, understood. Chief Abram still respected the Spirit Warrior of the Wataugans and was still concerned about how to deal with that. It was that same "Spirit" that animated Blackbeard the Pirate.

By lunchtime, the Indians had given up trying to lure a rescue party out of Watauga Fort. The children came out of the blockhouse in excellent spirits and filled with stories for their mothers of what they had seen concerning Blackbeard the Pirate. It became the scandal of the day. The leading actress encountered none other than Captain Jack Sevier, on her way back to the Sherrill wagon.

"Who is this so cleverly disguised?" the captain challenged.

"Blackbeard the Pirate," she answered, "is none other than your very own, Bonny Kate." She untied the ribbon at her chin and released her hair.

"You have trespassed against my property again, Miss Sherrill," he accused her with a grin. "I'll thank you for the return of my hat." He reached up and took it from her head.

"Thank you for the use of it. It served me very well in completing my costume."

"What is this about?" he asked.

"A diversion so the children would not be subjected to the terror outside this morning," she answered.

"Well done, Miss Sherrill," he praised her. "You saw a need and filled it. I consider that a great service to the community. Now what restitution shall be required of Blackbeard the Pirate for the theft of my hat?"

"How about dinner tonight?" she suggested. "We are roasting a lamb that Papa brought in last night."

"I look forward to that." He turned and walked toward Robertson's cabin. The day was half gone, and the night watch had not had any opportunity for sleep.

Another thunderstorm rumbled up the valley that afternoon, and the Indians returned to their camp without further harassment to the stubbornly defended fort.

Shortly after breakfast on the fourth day of the siege, two men rushed a wounded man to the bench outside Robertson's cabin. Word spread like wildfire that Lieutenant Sevier had been hit. Bonny Kate felt the pain of that news in her heart as though the victim had been her own father. She ran to the cabin where a crowd had gathered fearing the worst. Charlotte, Ann, and Kesiah were in action hovering over the wounded lieutenant, assessing the damage and ordering those nearby to fetch hot water, bandages and other supplies as might be necessary. Bonny Kate could only get close enough for a quick glimpse of her savior laid out on the bench holding his hand over his right eye. She saw no blood but heard someone say, "It's his eye." Several women wept openly because the polite, strong, handsome lieutenant was the favorite of all. Bonny Kate dared not approach closer but waited among the disturbed women for more news, hoping, praying, indeed, pleading with Divine Providence for mercy on behalf of the worthy man. Charlotte gently removed his hand from his face, and he moaned in pain.

"It's me, Jack," Charlotte said soothingly. "We'll get you patched up. Just tell me where it hurts."

"My eyes," he complained. "Thank God the rascal missed me."

"No bullet wound," Charlotte confirmed.

"They missed him by an inch," stated Jacob Brown who had witnessed what had happened. "He fired back even after being blinded."

"Did I do any good?" asked the lieutenant in a weaker voice than Bonny Kate had ever heard from her hero.

"I think you got him, Jack. He come out of that tree pretty quick, and I didn't see him move after that."

The information spread among the crowd rapidly that the bullet had missed the lieutenant's eye by an inch, but wood splinters may have blinded him. Charlotte and her helpers worked quickly to wash out his eyes and float out the debris. They soon determined that the eye itself had escaped serious injury. Charlotte worked delicately at removing splinters from his cheek and temple. Soon he was sitting up and resting, and the crowd left to return to their campsites and cook fires. Bonny Kate breathed a prayer of thanksgiving and approached him cautiously.

"Well, my Bonny Kate, you're a sight for sore eyes," he joked. "I've had another close shave, but this time it is not on your account. I very nearly became a one-eyed Jack. What good would I be without my shooting eye?"

"With the accessory of an eye patch, you can always come to work for Blackbeard the Pirate," she offered, trying to match wits with his humor.

John laughed. "That's a comfort, Miss Sherrill."

"I'm sure glad it worked out the way it did," she said with great relief.

"I hope this never gets back to Sarah," he said thoughtfully. "It would have worried her too much."

Bonny Kate curtsied and left him. She had just experienced a disproportionate measure of the worry that Sarah might have felt to have death come so close to her beloved. Bonny Kate was not even related to the man, and she felt a tight knot in the pit of her stomach. Deep breathing was required, or maybe her bodice was laced too tightly.

Chapter 9

Washday

The fifth day of the siege, Mrs. Susan Carter fell ill with the camp fever. She was a courageous woman, who had sacrificed much for the good of the country. Her husband, John Carter, led the Watauga Association and was its colonel, the top-ranking military leader of the community. He had left his military post vacant to promote the Watauga Petition to the General Assembly of North Carolina. Mrs. Carter had felt the sting of criticism from various women for his absence at a time when the military affairs had reached a crisis. Then her favorite son Landon had left her for the dangerous mission of a night ride to Eaton's station to secure help for the Wataugans. That was three days ago, and there was no word concerning his whereabouts or his well-being. These are the things that worried the worthy woman in her fevered state. The camp fever was a frightening thing because water escaped the body much faster than it could be replaced, and the caregivers had no pleasant task in keeping the patient clean. Luckily for the comfort of Mrs. Carter, she had her own cabin as the colonel's wife, but no daughters present to care for her. Bonny Kate was volunteered by her mother to care for Mrs. Carter. Mary Sherrill prescribed chicken broth as the most effective remedy, and it was Bonny Kate's job to keep the patient from becoming dehydrated.

After the night watch ended, Lieutenant Sevier came by for a visit. Bonny Kate stood as he appeared in the open doorway, holding a bouquet of wild flowers of mixed colors. He removed his hat, smiled, and nodded in greeting.

"Good morning, Miss Sherrill," he greeted her softly. "Is Mrs. Carter able to receive a visitor?" He was clearly very concerned for the sick and suffering.

"Hello, Jack," Mrs. Carter called out. "Come cheer me up."

"Good morning, Susan." He smiled. "I brought you some colorful flowers from the meadow. We ventured out again early this morning for water and firewood. I'm glad to see you have such talented care. Miss Sherrill seems to be very capable."

Bonny Kate took the flowers and arranged them for Mrs. Carter in a glazed clay pot with some water.

"She's a dear girl, Jack, but she insists on filling me with this infernal chicken broth!" Mrs. Carter complained. Bonny Kate smiled as her eyes met the lieutenant's.

"Do what she says, Susan. These Sherrills seem to have a lot of wisdom," he advised. "I've had some experience with the camp fever, and I know you can beat this thing."

"Bonny Kate said her family met my husband on their way out from North Carolina," Susan told him. "Her father and brothers signed the petition."

"Yes, and they volunteered for my night watch," he added. "They have been very helpful and useful to us."

"Any news from Landon?" Susan asked.

"I figure he'll be back any day now," John answered. "And he will bring the rangers, no doubt."

"Why did you send Landon?" she asked in despair.

"It was his horse we found, and he was eager to go," John explained. "Besides that, no man at Watauga Fort has a better sense of direction or a greater sense of mission than Landon Carter. I can trust him to get the job done."

"My husband may be gone for a year at General Assembly, and my Landon is all the family I have," Susan said.

"I realize that, Susan," John replied tenderly. "I would have gone myself, but Landon insisted I stay here and try to do some good. I hope I don't make a mess of things before he gets back. I would never want to disappoint Landon Carter. Why, the day is coming when I'll be addressing him as General Carter!"

"Horseradish," Susan exclaimed. "I know how things work around here. Take note, Bonny Kate. This man will get things all turned around, and in a twinkle of an eye, I'll be thinking it was my idea to send Landon for help."

They all laughed.

"Could you tell me where you got your drinking water, Susan?" John asked.

"From the barrel between here and Robertson's," she answered.

"Bonny Kate, would you please go get your brothers to dump that barrel," John directed. "I want it scrubbed out with lye soap before anybody takes another drink from it. Make sure all the water you use for drinking has been boiled. And when you are cleaning up around this house, use hot water as hot as you can stand. I'll give the order to provide the firewood to keep the fires burning."

"So you think camp fever comes from the water?" Susan asked.

"I'm sure of it," he answered.

Bonny Kate left on her mission. She admired his decisiveness, and his kindly use of authority, and moved swiftly to carry out his orders.

Bonny Kate sat with Mrs. Carter most of the day and much of the night for three straight days. She continued to encourage her to drink the chicken broth, which now Mary Sherrill alternated with beef broth and lamb broth for variety. Bonny Kate actively controlled the fever with baths and wet rags applied to Mrs. Carter's neck and brow. Others fell victim to the fever also. Sallie, the Robertson's servant was one, and then there were Mrs. Isbell, Mrs. Lucas, several children, and most alarming, five of the men from the day watch. James Robertson was very concerned about any reduction in troop strength. The women with the fever became the guests of Mrs. Carter and Bonny Kate cared for them all. The days dragged on but Mrs. Carter's condition improved and nobody died from the camp fever.

On the evening of the eighth day, Landon Carter rode in with ten pounds of lead shot that had been produced in Virginia. He reported that Colonel Russell was on his way with his frontier rangers. Sevier and Robertson received a tremendous boost in confidence that the community would survive. Mrs. Carter was very relieved at her son's safe return, and her lifted spirits began to restore her health.

One morning the women boiled water in two large washpots in order to do some laundry. John Sevier and James Robertson had just finished breakfast and walked over to speak with Ann Johnston.

"It looks like washday, Ann," James said.

"Ten days in July without washing is more than I can stand!" she replied. "Take off your clothes, James, and I'll wash them too."

"Sorry, sister, Charlotte is bringing over my dirty clothes. And what I put on this morning is what I'm wearing all day."

Bonny Kate brought over a basket of clothes. "Here is the Sherrill laundry, and I have the things to wash from Mrs. Carter's, but I need your clothes, Captain Sevier."

"Lieutenant Sevier can't take off his clothes either. He's going out hunting this morning for some fresh meat and is taking half my garrison," James informed her.

"They all volunteered, James," John corrected him. "It will do them good to get a deep breath of freedom in the open fields."

"I admire your activity," she said bravely, but she made no effort to conceal her concern by the look on her face. "Is it safe to be out?"

"Is it safe to be penned up in here?" he replied. "I'm not sure it's safe to be anywhere until Big Chief Robertson gets the Cherokees back to the peace talks. When are you going to get around to that chief?"

"Just as soon as War Chief Sevier puts a convincing whipping on the Cherokee war chiefs!" James countered. "When are you going to get around to that?"

"Well, you haven't exactly provided the tools for me to do the job, have you, Captain?" John turned to Bonny Kate and continued his rant. "First, he sends a company of our best men to Charleston, how long they will be gone is anyone's guess, then he musters our militia up to Eaton's Station, and leaves Watauga Fort undermanned."

"Don't pay any attention to him, Miss Sherrill," James cautioned with a big smile. "He's in a bad humor this morning. He has trouble following orders."

"I'm in a perfect humor this lovely morning, Miss Sherrill," John responded. "And I always follow orders."

"I gave him a simple order to fortify my trading post, but can he do the job right?" James complained. "Do you see my trading post fortified? No, he had to build the fort across the river, up here on this hill."

"The orders from Colonel Carter left the site selection to my discretion. Your trading post was indefensible, down there in that bottom," John argued. "This site is the best place for a fort in the whole valley."

"His failure to follow orders cost me my business," James continued. "The place has been ransacked, and all my goods taken!"

"The fortunes of war, Captain Robertson, are so unpredictable." John smiled. "Just like two years ago, Miss Sherrill, when he took our militia up to the Ohio. My brother Val got to go, but did I get a share of the glory? No, I stayed behind to nursemaid a whole community of women and children, while he became a war hero and earned the rank of captain. Get him to tell you about how he and my brother went out at dawn to take a piss and stumbled into the Indian attack."

"We were hunting," Robertson corrected him. "And because of the early warning, we alarmed the whole army to action and prevented a surprise attack. Val Sevier and I were responsible for the greatest victory Virginia ever won over the combined forces of the northern confederation."

"It takes a military genius to create a great victory out of a trip to the potty," John observed. The washing women roared with laughter.

"We were hunting!" James protested, but further discussion was impossible for the mirth that pervaded the whole fort as Lieutenant Sevier's joke was repeated for the benefit of those who missed it.

Bonny Kate had never imagined that she would ever find herself at the center of such a hot argument. She couldn't recall what she had said or done to cause the disturbance. But she had certainly stumbled upon some unresolved issues and long-standing resentments between two old friends. Her reputation in the community as a troublemaker was enhanced that day, through no fault of her own. Captain Sevier apologized to her privately for his crude language and explained that he and Captain Robertson remained the best of friends and meant no harm in their remarks.

"You see, Miss Sherrill, even best friends need to air out their dirty laundry from time to time," he joked.

"Oh, Captain Sevier, about your laundry," she remembered. "I promised I would wash for you."

"My extra shirts and things are in my pack," he instructed. "Just help yourself, as you have always done before."

"I resent that," she responded. There were limits to the indignities she would bear, and he would have to learn those limits.

"Miss Sherrill, on other occasions you have trespassed among my possessions," he stated.

"True," she had to admit. "But I have resolved to take greater care with my liberties in the future."

"Very well," he replied respectfully. "I apologize for my remark, and today I grant you permission to wash my shirts and other garments, if you are still so inclined."

"Thank you, Captain Sevier." She curtsied and he bowed. She ran to get his laundry from his pack. She found delight in speaking with Captain Sevier. His expressions and mannerisms were exquisitely entertaining. She often prolonged even the most mundane encounters with him; and he, although constantly busy and prone to vigorous action, gave generously of his time to converse with her. She had developed a dangerous fascination with a married man that was not unlike the obsession a kitten has for a string of yarn.

Back at the washpots, Bonny Kate busied herself among the women, with the chores of the day.

"Bonny Kate, how's your family this morning?" Charlotte asked.

"We are all well, just exhausted," she answered. "Papa struggles through the night watch and doesn't sleep well in the day."

"I know just how he feels," Captain Sevier enjoined. "James, couldn't we move Sam Sherrill to the morning watch?"

"I already offered, and he insists on serving with your watch. You save the life of a man's daughter, and you've got a friend for life!" James declared.

"An entire family of friends!" Bonny Kate exclaimed.

John bowed courteously to Bonny Kate, "You honor me, Miss Sherrill, to call me friend." She smiled at his gallant demonstration and curtsied in response. Charlotte didn't approve of such warm expressions being passed between her husband's old friend, and a girl she judged to be a haughty little home wrecker. Something ought to be done soon to prevent a scandal.

"Another case of camp fever," Charlotte announced out loud. Everyone turned to look at her. "Last night, it was the Jarrell boy. He's resting comfortably now but had a rough night."

"That's twelve cases in three days," Ann counted. "Is there any news this morning on Mrs. Carter?"

Bonny Kate supplied that information. "She's sitting up comfortably and still taking her broth. The fever just has to run its course."

"We can't afford any more cases weakening the garrison," John said. "I need everyone defending that wall."

Charlotte couldn't afford to have John Sevier so near to Bonny Kate Sherrill. They kept looking at each other, not staring but quick glances, so as not to be observed by the other. But they were observed by Charlotte.

"I thought you were going hunting," Charlotte said to John.

"Yes, we need to be going." John remembered his original purpose and left to assemble his volunteers.

The hunting party had been gone only about an hour when the few men left on the walls began firing steadily. They were trying to stop a group of Indians who were charging the wall at the vulnerable corner where the blockhouse overhang provided the attackers some cover up against the wall.

"Indians!" shouted Landon Carter. "They're charging the wall with brush and torches!"

James Robertson ran to the wall, and the women took positions for reloading. Then the firing stopped.

"James, what's happening?" Ann called up to her brother.

"They're piling brush against the blockhouse wall," he answered. "We can't get a shot at 'em!"

"Come on ladies," Ann shouted as she ran to the boiling washpots. "Everybody grab a bucket of hot water and follow me!" Ann and Bonny Kate were the first to fill two buckets each and they walked quickly to the blockhouse and entered. The smell of smoke was already filling the dark recesses of the largest building in the fort. The builder of the fort, with his attention to detail and his sense of accommodation to the comforts of a largely female community had provided a sort of public privy on the upper level of the blockhouse. There were several holes cut in a bench along the wall that allowed the waste to fall outside the wall of the fort. The Indians had chosen this area as their point of attack.

The smoke poured up through the waste holes as the Indian fires ignited. Ann and Bonny Kate could see the Indians below and Ann's first bucket of boiling water hit the brush and extinguished a section of the fire. Bonny Kate's first target was the back of one of the Indians. He howled with surprise at the burning pain. His fierce, war-painted face contorted with rage, looked up in time for Bonny Kate's second bucket, and he was done for the day. He quit the field of battle and ran for the safety of the rifle range where the riflemen along the walls added further injury to the insult the girl had delivered. There were no fewer than a dozen more warriors that needed to be flushed from the shelter of the blockhouse, and the work became desperate on both sides.

Bonny Kate bravely turned and received another bucket from Kesiah Robertson who stood behind her. "Keep 'em coming! I'll pour!" Ann saw the effectiveness of Bonny Kate's tactics and also took aim at the Indians. The brave girls moved from hole to hole pouring hot water on every target that presented itself. Every time Bonny Kate turned around, there was a different woman passing her up a bucket and taking the empties. She must have seen every woman in the fort supplying her with boiling water.

Once she turned, and there was Mrs. Susan Carter up from the sick bed. "I wish I could do this with that infernal chicken broth!" she shouted. Bonny Kate laughed as she delivered another hot bath on the stubborn attackers below. The water that fell on the fires became steam and combined with the smoke billowing up. It created a dark hellish scene as Ann and Bonny Kate fought like devils to keep up their defense. The screams of the Indians were frightening.

"More water, ladies, keep 'em coming," Ann shouted.

Some of the Indians fired their rifles up into the smoke above, and suddenly Ann fell screaming, clutching her left arm. "They shot me, Bonny Kate!" Bonny Kate scrambled to assist her friend. Mary Jane Sherrill stepped up to take her sister's place and kept the water flowing onto the fires below.

"Stay still," Bonny Kate instructed her patient. "Let me see. Move your hand . . . That ball grazed you." After a quick examination, Bonny Kate ripped some cloth from the hem of her petticoat and wet it in one of the hot water buckets. She applied it as a bandage to the wound.

Ann stood up and bravely said, "Let's finish the job, Bonny Kate." They continued their work in the clouds of steam and smoke until at last a great increase in firing outside the fort announced that the fire starters were retreating. A larger battle was taking place, because at that moment Lieutenant Sevier's hunting party had returned and joined the fray.

"Come on ladies, more buckets," Ann ordered. The only enemy now was the fire, which was soon extinguished.

Outside James Robertson was elated. "There they go! Look at them run!" He jumped down from the wall and gave the command to cease firing. The gates opened to admit Lieutenant Sevier's hunting party. The men congratulated themselves on their victory, but Robertson knew who the real heroes were.

On the main floor of the smoky blockhouse, Bonny Kate collected the last few empty buckets as Ann sat on a keg examining the wound on her arm.

"Come on, Ann, let's get out of here," Bonny Kate directed. "That's a keg of gunpowder you're sitting on!"

Ann and Bonny Kate, with clothes and faces grimy from sweat and smoke, emerged from the blockhouse to the cheers of the men and women of Watauga Fort. James Robertson and John Sevier were there to meet them at the door. Charlotte and the other women surrounded them to care for the wounded Ann.

"That was some heroic action! You did a great job, Ann; you too, Bonny Kate," Captain Robertson praised them.

Charlotte directed her medical team. "Let's get you patched up, Ann. My goodness, what quick thinking that was!" They walked toward the cook fires.

James laughed. "Those rascals ran like rabbits when the hot water hit them!"

John looked admiringly at the grimy bedraggled Bonny Kate. "If you hadn't put out those fires, we'd have been blown to kingdom come. All our gunpowder is stored in that blockhouse!"

"I guess it's time to redistribute those powder kegs," James recommended.

"Let's get it done right now!" John volunteered. "Come on, men." John led his men into the blockhouse.

Later that morning, Bonny Kate, Mary Jane, and Kesiah washed their clothes while Ann Johnston sat watching, giving her wounded arm a rest. Many other women were likewise engaged in what became kind of a community washday. Bonny Kate was wringing and hanging her family's wash, including a shirt of Lieutenant Sevier's.

"Whose fancy ruffles are you washing there?" Ann inquired.

"Captain Sevier's," Bonny Kate answered.

"I thought so." Ann laughed. "He's a gentleman who likes a little lace under his buckskin. And you do his laundry now?"

"I help him out a little, when I can," Bonny Kate replied.

Ann and Kesiah looked at each other and laughed.

"What?" Bonny Kate questioned their amusement.

"Bonny Kate, you are so obvious!" Ann observed.

"What do you mean?"

"You call him captain when he's just a lieutenant, you cook his meals, wash his clothes, follow him around when he's off duty, visit with him at the wall when he's on duty . . ."

"I'm just trying to be helpful," she tried to justify.

"Well, it's obvious to every woman in this fort that you are somewhat more than helpful," Ann accused. "I warned you on the very first day, Bonny Kate. He's married!"

"I know that," she admitted.

"You are playing a dangerous game," Kesiah said unkindly. "Most of these women here are friends of Sarah Sevier. Don't think for a moment they aren't watching you like a hawk. And when word gets back to Sarah about your shameless shenanigans, she'll scratch your eyes out!"

A concerned look crossed Bonny Kate's face. Yes, what woman wouldn't fight that hard to keep a man like Captain John Sevier!

Ann spoke more kindly than her cousin. "It doesn't look right. Folks are already talking."

Bonny Kate was generally irrepressible, and her confidence returned quickly. "I've always been one to make folks talk!"

"Then let's talk plain," Kesiah spoke venomously. "An unattached, unspoken-for beauty like you threatens married women."

"What about you, Kesiah?" Bonny Kate answered. "Aren't you a threat too?"

"I'm engaged, and that makes me acceptable," she proclaimed. "When this war is over, I'll become Mrs. Robert Sevier."

"Robert Sevier?" Bonny Kate asked.

"Yes, the lieutenant's younger brother," Kesiah answered. The warmth in Kesiah's voice surprised Bonny Kate. She discovered a new facet in Kesiah's complex character. The girl was smitten with love, and that fact redeemed her in Bonny Kate's estimation.

"Are there more brothers like the lieutenant?" Bonny Kate asked.

Ann and Kesiah looked at each other and laughed.

"John has four brothers, but there's not another one like him!" Ann replied.

"My Robert is very special in his own way, but you stay away from him, Bonny Kate!" Kesiah warned.

Bonny Kate became indignant. "I'm not that kind of girl!"

"I learned what kind of girl you are in the blockhouse today . . . brave and true," Ann declared.

"Thanks, Ann," Bonny Kate appreciated and valued her new friend on the frontier and would carefully consider her counsel. She finished hanging a line of clothes and walked over to the rinse pot to wring out another load. "Tell me about Sarah Sevier. What's she like?"

"Beautiful, blonde, bright blue eyes, shorter than you, and very shapely, even after eight children," Ann answered.

"She's the perfect wife and mother, cheerful, intelligent, witty, with a great sense for business," Kesiah added. "You'll see when they move here after the war."

"I hope this war ends soon," Bonny Kate said wishfully. "I'd like to bathe and wash my hair."

Ann and Kesiah laughed at the sudden change of subject in Bonny Kate's thinking, and this time Bonny Kate joined them. Ann dipped a bucket of cold water out of the water barrel. "Well, Bonny Kate," Ann declared. "Let's not wait for the war to end!" She threw the water at Bonny Kate hitting her full in the face with a sudden drenching of cold water.

"Oh yes!" she squealed in surprise. "Oh, that feels good! Somebody get me the soap!" Kesiah tossed her a cake of soap, which she caught in her apron. Fully clothed, Bonny Kate washed her hair with the soap as the girls supplied more buckets of water for the rinse. It wasn't long before all three girls were drenched and washing noisily in the same manner. A crowd of children gathered to watch, laughing with delight and great amusement.

Chapter 10

The Birthday Party

As long as the Indians stayed in the Watauga Valley, the settlers stayed in the fort. Lieutenant Sevier's nighttime patrols had discovered the fate of James Cooper, the man who went out looking for boards to build a shelter. His body was found shot and scalped on the banks of the river. Another man they identified as Mr. Clonse was found in the same condition in a thicket beside the river. He apparently tried to make it to the fort one night after the siege began. The boy, Sammy Moore, was assumed to be a captive, and Lieutenant Sevier still worried about his friend Lydia Bean who never showed up when she was expected. These were the only losses suffered by the settlers in the first two weeks of the siege. Lieutenant Sevier was already planning an expedition into the heart of Indian country to rescue captives, recover horses, and destroy the enemy's ability to continue making war. How and when he would be able to carry out his plan was still to be determined.

The thirteenth day of the siege happened to fall on Bonny Kate Sherrill's birthday. It was on August the third that she attained the age of twenty-two. The day dawned cooler because of a shower the night before. Bonny Kate and Mary Jane awakened under the family wagon beneath damp blankets as the wind had blown in the rain upon them.

"Katie?" Mary Jane roused her sister.

"What?" Bonny Kate answered sleepily.

"Happy Birthday," said Mary Jane.

"Thanks, Mary Jane." Bonny Kate sat up and reached toward her feet where Bounder lay. She stroked the silky long hair of the contented border collie. "I want it to be one I'll always remember," she said. "So I've made some plans." Back home at Sherrill's Ford, the family always made much of birthdays. Bonny Kate saw no reason not to continue her family tradition on this birthday.

"Do those plans include people outside the family?"

"Yes," she replied. "I want to have a dance tonight and invite the whole community."

"Are you planning to dance with the lieutenant?"

"If I can capture his attention," Bonny Kate schemed. "I would suppose he is an excellent dancer."

"He's the perfect gentleman," Mary Jane observed. "Every woman will be lining up for a dance with him."

"I know that's true, but it's my birthday party, so he should reserve some dances for me."

"You were so lucky to be rescued by him," her sister marveled.

"I'll tell you, Mary Jane, and never repeat this to any living soul, but I could gladly undergo that peril and effort again to fall into his arms and feel so out of danger!" Bonny Kate drew a deep breath and sighed dreamily.

"Too bad he turned out to be married," Mary Jane reminded her.

"A dance or two won't do him any harm," Bonny Kate reasoned. "And it will do me a world of good!"

Bonny Kate crawled out from under the wagon and knelt in prayer. "Our Father who art in heaven, hallowed be thy name. Thy kingdom come, thy will be done, in earth as it is in heaven. Give us this day our daily bread; and forgive us our debts, as we forgive our debtors; and lead us not into temptation but deliver us from evil. For thine is the kingdom and the power and the glory, forever. Amen." She rose and began what she hoped would be a very special day.

Captain Sevier ate breakfast with the Sherrills every morning, since Sallie had taken sick. He was animated and cheerful, as usual, and offered his best wishes on discovering it was Bonny Kate's birthday.

"So how old is our birthday girl today?" he asked.

"Twenty-two," her father answered for her. Usually this became an uncomfortable topic, because the next question always centered on why she wasn't married. At twenty-two, it was getting harder and harder to answer that question. But Captain Sevier acted surprised and channeled the conversation away from its usual course.

"My goodness, I never figured you for a day over seventeen!" he exclaimed. "She is a rare treasure, Mr. Sherrill. She has the beauty of a seventeen-year-old, but the wisdom and experience of a woman in full bloom!"

"Thank you, Captain!" she replied, appreciating his kind treatment of steering clear of her greatest embarrassment.

"I hope you have a very happy day!" he exclaimed.

After breakfast, Captain Sevier escorted Bonny Kate to Mrs. Carter's sick cabin, where they distributed broth, and some solid food to the women who were recovering ahead of the others. He told some jokes and entertained them with his good humor, good looks, and polite conversation for a while and then went to get some sleep. Two weeks of night watches had exhausted all who served with him, but nothing had changed in the situation concerning the standoff with the Cherokees. The night watch often traded shots in the open fields with the enemy who wanted to get close enough to shoot and scalp, but the vigilant long-rifle men, with a little more range than a musket, were able to keep them at bay.

In the middle of the morning, Bonny Kate put her plan for the day into action. She approached the cabin where James and Charlotte Robertson were sitting and talking.

"Captain Robertson, I'd like your permission to hold a dance tonight," Bonny Kate requested. "It's my birthday, and I want everybody to have some fun."

"Well, Miss Sherrill, that's not something we typically do during an Indian siege. Still, I agree the people could use a little fun."

"My folks can play the fiddle, so we have music," she promised.

"Music and dancing," Captain Robertson thought the idea over. "Imagine what our savage friends would think to hear us having a good old time, kicking up our heels, and making a ruckus with fiddle music! That might be more than they could stand. By golly, we'll do it!"

"All of us?" she asked thrilled at how easily her request was granted. "I mean . . . the night watch too?"

"Most can be available for at least a part of the time. We can take turns on the watch so everyone gets to enjoy the evening."

"Oh, thank you, Captain!" she exclaimed. "It will be a night to remember!" She rushed away to make the preparations.

"A night to remember . . . ," Charlotte said with disgust. "A fine trap she's laying for the unsuspecting lieutenant. My heart goes out to poor Sarah, completely unaware of her husband's peril."

"Charlotte, it's only a dance," James pointed out, still thinking it was a fine idea.

"Mr. Robertson, are you just going to stand by and watch your good friend's family be torn apart? Is that your idea of a civilized society, where a girl with stars in her eyes, can just steal any old husband to whom she takes a fancy?"

"Well, now that you put it like that, no," James replied. "We can't have that sort of thing going on in our community."

"Why, if she were after you," Charlotte threatened, "I would let the dogs out on her!" James liked Bonny Kate, and doubted very much if the dogs could catch her. He also had a lot of respect for the sacrifices the Sherrills had made in defense of Watauga Fort, but he wanted to avoid an unseemly scandal as much as he wanted to appease his wife.

"I suppose I could send Lieutenant Sevier out on patrol tonight," he said. "That would keep him out of harm's way."

"And that would put a stop to her little intrigue," Charlotte approved.

"Then you and I can enjoy the dance and not worry about the Seviers," James suggested. He was proud that he had solved the problem so quickly.

"And that haughty girl can spend her "night to remember" sitting on old maid's row!" predicted a thoroughly satisfied Charlotte.

Bonny Kate spent the afternoon happily making arrangements and telling every family in the fort about the dance. She found a few more musicians that could accompany the fiddle playing Sherrills, and excitement began to build.

Mary Sherrill and Mary Jane cooked the evening meal a little early and planned for the night watch to join their family for the special birthday dinner. When the dinner was prepared, Bonny Kate was sent on the delightful mission of waking Lieutenant Sevier for dinner. She would get to personally invite him to the dance and be the first to reserve a dance or two with him. She strolled over to where John was sleeping soundly, in a section of the open common ground that was used by the majority of the night watch.

"It's time to get up, sleepyhead," she spoke gently and endearingly.

John sat up and recognized the owner of the sweet voice. "You're mighty cheerful."

"That's because I have something special planned for my birthday—a dance!"

"Sounds like fun!" he sounded very interested. John Sevier was a man of action and fond of dancing from his earliest days.

Captain Robertson approached, acting quickly to interrupt any interaction between the two subjects of concern. He acted only for the good of the community. "Good evening, John. Hello, Miss Sherrill."

"What's up, James?"

"Special detail tonight," Robertson answered immediately.

"Bonny Kate was telling me about the dance," John said. "Does it have anything to do with that?"

"That's exactly right," the captain said. "Because of the dance, I want you to lead the men on patrol. There will be so much noise in the fort, you'll need to get out away from here where you can watch and listen, just so the Indians don't try anything." Bonny Kate's day-long happiness dissolved in disappointment.

"Yes, sir," John obeyed. "We'll leave just after dark."

"I appreciate your readiness to take on dangerous duty so the rest of us can have some much-needed amusement." James smiled.

"I'm happy to do it," John replied without hesitation. Bonny Kate was amazed that whatever enthusiasm he had for dancing vanished with the prospect of military adventures.

James tipped his hat to Bonny Kate. "Excuse me for interrupting, Miss Sherrill." He strolled away.

When the captain was out of earshot, she spoke angrily, "I can't excuse him for that! It's my party!"

"It's his command," John responded always mindful of duty.

"But I wanted . . . I mean, I had hoped . . . since it's my birthday . . . you would have danced with me."

"That's mighty thoughtful to include an old married fellow in your party, but duty calls, perhaps some other time."

"Perhaps," she pouted, and walked away clearly upset. John watched her go, shrugged, and strapped on his sword.

The dance began with everyone joining in the English country dances, circle dances, and contra dances to the exuberant tunes played by the Sherrills and their fellow musicians. All the families enjoyed the festivities. Bonny Kate participated among the children, teaching them the steps, but without her characteristic enthusiasm. As one dance ended, Mary sensed the sudden change in her daughter's mood.

"Katie, are you feeling well? You're not taking the camp fever, are you?"

"No, ma'am, I am well. The music is divine, but there are so few men."

"Ah, so men, is it?" Mary understood.

"With the men of this country off to the war, those remaining are either too old or too young."

"Or too married," Mary added.

Suddenly Lieutenant Sevier entered the gate, looking for the Sherrills. He approached them crossing the dance area. Bonny Kate's mood brightened noticeably.

"Good evening, Mrs. Sherrill," he greeted the mother. "May I have the honor of dancing with the birthday girl?"

"Oh, Captain Sevier," Mary responded. "You have come to the rescue again! Miss Katie faces the peril of becoming a wallflower if she cannot find a suitable dance partner."

John bowed politely. "Good evening, Miss Sherrill."

Bonny Kate beamed and curtsied, resplendent in her finest dress. "Good evening, Captain Sevier." She took his arm, and they walked to the dance line. "I presume your patrol was uneventful?"

"Completely unnecessary," John answered. "The Indians are content tonight at a dance of their own."

"How considerate of them," she returned. "No doubt to honor my birthday."

"No doubt," he affirmed. As her father, the fiddle player, began a slow tune, she reached the place she had longed to be all day, in the arms of her savior. They danced, and it was everything she had hoped it would be, a night to remember.

"How did he get back in here so soon?" Charlotte fumed.

"The man has trouble following orders," James said sourly. "Come, my dear, let's dance our troubles away, and let the Lord worry about the troubles of others." James Robertson and his lovely wife rejoined the other dancers.

Chapter 11

The Sherrills Find a Home

A week after Bonny Kate's birthday dance, she and her sister Mary Jane slept soundly under the wagon when Sam Sherrill knelt beside them and gently shook Bonny Kate to awaken her. She sat up to predawn darkness and heard her father's low voice trying to get her attention.

"What is it, Father?" she asked drowsily.

"Katie, two officers just rode in from the Holston with news from the outside."

"Are the Indians gone?" she asked.

"We think so. The Indian camp was dark all night. But these officers need some breakfast. Captain Bean and Lieutenant Shelby are good friends of Lieutenant Sevier's so make it special!"

"Yes, sir," she obeyed her father. She got up, dressed, and proceeded to join her father in the cooking area.

John Sevier built up the fires for the morning cooking. James Robertson stood conversing with two young officers, William Bean and Isaac Shelby.

"Good morning, gentlemen," Bonny Kate greeted the group.

John grinned at her. "Allow me to introduce Miss Bonny Kate Sherrill. This young lady can outrun and outjump most any Indian in all the backwater country! Bonny Kate, I want you to meet Captain William Bean and Lieutenant Isaac Shelby."

"Pleased to meet you, miss," Isaac said tipping his hat. Captain Bean also tipped his hat.

"Gentlemen." She curtsied. "I shall fix you a fine breakfast." Mary Sherrill arrived to help Bonny Kate prepare the meal. John greeted Mary with a smile as she walked by. His politeness charmed every woman no matter what her age and station in life. He was just that rare sort of man.

John's fire building cast a warm glow on the scene as he joined his friends. "Was there any action up at John Shelby's fort?" he asked.

"No, Jack, your family is safe and sound. There was no trouble at all on the upper Holston after the battle at Long Island Flats," Isaac Shelby answered. Lieutenant Isaac Shelby was numbered among John Sevier's closest friends. The ruddy cheeked, red-headed son of Evan Shelby had accompanied John on his first hunting trip into the Watauga district. He was a couple of years younger than John, but no man alive was more active and enterprising than Isaac Shelby. He had a keen intellect, a quick biting wit, and a desire to hurry up and move on when a guiding strategy was clear. He and John always worked well together, because Isaac could carry out plans and get things done while John could formulate strategies and persuade other strong men to cooperate with their designs. Isaac was abrupt and impatient at times, making him not so popular among the women, but none could deny he was destined to become a great and powerful man.

"The Indians have had us penned up here since the twenty-first of July," Captain Robertson explained. "What's happened to the rest of the country?"

"There is a lot going on!" Isaac began. "Governor Henry called out the Virginia militia under Colonel Christian. They will rendezvous at Long Island of the Holston next month along with troops from North Carolina. We got more news from the east when the Williamsburg courier arrived. It seems that the Congress in Philadelphia has declared all the colonies free and independent states. Virginia's resolution for independence passed on July second, and Thomas Jefferson wrote a declaration to make it official."

"I wonder if it's as eloquent as our Watauga Petition," John joked.

"But there's bigger news than that," Isaac continued. "The British invasion fleet was repulsed at Charleston!"

"Whoa, that is big news!" John exclaimed.

"How did that happen?" James questioned.

"The defenders built a fort of palmetto logs at the entrance to the harbor. From there they fired on the ships so furiously that the British had to withdraw," Isaac recounted. "At one point in the battle, the British landed troops to take the fort by storm, but they met with our overmountain riflemen. And the British sure got a good whipping!"

"Hurrah for the overmountain men!" John rejoiced. "They saved the whole city of Charleston!"

"Well, they had a big part in it, but the heroes of the day were some mighty determined artillerymen in the fort and their commander Colonel Moultrie."

"When was this great victory?" John asked.

"June it was, the last week of June," Isaac replied.

"I now see why the Indians attacked us this summer. The British timed it to coincide with their invasion of South Carolina," James observed.

"Except our riflemen stopped the invasion at Charleston and we stopped the invasion of Indians here!" John exclaimed. "Old King George will learn not to tangle with us anymore!"

Bonny Kate got a good lesson in war and the events of the day as she cooked and listened to the discussions of the men. As the sun colored the eastern sky, she brought plates of food to the officers and served them hot drinks. The men sat Indian style around the fire and began to eat.

"The Indian camp was quiet and dark all night," John volunteered. "I think they pulled out yesterday, late."

"Why didn't you wake me to report that?" James challenged.

"It didn't seem urgent enough to lose any sleep over," John replied. "Besides, it could be just another trick." John savored another fluffy hot biscuit. "These are mighty good biscuits, Miss Sherrill!"

"Thank you, sir," she called back.

"I hope you will share your secret with my Sarah when she moves down here."

Every mention of Sarah Sevier hit Bonny Kate like a bucket of icy water in the face. She was completely unwilling to share any of her secrets with Sarah, neither the secret of her biscuits nor the secret desires she held so deeply locked in her heart.

"Maybe after twenty days, old Chief Abram got tired of this as a business gone badly," James suggested.

"After breakfast, I'm taking a patrol over to the Indian camp," John proposed. "I want to find out what direction they headed when they left."

Bonny Kate carried a kettle of hot spice-wood tea to serve to the men. "How can we be sure it's safe to go out?" she inquired.

"Why should you care? You're not going out anyway," Captain Robertson told her. "It was you that started all the trouble in the first place. What did you do, trade the Indians some sour milk?" The men laughed as she stuck her tongue out at Captain Robertson. It was a disrespectful, girlish gesture that seemed so out of place on a full-grown woman that even Robertson had to laugh.

She stood erect with the hot kettle in one hand and her left hand on her hip, looking directly at Captain Robertson. "You are a bold one to be talking about bad trades. Aren't you the one who made the peace treaty?"

The men enjoyed another good laugh, this time at Robertson's expense.

"If you are finished with your little morning show, Miss Sherrill, it's back to the pots and pans with you!" Captain Robertson dismissed her. She drew up indignantly.

"Hold on, Miss Sherrill," John interjected. "The military emergency is over. Before you take any direction from him, just ask him about the time he got lost."

The men that knew the story began laughing.

"You got lost?" she asked Captain Robertson.

"He was lost for three weeks between here and the Yadkin." John laughed with great relish. "He nearly starved before he wandered his way out."

"I was never lost," James bellowed his denial. The men quieted quickly to hear what would come next. "But for several days, I was a might bewildered."

The men roared to hear an old joke, common among hunters, so perfectly delivered.

Bonny Kate resumed dispensing refills of the steaming hot spice wood tea. "More tea, Captain Sevier?" she offered.

"Please, ma'am." He held out his cup, and she poured. She glanced from the cup up to his eyes and gazed a little too long. The tea overflowed onto his hand.

"Whoa! That's hot," he reacted loudly.

"Oh, I'm so sorry, Captain! Oh my! I'm so clumsy! I'll get you a cold rag!" She rushed to the water barrel and dipped a towel into it. John sprang up and followed her.

James Robertson called after him, "John, you'd be safer out there with the Indians!" The men enjoyed another good laugh, but John ignored it. John met Bonny Kate at the water barrel, and she gently pressed the wet rag on his injured hand. Their eyes met again, and she blushed.

"I'm very sorry," she repeated with all sincerity.

"That's all right," he assured her.

"I noticed that Captain Bean hasn't touched his breakfast," she said. "Is there something wrong with it?"

"Breakfast was wonderful!" he declared. "Captain Bean is concerned about his wife. Lydia was on her way to this fort but never arrived. We are afraid the Indians got her."

"Oh, how terrible! I will pray for her safe return," she empathized.

"I was the last person to see her at her home. I should have insisted that she travel with us to the fort. I made an error in judgment."

"Then I'll pray for you too," she offered.

"Bonny Kate, we have other folks to feed," her mother called to her.

"Yes, Mama." She returned to her work, and John returned to the men.

"Riders coming from downriver!" announced Landon Carter from his post at the wall. John Sevier, Isaac Shelby, William Bean, and James Robertson ran to open the gate. Outside they gazed down the valley.

"It's Russell's rangers!" Isaac Shelby identified the unit. The rangers rode up to the fort as all the people cheered.

Bonny Kate spent the morning cooking, serving breakfast, and cleaning up. She went to Mrs. Carter's to tend to the feeding of the sick and then worked to serve breakfast to the fifty men who rode in with Colonel Russell. She conversed with the rangers who she found were not Watauga men but Virginians. Almost all of them had wives or sweethearts back home, and not a one of them seemed a likely prospect for her. Colonel Russell, an impressive officer with a great deal of life experience, was deeply concerned about his daughter, Lydia Bean. Colonel Russell, Captain Bean, and Lieutenant Sevier conversed quietly at great length about possible courses of action. At one point, Captain Robertson joined the group, and an argument ensued. The best Bonny Kate could make out from what she heard was that Captain Sevier volunteered his company to join the rangers in pursuit of the Indians to recover the captives and the stolen horses. Robertson considered the plan impulsive and dangerous and refused to release Lieutenant Sevier's company to the command of the armed services of another state. Colonel Russell and William Bean had strong personal reasons to urge such action, while Lieutenant Sevier felt responsible for losing Mrs. Bean in the first place. Nobody was happy with Captain Robertson's position, but because he was the highest-ranking North Carolina officer in the Watauga jurisdiction, he prevailed, and no expedition rode out that day.

Later that morning John Sevier and Isaac Shelby relaxed in the area where John and his men slept. Having been denied the chance to pursue the Indians, their exhaustion crept up on the usually active men. They could see Bonny Kate working in the cooking area.

"I've heard some talk today about that Bonny Kate girl," Isaac remarked. "So naturally, I've been watching her. The thing I notice most is how she watches you."

"You're imagining things," John answered.

"They say she regards you as a hero for saving her life. Is it true she washes your clothes and cooks your meals?"

"The Sherrills have shown me great hospitality."

"I can just imagine. Tell me more."

"I'm not telling you nothing!" John reacted.

"Then I'll tell you something, John. You're going to break that girl's heart when you run home to Sarah. You may charm the ladies, John, but Sarah always wins."

"There is no one living in the whole wide world that compares to my Sarah!"

"Bonny Kate knows you are married, doesn't she?"

"Of course she does. That's no secret."

"Then she's just a romantic dreamer, the poor girl. It seems such a waste for a beautiful girl like Bonny Kate to get her hopes and dreams up about a hero who's just going to cast her aside."

"Why don't you step in and rescue her from that sad fate?" John challenged him.

"I can't compete with you, John, in any kind of race," Isaac declared.

"I assure you, Isaac, I'm not in the race," John insisted. "I welcome anyone to take my place as her hero."

"There's not a man in this country that could do it, John." Isaac laughed. "You are stuck with it. What terrible luck, old man." Isaac continued laughing.

John lay back against his saddle. "Guess how old she is, Isaac."

"I don't know . . . sixteen, seventeen maybe?"

"Nope, she's twenty-two," John informed him.

"An old maid?" he asked in disbelief.

"Practically," John affirmed. "That's why I think she won't waste much time on me. Now, if an old bachelor like you were to hang around long enough, I think she'd rope and hog-tie him right quick. Why the first thing she asked me this morning, after she met you, was if you were married. She's on the prowl, Isaac, so watch your step!"

"I'm too busy for that," Isaac reacted quickly. "I'm leaving tonight to scout for the rangers."

"I'd appreciate that, Isaac. The sooner you Virginians chase away these Indians, the sooner I can get home to Sarah."

"Mr. Sherrill, Mr. Sherrill!" called Jacob Brown as Sam Sherrill was heading out the gate of the fort. "May I have a word with you?" Sam turned and waited while Mr. Brown caught up with him.

"I was just going out to see what is left of my livestock," Sam told him.

"I'll walk with you," said Jacob and they proceeded down the hill, into the fields. "Mr. Sherrill, I wanted to tell you about the prospects down in the Nolichucky Valley. Only about twenty-five miles to the southwest of here, spreads the most beautiful land on earth. Nestled beside the lofty mountains, along a fast tumbling river, the greenest forests tower over the most fertile soil anyone has ever seen. Game abounds in great profusion and a man like you could easily support a family just by hunting!"

"That sounds mighty good," Sam said. "But an opportunity like that would probably cost me a great deal."

"Of course it would," Mr. Brown agreed. "But for a family like the Sherrills, I could work a very attractive deal for you."

"Mr. Brown," Sam spoke cautiously, "I don't like to be pushed, prodded, or persuaded with any fast talk. Personally, I like you, and Mary likes Mrs. Brown, but when it comes to selecting land for a farm, I'm a hard man to please. I like to walk it, measure the soil depth, taste the water, and choose my own homesite. I want to know who the neighbors are and how safe we would be from the Indians."

"You are a wise man, Mr. Sherrill," Jacob complimented him. "I will be perfectly honest with you and show you every part of the property you want to see. As for your neighbors, my farm is the biggest at the head of the valley, and I'll be subdividing it as new settlers come in. Downriver from me is John Sevier's new place. He intends to live on it, make crops on it, and raise horses on it. The next property downriver from Sevier's is now available. I was thinking it would be ideal for you."

"Next to John Sevier, you say?"

"Yes, sir," Jacob confirmed, "your new friend, the man who saved your Bonny Kate. Now, Sevier is a man who knows how to choose land, and if he's excited about the Nolichucky that is the highest recommendation I know."

"I'd like to look at that property," Sam said.

"Captain Robertson wants me to ride over and scout the valley as soon as I can get a horse. If you were willing to go with me on a four-day trip, I could show you the property then. The only delay is finding some horses."

"I know where to get the horses," Sam volunteered. "I have two horses within a walking distance of here. We could leave for the scouting trip tomorrow if Robertson allows it."

"Excellent!" Jacob exclaimed.

"I intend to pay you in full your fair asking price," Sam declared. "I have never underpaid for anything in my life and have never cheated any man. So when you quote me a price, it better be your very best offer because I'm not going to haggle. Now let's hear about this deal you mentioned."

"Mr. Sherrill," Jacob said. "I won't sugarcoat it with fancy talk. Every time the Cherokees are beaten in battle, my land values go up. It gets safer and safer to settle this country."

"The Indians aren't beaten yet," Sam pointed out. "And none of your land titles are clear until the issue with Great Britain is settled. But that is a risk I'm willing to share with you and all the others. You must know that as a family, we made great sacrifices in defense of the community. I am about as ruined as a man can be because of the Indian trouble."

"I understand that," Jacob said. "But I really value you and your family and would love to see you as a citizen of the Nolichucky. I'm offering you 312 acres at the same price John Sevier paid, and I'll give you six years to pay me for it, but I have one additional consideration."

"Sounds good so far," Sam said. "And what's the other consideration?"

Mr. Brown drew a breath before continuing, "Make sure your Bonny Kate enters every turkey shoot or target shooting contest for the period you owe me the money for the land."

"What kind of a deal is that?" Sam asked, completely surprised by such a strange condition.

"I'm betting on her to win them all!" Jacob exclaimed. "I'll make more profit on this one condition than the land will ever be worth."

"Well, sir, she would never go for that," Sam hesitated. "She and her mother have got too much religion to allow such wagering."

"They wouldn't have to know about my wagers or about the terms of this land agreement. This is the best price for land you'll ever see. What do you say, Sam? Do we have a deal?"

"I'll look the land over and make my decision," Sam told him.

When the two men returned to the fort about an hour later, Mr. Brown seemed very pleased with his possible land sale. The quality of the parcel would certainly exceed his glowing descriptions, and the possibility for profits at the turkey shoots were a sure thing. A flood of brand-new settlers would provide him a steady stream of pure profit for years as the newcomers would place their bets against the shooting skills of an unknown frontier girl. Sam Sherrill, on the other hand, was greatly discouraged at finding only Fowerbell, the milk cow, and a half-dozen sheep as the remnants of his once great fortune. The Sherrills could not survive the winter on what was left; and the seed stocks he brought for next year's corn, wheat, barley, and oat crops had been consumed as food during the siege. Regardless of his prospects, Sam Sherrill still prepared for his trip to scout the Nolichucky with Mr. Brown.

Several days later, Sam Sherrill and Mr. Brown returned to Watauga Fort with their deal done. Sam Sherrill had recovered his horses from Mr. Miller in fine condition and had renewed Mary's promise to Eliza Miller that she and Katie would be present for their baby's birth. Mr. Brown reported to Captain Robertson that the Nolichucky was clear of Indian activity as far down as the crossing of the Warriors' Path. They dared not go any farther.

The Watauga community they found upon their return was much more relaxed. The rangers had moved downriver closer to the Indian towns to watch for any possible hostile intent. The camp fever was gone, and several families had moved back to their homes. It amazed the military leaders of the community that very little property destruction had been carried out by the Indians. Crops were untouched and plentiful with harvest time approaching.

Lieutenant Sevier had been away on leave to spend time with his family. Bonny Kate knew for the first time what it was like to go a day, then two, then three, then weeks without seeing him and speaking with him. She agonized with those feelings and struggled to banish them to their proper place, out of her mind; but it was not easy.

Sam Sherrill immediately found work hauling loads of freight in his wagon, now drawn by his horses. He worked for food stocks and supply items.

At the beginning of September, Captain Robertson called a meeting of the Watauga Association and the families gathered as before. Lieutenant Sevier came back for the meeting also, as dashing and handsome as ever. Bonny Kate was again captivated and waited for opportunities to converse with him as often as she could.

After the business meeting where Sam Sherrill had been introduced as a new member of the Association, and he had exercised his rights as a landowner to vote, John Sevier came over to the Sherrill wagon to visit and enjoy a meal. As John and Sam conversed, darkness overtook the land, and they turned to discussing the future.

"I'll have to get used to sleeping at night again," John said yawning.

"I won't have any trouble," Sam said. "I'm glad night watches are a thing of the past. I'm ready to get on with my life."

"I'm sorry we ate up your seed stock and livestock during the siege," John said. "We used your furniture, consumed your powder and shot, and everyone enjoyed the fruits of your family's labors."

"Well," returned Sam, "you gave us protection and saved our Katie. You can't put a price on that!"

"So where will you go now?" John asked.

"I bought a place from Jacob Brown, on the Nolichucky, next to yours; but I'm thinking it's still unsafe to move any closer to the Indian towns."

"You're right," John agreed. "Do you have a place around here?"

"No."

"Then you'll stay with me," John invited. "I've got a new farm opposite Stony Creek just four miles up the Watauga that's plenty big for two families. I need help making next year's crop on it. Do you think you could help me out for half the farm's yield?"

"Half?" Sam asked very surprised. "That's mighty generous, John, but my business requires quite a lot of space. You see, I'm not so much a crop farmer as I am a horse breeder."

"By the grace of the Almighty!" John exclaimed. "A horse breeder! Man, you shall prosper out here on the frontier. Men are willing to pay hard silver for good horses. Where are your horses? You didn't lose them to the Indians, did you?"

"No, I left most of them back in Rowan County. My other sons will bring them out when I get settled on a farm."

"Why not run your horses on my new farm?" John suggested. "I have plenty of room, even for horses. There's no cabin on the place yet, so you're welcome to build anything that suits you. I'll be going on the Indian campaign for a month or so, then Colonel Carter wanted me to join him in Halifax to push our Watauga petition through the General Assembly. I'll be moving Sarah and the children down here before the first snow. I'll build a house too and we'll be neighbors. What do you say, Sam?"

"I'd say that's mighty kind of you, John," Sam replied. "I accept on one condition, you let me and the boys build both houses. It sounds like you're going to be too busy."

"Sam," John said. "Every time I try to help you, you end up helping me. I want you to know I appreciate it. We'll pack up your wagon and go to the farm tomorrow."

Bonny Kate's spirits soared. Surely, this was a sign of favor from Divine Providence. Nothing could be more perfect than settling on the Sevier farm at Stony Creek and seeing the captain every day and trading words with him as she delighted in doing. In addition to the temporary arrangement at Stony Creek Farm, there was the future prospect of living as Captain Sevier's neighbors on the Nolichucky.

The Watauga Association hosted a dance that night as Sam and Mary and some of their new friends provided the music. Bonny Kate had only two opportunities to dance with Captain Sevier that night, because so many other women of his acquaintance made requests for dances, and he politely indulged them all. That didn't matter to the romantic Bonny Kate. She knew that in the morning he would take her home to his farm at Stony Creek, where she would begin a new life as his . . . his . . . what . . . guest, maybe, or the daughter of his sharecropping partner or tenant? The roles were rather undefined and probably would never have worked in the Old World, but this was a New World. Bonny Kate and all the Sherrills felt that they had arrived in a new home and because of the kindness and hospitality of the people of the new community they would make a good living and eventually thrive.

Chapter 12

Mrs. Sevier's Homecoming

Four miles up the Watauga River from Sycamore Shoals, on the south bank, opposite the mouth of Stony Creek, John Sevier owned 312 lovely acres in a bend of the river. The property included a broad plain along the river and rose on its southern side to the heights of Lynn Mountain. Sam Sherrill and Captain Sevier selected a cabin site on a gentle hill that commanded a magnificent view down the Watauga Valley to the west.

"It's a fine place for a home, Sam," John complimented his choice. "I like a fortified hill for defense, and it's not too far from that spring where you'll have sweet water year round. You and Mary will have a fine view from up here."

"No," Sam corrected him. "This one will be for you and Sarah. After all, you are the owner. I'll build the guesthouse over beyond the bend in the river so you folks can enjoy your privacy."

"You are most kind, Mr. Sherrill, but remember we are only going to be here for one or two years. Don't build big or clear too much cropland. Save that effort for your Nolichucky farm."

"Mr. Sevier." Mary laughed. "You have much to learn about the Sherrills. They never do anything halfway!" John looked around the circle of smiling Sherrills—Sam and Mary, Sam Junior and Bonny Kate, Adam and Mary Jane, George and William, all new citizens of Watauga. John Sevier realized that his efforts of the last four years to build a strong community in the overmountain settlements were finally bearing great fruit. With a few more families like the Sherrills, he and James Robertson could realize their dream of building the settlements into a great commonwealth.

"I'll see that you get top price for this place when you sell in two years," Sam promised. "I can already envision the improvements I'll make."

John thanked Sam and all the Sherrills and bade them farewell. He mounted his horse, waved his hat, and rode down the valley trail.

"When will we see him again?" Bonny Kate asked her father.

"After the Indian campaign," Sam replied. "That's when he plans to move his family down here."

"What sort of duty will he be assigned on this Indian campaign?"

"He has been promoted to captain and will lead a light horse company for scouting and skirmishing," Sam explained.

"I figured they would give him the most dangerous job," she worried.

"After that he has plans to go to Halifax as our representative to General Assembly. Did you know that he was the one who wrote most of that petition we signed?"

"No, sir, but it doesn't surprise me," she answered. Sam looked at his daughter and saw a tear roll down her cheek.

"What's this?" he asked, gently touching her face to brush away the tear.

"Good-byes always make me cry," she answered. "I'll help Mama with the lunch." Bonny Kate turned away to keep herself busy. She would have to do a better job of hiding those feelings.

Sam wondered about the condition of Bonny Kate's feelings since her rescue from the Indians. Those feelings would run high and low, unpredictable like the weather. It had gotten worse since she turned twenty-two and felt the sting of being labeled an old maid by some of the gossipy women at Watauga Fort. He knew the season had arrived, and indeed was passing, when she ought to be married off; and the rapid rise and fall of her feelings was proof of her readiness for that. But Sam had a selfish reason for holding on to his favorite daughter just a little longer, and for that reason, he would take her out hunting every day and sharpen her shooting skills. There was a gathering coming up in October where he would enter her as a contestant in the turkey shoot.

On the last day of October, a chilling wind blew out of the north late that afternoon as the heavily loaded Conestoga wagon of household goods and furniture pulled into the yard of the new Sevier cabin at Stony Creek. John Sevier drove the team of horses; and beside him sat his petite, blond, blue-eyed wife Sarah Hawkins Sevier.

"Here's our new home in the Watauga valley!" John exclaimed. "It looks like the Sherrills are here to welcome us."

Sam Sherrill walked out on the porch. "Hello, John, welcome home!"

"Hello, Sam, any news since I left?" John said climbing down to assist Sarah.

"I think you are making all the news with your military exploits among the Indians. Is this the celebrated and beautiful Mrs. Sevier?"

"She is indeed," John declared. "Sarah, my dear, meet Mr. Samuel Sherrill who stood by me through many long night watches."

"I'm delighted to meet you, Mr. Sherrill." Sarah smiled, offering her hand. "John has told me so much about his warm friendship with your family." As they shook hands, their eyes met and Sam was impressed with the youthful sparkle in her eye and her broad smile.

"Thank you, ma'am, the feelings are mutual," Sam replied. Mary Sherrill emerged from the cabin, wearing a cooking apron. "Mrs. Sevier, this is my wife, Mary."

"Hello, Mary," Sarah said, stepping forward to hug her.

"It's a pleasure to finally meet you, Sarah," Mary said.

"I appreciate all you did for my husband during the Indian troubles," Sarah responded.

"My goodness!" Mary exclaimed. "We could never do enough to repay him for what he did for us! Come see your new home. We have prepared a homecoming dinner for your family."

"You are so thoughtful," Sarah replied.

"My dear, we must observe tradition," John announced. He picked up Sarah and carried her across the threshold of their new home. Inside he passionately kissed her, and she responded until her eyes became used to the darkness of the firelit room, and she saw a tall feminine form watching them from beside the hearth. Sarah reacted quickly.

"Oh, John, we are not alone!"

Bonny Kate returned to her work at the hearth, taking hot pots of food off the fire and placing them on the table all set for a dinner. John put Sarah down gently, and Mary Sherrill entered the room behind them. As Bonny Kate completed her tasks, she looked up, and her eyes met Sarah's. Sarah smiled. "Who is this lovely lady?"

Mary stepped over to the table. "Sarah, this is my daughter, Catharine."

"Catharine, it's a pleasure to meet you."

Bonny Kate curtsied politely. "Pleased to make your acquaintance, Mrs. Sevier, but folks just call me Bonny Kate."

"Yes, of course, you are the one," Sarah made the connection. "The Bonny Kate of legend, rescued at Watauga Fort after outrunning all the Indians."

Bonny Kate blushed, "Yes, ma'am, pulled over the wall to safety by the gallant Captain Sevier." Sarah crossed the room and embraced her. Bonny Kate was surprised by the affectionate gesture. She was also surprised at how short Sarah was, a good three or four inches, shorter than she. The child bride had never grown up; but she was fit, firm, friendly, and formidable.

"I'm sure it was the hand of Providence guiding my husband that day." Sarah released her and stepped back grasping Bonny Kate's hands in hers. Their eyes met again. Sarah said with a sincere smile, "I know we are going to be great friends."

"I'd like that, ma'am," Bonny Kate replied with an equally warm smile.

"Oh my, what a feast you have prepared!" Sarah exclaimed. "I'll get my children rounded up and washed for this wonderful dinner."

"I'll help you," John offered, and the lovebirds left the room.

The fight was over. Sarah had won it in less than a minute and walked out with the prize. Bonny Kate felt ashamed for every encounter she'd ever had with Captain Sevier. Her feelings for him had been a burden to her ever since the first meeting. For purposes of amusement, the community had invented ridiculous rumors of a relationship that never was. She had been moved to desire the perfect man within the context of dire circumstances, at a time of extreme emergency, and had denied the existence of Sarah whom she had never seen. She had prepared herself for this meeting, by hoping for a reason to hate the woman, and hoping she could somehow prove superior to her in beauty, ability, virtue, faith, or force of personality. Now there was no hope.

Sarah and John walked out to the yard where the Sherrill and the Sevier boys unloaded the wagon and tended to horses under the direction of Sam Sherrill. Sarah paused beside the wagon and turned to John. "You said she was just a girl," she teased. "Why, she's full grown and beautiful! You didn't tell me she was beautiful."

"That made no difference to me," John defended himself. "She was the only one shut out of the fort needing a rescue."

Sarah laughed. "Since when does feminine beauty make no difference to the gallant Captain Sevier?"

"There's only one beauty I care anything about, and she's all mine." He took her in his arms and looked lovingly upon her. She laughed softly with her arms around him.

"I wish I could have been there to see it. Folks will never tire of telling the story of the rescue of Bonny Kate."

"Well," said John, "I'm tired of hearing it."

"Is she spoken for?"

"Not yet," he replied.

"I bet I can find her a husband."

"Aim high. Everybody says she's one to watch out for."

"I can see that already," she agreed. "Thank you for moving us here. I love you so much, and I'm so proud of you."

"I love you too," he said and kissed her again, passionately in the yard of their new Watauga home.

The dinner was grand, and Sarah entertained most graciously, telling story after story about their life together. John was involved with the entertainment sometimes adding a humorous episode, or lovingly correcting her details, and they played off each other perfectly, delightfully, and passionately. She seemed the perfect mate for him, bringing out the best in his personality. She was smart, well informed, polished in her manners, confident in her relationships, and very interested in the welfare of others. Her world was not about her. It was about him, their children, their extended family, and their close friends. Bonny Kate was fascinated with her and could feel her family being drawn into Sarah's world. By the end of the evening, Sam and Mary Sherrill felt very good about their new neighbors, but Bonny Kate's mind was in turmoil. She had not seen Captain Sevier for almost two months and wanted so badly to speak with him as they had those many evenings at Watauga Fort. There was no opportunity. He had not changed a bit. Still polite, funny, charming, but a world away from her as he sat across the table beside his perfect wife.

In the cold-night air, Bonny Kate walked home beside her mother at the end of the line of Sherrills that Sam led, lighting their way with a lantern.

"You were strangely quiet tonight," Mary observed. "Are you feeling all right?"

"Oh, I never felt better," Bonny Kate lied.

"I am very impressed with Sarah Sevier," Mary said. "She's a very strong personality, but she never makes others feel as though she's better than them. She uplifts those around her, and that is a rare gift."

"I know," Bonny Kate agreed.

"Having her as a friend could be quite beneficial for you, my dear," her mother advised.

"Why do you say that?" Bonny Kate asked.

"The Seviers have a wide circle of friends and connections with a great many families of quality."

"I've noticed."

"And Sarah is admired by all as one of the most accomplished matchmakers in all the backwater country," Mary declared.

"Mother, I'm surprised at you!" Bonny Kate exclaimed. "After all your teachings about natural love and how we should trust to Divine Providence and how it will happen when it happens and just be patient, dear, now you advise me to submit myself to a contrived relationship with a complete stranger, or maybe I should just sell my heart to the highest bidder, like so much horseflesh?"

"Did somebody say horseflesh?" Sam called back.

"Never you mind, father," Bonny Kate returned. "Mother and I are just discussing women's business."

"I thought I heard you say horseflesh," Sam mumbled. "I have an interest in that business."

"Let me listen," Mary Jane spoke up. "I have an interest in women's business."

"Stay out of this, Mary Jane," Bonny Kate warned her.

"I can tell the idea excites you," Mary continued. "When things don't seem to be working for you, sometimes it's best to accept the help of an expert when it's offered."

"Oh, Mother, I couldn't," she moaned. "I just couldn't go to Sarah Sevier and ask for that kind of help!"

"Wait until you know her better," Mary advised. "Give her a chance. This friendship may just be the workings of Divine Providence!" Bonny Kate trudged on in silence feeling lower than, ever she had, in her entire life.

At home, Father Sherrill built up the fire and retired to the comfort of his bed, and Mary joined him snuggling close for warmth. The siblings were in bed in the loft above where Bonny Kate's soft bed awaited her. But she had one more task to complete that night. In the light of the cheerful fire, she sat at the dining table with a bowl of water and a dish of soap. She scrubbed vigorously at the stubborn bloodstain on her good lace cap. She would wear that cap again, proudly, without the significance she had once attached to it. She was done with Captain Sevier and Mrs. Sevier too. She couldn't bear to imagine going to Sarah Sevier for matchmaking services as her mother proposed. Humiliation heaped upon humiliation would accompany such a desperate move.

Tears of shame fell into the washing bowl. How could she be done with the Seviers? They were living on the Sevier farm. They would see Seviers every day. Her father had allied himself with the Sevier family, all because of the obligation he felt for the daring rescue of Bonny Kate. Yes, Captain Sevier had saved her life, but he had also ruined it. After all the trials and temptations she had suffered with that man, and after seeing what possible perfection Providence could create in a man, and after seeing one fortunate woman possessing that perfect man, a great sad despair enveloped her. Knowing all that she knew, how could she ever love again? One thing was certain, she told herself over and over again, she didn't love any man, now.

Chapter 13

The Housewarming

The next morning was cold for the first of November but clear. The fire felt good to Bonny Kate after her trip to the spring for water. She was thankful she had on a pair of wool stockings inside the moccasins she always wore. They were the same moccasins she had worn since the morning of the rescue, the lieutenant's moccasins that she had been meaning to return to their rightful owner. Perhaps today might provide an opportunity for that encounter, but who could tell?

No sooner had the Sherrills cleaned up after breakfast than Captain Sevier came calling with three of his sons: fifteen-year-old Joseph, thirteen-year-old James, and eleven-year-old John Junior. They were all dressed out for hunting but easily availed themselves of the invitation to come in and see where their new neighbors lived. The captain's sons removed their hats and smiled broadly as their father reintroduced them. They were fine specimens of blooming manhood, blond, handsome, polite, good humored, and so far, unspoiled by the hardships of frontier life. Joseph and James took a more than passive interest in the raven-haired, blue-eyed beauty and sweetness of Mary Jane Sherrill. John Junior's attention, however, was reserved for Bonny Kate. She was, for him, an awe-inspiring heroine of the frontier, from the stories he had heard about her rescue before the walls of Watauga Fort and the other shenanigans that had been attributed to her in the fertile fields of storytelling. Her reputation for aggressive competitiveness had been enhanced by her successes at foot racing and turkey shooting at the October Harvest Gathering down at Sycamore Shoals. The Seviers had missed that event because of Captain Sevier's participation in the Indian campaign. Despite the admiration in the eyes of John Junior, she envied the attention Mary Jane received from the elder boys. It was another reminder that her charmed youth was passing without the discovery of her desperately desired destiny.

"I'm showing the boys our new farm," Captain Sevier addressed Sam. "Would you like to go with us on a little morning hunt?"

"I sure would," Sam replied. "George and Billy can go too." The Sherrills made ready while Captain Sevier complimented Mary on the neatness and organization of her home.

Mary smiled and thanked him for his kind observations and asked, "Does Mrs. Sevier need any help unpacking and getting organized?"

"Oh, she loves company, and any help you could give her would be greatly appreciated," the captain replied.

"Then we will go to her at once," Mary announced. The Sherrill women made ready to leave for the day as well.

The morning sun felt good as Bonny Kate accompanied her mother and Mary Jane up the hill to the Sevier cabin. Behind them walked Sam Junior and Adam Sherrill, each leading a horse harnessed for pulling the Sherrill wagon. They were excited by the prospect of a freight-hauling trip up to Fort Patrick Henry to pick up supplies destined for Captain Robertson's trading post. The wagon was left at the Seviers' cabin the previous night. Despite the difficulty of bringing the wagon over the North Carolina Mountains last summer—where at times they were forced to unload it, take it apart, and hand carry the pieces over steep rocky narrow portions of the trail—it had proved to be a valuable asset in the valley of the Watauga. The wagon had been employed continuously by the enterprising Sherrills ever since September and added daily income to the recovering family. Bonny Kate wished that she might travel with her brothers to see something of the other communities; but she was employed continuously, carding, spinning, weaving, sewing, cooking, cleaning, herding, hunting, fishing, milking, churning, candle-making, soapmaking, and wondering about her future. The prospect of a cold day with Sarah Sevier at Stony Creek had no particular appeal to her, but out of a sense of duty to her family, she went forward bravely.

The welcome at Sarah's door was warm, enthusiastic, and friendly. Bonny Kate received another sisterly hug from Sarah and was immediately surrounded by adoring little children whom she wasted no time entertaining. Mary Sherrill went right to work beside Sarah, and Mary Jane was very helpful unpacking things and arranging them as Sarah directed. The morning passed pleasantly enough for all. Sarah's five younger children were as fine looking a group as her elder boys. Betsy was eight, little Sarah whom they nicknamed Dolly was six, Mary Ann was four, Valentine was three, and Richard whom they called Dicky was a year old. The three girls looked a lot like Sarah, fair, blonde, beautiful, slender, and alert. Bonny Kate imagined they would all grow up to be taller than their mother and figured they would all marry well. Sarah glowed with happiness in her new surroundings and admitted to Mary that she and Captain Sevier had lain awake late last night to enjoy the delights of marriage in their comfortable new home. Mary appreciated that Sarah had discretely lowered her voice to prevent her daughters from hearing that information. Her unmarried girls were much too curious about such things.

At midday, Colonel and Mrs. Carter arrived for a visit, paying their respects to their new neighbors. They brought a pair of turkeys fresh killed that morning and called it a housewarming gift. Sarah invited them to stay for a dinner that she was planning to serve around two o'clock. Bonny Kate volunteered to prepare the birds for roasting. She received the game from Colonel Carter and stepped toward the door.

"My dear girl," Mrs. Carter stopped her. "Don't you dare come near me today with any of that turkey broth!" She and Bonny Kate laughed as Mrs. Carter hugged her tightly. Bonny Kate was pleased that Susan Carter's health and vitality had returned so completely. She went out to her task cheerfully.

While Bonny Kate was busily preparing the fowl for the spit, the men returned from their hunt with plenty of pheasants, grouse, and quail.

"We found a little bit of everything," Captain Sevier announced. "But I see you already have some fine-looking turkeys there, Miss Sherrill."

"Compliments of Colonel Carter," she informed him. "The Carters are here and staying for dinner."

"That's wonderful!" Captain Sevier exclaimed. "Come on, Sam, let's greet our guests." They left their game on the workbench beside Bonny Kate. George and Billy Sherrill followed the example of their father and started to leave as well.

"Boys," Bonny Kate said sternly. "Get to work on those birds." Without objection, George and Billy began to help. Surprisingly the three Sevier boys, over whom Bonny Kate had no authority, pitched in cheerfully as well; and the six of them soon had the bounty of the day ready to cook. "I'm collecting those feathers to use later," Bonny Kate directed. John Junior found an empty meal sack and stayed behind to help her bag the feathers.

"Miss Sherrill," John Junior said. "Could you teach me to shoot as good as you did to win the October Turkey Shoot?"

"You know, Johnny, I don't much care to have you call me Miss Sherrill," she said "Why don't you just call me Bonny Kate as my closest friends do."

"You mean it?" he grinned.

"Of course I do," she replied. "And why are you asking me to show you how to shoot when the best marksman in the west is none other than your own father?"

"That's true," answered Johnny. "But Father rarely has the time these days to spend much time with any one of us." There was a regretful sadness in the voice of the youth. It was the first visible sign that the Seviers were not so perfect a family as they appeared to be.

"I would be delighted to show you the secrets of fine shooting," she promised.

"Thanks, Bonny Kate!" he exclaimed. "What about tomorrow?"

"What about today?" she suggested. "I have some time late this afternoon after the chores are done."

"Well, Father leaves in the morning, and I would rather spend my time today with him," Johnny told her.

"Oh my goodness, he just arrived and he's leaving again so soon?"

"Yes, ma'am. The men are going to the General Assembly at Halifax to write the new state constitution."

"That's fine," she said. "We can just make our date for tomorrow after the chores."

"Sure, and I'll help you do your chores," the boy promised.

She smiled at the child, so willing to improve his skills, that he would seek her help. She couldn't help liking John Sevier Jr., and they would become regular hunting partners.

The guest list for dinner expanded when the Charles Robertsons, the John Hailes, and the James Robertsons arrived. The Sevier home had become the meeting place for the leading men of the Watauga Association and the delegates of the western people to the North Carolina General Assembly. Bonny Kate observed the discussions and relationships closely as she helped the women complete the preparations for the meal. When it was time to seat the guests around the dinner table, the great men and their ladies took their places including Sam and Mary Sherrill. Bonny Kate appreciated the high honor paid to her parents by captain and Mrs. Sevier. This would never have happened in Rowan County where the Sherrills had been the earliest settlers, but certainly not numbered among the elite ruling class of landed power and privilege. When all the dishes of steaming food had been laid out on the tables, Bonny Kate searched for a place at the children's table with all the younger Seviers and Sherrills.

"Oh, Bonny Kate," Sarah called to her. "Your place is here beside me." Bonny Kate turned and saw that Captain Sevier, Sarah, and she were the only ones left standing. Sarah waited for her at the end of the table, and sure enough, there was an empty place of the highest honor at the right hand of the hostess. In an awkward moment, when all were silently watching her, she walked down the table and seated herself between Sarah and Mrs. Carter. Sarah did not sit until Bonny Kate was seated, another sign of favor. As John Sevier gave thanks to God for the blessings of Divine Providence, Bonny Kate's mind raced with all possible reasons why Sarah was doing this to her, and what might she have in mind to do next. A great lady like Sarah Sevier had the power to completely humiliate, and strip away all the dignity of a simple uninformed country girl like Bonny Kate Sherrill. In front of the most powerful people of the Watauga District, she was now completely at the mercy of a woman she knew she had wronged. As the guests began to eat, she looked down the table at Captain Sevier, and he smiled at her. What had he told his wife about her outrageous behavior during the perilous days at Watauga Fort? She glanced across the table at the cold disapproving Charlotte Robertson and found her smiling at her. That made her even more uncomfortable. What had Charlotte Robertson told Sarah about her?

Sarah smiled. "Bonny Kate, this a perfect time for you and I to get better acquainted. This is the first time that the winner of the Watauga Turkey Shoot is a member of the fairer sex. I should like to know how you did it."

Bonny Kate was on familiar ground as she explained how her early years at Sherrill's Ford had given her the skills that allowed her to compete in a man's game. She gave credit to her father for his encouragement and to Divine Providence for a good eye and steady nerves.

"Well, I think Divine Providence has been very generous to you," Sarah concluded. The conversation at Sarah's end of the table then took its normal course as the other women participated, and Bonny Kate warmed up to them. Sarah addressed her witty side comments to Bonny Kate for great effect and she was completely captivated by Sarah's social skills. As the dinner progressed and the men enjoyed their second helpings, Bonny Kate's apprehensions melted away.

"Mrs. Sherrill, do you think that we women can manage while our men are away?" Sarah asked suddenly.

"I think so," Mary replied. "We'll just keep a rifle in Bonny Kate's hands to protect us."

As the women laughed, Bonny Kate looked confused. She had missed much information by entertaining the children that morning. Mary explained, "Your father is going with the men to guide them through the mountains on their way to Halifax. Then he will stop at Sherrill's Ford and bring back our herd of horses with your brothers and Sister Susan." That was great news to Bonny Kate. She had longed to have Susan, her husband Leroy Taylor, and their brothers Uriah and John reunited with the western pioneer portion of the Sherrill family.

The rest of the day was delightful as the Sherrills were welcomed into the tight-knit mountain community through the influence of Sarah and John Sevier. As Mary Sherrill predicted there would be great advantages in friendship with the Seviers.

As the Sherrills were leaving to go home that evening, Sarah took Bonny Kate by the hand and led her aside. "Can you come back tomorrow?" she asked. "We really need to talk, just the two of us. The menfolk will be on their way east, and I'll send the children out to play when the sun warms up."

"Oh, Sarah," Bonny Kate hesitated, unsure of Sarah's purpose. "I'm behind on my spinning."

"Bring your spinning here," Sarah persisted. "You can use my wheel. It's a really fine one and runs so true. Please, Bonny Kate, at least spend the morning with me."

"I'll come over with Papa for the sad good-byes," she promised. "But I'll just stay the morning."

"Thank you, Bonny Kate." Sarah smiled. "I'll set up my wheel for you."

Bonny Kate remembered to take her sack of feathers home with her, and it occurred to her that the men leaving in the morning would need several sets of pen feathers to write home to their loved ones and also to write that state constitution. That night, she took out her knife and trimmed the pen feathers from the turkeys and prepared several nice writing quills to send with the delegates in the morning.

Bonny Kate didn't sleep very well another night. Out of all Sarah's friends and close family members that she could call upon to spend the day with her, why did she insist on having Bonny Kate? Her urgency about this visit where it would just be the two of them gave Bonny Kate an uneasy feeling. The guilt she carried for the things she said and did at Watauga Fort had always been a burden. Maybe tomorrow she could confess all that had gone on in her own mind and find some peace. To be at peace with Sarah Sevier would be the end of all her problems, except, of course, the problem of finding a new man in her life. Next time it would be a man destined for greatness and power like Granny Sherrill had foretold, but one unencumbered with wife and children. "Please, Divine Providence," she entreated in the quiet time of her night prayers. "I trust entirely on your mercy. Take the veil from my eyes, and let me see clearly my destiny!"

The familiar voice in her head, the one she was sure did not belong to her, the one that always answered immediately, when she was deep in prayer, came again, "In time, my child, in the fullness of time!"

Chapter 14

Confessions

Bonny Kate walked up the hill to the Sevier cabin with her father. It was hard to explain to her mother and Mary Jane why Sarah had invited her for the morning and not them, but Mary accepted it and used her authority to keep Mary Jane at home as well. Sam had sent his only two horses with Adam and Junior for the freight run, so he had to borrow an extra one from Captain Sevier. The animal the captain provided was beautiful and spirited, and Sam liked the look of him. Captain Sevier planned to travel down the valley to pick up Colonel Carter at his home and Captain Charles Robertson at Watauga Fort. John Haile would also meet them at the fort and they would all travel up Gap Creek.

Bonny Kate's farewell to her father was a simple smile and a kiss on the cheek. Sarah's demonstration with her husband was much more elaborate. There were tears and hugs and kisses and clinging that went on for some time. He treated her tenderly and held her a long time.

Bonny Kate turned to her father and handed him a paper package tied up with a ribbon she had brought along. "I made these quills for the men to write the constitution. Please make sure Captain Sevier gets them when he is able to concentrate on more than one thing." Sam took the package and promised he would deliver it at a more opportune time.

When Captain Sevier was mounted, he raised his hat in farewell. He looked back several times as if wishing he didn't have to go and waved each time. Sarah remained before the house until the men were completely gone from view. She turned her tear-streamed face toward Bonny Kate and welcomed her.

"Come on in, Bonny Kate," Sarah invited. "I always have trouble saying good-bye, but homecomings are wonderful!"

Sarah went to the washbasin and washed her face. Six-year-old Dolly, concerned about her mother's tears, asked, "Will Papa be all right?"

"Yes, dear," Sarah answered as she patted her face dry. "Your father is in fine company, doing important work for the good of the whole country. You should be very proud of him."

"Why are you crying?" Dolly asked.

"Because I will miss him while he's gone," Sarah answered.

"I'll miss him too," Dolly declared. Sarah dropped to her knees and hugged her sensitive daughter. At that moment, the three elder Sevier boys excused themselves, eager to start their day. They had been instructed to join William and George Sherrill cutting trees in the forest to make logs for the construction of a smokehouse near the Sevier home.

"Oh, but we have Miss Bonny Kate to cheer us up this morning," Sarah announced. The mood of the household changed rapidly as the children became excited and looked to Bonny Kate for entertainment.

"I brought my spinning to do," Bonny Kate reminded Sarah. "But I like to sing while I spin so that may cheer them up."

"There's my wheel," Sarah indicated, then she turned to the table where the breakfast dishes lay and began to clean up the morning mess. Sarah worked quickly and efficiently. Bonny Kate pulled the wheel away from the wall and began her work. It was an exceedingly fine wheel, well balanced and well joined. She never saw the equal of it in North Carolina, not even at the Lincoln Town Fair where Granny Sherrill had taken her as a girl. The memory of those trips prompted her to tell stories of those long gone days, and the children were fascinated. She worked at spinning some fine linen thread while she spun tales and sang songs, and two hours sped by before she knew it. Sarah had finished all her morning tasks and had done some letter writing and journal entries related to the family businesses.

At midmorning, Sarah announced it was time for the children to go play outside. The day was warming up and children needed some sunshine and exercise. "Can Bonny Kate come out and play with us?" eight-year-old Betsy asked.

"No, dear," Sarah answered. "We have important grown-up business to discuss. You can see her again at lunch." The four children went out, leaving little Dicky inside to take a nap.

"Thank you for coming this morning," Sarah began. She sat on a chair beside the hearth. "I have managed to get so much done."

"I enjoyed it. Your children are very sweet," Bonny Kate complimented her.

"Please sit for a while. All that spinning can wear a girl out." Sarah offered a chair close by, and Bonny Kate took it. An awkward moment of silence followed.

"Mrs. Sevier, there is something I must say to you," Bonny Kate struggled with the words.

"Well, you can begin by addressing me by my Christian name. All my close friends call me Sarah."

"Sarah," Bonny Kate began again. "I am not deserving of the friendship you have so kindly offered."

Sarah laughed. "Oh my, dear girl, who could be more deserving? I owe you so much for what you did for my husband."

"What I did?" she wondered.

"You risked your very life to provide him the opportunity to be used as the instrument of Divine Providence. That event is working in his life even now to transform him into an even more useful tool for the Lord. The world will see great things from him because of what you did."

"I don't understand," Bonny Kate said.

"Before the rescue, John Sevier was considered a dreamer, full of impossible ideas about individual freedom, economic self-determination, and respect for all human beings as equals. Those ideas have a divine source; but when he expressed them among his friends—the practical powerful men—they laughed at him, gave him the rank of lieutenant, and made him a laughingstock for their practical jokes."

"Oh, I'm sorry," she empathized. "They continued to play jokes on him the whole time we were in the fort, all because of me."

"So you see what I'm talking about?" Sarah said.

"Yes, ma'am."

"Well, things have certainly changed!" Sarah exclaimed. "Look at him now, a captain of the light horse, an elected delegate to the General Assembly, and the Robertsons, the Carters, and the Shelbys of the world have accepted him as their equal. I've never seen him happier!"

"I'm very happy for him and for you."

"I am delighted to finally meet you and learn what a remarkable lady you are," Sarah continued. "That is so like Divine Providence to select for his purposes another great and worthy soul. I believe you are destined for great things too."

"My Granny Sherrill always told me the exact same thing," Bonny Kate marveled.

"Well, I'm not surprised."

"Sarah," Bonny Kate began once again, now feeling a great need to unburden her great and worthy soul. "I must seek your forgiveness for the way I have trespassed against you. I kissed him on his wounded cheek, before I knew he was married. I flirted with him shamelessly every time I met him."

"Did you ever feel weak in the knees?" Sarah asked.

"Yes."

"And that knot in the pit of your stomach?"

"Oh Lord, yes."

"He has that effect on every woman. We have known about that for a long time. We call it the Sevier effect."

"I borrowed his rifle without asking in the middle of a war," she admitted.

"Now that's a new one we haven't seen before," Sarah mused.

"I fell for the sweet lips joke."

"They've done it to me," Sarah admitted.

"I washed his laundry, I cooked his meals, I did his mending, I borrowed his hat without permission to play Blackbeard the Pirate . . ."

"Another first." Sarah nodded patiently.

"I danced with him and enjoyed myself."

"That is to be expected," Sarah replied. "He's a wonderful dancer."

"And, dear Lord, forgive me, I treasured a drop of his blood that fell on my cap from his arrow wound and I called it the blood of my savior."

"There's actually a good reason for that," Sarah explained. "The name Sevier came from John's French ancestry. It was originally Xavier which means savior."

"Sarah, they gave me his moccasins for my wounded feet, and I never returned them."

Sarah looked down at Bonny Kate's feet. "Those are my moccasins!" Sarah exclaimed. "I always wondered what happened to them. John had carried them down to Charlotte Robertson to restitch. Say, she did a really fine job."

Bonny Kate removed the moccasins to give them back to Sarah, but Sarah did not reach out to take them. She pushed them away.

"I want you to keep them. From what you have told me, you are the only woman in the world who knows what it's like to walk a mile in my shoes," Sarah said quietly.

"Quite a few miles actually," Bonny Kate informed her. "And I regret every step."

"No, you don't," Sarah said wisely. "And I have no regrets either."

"Before I met you, I hoped I could be a better woman than you, but I'm not. And I hoped I wouldn't like you."

"But you do like me, don't you?" Sarah asked.

"Yes, ma'am, very much," she admitted.

"Is that all you have to tell me?" Sarah waited patiently.

"I'm pretty sure," Bonny Kate sighed.

"Well, I'm glad it was you, who cared for him and entertained him, and not some licentious floozy," Sarah declared. "If it is forgiveness you want, you most certainly have it. I believe you are a normal hot-blooded woman, with a divine purpose for your life. We just have to find you the right man to fulfill it. Now that we have covered all this ground, is there any reason why we can't be friends?"

Bonny Kate laughed so hard that the tears came. She threw her arms around the little woman in great relief. "Sarah, there's no reason in the world, why we can't be the best of friends!"

Sam Sherrill returned within the month with a dozen fine breeding horses, his son John Sherrill, and his married daughter Susan Taylor with husband Leroy.

They had a joyful homecoming for their reunited family. The other son Uriah did not make the journey. Sam could not persuade him to leave a good farm he had acquired from an uncle. There was also another reason to consider. Uriah was courting a pretty little thing who lived not far from Sherrill's Ford.

The new residents of Stony Creek made daily progress in developing the farm. The Seviers' smokehouse was completed, and the Sherrills put in a garden of greens that would bear all winter. The Sherrills added a second pen to their house for Susan and Leroy, and Sarah Sevier made another new friend in Susan Taylor. The women of Stony Creek spent their afternoons quilting, sewing, weaving, spinning, singing, talking, and laughing at the jokes they all shared until the sun went down a little earlier each day than the day before.

One day Ruth and Jacob Brown came calling. Sam wanted to see if Mr. Brown could carve out another good farm, one for Susan and Leroy. While the men talked, Ruth visited the women in the main house.

"Ruth, we need to throw a big gathering in the spring," Sarah remarked.

"I'm all for that," Ruth agreed. "Mr. Brown made a tidy fortune at the October Gathering, wagering on what he called a sure thing." The women laughed.

"Have you discovered what that sure thing was yet?" Sarah asked.

"No," Ruth replied. "But I'm not about to spoil a good thing by asking too many questions." The ladies laughed again. Bonny Kate kept stitching, unaware of her part in Mr. Brown's tidy fortune. She was still naive to the ways of men.

"I have two fine-looking ladies in this room that still need good husbands," Sarah informed the group. "A lively dance is needed to promote the product." Sarah smiled at Mary Jane and Bonny Kate, and they smiled back at the exciting thought.

"I should say so," Ruth agreed. "We'd better start now to make some designs in that direction."

"Ladies," Sarah announced. "Ruth Brown has made more successful matches than anyone in the west! You should consider yourselves fortunate that she takes such an interest in helping you."

"Yes, but Sarah always finds the rich ones!" Ruth reciprocated. Much more laughing and good-natured joking went on that fine December afternoon.

Before the last day of the year, John Sevier came home to another sweet reunion with his wife. The state constitution was complete and upon the motion presented by delegate John Sevier, Watauga territory was renamed Washington territory and included in the boundaries and provisions of the State of North Carolina. A territorial court was established with Colonel John Carter as Judge and John Sevier as Clerk of the Court. They also had promoted John Sevier to lieutenant colonel of the militia, a post he was very pleased to have.

"Why doesn't Colonel Carter step out of the way and let you run the militia?" Sarah complained. "He's not a military man. There they go again, holding you back with this lieutenant thing!"

"Sarah," John tried to calm her. "Don't be ungrateful. I'm very happy to be a lieutenant colonel. And my time will come. Colonel Carter has been very good to me, and I will always support his leadership."

"You are too nice, John Sevier," she gently criticized him, "too nice for your own good."

He took his sweet wife in his arms. "Tonight, when the children are sleeping soundly, I'll treat you to something nice!" he whispered.

"Oh?" she purred. "Give me a little sample." He lovingly kissed her.

Chapter 15

The Beauty and the Beast

On a cold January morning, Sarah Sevier was hosting a breakfast party with guests Mary Sherrill and her three daughters, Bonny Kate, Mary Jane, and Susan Taylor. James Robertson rode up to the Sevier cabin, secured his horse, and knocked on the door. Sarah opened it and admitted him into the warm room.

"Hello, Mr. Robertson," Sarah greeted him. "Come in and warm yourself at the fire."

"Hello, Mrs. Sevier, and good morning, ladies." James nodded to all the ladies present and walked across the room to the fireside. "Is Jack here?"

"No, sir, he's out with the light horse company patrolling for Indians on the Nolichucky. Do you need him for something?"

"No, I just like to know where he is and what he's doing, and that is a hard trail to follow!"

"Yes, I know how you feel." Sarah smiled.

"The reason I called on you so early is to deliver an urgent message to Mrs. Sherrill."

Mary looked up from the quilt she was stitching. "What's the message, Mr. Robertson?"

"Charlotte wanted me to tell you that Mrs. Eliza Miller is expecting her baby within the week," he replied. "Charlotte thinks you ought to make all haste to get up there. The Millers sent the message by way of some settlers descending Gap Creek, so it took two days to reach us. Today makes the third day."

"Oh my goodness," Mary exclaimed.

"Who is Mrs. Miller?" Sarah asked.

"She's the young wife of a blacksmith that settled up on the Little Doe River," James answered.

"I promised Eliza, who is a first time mother, that Bonny Kate and I would attend her at the birth," Mary explained. "She has no womenfolk to help her, and the poor little thing is scared to death."

"What a sweet promise!" Sarah exclaimed. "That's exactly the kind of neighborliness that builds up a community."

"Charlotte thinks you should travel today before any snow comes." James stressed the urgency. "Those high clouds moving in usually mean snow in a day or two."

"Mr. Sherrill took all our boys on a hunting trip this morning," Mary worried. "I can't leave until he returns."

"What kind of hunting trip?" James asked.

"Mountain lion got one of our ewes last night," Mary explained. "It's a mighty big cat that can take down a full grown ewe. Sam went after it immediately with all of our young fellows."

"They could be gone two or three days," Bonny Kate observed. "Mountain lions are crafty, fleet of foot, and not easily brought to bay."

"I wouldn't wait for the men to return," Sarah advised. "That baby could come any day. I think we ought to leave straight away."

"We?" Mary questioned. "What are you saying, Sarah?"

"I'm going with you," Sarah answered. "And James can escort us."

"I'm sorry, Sarah, but that's impossible," James declined. "I am traveling this morning to Fort Patrick Henry to meet with other commissioners appointed by the governor to plan a parley with the Cherokees. The peace of the whole country depends on it."

"Who would keep your children, Sarah?" Mary asked.

"I will, and Mary Jane can stay here to help too," Susan volunteered. Sarah looked at Susan Sherrill Taylor—the twenty-four-year-old, somewhat shorter, more serious, married version of Bonny Kate—and accepted that idea instantly.

"That's settled," Sarah decided. "Now we just need a man to escort us. Three unescorted women would be too easy a target for the scoundrels of this wild country."

"Let Bonny Kate play the man," Susan suggested. "When she dresses in Father's hunting breeches, hunting shirt, and broad hat, no one can tell she's not a man!"

"Thank you, dear sister," Bonny Kate said. "I love you too."

"Let her carry the rifle," James added, "and you would be safer than traveling with a man."

"I don't have a rifle," Bonny Kate remembered. "Papa took all our shooting irons on the cat hunt."

Sarah walked over to the front door and reaching up to the rack over the door, lifted down John's rifle Sweet Lips and presented it to her friend.

"Now you have a rifle," Sarah declared. "Bonny Kate will make an excellent man."

"I much prefer being a woman!" Bonny Kate protested.

"There's no time for that!" Sarah rushed everyone into action. "Please hurry, Bonny Kate, we have to leave immediately." While Mary Sherrill and Bonny Kate returned to the Sherrill cabin for Mary to pack some things for the trip and Bonny Kate to dress for her role as the man, James Robertson stayed for a breakfast and a visit with Mrs. Sevier. He wrote out detailed directions for a short cut through the wilderness that would make the trip shorter by half the distance than by following the established route through Sycamore Shoals, and up Gap Creek. He recommended skirting Lynn Mountain on the eastern end beside the Watauga River and entering the forested valley on the north side of Iron Mountain. Following the valley all the way to where the Doe River cuts through Iron Mountain would allow them to find the home of a trustworthy man named Jenkins who could show them the best way over Iron Mountain into the valley of the Little Doe. From there, it was only a half dozen more miles to Miller's cove. In addition to being shorter, it would provide a route not frequented by robbers and Tories.

Part of Bonny Kate's job of being the man was to catch and saddle the horses. Mary had instructed her carefully as she sent her out to the horse pasture.

"I don't know how Mrs. Sevier sits a horse," Mary cautioned. "So be sure to get her a gentle, sure-footed one. She is so kind to be going along with us. We have to take especially good care of her." Bonny Kate had not even considered the possibility that Sarah Sevier, in a rugged, outdoor setting might become a liability and exhibit weakness in measure enough to need to be cared for by stronger women. That idea appealed to her. Bonny Kate having trespassed her way into Sarah's world had proved unequal to the great Sarah Sevier, and although Sarah had dealt with her kindly, and forgivingly, the experience still hurt. Now came the opportunity for Sarah to find herself trespassing in Bonny Kate's world, and nothing in the nature of Bonny Kate's wild and free world was kind or forgiving.

It was no easy task catching the Sherrill horses that day. They were still kind of spooked from the night visit by the mountain lion. She wondered where that cat could be lurking. Cats had the nasty habit of circling back and revisiting territory a second or third time.

Bonny Kate took to heart her mother's instructions and selected for Sarah a small gentle horse named Paddy that had served the succession of Sherrill children but was still a serviceable animal. Sarah would look like a child herself on such a mount compared to Bonny Kate's towering black stallion and matching mare she chose for her mother. By the time, Bonny Kate had caught and saddled the horses, Mary was back at the Sevier cabin waiting with Sarah. James Robertson continued his visit, lounging on a bench beside the cabin despite his pressing engagement at Fort Patrick Henry doing the governor's work.

Sarah laughed when she saw the little horse and declared how adorable it was. Mary was embarrassed at her daughter's behavior and immediately sent her back after Belinda, a gentle but full-sized mare. "I'm sorry, Mrs. Sevier, I was the one who told her to fetch you a gentle horse, but I'm afraid she over did it."

"That's understandable, Mary." Sarah laughed. "I am constantly underestimated in my abilities on account of my girlish figure." James Robertson was amused at the ladies' conversation but wisely did not make any comments.

After the short delay, the ladies were packed and ready for the journey. Susan and Mary Jane conducted the ceremony of farewells, parading all the young Seviers past to bid their good-byes to their mother and her travel companions.

James Robertson presented the directions to Miller's Cove to Bonny Kate. "Here, good sir, are the directions to Miller's Cove, by the most direct route," he teased her.

"I'm not convinced it's such a good idea taking directions from a man who got lost on his way to North Carolina," Bonny Kate joked.

"You got lost?" Sarah asked of James.

"I was never lost!" he exclaimed. "But for about three weeks, I was a might bewildered."

The ladies laughed and mounted their horses, beginning their journey in excellent spirits. Sarah's horsemanship left nothing to be desired, and she handled the gentle Belinda with grace and skill. They skirted the eastern end of Lynn Mountain and entered a wide forested valley. On their left towered Iron Mountain, a formidable barrier that they would have to cross at a point many miles ahead, but the first hour of their trek was smooth enough for conversation.

"This is a beautiful valley!" Sarah exclaimed. "It reminds me of our home in Holly Bottom."

"Holly what?" Bonny Kate laughed.

"Holly Bottom," Sarah repeated. "Our farm was called Holly Bottom."

Bonny Kate laughed again. "Whose idea was that?"

"John's," Sarah revealed, still not seeing the humor.

"Where did he get a name like that?" Bonny Kate chuckled.

"Our neighbor, Mr. Cawood, named the head of the branch Holly Springs, so when John built our cabin on the broad bottom land, he named it Holly Bottom."

"Oh, that's rich." She laughed. "Holly Bottom Farm in the broad bottom."

"What's so bad about it?" Sarah wondered.

"Nothing," replied Bonny Kate, "if you fancy being known as the mistress of the broad bottom."

Sarah laughed. "I hope you are not making reference to my figure!" Mary and Bonny Kate joined her in laughter.

"The next time a farm is to be named don't let Mr. Sevier do it!" Bonny Kate warned her.

"I know," Sarah agreed.

"Stony Creek Farm, for example," Bonny Kate continued. "Farmers hate stones in their fields. He will have trouble selling a farm called Stony Creek Farm."

"Oh, Bonny Kate." Sarah realized. "You have discovered a rare flaw in the character of my husband, and I always thought he was the perfect man!"

"A flaw?" Bonny Kate asked.

"Yes, for the first time in my life, I realize my dear man has a pattern of picking unfortunate names. I can think of other examples like Fort Caswell. That never caught on; people still call it Watauga Fort. And Washington District he named for General Washington whose only claim to fame is being kicked out of New York by the British. Then he named my son Richard, but we all prefer to call him Dicky, and little Sarah, we call her Dolly to keep her from being confused with me."

"And he changed the name of my Katie to Bonny Kate," Mary added.

"He didn't!" Sarah gasped.

"He certainly did," Mary confirmed. "And that's a name that did stick."

"Well, I declare, my man is a wonder!" Sarah exclaimed. "He named you Bonny Kate after his favorite song! Do you know that song?"

"No," Bonny Kate admitted.

"Well, if you have never spent much time in Virginia taverns, I suppose you wouldn't."

"He named me after a tavern song?" she asked.

"Yes, and it is quite naughty," Sarah answered.

Bonny Kate fell into a distressed silence. A name she had received from her savior at a life-changing moment, that she intended to make great in all the frontier communities, now appeared to be tainted in the context of its origin. "Just my luck!" she exhaled. She needed to know how bad it was but was afraid to ask. Thankfully, her mother pursued it.

"What is the song about?"

"Bonny Kate, the Bonny Lass of Fisherrow, it's a very lively tune," Sarah explained. "Mr. Sevier and I dance to it with such pleasure until we wear ourselves out!"

"But what's it about?" Bonny Kate persisted.

"A beautiful young girl working in the fish stalls of New Market is seduced by a lawyer to accompany him to a tavern where he tries to fill her up with liquor so he can take her upstairs and have his way with her. She holds her liquor like a man and resists his advances, so he pursues her by showing her a stack of silver coins. She takes the coins and dashes out the back door into the alley and makes her escape through a part of town she knows so well."

"That is a naughty song," Bonny Kate sighs.

"Yes, but the girl escapes with her virtue intact," Sarah observed, "just as you did when you escaped from the Indians. Mr. Sevier loves that song because it presents two of his deeply held convictions. He has a high regard for active, enterprising, virtuous women, and a low regard for lecherous lawyers." The explanation of the song and the realization that Captain Sevier had imagined that Kate Sherrill possessed traits he greatly admired did little to ease her mind.

"The town we started in Virginia he named New Market, after the town in the song," Sarah added. "Names are very significant to my dear husband, but now as Bonny Kate has pointed out, the poor man has a dismal history of naming things. I'm sorry, he did that to you, Bonny Kate, or should I just be calling you, Kate?"

"No, Bonny Kate is my name," she sighed. "I'm stuck with it. Nobody in Washington District would know who I am without it."

Sarah laughed. "I don't know when I've enjoyed so much laughter and good company."

Mary's good company had to suffice for the next half hour, as Bonny Kate rode out front by herself and wrestled with her reflections concerning the Bonny Lass of Fisherrow. John Sevier was a deep man with great imagination and a sense of the significance in the names he applied to people and places. Sarah was the only one who came close to understanding the man, and even her perceptions were imperfect. Bonny Kate's yearning for moments with him returned as she wished to know him on deeper levels of understanding that escaped most of his acquaintances. Sarah appeared to be the only conduit Bonny Kate had available to the object of her fascination. There was no contending with Sarah, not in her home and not on this wilderness journey. Bonny Kate felt the sting of defeat as before. She had started a conversation that Sarah skillfully deflected, hurting only the lady who began it.

"Bonny Kate," Sarah called. "Are you all right?"

"Pay no attention to her, Sarah," Mary said. "Bonny Kate likes to get off by herself sometimes and think about things."

"I wanted to compliment you on the comfort you seem to have with the directions Captain Robertson gave you," Sarah said.

"Father and I went up this valley on one of our October hunts. There is a narrow hollow at the other end that leads down to the Doe River."

The women halted and rested the horses at a sulfur spring. The water didn't taste as good as the springs at Stony Creek, but the horses didn't seem to mind. In the soft mud around the spring, Bonny Kate saw something that chilled her more than the January wind. She reached down and placed her hand in the deep track of an animal. Her hand could not even span the largest paw print of a mountain lion she had ever seen!

"This would be a pleasant place for lunch," Sarah remarked.

"We will eat in the saddle," Bonny Kate said quickly. She pulled the rifle, Sweet Lips, and checked the priming. She scanned the winter forest and had a long view of gray sticks towering over the leafy floor as far as she could see. She listened hard for any distant rustle in those loose dried leaves.

"What are you doing there?" Sarah asked.

"Checking the rifle," she answered cheerfully. "Always be prepared, that's a creed I live by."

"Do you sense that something is wrong?" Sarah persisted.

"I'll feel better when we are moving again," she replied calmly. "Remember to hold on to your horses. The least little bird rustle will spook them in a place like this, and I don't want to waste any time running them down." The horses had given no indication of the presence of danger. That meant the lion had stopped at the spring some time ago and left in a downwind direction. Since that was the direction from which they had just come, she figured the lion circled around somewhere behind them, and was stalking them, looking for an opportunity. She resolved to meet the danger here at the spring rather than enter the narrow hollow further on, a place that would favor the predator.

"Mother, why don't you and Sarah ride on a little ways, while I stop here for a little woman's business," she suggested.

"We can wait," Mary offered.

"No," she answered sternly. "My modesty forbids it. Go on and find Mr. Jenkins's place if you can. I'll be along directly."

"Bonny Kate, is it Indians?" Sarah asked, scanning the woods for herself.

"No, game, I think," she answered, her attention focused on the way they had come. "Now move on. I don't want you scaring him away."

"We better do what the man says," Sarah advised Mary.

"Honestly, the lengths to which she will go to take a little squirrel pelt," complained Mary. "Do you see why she's so hard to marry off, Sarah? She plays the man part too well, I think. I'm hoping you can straighten her out and find her a good husband."

"I agree with you, Mrs. Sherrill, she represents quite a challenge to me."

The voices of her companions faded into the distant parts of the forest as she tied her black horse securely to an oak tree.

"I'm sorry, Blackie, I know you're in for quite a scare, but give him a good fight, and I'll try to finish him in two shots." She took some rope and tied the rifle to one end, leaving the gun leaning against the tree. She climbed up on the horse's back, reaching for the lowest limbs to pull her body up.

"Easy, Blackie, don't upset me while I get into position. I'll post myself right above you, boy." Bonny Kate found a good position in a fork of the tree. She pulled the rifle up with the rope and prepared it for firing. She put a second rifle ball in her mouth for the second round and settled in to await the action. She had second thoughts about how many shots it takes to kill a big cat and placed a third rifle ball in her mouth. The waiting was her least favorite part. She turned to see where her companions had gone, and there was no sign of them, not even a sound. She waited, hoping her instincts had been correct. After about a quarter hour had passed, she began to have doubts. What if the big cat had bypassed her for a softer target? She worried about her mother and thought of Sarah, so well beloved by her family and friends. Had she miscalculated the crafty cat and put her companions in danger, without even warning them about the nature of the threat? Had she wasted enough time on the trail to invite greater dangers after sunset on the cold, dark road into Millers Cove?

Blackie sensed something evil and became restless. That aroused her from her dark thoughts into a darker reality. The horse shifted nervously and pulled against his lead rope. Something was there! In an instant, a golden-coated lion bounded out of a draw to her right and crossed obliquely her field of fire. She expected a straight-on charge and couldn't draw a bead on it as it came across. Blackie was in a panic down below, and she even felt her tree shudder slightly in his struggle to be free. Suddenly the cat turned straight on much closer than she had expected. She brought her barrel down to a spot between the cat's shoulder blades and fired. Smoke blocked her view, and whole lot of racket in the forest behind her told her that Blackie had broken free and was trying his best to gain some distance between him and trouble. The tawny-coated beast flashed beneath her tree.

"Confound it!" she cursed as she struggled to pour her powder and ram another ball down the barrel. Blackie would never outrun that cat if she missed her shot. Maybe her second shot could still reach the cat before he bounded out of range. In any case, she was stranded, and all the action had moved in the direction of the helpless women. Her perch was no longer an advantage, so she dropped to the ground and primed the pan for a second shot. She peered around the tree with no idea where that darn cat could have gone. What she saw surprised her. Not a dozen yards away, the cat thrashed about in obvious pain. She raised her weapon, looking for a head in all the confusion of movement that presented itself. Wounded lions are the most dangerous she had always heard. If the second shot didn't kill, the cat would turn on her viciously. She fired again on what she thought was a head and stepped behind the tree to reload for a third shot. When she stepped out to deal another blow, the cat lay motionless. The head was as big as a pumpkin, with teeth like daggers. The paws were massive with claws as sharp as sickles. She fired her third shot at the place where she thought its great heart pounded and nothing indicated there was any life left. She remembered to breathe again and took great breaths of cold air. She went through the motions of reloading again as a precaution, but the shooting was done for the day. She leaned against the oak tree and felt the rush of hot blood through her veins. The nerves in her extremities tingled, her breathing was ragged, and the sweat that had poured from her pores left her hunting shirt wet and cold in the January wind. She took the shirt off and sat Indian style beneath the tree in her lacy shift and her buckskin breeches. She breathed a prayer.

"Forgive me, Lord, for destroying this magnificent handiwork of your creation, but I truly believe he meant to do me mischief. Thank you for your saving grace, and may all the things that I do, be to thy glory, Amen."

Bonny Kate sat and waited and listened to the forest all around her, and there was silence and a spirit of peace returned to her, but nothing was spoken.

Chapter 16

The Snow Baby

Bonny Kate sat beneath the oak near the sulfur spring and recovered from her encounter with the mountain lion. She had not ventured near the big cat but knew he was dead. It was not long before Sarah and Mary returned bringing Mr. Jenkins and his son, looking for her. They had recovered her runaway horse, and the women were in a near state of hysteria over Bonny Kate's well-being. After a tearful reunion, the travelers gathered their things and prepared to move on.

Mr. Jenkins examined the mountain lion. "Stock Killer, they call him. He's the terror of the night. We've been trying to get this one since before the Indian war. How did you do it?"

Bonny Kate explained how the event took place, and Mr. Jenkins and his son listened to every detail.

"Good Lord, girl, you used your own horse to bait that cougar, and shot him from the tree?" Mr. Jenkins was clearly impressed.

"It didn't go as I planned, but I'm glad Blackie broke away. My first shot was late and hit further back than where I aimed. Everything happened so fast and unpredictable!"

"You hit his spine and disabled his hind legs." Mr. Jenkins explained, pointing to the wound as though the women were interested. "You are lucky he couldn't get up, or this fight could have gone the other way."

"I know it," she affirmed.

"You are, Bonny Kate Sherrill, aren't you?"

"Yes, sir," she answered. "How do you know me?"

"I saw you at the turkey shoot last fall, and my wife Irma was at Watauga Fort last summer. You have made quite a name for yourself," he declared with admiration.

"Thank you, sir." She smiled. "This is my mother, Mary Sherrill."

"How do, ma'am." He nodded.

"And my dear friend, Sarah Sevier," she completed the introductions.

"Jack Sevier's wife?" he asked.

"Yes, sir, the very same." Sarah smiled.

"I've been hunting with Jack, and he's fine company!"

"We can all agree on that." Sarah laughed.

"So why are you ladies traveling through such a remote part of the country?"

"We are going to help deliver Mrs. Miller's baby."

"Miller, the blacksmith?" he asked.

"Yes, sir, do you know the best way to get there?" Sarah asked. "We had hoped to get there by dark."

"I can get you over the mountain and back on the main road, but you'll have to move fast to get there before dark."

Mr. Jenkins and his son loaded the huge cat on one of their horses, and the party left the sulfur springs. It was two miles down to the crossing of the Doe River and another half mile up to the Jenkins place. They had lunch during a brief visit with Mrs. Jenkins whom Mary and Bonny Kate remembered from Watauga Fort days. Sarah was a new acquaintance, but her social skills and graceful ways naturally dominated the conversation. Bonny Kate's exploits of the morning were barely mentioned, so she played the man's part, strong and silent.

It was Mr. Jenkins who called the ladies back to the tight travel schedule and after good-byes and promises of future visits and closer ties between the Jenkins family and the Sevier clan, Mr. Jenkins led the intrepid ladies over the high mountain and put them on the main road.

"Bonny Kate, I'll skin that cat and take the hide down to Robertson's trading post," Mr. Jenkins promised. "I'll tell everybody what happened, and that way you can collect the bounty."

"What bounty?" Bonny Kate asked.

"Oh, didn't you know?" he expressed surprise. "Colonel Carter offered a very generous bounty on the Stock Killer, highest I've ever seen, and it's probably gone up since I last heard."

"Thank you, Mr. Jenkins. You have been most kind." Bonny Kate thought about the value of the hide of that cat. The coat was a winter coat, thick and full, and the bounty would make her father proud and help with his debt to Mr. Brown for the purchase of the Nolichucky farm.

Mr. Jenkins took his leave of the ladies, and Bonny Kate resumed her role as the man of the party. They made their way rapidly up the Little Doe River on a well-traveled road. Cloudy skies hastened the coming winter darkness that was nearly complete when they reached the Miller cabin.

Eliza Miller had already gone to bed, and Mr. Miller had several candles lit and a fire going for warmth in the cozy cabin. He was surprised and relieved to welcome Mary and Sarah as they introduced themselves. They had indeed arrived in time, before the birth of the baby.

Bonny Kate unsaddled the horses, gave them a good brushing, found them some feed, and secured them for the night in the blacksmith's well-equipped, well-organized horse barn. She made her way to the cabin and entered as Sarah was examining Mrs. Miller. She walked over to Eliza's bed to join the other women, but Mr. Miller grabbed her and pulled her back a little roughly.

"Hold on there, fellow, that's woman's business," he said firmly. "Don't be looking at my wife!"

Bonny Kate smiled and removed her hat and undid the ribbon that held back her hair. "I am a woman, Mr. Miller," she purred in her sweetest feminine voice. "We met last summer, I'm Kate Sherrill, but now folks just call me Bonny Kate."

Mr. Miller recognized her and apologized for his mistake. "I thought you were a man sure enough when you came in dressed that way."

"That's the illusion we wanted to create," Sarah explained. "We needed a strong man to escort us and so we made her up to appear like one."

"That's a pretty good trick," Mr. Miller agreed.

Mary volunteered to make some supper, while Sarah asked Mrs. Miller some questions about her experiences of the last few days. Sarah also answered the many questions that had burdened Eliza and each answer gave her greater peace of mind. As they all enjoyed their dinner, Sarah made an announcement.

"From everything you have told me, your pregnancy has been very healthy and normal. We have arrived at the most opportune time, and I am confident of an easy delivery!"

Mrs. Miller was very pleased and happy to have Sarah on one side of her and Mary on the other, and Bonny Kate lightly moving around the cabin performing useful tasks.

"Mr. Miller, our prayers are answered, with the arrival of three angels of mercy!" she beamed. He smiled and nodded. The evening passed pleasantly, and the night passed restfully even for the angels of mercy who made their beds in the loft overhead.

The morning was bitterly cold and cloudy and smelled like it might snow. Mr. Miller built up the fire, and then accompanied Bonny Kate down to the horse barn to feed the livestock.

"Good morrow, Kate, for that's your name, I hear," Mr. Miller pronounced dramatically.

"Pardon me?" Bonny Kate responded.

"I'm quoting a favorite passage from Shakespeare," explained Mr. Miller. "Here's Katharina's part." In a falsetto voice, he continued:

> Well, have you heard, but something hard of hearing:
> They call me Katharina that do talk of me.

In a deep booming male voice, Mr. Miller went on as Bonny Kate stopped her progress to the barn and just listened.

> You lie, in faith; for you are call'd plain Kate,
> And Bonny Kate and sometimes Kate the curst;
> But Kate, the prettiest Kate in Christendom
> Kate of Kate Hall, my super-dainty Kate,
> For dainties are all Kates, and therefore, Kate,
> Take this of me, Kate of my consolation;
> Hearing thy mildness praised in every town,
> Thy virtues spoke of, and thy beauty sounded,
> Yet not so deeply as to thee belongs,
> Myself am moved to woo thee for my wife.

"Here's the answer Katharina gives," explained Mr. Miller, returning to his falsetto voice.

> Moved! in good time: let him that moved you hither
> Remove you hence: I knew you at the first
> You were a moveable.

Mr. Miller stopped and returned to his own voice. "Isn't that wonderful?"

"Yes," she answered. "But what is it?"

"My favorite play from Shakespeare," he explained, "the *Taming of the Shrew*. That's where your name Bonny Kate comes from, is it not?"

"Who is the shrew?" she asked.

"It's Katharina, the one he called Bonny Kate."

"So Bonny Kate is the name of a shrew?"

"Yes, I think it's wonderful that you have adopted a name that honors the great playwright Shakespeare," Mr. Miller could not contain his enthusiasm. "It speaks volumes about your character, Bonny Kate. When I saw you dressed as a man last night, I was so impressed with your boldness. Bonny Kate is a name that makes a statement: here I am world, accept me for who I am. I am one to watch out for! It's a rare honor to have you and your mother present at the birth of my child," Mr. Miller concluded.

They completed the morning chores at the barn then Mr. Miller left to tend some livestock he kept in the cove. Bonny Kate wondered at a blacksmith that could quote such pretty words. She had heard of Shakespeare's plays from her mother, but never read one. All the reading she had ever done was in the Holy Bible.

Bonny Kate returned to the cabin where she walked in on one of life's greatest dramas. Eliza had risen that morning to her regular activities when the contractions began. Mary and Sarah, went right to work, while Bonny Kate, the shrew, performed every command she was given. They propped up Eliza with whatever pillows they could find and coached her through the first several sets of contractions.

When Mr. Miller came back from feeding his livestock, he found the women hard at work. Bonny Kate's job was to keep him out of the way.

"Today is the day, Mr. Miller," Bonny Kate informed him cheerfully.

"What should I do?" he asked.

"Nothing you can do," she replied. "Just let nature take its course."

"I've got to be doing something, Miss Sherrill."

"Why don't you go down to the forge and work some iron. I'll call you when there's anything to report."

"Will it take long?" he asked.

Sarah stepped over to him to answer the question. "First babies always take longer than any other. It could be all day. Go over and give your wife some encouraging loving words, then just give her some time."

Mr. Miller sat with his wife a few moments while the three women went out on the porch.

Mary knew something was amiss. "Sarah, what's wrong?"

"I'm not sure," Sarah replied. "Last night the baby was in perfect position for a normal delivery, but it moved in the night."

"Is it breech now?" Mary asked.

"No," Sarah replied, "cross-birth, I think."

"What's that?" Bonny Kate asked.

"The baby is side to side," Sarah explained. "If it doesn't return to normal before long, we could lose them both."

"What can be done about it?" Bonny Kate continued.

"Watch and wait, hope and pray," Sarah answered. "Don't let on that we have concerns. That would only make matters worse."

Eliza started screaming again, and Mr. Miller came to the door. Sarah calmly walked into the cabin. "We will take over from here, Mr. Miller." The little woman reached up to pat the burly blacksmith on his shoulder. "Don't worry about a thing!" Mary followed Sarah to the bed.

Bonny Kate stayed on the porch with Mr. Miller as the women inside worked through another set of contractions.

"We will need more firewood up here close to the door if those clouds bring us any snow," Bonny Kate suggested. Mr. Miller agreed and went right to work, glad to have something to do to keep himself busy. Several errands later, Bonny Kate persuaded Mr. Miller to fire up his forge and work some iron. She operated the bellows while he quoted Shakespeare and hammered out some door hinges. They spent the morning engaged in useful activity. He told the story of how he met his wife and how they came to settle in the remote part of the mountains. Bonny Kate let him talk on and did a good job of concealing the concerns Sarah had shared earlier. At midday, Bonny Kate returned to the cabin to check in with Sarah and prepare a lunch. Her mother met her at the door, and they conversed quietly outside.

"Any news?" Bonny Kate greeted her.

Mary shook her head sadly. "No change. She's done all that work for nothing. At least, she's still in good spirits; Sarah has seen to that. I'm so glad Sarah's here with us. She provides such a calm, confident influence."

"We need to pray," Bonny Kate decided. Mother and daughter knelt on the porch and lifted up Eliza and John Miller in prayer. They prayed for Sarah also in her activities to provide comfort and encouragement to the would-be mother. When they had finished, they went inside and prepared a lunch. Mr. Miller came in to eat and spent some more time with Eliza. He tenderly encouraged her, and they still assumed that everything was proceeding normally.

The afternoon went the same way, and by dinner hour, Sarah told Mary they would have to tell Mr. Miller to prepare him for the worst. Sarah took Bonny Kate, and they found Mr. Miller tending his animals at the horse barn. He took the news very hard but expressed his gratitude for the way Sarah had explained everything and the comfort she had given his wife all day.

"Isn't there anything else we can do for her?" he asked in his despair.

"Yes," Sarah replied confidently. "You can join Bonny Kate and Mrs. Sherrill in a prayer circle. These Sherrills have considerable influence with spiritual matters, and I have personally seen many instances where they have been used as instruments in the hand of Divine Providence."

As Bonny Kate looked at Sarah in wide-eyed surprise, Mr. Miller exclaimed with hope born of desperation, "Yes, I'll try anything!"

The three of them returned to the cabin. Sarah entered to work with Eliza, and Bonny Kate called her mother out to the porch for another round of prayer. They knelt and joined hands with Mr. Miller.

"How do we begin?" Mr. Miller asked.

"Mother will begin," Bonny Kate explained. "When she finishes, you just say what is in your heart. Use your prettiest words, like your Shakespeare, and be sure to ask clearly for deliverance for Eliza. Then I'll finish the prayer with one more appeal to Divine Providence. Let us pray."

In the gloom of gathering dusk one very worried man, a mother named Mary, and her daughter prayed earnestly and beautifully outside the lonely cabin in the mountain fastness. As their prayer rose to the heavens, a light snow began to fall. On the road below, a solitary figure approached leading his horse. He came up to where he could see what was going on and stopped to listen reverently. When Bonny Kate finished and said Amen, the solitary man called out.

"Amen," he said.

Mary and Bonny Kate recognized the newcomer as Sam Sherrill.

"Father!" Bonny Kate rose and flew into his arms. Mary came to greet her husband just a little slower.

"Mary!" Sarah called from inside the cabin. "Mary, come quickly! This baby has moved again! We have work to do!"

Mary rushed inside to help with Bonny Kate right behind her. The two men shook hands and stayed out on the porch.

"Good thing, you got up here before the snow," Mr. Miller remarked.

"I'm thankful for that," Sam replied. "Sounds like you have a birth underway."

"I hope so." Mr. Miller breathed out. "It's been a long day of trying."

"It won't be long now," Sarah called out cheerfully.

The snow fell all evening and covered the valley of the Little Doe River. By midnight, all the excitement and work associated with birthing was over. Eliza—happy, proud, and exhausted—held her little baby girl. She looked at the tired faces of her new friends in the warm firelight and felt truly blessed by those brave women who had come to her rescue. She was unaware that the birth had been anything but normal.

"Have you thought of a girl's name for your precious baby, Mrs. Miller?" Mary asked.

"Mr. Miller wanted to name her Katharina, because of his fondness for that Shakespeare character, but I have decided on another name if he will allow it."

"Whatever you want, my dear," Mr. Miller answered. He was a relieved man who fully realized that a miracle had occurred under his roof that evening.

"I would like to name her Sarah, for the lady who delivered her." Eliza smiled.

"Sarah Miller is a fine name, my dear," Mr. Miller approved.

Sarah Sevier smiled. "Thank you, but I am the least deserving of that honor," she acknowledged. "It was Mary Sherrill who organized this mission, and Bonny Kate who escorted us here safely."

"My dear, to honor all three of your helpers we should have had triplets," Mr. Miller joked.

"Maybe next time." Eliza laughed.

The Millers and their guests were snowbound for a week. Sam Sherrill and John Miller waded through deep snowdrifts to tend the livestock and accomplish the other necessary farm chores. Mary and Bonny Kate provided excellent meals and Sarah took good care of her little namesake. Eliza Miller recovered quickly as young women so often do and was as active as the other women by the end of the week.

One morning, Bonny Kate and her parents rode up into Miller's cove to see what it looked like in winter. They held fond memories of camping in the beauty of the place and dancing there with the Millers in the splendor of a midsummer night. The winter appearance did not disappoint. The sun sparkled on the icicles that adorned the trees and the bright snow illuminated even the shaded parts of the valley. The waterfall was spectacular plunging into the icy pool as the creek was already beginning to carry the runoff of snowmelt from the sunny slopes above.

"Is there a place like this on our new farm?" Bonny Kate asked her father.

"No, my dear, we will have rolling pastures and thick forests along the Nolichucky River, with deep soil in the bottoms for our crops."

"I wish we could go out there this year and plant, even if it's still unsafe to live there," she remarked.

"Say, that's a good idea," Sam declared. "We could start a crop of wheat and corn out there and leave it untended. In the fall, we could go out there and harvest whatever we can. The peace with the Indians may be arranged by then, and we would have the yield of two farms to live on. I believe we will try that!"

On the ride back to Miller's cabin, the three of them talked about their new farm and planned big things.

When the snow melted enough for travel along the roads and trails, Colonel John Sevier made his way up the valley of the Little Doe hoping to join his wife and her friends for their journey home. He had come back from his service with the light horse company to find his children missing their mother but thriving under the excellent care of Susan Sherrill Taylor and Mary Jane Sherrill. John had heard of the women's adventure with the mountain lion from Charlotte Robertson, who heard it from Mr. Jenkins, and knew the story would soon be told in every home in Washington District.

There was a joyous reunion for John and Sarah Sevier in the snowy yard of the Miller home. Mr. Miller was honored to have Colonel Sevier as his guest and delighted to meet him personally, having heard so much about him. The evening of the colonel's arrival, the Millers had a celebration marking the one-week-old age of their healthy daughter. They also celebrated being surrounded by such warm friends. Eliza had the constitution of most frontier women and had returned to a fully active involvement in the business of life. She and Sarah Sevier had plans to meet at the spring gathering and spend some time together, and in the meantime, they would write letters to keep up their friendship. Bonny Kate was amazed at how easily Sarah made loyal friends and brought them under her influence so quickly.

That night every woman had her man, except for Bonny Kate. John and Eliza Miller were extremely happy, Sam and Mary Sherrill were unusually affectionate, and John and Sarah Sevier were very much in love. Bonny Kate was acutely aware of the loneliness of being the old maid. She watched Colonel Sevier's attentions toward his wife in the firelight. They sat together touching, cuddling, and whispering sweet secrets to each other. It had been so long since

Bonny Kate had seen Colonel Sevier; he was like a stranger to her. The silly girlish infatuation with him was but a distant memory, but she still carried a name that he had bestowed upon her. Someday, she would get around to asking him whether he had named her after a fish maid in a tavern song or for a Shakespearian shrew.

Chapter 17

Trouble with Tories

Robertson's Trading Post situated on the north side of the Watauga River, across from Watauga Fort, was a row of log rooms consisting of two storerooms, a trading room where the Robertsons displayed goods for sale, and another room served as living quarters for the Robertson family. Even though the Carters had a store just two miles up the river and the Browns ran a store on the Nolichucky, most Wataugans were willing to pay a little more for the variety and availability the Robertsons offered; and Charlotte was almost always available to open the store and trade, morning, noon, or night.

One day early in the month of March 1777, Bonny Kate rode one of her father's finest horses down the Watauga Valley to do some trading. She was an imposing lady on horseback, straight and tall, yet moving with a fluid grace that responded to the motions of the magnificent animals the Sherrill horses were known to be. She carried three dozen spools of fine linen thread, a couple of dozen writing quills, and a sack of woven goods the ladies of Stony Creek had produced, which she intended to trade for a long list of goods the ladies wanted. Bonny Kate's top of list items were flax seed for her spring planting and maple sugar drops, a surprise for the little Sevier children. She stopped at Carter's store to visit with Mrs. Carter but soon learned the Carters didn't have many of the needed items including the maple sugar drops, so after a pleasant conversation, she rode on to Robertson's.

The Watauga Valley had changed a great deal in the eight months since the Sherrills had first arrived. New farms were being established all over the valley and the great wild forests were retreating back up the tributary valleys as pastures, fields, and gardens were opened up. When she arrived at Sycamore Shoals, she decided to ride up to Watauga Fort and have a look around. She wanted to refresh some fond memories. She rode around the outside first looking at the tall palisades. She stopped at the place where she had struggled desperately with her last pursuer and heard the lieutenant call "Jump for me, Kate!" She looked at the place, she had clambered over the wall. It all seemed so long ago. She was a different person then, yet still the same problems persisted. No husband, no sweetheart, and no prospects yet. Sarah had been a great comfort to her in that department and a great friend. She exuded great confidence that the right men would soon come along, and Bonny Kate would have many from which to choose, and not a bad choice in the lot! Sarah's spring gathering was just weeks away, and Bonny Kate's lovely party dress was nearly ready. Sarah had sent letter after letter to relatives as far away as Augusta County searching for referrals of appropriate matches for that lovely frontier princess Catharine, lady in waiting to Queen Sarah of Stony Creek. Sarah had high hopes for the happiness of her friend. Bonny Kate harbored apprehensions.

"What about love in all this?" she frequently asked Sarah.

"Oh, that comes along later," Sarah always answered confidently. "Love takes its own sweet time!"

"Just like Divine Providence, I suppose," Bonny Kate would say to herself.

Inside Watauga Fort people were living in the cabins—people she didn't know, new people, probably paying rent to Captain Robertson. There was an untidy appearance to their manner of dwelling, and when she bade them good morning, they answered with silent stares. She toured the fort without dismounting, remembering so many good times, even in the midst of ever-present danger. She had much for which to be thankful. The idle, staring persons occupying the fort made her uneasy; so she turned her horse, rode out the gate, and headed down the hill toward the trading post.

John Sevier walked into Robertson's trading post and immediately noticed a half dozen tough-looking characters loitering suspiciously. Charlotte Robertson, alone at the store, looked relieved to see him. John quickly sized up the situation and eyed the men with a hard look.

"Good day, Colonel Sevier," Charlotte greeted him.

"Hello, Mrs. Robertson," John greeted her. "I'm expecting to meet a dozen or so militia men, armed to the teeth and ready for action about midday. Is anybody here yet?"

"You are the first," Charlotte answered.

"I'll just wait here in the store, if you don't mind."

"Not at all, Colonel," Charlotte replied. "Is there trouble brewing?"

John spoke boldly, with a lot more swagger than Charlotte had ever seen in the man, for John had never been ordinarily prideful. "We heard reports of Tory outlaws moving in with all these new settlers. The militia has been called out to capture them. Judge Carter says we will bring these men to justice." He drew one of his pistols and prepared it for use, steadily watching the strangers.

The leader of the men stood up from a barrel where he had been lounging and slouched out. The others followed him. John looked at Charlotte.

"Rough-looking customers," he observed. "Who are they?"

"They claim to be hunters," Charlotte informed him. "But I suspect they're the same Tories your militia men are looking for."

John leaned toward her and said in a low voice, "That was a bluff, Charlotte."

"Oh . . . ," she realized. "Then we can expect no—"

"No militia," he finished her sentence, working rapidly to finish loading and priming his pistols.

"But I heard a horse coming just now," she said hopefully. They crossed the room to the window in time to see Bonny Kate Sherrill ride up to the yard.

"There's trouble," Charlotte almost growled in John's ear.

"She's one who can find it," John agreed. "Charlotte, is your boy close by?"

"I'm here, Colonel," Jonathan Robertson responded from the back of the room. The eight-year-old son of Charlotte and James Robertson emerged from his hiding place with a long rifle that was probably a little more gun than he could handle.

"Good!" John exclaimed. "Bring your rifle to the window and cover me, but stay out of sight." John walked to the open door with a cocked pistol in each hand.

"Good luck, John," Charlotte said as he stepped out.

Bonny Kate tied her horse to a tree and unloaded her trade goods as the Tories moved toward her menacingly.

"Well, look here, fellows, here's a fine sight for men so long gone in the wilderness," leered the leader of the Tories. "Hey, missy, you live around here?"

"I mind my own business, and so should you," the bold girl replied.

"Your own business is it?" the Tory remarked insolently. "We could sure enough show you some business." The man moved to block her progress toward the store.

"I don't think so," the brave lady held her ground.

The Tory reached out and grabbed her by the left wrist. Instinctively she reacted, driving the heel of her right hand into the Tory's nose. He fell to the ground, releasing his hold on her. She reached for the rifle hanging on her saddle. The other five men rushed her, but a powerful voice boomed out, stopping them in their tracks.

"Bonny Kate, please don't lose your temper and shoot anybody!" The men looked around and saw John Sevier approaching with pistols leveled, one in each hand. He continued, "I'm sworn to keep the peace, protecting life and property. You boys slowly back away from that dangerous gal."

The Tory leader struggled to get up on his knees as John arrived beside him. John placed the barrel of his pistol directly on the end of the Tory's injured nose.

"No, you stay right there for now," John ordered. "I'll protect you. But if I hadn't come over when I did, she might have shot you all down."

"Foolish talk!" another of the gang spoke up. "He's outnumbered, and he knows it."

"I was only trying to save your lives," John declared. "You don't want to tangle with her. She kills mostly lions and bears, but I suspect she's killed more than a few skunks and Tories here lately."

Bonny Kate leveled her rifle at the Tory who spoke. "That's right, Colonel, but I haven't shot one in over a month. I was afraid this country was running out of Tories. Can I shoot this one now?"

"Hold on there, Bonny Kate," John said. "How do you know these fellows are Tories?"

"They have the same disgusting smell," she replied.

"That evidence is not enough to convict them in Judge Carter's court," John cautioned her. "I am not convinced these fellows are really looking for trouble."

"Back off, boys," the Tory leader ordered his men. "We don't want any trouble with these people."

"That's easy for him to say. He smells the gunpowder, but what about you boys?" John studied the other five men. Bonny Kate had one covered, and he could take out the leader and one other with his pistols. The Robertsons would have to deal with the other three if these bullies wanted to push this thing.

"No, mister, we don't want no trouble," one of the men spoke up. "We are not Tories. We were just out hunting and trapping in Kentucky. We didn't mean no harm to this girl."

"Did you hear that, Bonny Kate?" John asked. "They're not even Tories. I sure wish you wouldn't shoot them. Don't rile her boys, better put down all your knives, tomahawks, and shooting irons. And be quick about it." John nudged the gun on the Tory's nose.

"Do as he says!" the leader ordered. The men dropped their weapons and stepped back. Charlotte and her son emerged from the store covering the Tories.

"I sure do love the peace and quiet," John declared. "Don't you?" He nudged the Tory again.

"Yes, sir, peace and quiet suits me fine."

"Why can't I just shoot them and be done with it?" Bonny Kate persisted.

"Because they say they're not Tories."

"But that man bullied me, and I won't tolerate a bully!" she exclaimed.

"She has accused you boys of assaulting and insulting a lady. Now that's a serious charge in this country. We hold a much higher regard for our womenfolk." John turned to Bonny Kate. "Do you want to bring charges against these fellows, Miss Bonny Kate?"

"Yes, sir, I do!"

"Very well, as an officer of the court I arrest you boys and charge you with assaulting a lady. Court is held next Thursday over there at Watauga Fort. Your weapons are confiscated by the court until you prove your innocence."

Charlotte and her sons quickly gathered up the weapons, taking the rifles and powder horns from the saddles and gathering up the weapons on the ground. John backed away keeping his guns trained on the men.

"Well, that's it until Thursday. Be there for the trial or we'll hunt you down."

"You're not holding us?"

"We have no jail," John replied. "Usually justice here moves faster, but Judge Carter is away on business, so you fellows just have to wait and show up on Thursday."

The Tory leader stood and made for his horse. "Come on, men, we don't need no second invitation." The Tories mounted their horses and rode away.

"Do you think it was wise to let them go like that?" Bonny Kate asked.

"I think they'll clear out for good and go back where they came from," he replied. "Maybe they will spread the word that Watauga valley is no place for Tories and outlaws."

"Colonel Sevier, it seems I'm once again indebted to you for preserving my life and my dignity."

"That's what neighbors are for, Miss Sherrill," John answered. "And I am indebted to you for distracting them long enough for me to get the upper hand."

They walked toward the porch of the trading post where Charlotte waited. "Bonny Kate, you invite trouble when you ride around the country without an escort. These are dangerous times!"

"I'll make it dangerous for anyone who wants to mess with me!"

Charlotte disapprovingly ignored her bravado and turned to John. "Colonel Sevier, thank you for settling that matter. I was very uncomfortable having those men loitering around my store. I don't know what might have happened if you hadn't arrived."

"I'll call up a militia patrol to make sure that bunch doesn't come back," he assured her.

"Come on into the store for some refreshment," Charlotte invited. "I think we can safely get back to the trading business. But when the trading is done, I'm going to insist, Colonel Sevier, that you escort Miss Sherrill home safely."

"If she will allow me," John looked at her as they followed Charlotte to the store.

She smiled as their eyes met. "Nothing would give me greater pleasure, sir."

Inside the trading post on one of the walls, hung the skin of the mountain lion called the Stock Killer. She walked over to it and ran her hand over the thick furry coat.

"He was a magnificent animal," she marveled. "It all happened so fast."

"What did you do with the bounty money?" Charlotte asked. "It would have made a fine dowry for a young woman hoping to get married."

"Papa made another payment to Mr. Brown for the farm on the Nolichucky," she answered. "Have there been any interested buyers for the lion skin?"

"Lots of interest but nobody buying," Charlotte replied. "Mr. Robertson mentioned buying it to give as a gift to Chief Attacullaculla. This cougar gave the Indians as much trouble as it gave the settlers. They believe that only a spirit warrior could have killed it. Watch out, Bonny Kate, the Indians are talking about you."

The thought of that kind of notoriety caused a cold shiver. "I'd rather not come to the attention of our savage friends," she said. "I hear they'll steal a woman as easily as they'll steal a horse. Whatever happened to Lydia Bean?"

"I'll tell you," John volunteered. "They were about to burn her at the stake when Nancy Ward climbed up atop the burning pyre and kicked away the firewood. She ranted at the braves and shamed them for the cowardice of making war on women. Lydia still lives a captive but under the kind protection of Nancy Ward. When the peace treaty talks begin we will arrange a trade to get her back home."

"I could have ended up the same way, or worse, if you had not been there to pull me over the wall," Bonny Kate reminded him.

"Sarah calls it the workings of Divine Providence," John explained. "And I believe she is right."

"I am sure she is," Bonny Kate agreed.

Bonny Kate found everything she needed at Robertson's Trading Post and rode home to Stony Creek with Colonel Sevier as her escort.

"I haven't seen much of you lately, Mr. Sevier," she commented. "Where do you go every day?"

John laughed. "I go out and rescue damsels in distress. Aren't you glad I came to your rescue this morning?"

"Yes, sir, but doesn't your family suffer by not having you home?"

"I'm home every night for dinner, and I never miss my breakfast," he replied.

"What about your farm?" she persisted. "How are you going to make it work?"

"Miss Sherrill," he explained. "Sarah is the most excellent manager of our home affairs. I think she would be very hurt to hear that a close neighbor and friend questioned her abilities."

"That is not my intention," Bonny Kate reacted. "I am not questioning Sarah's abilities. I'm just curious to know how you make your living, sir."

"Well, Miss Sherrill, I'm what you might call a public servant. My offices include lieutenant colonel of the County Militia, Clerk of the County Court, and friend to the honest hardworking yeoman farmer."

"Is there enough fighting and court business to make an honest living?" she asked.

"Lately, there has been enough to keep me very busy," he replied. "We are working harder than ever to restore the peace with our Indian neighbors, and our efforts have rewarded us with a chance, later this month, to meet with the chiefs up at Long Island of the Holston. The members of the Watauga Association are also hard at work to encourage settlement, provide economic opportunity, and promote prosperity throughout the backwater country. I'm doing all this to bring peace to the country so our families can settle on the farms we have bought on the Nolichucky. I'm a little surprised that you of all people would question how I'm going to make my farm work. Don't you know that your father and I have an agreement to split the yield of Stony Creek farm half and half for the coming year?"

"Yes, sir, I understand that, but won't you be working there with us also?"

"I trust your father does not need another manager to help him oversee the operations. If he needs me to make any decisions, Sarah can advise him better than I can. I'll be the first to concede that!"

"So you get half the farm's yield for staying out of my father's way?"

"I'll work on the farm whenever I'm home, but Public Service is unpredictable in the demands it imposes on my time. The involvement of your family in my farming enterprise seems like a complicated arrangement but hopefully it's only for a year or two, until the peace is achieved."

Bonny Kate began to realize that her hero, the husband of her friend Sarah, was playing on a bigger stage than she ever imagined. Colonel Sevier was what her Granny Sherrill would have called a great and powerful man.

"I'm sorry I questioned you about your business," she said. "I imagined you being more involved in the farm. You have been very patient in explaining all this to me, and I appreciate that."

"Is there anything else about my life that might be of interest to you?" He smiled.

"Well, actually there is one other thing. I wanted to ask you about the name Bonny Kate. Where did you come up with that?"

"Why do you ask?" he returned.

"Well, Sarah told me it was from your favorite song, but there is also the Bonny Kate in the Shakespeare play *Taming of the Shrew*. Which one were you thinking about when you called me that name?"

"The song," he replied. "It was appropriate when you made your escape from the Indians. Without thinking, the idea just popped into my head. Everything happened so fast that morning."

"So you did not think me a shrew?" she asked.

"I never regarded you a shrew." He laughed. "And I never will."

"Thank you, Colonel Sevier, that is a relief," she declared with a smile. "But I'm not so sure I like being named for a fisher woman in a naughty tavern song."

"If you don't care for the name Bonny Kate, I'll call you whatever you like," he offered.

"The problem is, I can't think of any name I like better."

"Well, keep me informed," he said. "I shall enjoy helping you get accustomed to the new name of your choice. Sarah tells me you have some skill in naming farms."

"Oh yes! We are going to call Papa's new farm Daisy Fields because of the wild daisies that grow there in such abundance. Every great estate should have an appropriate name."

"I like the name Daisy Fields. You have a romantic imagination," he approved.

"Papa says that's one of my most obvious faults." She laughed.

"And what would you name my new farm?" he asked.

"Think about the one feature that makes the farm unique or special."

"Well, the homesite is located near an old plum orchard left by the Indians. Sarah will be making some mighty fine plum preserves."

"There's the idea, Plum Orchard or Plum Grove," she suggested.

"I like the name Plum Grove Farm," he decided.

"No, no, Plum Grove Plantation," she corrected. "You have to think big!"

"Plum Grove Plantation is what we will call it. Thank you, Bonny Kate."

Bonny Kate and Colonel Sevier arrived at the Carter home in the course of their progress up the Watauga Valley. Landon Carter came out to greet the colonel.

"Good morning, Jack! What's the news?"

"A gang of six Tories attacked Miss Sherrill down at Robertson's this morning. I stopped them short of doing her any harm, and I took away their weapons, but I think they will cause more trouble for the community if they are allowed to loiter in the vicinity. I suggest you round up a dozen men and track them out of the valley. I'm curious to see where they are headed."

"They are headed for Judge Carter's court," Bonny Kate declared. "I'm pressing charges against them."

"You want them arrested, Jack?"

"Not yet, just track them for now. I need more evidence of their intentions in this territory."

"I could leave immediately if I had a good horse. Mine is being reshoed today," Landon explained.

"Better take mine," the colonel offered. "There's no time to lose." He dismounted and removed his rifle and other personal effects.

Landon Carter gathered his things in preparation for his mission. Colonel Sevier thanked him for his service, and he was gone in the next instant.

"Good lad, that one," Colonel Sevier commented. "Miss Sherrill, you would do well to marry such a fellow as that. He's dependable and solid as a rock. He's also likely to become very rich from his inheritance."

"And much too young for this old maid," she sighed. "You forget, Colonel Sevier, I'm twenty-two years old, and Landon is how old?"

"Oh, I think he's about sixteen," he guessed.

"It would never work," she told him. "But thanks for thinking of me as an eligible lady. Just find me someone a little older."

"I'll work on that." John began the two-mile walk to Stony Creek. Bonny Kate rode beside him and watched his rapid stride. He moved with supple power in his muscular legs. He was fit and well used to physical activity.

"Colonel Sevier?"

"What is it, Miss Sherrill?"

"We could travel faster if we rode double," she suggested.

"It's only two miles home," he answered. "If I am delaying you, please proceed without me."

"Those boots of yours were never meant for walking," she observed.

"My boots fit me quite well," he responded.

"I'm afraid you will tire yourself out walking all that way."

"I'm very happy to have the exercise."

"You are such a busy man," she persisted. "You could save much time by riding with me."

John stopped and looked at her. "You are determined to have me ride with you, and you are not going to leave me alone until I consent to it."

"I only suggest it out of respect for your position in the community, and my personal gratitude for your gallant service to me this morning," she explained. "Please climb up behind me."

"That would be inappropriate, Miss Sherrill," he objected. "Where would a gentleman place his hands to hold on? There are too many soft and ticklish places on the feminine form to afford me a secure hold."

"Then you ride ahead of me and handle the horse while I worry about holding on," she offered.

"Very well," he agreed. "That is acceptable to me."

She slipped off her horse, and he caught her politely at the waist and lowered her feet to the ground. The thrill of his touch was still there! What did Sarah call it, the Sevier effect? Yes, and she felt it powerfully as he mounted the horse and pulled her up to seat her behind him.

She wrapped her arms around his waist as he urged the beautiful stallion home. The trip was too short as the colonel set a fast pace for the powerful animal. Bonny Kate held on tightly with her bonnet pressed against the warm wool of his coat. The galloping movement of the horse and her contact with the handsome, gallant man was exhilarating. She supposed he was intentionally trying to be rough with her to prevent her from enjoying the ride too much, but the action had the opposite effect. It took her breath away and heightened her desire for such a man as she now held. As the horse charged up the hill to the Sevier cabin, she looked over his shoulder, and the hair of his queue brushed against her face, and she again thrilled at the closeness. She saw Sarah standing at the door watching their approach and knew there was now one more trespass to confess. The horse slowed to a trot, and Bonny Kate released her hold on the colonel's waist and regained her erect riding posture. She removed her bonnet and cap to release her disheveled hair and was breathlessly trying to compose herself. When the horse stopped, Colonel Sevier lifted his right leg over the horse's head and bounded to the ground.

"Bonny Kate was attacked by Tories this morning down at Robertson's," he announced.

"Oh, the dear girl," Sarah exclaimed. "What did they do to her?"

"They roughed her up a little," John explained. He helped her off the horse and she weakly leaned on him as Sarah and he assisted her into the house.

"Oh, how dreadful," Sarah continued. "What are you feeling, my dear?"

"I'm weak in the knees," she breathed heavily. They laid her on their bed. "I feel as limp as a rag doll, with a knot in the pit of my stomach."

"You rest, my dear," Sarah instructed. "Betsy, run down to the Sherrills and fetch back Mrs. Sherrill." Sarah left the patient and accompanied Mr. Sevier back out into the yard.

"John," she asked earnestly. "Was she violated?"

"No," he replied. "But she would have been if Charlotte Robertson, and I hadn't come to the rescue. There were six of them trying to drag her down to the canebrake, and she was putting up one heck of a fight. She broke one fellow's nose."

"Good for her!" Sarah cheered.

"See if you can calm her down," John recommended. "She had a terrible scare, but with your gentle attentions, she should recover quickly."

"I'll do my best," Sarah promised.

John reached for Bonny Kate's horse. "I have called out the light horse to track them down. I suspect they are looking for more trouble. She wants to press charges and Tories are bad about finishing the mischief they start. Have Mr. Sherrill guard the place well until we apprehend this gang."

"I will. You be careful, John." She embraced him, and they kissed.

He looked lovingly on her. "I have a very strong desire to stay here with you tonight."

"Handle the emergency first, my love," she spoke sweetly. "Then there will be time for us."

John leapt into the saddle and noticed the sack of trade goods Bonny Kate had left hanging on the saddle. He took it and handed it to Sarah. "Bonny Kate did some trading this morning. See that she gets this." Sarah nodded and received the sack. John raced back down the trail to join the action.

Chapter 18

The Beloved Woman

The month of March was nearly over when Colonel Sevier came riding home on a well-spent mount. He unsaddled the horse to cool it down, brushed it, and put it out to pasture. He enjoyed the homecoming with his family, but his stay was to be one night only. As soon as he could untangle himself from the loving arms of wife and children, he made his way down to the Sherrill cabin to pursue the real purpose of his visit home.

Sam Sherrill and his sons were attending the birthing of a spring colt. Bonny Kate was there too, in the midst of the action, directing the boys on how to assist the mare. She was keenly interested in the racing qualities of the colt. Colonel Sevier watched her for a moment before getting Sam's attention.

"Welcome home, John! How did the Indian talks go?" Sam was glad to see his friend but soon saw the weight of the world burdening him. John drew him aside where they could converse privately.

"The talks are a disaster. Only the Virginia commissioners showed up. The Carolinas haven't gotten around to appointing any representatives. The friendly Cherokees are wondering what the deal is and Dragging Canoe and his war party are still working for the British. The talks can't move ahead without some sign from the Great Spirit so neither side is moving," John admitted. "I'm going back in the morning, and I'd like you to go with me."

"What could I possibly do to help the Indian talks?" Sam asked.

"Bring Bonny Kate." John was more serious than Sam had ever seen him.

"What?" Sam reacted.

"I know it's a strange request, but the Indians want to see her. It has something to do with their religious beliefs, some kind of magic, or medicine they call it. Robertson and Brown think it may move the talks forward if Bonny Kate were to go up to Long Island and perform some of her shooting tricks, run a race or two, and show off some of her natural charms."

"That sounds pretty doggone dangerous," Sam declared. "Bonny Kate is more likely to start a war, than secure a peace!"

John laughed. "That's exactly the argument I used, but Brown and Robertson are running the show, and they have the powers of the Virginia commissioners backing their play. I'm a very small player in all this except for one thing. The ace they think they hold in their hand, lives on my farm."

Sam had a debt to pay Mr. Brown and nobody in the Watauga community ever refused a request from the worthy James Robertson. These were good reasons for going along with the strange request. Sam inhaled deeply and exhaled his answer, "You'll have to ask her."

Bonny Kate was anointed in horse blood as she worked to clean up the little colt. She smiled when she saw Colonel Sevier present at the birth of her new racing champion. "Here's a fine little fellow that can beat anything in the Sevier stables in a year or two!"

"Don't bet the farm on it, but I'll admit he's one to watch out for," John replied.

A few moments passed as they all admired the new little racer.

"Bonny Kate," Sam broke the silence. "Colonel Sevier has something important to ask you."

"What is it?" She smiled.

"I'd like to invite you to come up to the Indian talks at the Long Island for a few days." John had decided to keep the complicated request as simple as he could make it.

"What's it like?"

"It's just like one of our gatherings," John explained. "There's feasting and games and races and shooting matches and dancing."

"That sounds like fun!" she responded. "I'll take my new party dress and be the belle of the ball."

"No," John corrected her. "Better leave the party dress at home. Everything has more of an Indian influence."

"Then what should I wear?"

"Buckskin hunting shirt, buckskin skirt, leggings, and your moccasins," John answered. "That's more like what the Indian women wear."

"That's kind of mannish, don't you think?"

"Yes, that's the look we are trying to achieve," John approved. "Mannish is good."

Sam agreed, "Yes, definitely mannish."

"I'll consult with Sarah and mother and see what they are wearing," Bonny Kate decided.

"Your mother is not going," Sam declared.

"And Sarah?" she asked looking at John.

"She's not going either," John informed her.

"Say, what is this?" Bonny Kate began to have suspicions.

"It's a complicated mess," John admitted. "I'll explain it all tomorrow as we make our way up to Fort Patrick Henry. Your father and I will be with you the whole time, and it will be a good opportunity for you to get out and meet some men."

"Oh, so that's what this is about," she guessed. "Was this Sarah's idea?"

"No, it was mine," John said. "There are four companies of Virginia and North Carolina regulars stationed at Fort Patrick Henry, and a great many fine young officers among them."

"Are you sure I won't need my new party dress?"

"I'm sure," John replied. "You should dress for comfort, not show. So will you go?"

"I haven't anything better to do," she sighed, still misunderstanding the purpose of the trip.

The morning was chilly as the three travelers set out from Stony Creek. They moved slowly at first so John could explain the situation more fully and make Bonny Kate understand that she was the centerpiece of a diplomatic mission and not a spinster on a manhunt.

"The Indian chiefs first noticed Bonny Kate at Watauga Fort," Colonel Sevier began. "The day she escaped their fastest warriors and flew up to the top of that wall in a hail of arrows and bullets, convinced them that she was under the protection of the Great Spirit."

"Don't you mean the Holy Spirit?" she interrupted.

"The Indians call God the Great Spirit, so in many ways, their beliefs are similar to ours, and their medicine men attach great significance to events that we often ascribe to Divine Providence."

"If we can agree in religious matters then we are halfway to a lasting peace." Bonny Kate declared.

"Miss Sherrill, it's been my experience that the more affinity there is between theological parties, the greater commonly is their mutual animosity."

"That is why we cleave so to the Presbyterian persuasion," Sam declared. "There we can keep all the fighting in the family, decently, and in order."

They all laughed, and then John continued. "Jacob Brown has made the Indians understand that it was Bonny Kate who shot and busted their powder horns at such an extraordinary range. The Indians concluded that the Spirit Warrior had done it and so now Bonny Kate is associated with the Spirit Warrior who favored the settlers over the Indians during the siege of Watauga Fort."

"Oh, that was nothing. I can make shots like that all the time."

"I hope so," John said. "You may be called upon to prove it this week."

"Will there be a prize?" she asked.

"Try this," John said. "Peace with the Cherokees, an alliance against the British, freedom for the new United States, full membership as a North Carolina county for Washington territory, validation of our land claims, and full rights of land ownership for thousands of settlers, and enough land to make three new states, where Cherokees will enjoy the blessings of citizenship living alongside us in peaceful commonwealth. Is that enough of a prize?"

"More than enough for a simple uninformed girl like me," she admitted.

"Well, you are the one who has to win it," John charged her.

Bonny Kate breathed deeply. "Oh, dear Lord, why has this portion fallen to me? I am your least worthy servant and this task is too great for even the armies of men. Protect me, O Lord. Do not put me to the test, for in failing this I would become the scorn of nations. Amen."

The trio rode on in silence until John stopped his horse. Sam and Bonny Kate stopped likewise.

"Your prayer is an honest response to the responsibilities the Watauga Association has placed on you, Miss Sherrill. Robertson and Brown told me not to explain any of this to you. They reasoned that the high stakes of this mission would cause you to fold under the weight of the gravity of this situation. In opposition to their view, I believe that you should know the entire truth and decide for yourself whether to attempt this challenge or not."

"Is there anything else I need to know?"

"Yes," John answered. "The skin of that mountain lion you killed was taken by James Robertson and presented to Chief Attacullaculla. The gift pleased him greatly, but he assumed the gift had come from the Spirit Warrior as a mark of your favor towards him. That small misunderstanding resulted in the demand that you come to meet with Attacullaculla to receive his thanks and give him your blessing."

"Whoa," she said with rising reluctance. "They think I'm a Spirit Warrior?"

"No," John answered. "That's not exactly the way they see it. They believe the Spirit Warrior has taken up with you and goes about with you as kind of a companion. They think that you can listen to the Spirit Warrior and be guided by it to great feats, like killing the lion, and hitting targets beyond the range of ordinary marksmen."

"Kind of like the Holy Spirit?" she observed.

"Yes," John answered. "Not unlike the powers of their own Beloved Woman, Nancy Ward. They will be watching you and looking for signs that your medicine is stronger than that of Nancy Ward's. That will influence their decision whether to ally themselves to the British or to choose us as their allies."

"John, this isn't fair," Sam Sherrill protested. "We can't pass her off as some kind of prophetess to a bunch of savages. The whole thing is paganism."

"You are right, Sam," John agreed. "It is unfair to your daughter. But the stage was set for this huge gamble by the Indians themselves. They are predisposed to believe your daughter's skills come from a divine source, and who are we to question their beliefs? I've seen enough to know Bonny Kate's skills are real enough no matter what the source."

"Bonny Kate, we should go home now," Sam declared. "You don't need to be doing this."

"But I want to, Father," she said. "It is a way for me to be useful."

"Daughter, I don't want all this Indian hocus-pocus to give you the big head," Sam cautioned her. "Remember your Christian upbringing and how we live in the truth."

"Maybe the truth can enlighten the savage world and bring peace to the land where we live," she ventured. "I'll place myself under the protection of Colonel Sevier. I trust his judgment. He has been completely honest with us about this mission and is worthy of our trust. Are you coming with us, Father?"

"I suppose so," Sam answered. "But if anything goes wrong, we cut our losses and head for home!"

"I'll be right there with you, Sam," John assured him.

The ride continued, and so did the useful information. John did most of the talking. "Do you remember those Tories who accosted you at Robertson's store?"

"Yes, sir."

"My brother Robert and his men of the light horse caught them trying to break into Robertson's to recover their weapons. He found documents from the British governor in Canada promising big shipments of weapons and trade goods to the Cherokees in exchange for their loyalty to the king. The British were trying to prolong the war here to make it easier for the king's forces to defeat the seaboard states."

"My goodness," Bonny Kate exclaimed.

"If you hadn't insisted on pressing charges against those bullies, I wouldn't have confiscated their weapons. Then they wouldn't have attempted to break into Robertson's store and Robert wouldn't have arrested them and discovered the nature of their mission."

"My goodness," Bonny Kate repeated. "What a complicated chain of events!"

"Yes, Miss Sherrill, you have already served your country in the most amazing ways; and I bet you never realized it."

"No, sir, I never knew any of this."

"If it hadn't been for you, the peace talks going on now would never have taken place. The Cherokees would have received the Canadian governor's gifts and remained hostile."

"That's how Divine Providence works," Sam declared. The trio continued their journey in high spirits.

As John, Sam, and Bonny Kate approached Fort Patrick Henry a troop of Rangers rode out to meet them. They were North Carolinians from Wilkes County. They were led by young Lieutenant William Lenoir. John handled the introductions.

"Lieutenant Lenoir, I'd like you to meet Miss Bonny Kate Sherrill and her father Sam."

The polite lieutenant greeted Sam first with a nod and then turned his attention to Bonny Kate.

"My great pleasure, Miss Sherrill," Lenoir said as he rode his horse up close beside hers. He extended his hand, and she took it. It surprised her when he raised her hand to his mouth and kissed it. John noticed her reaction.

"He's French Huguenot a couple of generations back, just like me," John explained. "A hot-blooded race we are, eh, Bill?"

"*Qui, mon ami*," the lieutenant agreed. "So, Colonel, is this the lady we are assigned to guard for the next couple of days?"

"I guess so," John replied.

"I never would have imagined that the lady with the magic charms would also possess such charming beauty."

"Why, thank you, Lieutenant Lenoir." She smiled.

"Who assigned you this duty, Bill?" John asked.

"Robertson," Lenoir replied. "He said we have to make it look like she's so valuable that soldiers guard her day and night. I think I'm going to enjoy this assignment."

Bonny Kate was given her own cabin at Fort Patrick Henry. John shared quarters with Sam Sherrill in a building the soldiers called the barracks. That evening they went over to have dinner with Bonny Kate. James Robertson came by while they were eating and sat at the table with them.

"James, what's the plan?" John wanted to know. "Now that we have Miss Sherrill here what happens next?"

"Tomorrow morning, we meet the council of chiefs. We take Miss Sherrill with us and regard her the way they regard Nancy Ward. I'm hoping Miss Sherrill can get right friendly with Nancy and get the talks back on track."

"Will I have the same right to express my opinions to the leading white men as Nancy Ward has the right to speak to her chiefs?" Bonny Kate asked. John looked at Sam in surprise, and Sam smiled and shrugged.

James Robertson laughed. "So you know something about Nancy Ward and her position on the council?"

"Colonel Carter told me her entire story," she answered. "Will I have the same right?"

Robertson looked at John. "What does she know about our strategy?"

"Everything," John replied. "And she knows how important this is to the country."

"Look, Miss Sherrill, we brought you here to put on a show, not to participate in the talks," James Robertson explained.

"What show do you want, Blackbeard the Pirate or Beloved Woman of the Spirit Warrior?" she asked. John laughed, but James did not.

"I was hoping you would assist us in this deception without causing us any trouble," Robertson spoke seriously.

"Why must we use deception?" she argued. "If it be God's will that this land become the inheritance of our children living in freedom alongside their Cherokee neighbors in peace and prosperity as citizens in three new states, why not propose that now in good faith?"

James stood up and faced John. "I wonder where she gets her ideas about the future." John grinned back at him.

James continued, "Miss Sherrill, I have taken a great personal risk by bringing you here, and my powerful skeptical eastern friends have all but dismissed my idea as foolishness. But I know the power of these Indian beliefs, and we can use them to motivate the chiefs to peace."

"Why not place your faith in the power of our own beliefs?" she persisted.

"She's right, James," John asserted. "We will never pull this thing off unless we ourselves believe in what we are doing. We have to place our faith in Divine Providence in greater measure than the Indians trust in their beliefs."

"I always trust in Providence," Bonny Kate affirmed.

Silence fell over the room as Robertson, deep in thought, paced up and down the floor beside the cheerful fire. At long last, he spoke. "I am going ahead with it."

"Do I have the right to speak?" she asked.

"You shall," he promised.

"And you will convince Colonel Christian, Evan Shelby, and all the other Virginia commissioners to treat our Beloved Woman with deference and reverent respect?" John insisted.

"I can't do that," James stated flatly. "Our friends from the east are not play actors, and they were lukewarm to the idea of having Bonny Kate here in the first place. If they are going to show her any respect at all, she'll have to earn it."

"There's no time for that," John declared.

James Robertson stood and walked toward the door. "I'll invite them all to breakfast here, and Bonny Kate can entertain them and gain their confidence."

"That's not fair to my girl," Sam protested.

"I realize that, Mr. Sherrill," Robertson admitted. "But under the circumstances, it's the best we can hope for." He put on his hat and walked out.

"So how many am I supposed to cook for?" she asked, somewhat dazed by the speed of Robertson's decision making.

"I'll take care of the breakfast cooking," John volunteered. "You just say your prayers and get a good night's sleep. In the morning, be dressed and ready to entertain by sunup, and we will all trust in Providence." John stood up and cleared the table of the dinner mess dropping the utensils and plates in the washpot to soak. Nobody said a word until John finished up and walked to the door. "Good night, Miss Sherrill. See you back at the barracks, Sam." Then he was gone.

The next morning, Bonny Kate was awakened from a deep sleep by Lieutenant Lenoir's men knocking on her door. It took her several seconds to realize that she was not in the comfort of her cozy loft at Stony Creek Farm with Mary Jane and her brothers.

"Just a moment," she called out to the soldiers as she rushed to pull on and fasten her buckskin skirt. She straightened her shift and laced up the neckline for a modest appearance and opened the door. The first group of soldiers brought firewood and buckets of water. They went right to work on the business of preparing breakfast.

"Do I need to help in any way?"

"No, ma'am," replied a young corporal. "Colonel Sevier gave us complete instructions on what to cook and when, and all you have to do is entertain your guests. You have some pretty important friends. I heard that all the commissioners and their assistants will be coming over here."

Bonny Kate washed her face, brushed her hair, and finished dressing as the young soldiers worked at the hearth and at the table. They glanced her way frequently, especially when she lifted her hem to put on her moccasins and leggings.

"Seems a shame to cover up those legs like that, ma'am," the corporal said brazenly.

Bonny Kate smiled. "Not if it helps you stay focused on your work, young sir," she admonished him gently. A buckskin hunting shirt completed her mannish outfit. The shirt was Sarah's contribution, finely made to better fit a woman. It was much finer than anything she owned and gave her confidence in her appearance.

Colonel Sevier appeared in the doorway in full uniform and armed with his favorite rifle. "Good morning, my Bonny Kate," he greeted her warmly. "Are you ready for another exciting day?"

"I suppose so," she said as she recognized the rifle. "Do you have Sweet Lips?"

The soldiers all turned to stare at the couple.

John grinned. "Sarah always says I do."

Bonny Kate smiled at the effect her teasing had on the young soldiers. "You know I mean the rifle," she said.

"Yes," he responded. "I thought you might like to use it in your shooting demonstration today, since it's the same gun that killed the mountain lion."

"That's very considerate of you, Colonel Sevier."

Sam Sherrill arrived and greeted his daughter with a kiss. Then the commissioners began to arrive. Colonel Sevier was a big help to Bonny Kate introducing each guest and telling her something about each man's position, home county, and relationships on the western frontier. He enabled her to make conversation with each one and take a personal interest in their families and their experiences. The breakfast hour flew by in a blur as the men feasted on the full breakfast while feasting their eyes on the lovely, lively hostess. She did much to build community among those important men and many of them remarked on what a wonderful time they had at the breakfast. Robertson arrived dressed in buckskins, more like an Indian trader than a state-appointed commissioner, but it worked for him and his relationships with the chiefs. He kept an eye on the time and moved everyone out as the meeting time with the chiefs came all too soon. Bonny Kate had the strongest desire to stay and clean up the cabin as the commissioners filed out, but Colonel Sevier caught her and moved her out the door as well.

"Colonel Sevier, I haven't eaten anything yet," she protested. Half a dozen soldiers filed in around her as escorts, and they crossed the commons of Fort Patrick Henry giving her the feeling of a convicted criminal, being marched out to execution.

"I saved you a biscuit and a sausage," Colonel Sevier offered. He handed her the food wrapped in a napkin. "Eat it quickly before we arrive at the council meeting. It's very rude to be eating anything in front of the chiefs while we are discussing terms."

She ate the sausage and the biscuit as they marched down the hill to the river where they would ferry over to the Long Island, sacred meeting place of the Cherokees. The biscuit made her mouth very dry. It would be impossible to speak at the council with dry biscuit mouth and she expressed that to Colonel Sevier.

"Canteen for the lady!" ordered Colonel Sevier and at once one was offered to her by a soldier marching next to her.

She looked at the face of the soldier and saw a familiar smile. "Why, good morning, Lieutenant Lenoir!" She took his canteen and drank deeply.

"Good morning, Miss Sherrill. Fine day isn't it?"

"Oh yes, I feel that spring is just around the corner. I can't wait to see the fields blanketed in spring flowers."

The Chiefs of the Cherokee nation were seated on blankets beneath the council oaks. The commissioners of Virginia were directed to blankets across an open area where in times past council fires had burned, but in the light of day, there were no fires burning. The commissioners took their seats. Their advisors and assistants sat behind them.

Bonny Kate's escort company stopped well beyond the boundaries of the council area, and Colonel Sevier reached out and took her arm.

"Hold up right here, Miss Sherrill," he said quietly. They stopped. All eyes were watching her. Colonel Sevier dismissed the escort, and they marched away. "No woman may enter the council area without permission. When you are close to a Cherokee, do not make eye contact. That is insolence. You may, however, look into the eyes of the Beloved Woman. Here she comes now."

Nancy Ward stepped over to them carrying the symbol of her authority, the wing of a swan. "Hellooo, Jack," she purred seductively.

"Hello, Nancy," John replied.

"Is this your Beloved Woman?"

"Yes, she is," John replied. Bonny Kate was struck by that term applied to her from a man she might have easily fallen in love with if it hadn't been for Sarah. She fought off the distracting thoughts.

"How are you called, Beloved Woman?" Nancy asked, but Bonny Kate wasn't concentrating.

"Tell her your name," John prompted.

"Bonny Kate," she said clearly and confidently.

Nancy looked at John and then again at Bonny Kate. She placed her hand on Bonny Kate's face. It was warm and soft against her cheek.

"Where do you see the medicine in her?" Nancy asked.

"It's in her smile," John replied. Bonny Kate smiled.

"Yes, there it is," Nancy agreed. "The medicine is strong in her."

Nancy Ward made her way into the council circle and addressed the chiefs in Cherokee. Jacob Brown walked over to Bonny Kate and translated for her. "Here is the Beloved Woman of the Hunakas. She asks to speak in council as their representative. What is the pleasure of the chiefs?"

Bonny Kate smiled at Mr. Brown and took his hand in welcome.

One chief after another nodded his approval until it came to one old sad-looking chief. He gave a negative vote. "Oconostota, the stubborn old war chief," Mr. Brown explained. "He is the holdout on every issue. Win him and there's a bright future for everyone."

Nancy Ward returned and took Bonny Kate by the hand and welcomed her to the council. "The Beloved Woman will sit beside me."

"No," John objected. "The Spirit Warrior desires the Beloved Woman to sit in council among her own people."

"I'm sorry," Bonny Kate smiled at Nancy. "Maybe we can visit later."

Nancy Ward backed away respectfully as Mr. Brown and Colonel Sevier escorted Bonny Kate to a blanket on the front row across the way from Nancy Ward's place. She wasn't sure how a woman in a long buckskin skirt was supposed to sit among Indians, so she stood waiting until Nancy sat and did likewise. Sevier and Brown sat behind her to translate for her and coach her.

"That was a brilliant move, Bonny Kate!" John whispered in praise. "You just paid Nancy Ward the highest compliment. The chiefs are very impressed."

"What did I do?"

"You waited for her to sit."

"Why couldn't I sit over there with her?" Bonny Kate whispered.

"The Spirit Warrior goes where you go," John answered. "You have to stay on the proper side to maintain the balance of power."

Nothing was what Bonny Kate expected. The rules and customs were strange, and it was very easy to offend without realizing it. Nancy Ward had already tried to trick her into sitting on the wrong side, and she would have blundered into it if Colonel Sevier had not prevented her. The space between the two parties seemed like a mile. The talks were slow and boring, and much time was lost in translations.

She turned to Mr. Brown and noticed a strange Indian woman sitting beside him. The woman was strikingly beautiful, perhaps in her thirties, and staring at her intently. "What are they saying, Mr. Brown?"

"Nothing we haven't heard before," he responded. "They are relating the entire history of their people and the battles they have won against the various neighboring tribes. If you know how to sleep sitting up, this would be a good time to take a nap."

Bonny Kate scanned the line of a dozen chiefs until she found one who sat upon a fine lion skin, her lion skin. That chief must be Attacullaculla, the Little Carpenter as he was called by the whites. Behind each chief, stuck in the ground, was a long war lance. It shocked her to note that the war lances were festooned with human hair, trophies of long past battles, or were they? It was one thing to take a scalp as a trophy from an armed warrior, but some of those lances displayed the unmistakable long red or blond hair of white women. She was sickened by thoughts of the suffering and killing of innocent women and children that those trophies represented. She resolved to speak out against such savagery if ever she had the opportunity.

Just before lunch, Attacullaculla looked in Bonny Kate's direction and gave a command to his assistants.

"Straighten up there, Miss Sherrill, they are talking about you," Colonel Sevier warned from his seat behind her. She sat up taller and looked over at a grinning Nancy Ward.

"Mr. Brown, what are they saying?" Bonny Kate asked in a low tense voice.

"He has proposed a little shooting match," Jacob told her. "He's called for his best marksman, against you."

"Colonel Sevier, do you have Sweet Lips?" she asked.

"Sarah says I do," John joked. "But this is hardly the time for you to be thinking about such things." Jacob and John had a good chuckle before Nancy Ward rose and approached them.

"Get me the rifle!" she pleaded nervously, standing to meet the Beloved Woman.

"Lenoir's bringing it," John reassured her.

Nancy led her to the center of the council area. A stocky well-built warrior, a head shorter than she, emerged from the ranks of spectators. He wore the breechcloth and no shirt. His face was scarred from burns. She guessed that some sort of inferior firearm often traded to the Indians might have exploded in use at some time in his past. He was very serious about his task, and she remembered Colonel Sevier's warning about not making eye contact.

When Lieutenant Lenoir delivered Sweet Lips with the powder and shot, she felt her confidence return. "Good luck, Miss Sherrill," Lenoir wished her, and he quickly retreated. Two braves walked out of the council circle holding goose feathers. At one hundred paces, the braves stopped and held up the feathers.

"The Beloved Woman of the Hunakas will shoot the feather in half," explained Nancy. "Watch as he performs this for you." The Indian sharpshooter took aim and trimmed his feather neatly in two. The Indians cheered at his accomplishment, as Bonny Kate loaded Sweet Lips and primed the pan. She judged it an easy shot.

"Come, Holy Spirit, help me accomplish the will of the Father," Bonny Kate prayed out loud.

"You speak to the Spirit Warrior," Nancy Ward observed. "And does he speak to you?"

"Sometimes," she replied.

"Does he stay with you all the time, or does he come and go?"

"All the time," she answered.

"Will he punish you severely when you miss this shot, or will you say he betrayed you?" Nancy continued. Bonny Kate ignored her as she aimed at her mark. The brave holding the feather was twisting it slightly, making it dance side to side. The common idea of the noble savage, honest, childlike, always playing fair was hogwash, Bonny Kate realized. Nancy Ward continued to taunt her. "Take your shot, Beloved Woman, so you can miss and go home in disgrace. Your father can take you back and beat you for disgracing his house. You do not belong among these people. If you have any medicine in you, it is no stronger than mine."

"Bang!" spoke Sweet Lips, and half the feather floated to the ground beyond the holder. Bonny Kate grinned at Nancy as the commissioners and the white audience cheered. "Can your medicine do better than that?" she gloated.

"We shall see," Nancy replied. The feather holders walked fifty paces farther. "The Beloved Woman will shoot the feather in half again," instructed Nancy.

The Cherokee marksman fired and missed. Bonny Kate looked at his firearm and recognized that it was a smoothbore musket of British manufacture, unreliable at ranges over one hundred yards. She looked downrange at her twitching target and decided this kind of cheating could not be tolerated. As she turned to Nancy in protest, she noticed her adversary was reloading for another shot. She waited quietly while he took it and cut the feather in two.

As the crowd cheered, Bonny Kate spoke up, "Do I get two shots?"

"No, one shot," Nancy replied. "If you miss you lose."

"Why did he get two?" Bonny Kate was outraged.

"One practice shot," Nancy declared. "It didn't count."

"Why don't I get a practice shot?"

"Why does the Beloved Woman of the Spirit Warrior need a practice shot?"

"I don't," Bonny Kate declared, as she primed the pan. "Beloved Woman of the Cherokee will tell my feather holder to hold that feather still. If I see any movement I'll shoot away his thumb!"

"You cannot send a message like that to the grandson of Oconostota," Nancy objected.

Bonny Kate smiled. "The words of the Spirit Warrior have come to me as a fair warning to the grandson of Oconostota. Now tell him!"

Nancy hesitated, measuring the white woman's resolve. She turned to one of the braves nearby and spoke the warning in Cherokee, and the brave ran the message out to the feather holder. Whatever she said worked. The feather stopped twitching and Bonny Kate fired, cutting her feather easily. The feather holders walked out another fifty paces.

The commissioners were really enjoying the show now, and many of them were putting up big wagers on whether the girl could hit a three-inch piece of feather at two hundred yards. Many admitted that they had never seen anyone do such a thing. The feather holders arrived at a spot, two hundred paces away as the shooters loaded. Bonny Kate overcharged the magnificent Dickert rifle as was her practice for long-range shots. She would also aim a little high to make sure the ball carried to the target.

The Cherokee marksman was sweating as he loaded his inadequate musket. Bonny Kate watched him, figuring they would probably allow him three shots to hit his mark. His first shot hit the dirt short of the holder who instinctively jumped to avoid the skipping grounder. The Indians laughed at his reaction as Bonny Kate realized how dangerous the game had become to the poor feather holders. Her adversary's second shot hit the ground a little closer to the holder, and he quit the field. He didn't care for any more sport of that nature. Bonny Kate's holder dropped his feather and quit the field as well. His courage had been shaken by what he had seen and wasn't about to help a wild-looking white woman win the contest.

"Wait," she protested. "I haven't had my turn yet!"

"It's over," Nancy declared. "There is no need to test you any more. The chiefs are satisfied."

"Well, I'm not satisfied," she shouted in rage. "Tell that boy to pick up that feather and hold it still!"

Nancy just looked at her. All the Indians just looked at her. They had rarely seen such passion in any white man before, certainly not in the council circle. Some of the Indian translators tried to convey her demand but no one moved to meet it. A silence fell over the Council.

"This isn't fair!" she insisted. "Are there no men among the Cherokee who have the guts to hold my feather?"

"Oh, hell, Bonny Kate," Jacob Brown cursed. He turned to John Sevier. "John, somebody's got to shut her up!"

"I'll hold your feather!" John declared boldly, walking out into the council circle. All eyes turned to him, the small player in a big game, taking a big gamble. He walked out to Bonny Kate and smiled. "Don't miss, Miss Sherrill."

"Oh, dear, was I too forceful?" she worried.

"You forced us into a tight spot," he surmised. "Luckily, your meaning of the word 'guts' does not translate into Cherokee."

"I've overcharged, and I'll aim high," she advised him.

"Sweet Lips will do the job," he assured her. "One thing I've learned this trip, we have to believe that what we are doing is the best thing for everybody concerned. And I believe in you, Miss Sherrill." He walked down range.

As he walked the two hundred yards, Bonny Kate had some time to think. She admired his courage and regretted her foolhardiness, her sharp sense of fairness, and her hot temper. Nancy Ward had removed herself to watch from her side of the council ground. A hush fell over the Long Island in the midday sun as all men stood watching. John found the small piece of goose feather and held it out from his body in his left hand facing the assembly. He was amazed at the breathless silence and steeled his nerves to be absolutely still. He could barely make out the Beloved Woman of the Hunakas in the middle of the crowd, but saw the movement as she shouldered the rifle. He saw the gun belch smoke; and almost immediately, he felt the feather shudder in his fingers as the ball whistled by, hearing the rifle report a second later. He looked out to his hand and the upper half of the feather was gone. The cheering was wild on both sides of the council ground. How she did it, John could not fathom, but the nature and progress of the peace talks changed completely from that moment forward.

Chapter 19

The Words of the Beloved Woman

In the afternoon, the Indians planned a footrace and many of the young people would participate. Mr. Brown talked Sam Sherrill into letting Bonny Kate run. Next Mr. Brown had to persuade Bonny Kate to run. Bonny Kate thought she ought to clear it with Colonel Sevier to see what he thought.

"I'm running today," John answered. "If you can keep up with me, I'll keep you safe, but I'm not going to stop and help you if they knock you down. Indian races are very rough and tumble. There's a lot of shoving and tripping involved back in the pack, but luckily they no longer run with war clubs."

"I'll keep up." She smiled.

Mr. Brown and Sam Sherrill did their best to coach her in the finer points of running the Indian race.

"Get to the front fast and stay out there, but don't wear yourself out in the first half of the race," Brown cautioned.

"The island is a full four miles from one end to the other," Sam told his daughter. "That's like running from Stony Creek to Robertson's store and back, so I know you can do it."

"Watch out for the spectators, lining the route," Mr. Brown warned. "Sometimes women and children will throw stones at you or try to trip you by tossing branches out in front of you. Don't look back, and don't stop to settle the score. Just forgive and run faster."

"I don't know anything about the Indian runners, I'm sure they have some good ones, but Carter and Robertson are betting on Sevier," Mr. Brown declared.

"Colonel Sevier?" she asked surprised.

"Honey, he was the fastest man on the frontier not too many years ago," Mr. Brown affirmed. "He doesn't know it yet, but sitting at General Assembly, and Sarah's good cooking when he's home, have put a few pounds on his frame. He'll find out today what he's good for. Then I'd watch out for Louis Wentzel, the favorite of the Virginians. He's a tall lanky Kentucky long hunter, who not only outruns Indian warriors but can reload his rifle in stride at a dead run, keeping up a deadly fire at his pursuers. The Shawnees call him Deathwind."

Bonny Kate appreciated the skills attributed to Deathwind and thought about how useful that would be. She wondered how he poured the powder and primed the pan on a dead run, in a stiff headwind. She would like to see how he did that.

"He won't be carrying his rifle today will he?" she asked.

Mr. Brown had a good laugh. "No, Bonny Kate, not today; you have nothing to worry about."

Bonny Kate was not worried. Her goal was to keep up with Colonel Sevier and watch him run. She had never thought of him as a runner; but his good looks, attractive proportions, and easy grace could naturally have come from the benefits of running. She had most always seen him in uniform, with his shiny leather-riding boots, hardly a runner's livery. He would need moccasins laced up tight for an Indian race, and that's what he wore when she saw him next.

The racers milled about waiting for the starting gun in the council circle. Bonny Kate had put off her buckskins for lighter weight linen. She wore a simple petticoat and shift as she always wore for comfort and freedom of movement in her farm work. Her hair was tied back so as not to interfere with her side vision, remembering Mr. Brown's warning about the spectators getting involved. She became the center of attention again as she stretched her muscles and warmed up for the race by taking short runs around the council ground. She became aware that she was the only woman running among some very serious men. At gatherings of white settlers, she could almost always get her sisters or young girl friends to run with her as a lark. Of course they couldn't keep pace with Bonny Kate and usually put on the show of twisted ankles and fainting from exhaustion or heat or some such game as attracted the attentions of gallant men. Those girls played a different game and usually won better prizes, but Bonny Kate was too honest with men and with herself to play that way. Besides, Colonel Sevier had already told her he would not stop to help her if she went down.

At the starting gun, Bonny Kate accelerated to her usual race pace; and only Colonel Sevier, Deathwind, and a half-dozen Indian men could stay with her. She flew through the grass of Long Island with the wind in her hair and soft island soil cushioning her steps in what seemed an easy run. The woods and fields of the sacred island and campgrounds of the Cherokees presented no obstacles. The women and children threw no stones at her and no branches in her path and shouted no Indian curses as she had been warned about. Her breathing was easy and deep, from much practice in chasing after sheep in the woods and meadows of Stony Creek. At the lower end of Long Island, the course turned and came back up the north bank of the island. The same spectators who had watched the downstream race crossed the narrow island and watched the racers run upstream.

The lead never changed hands. Bonny Kate seemed stronger in the fifth and sixth miles and stretched out her lead over Colonel Sevier who kept company with Deathwind and the fastest Indians. The finish line came into view, with cheering crowds of settlers, commissioners, and Indians; and she felt the rush of victory, the exhaustion, and the sick stomach that always followed such an effort. Her father and Mr. Brown celebrated as she walked around to cool down and regain her breath. There was great interest in second place, and she was proud to see Colonel Sevier edge out the competition. To the delight of the home crowd, two of the Indians beat out Deathwind. Bonny Kate thought they might have been dead Indians if Deathwind had run his usual race equipped with his hunting gear. The thought reminded her that the footrace to the Indian was the deadly serious warrior's exercise and not the realm of a silly spinster on a manhunt. She put her victory into proper perspective and offered thanks to the Lord.

It rained later that afternoon, and Bonny Kate enjoyed the comfort of the dry little cabin in Fort Patrick Henry. Mr. Brown and Sam Sherrill were her guests as she ate to regain her strength and lay on her bed to rest. Mr. Brown had a large quantity of Virginia money to count, and he was recalculating Sam Sherrill's remaining balance of the amount he still owed on the new farm. Her father seemed happy, and she drifted into dreamless sleep to the sound of rain pitter-pattering on the cedar shingles.

The next morning began again with soldiers knocking on her door. The commissioners had so enjoyed breakfast with Bonny Kate that they resolved to a man to repeat the pleasure. She rushed to make herself presentable and received her guests as before.

The breakfast conversation was full of high praise for the enterprising young woman they all knew as Bonny Kate. She accepted the accolades with modesty and humbleness, deferring all credit to her mentor and sponsor Colonel Sevier. The colonel's second place finish had enhanced his reputation among the commissioners.

"Father, where is Colonel Sevier this morning?" Bonny Kate asked.

Sam laughed. "He's hurting this morning, my dear. A grown man ought not to make such a fool of himself. He could hardly get out of bed without my help."

"He had better show up at council this morning," James Robertson declared. "The chiefs are giving him a special place of honor for his first place finish yesterday."

"You mean second place," she corrected.

"No, the Indians declared him the winner," James explained. "Everyone knows that the Beloved Woman was carried along by the Spirit Warrior, so Colonel Sevier actually won the race, according to the way Indians judge things."

"Well, I never have been so unfairly treated in all my life!" she exclaimed. "This is outrageous! I ran the best race of my life, and they declare him the winner? Oh, there is no justice for women, whatsoever, in the land of the Cherokee. I'm so sick of all this double-dealing, Indian Spirit thing . . . all this Indian . . . this Indian . . ."

"Hocum pocum?" Sam helped her find the right words.

"Yes," she agreed. "All this hocum pocum, I'm sick of it!"

Sam and James laughed loud and hard, along with all the commissioners who overheard the ranting of the spirited girl. For James Robertson, no outcome could have been more perfect. He was very pleased with the reactions he had heard about from the Indian Camp. Some of the chiefs were ready to break with the hardliners and make concessions to the whites who enjoyed such favor from the Great Spirit evidenced through the feats of their lovely, young, recently discovered, Beloved Woman.

Despite the progress James Robertson was making for the Watauga party, the Virginia commissioners were not satisfied. The process was too slow, and they grumbled.

Colonel Christian, the military leader of the Virginians, who came to the aid of the western settlers during last summer's war, expressed his disgust. "The Cherokees don't seem much like a conquered people to me. Robertson lets them run the show too much. The girl is right, there's too much of that hocum pocum and not enough agreement to our terms." Colonel Christian had taken some criticism from other commissioners for his restraint in conducting the campaign. He spared the Cherokee capital, Chota, and refused to allow the killing of women and children. They also criticized Captain Sevier the leader of the Light Horse Company of Wataugans who had supported and encouraged the gentler policy. Bonny Kate was proud of Colonel Sevier for his kindness toward women and children.

John Sevier couldn't attend the breakfast but joined the procession on the way down to council. Today it was Bonny Kate's turn to save him a biscuit and sausage. He received it gratefully.

"Congratulations, on the race yesterday," she told him. "First place is quite an honor for you."

"You mean second place," he corrected.

"No, the Indians declared you the winner, because everyone knows the Spirit Warrior carried me along. That's just the way Indians judge things, I'm told."

"Miss Sherrill, I'm so sorry," he empathized.

"Just wait until next time," she warned.

"Next time?" he questioned.

"Yes, the spring gathering next month. There isn't going to be any Spirit Warrior to help me cheat. I'll beat you fair and square; you can depend on that!"

John laughed. "Oh, Miss Sherrill, I'm already feeling as though I've had a good beating. I can hardly move, I'm so sore." She laughed too as they approached another hard day of negotiating the future of the country.

The night rains had left a gray overcast as low clouds moved swiftly with the cold northwest wind. At the council ground, Nancy Ward met Bonny Kate's party.

"We have a new chief among the whites today," Nancy explained. "Beside the Beloved Woman of the Hunakas is a place for her feather holder and winner of the footrace. Carter is called Chief John, so we will call you Little John."

"You will call me many things before I'm done," John said.

Nancy looked at him and then looked at Bonny Kate. "He has much ambition, does he not, Beloved Woman?"

"Yes, he does, but it is noble ambition."

Nancy walked into the council circle and announced the arrival of the new chief.

"What do we do now?" Bonny Kate asked.

"Wait until everyone sits, then we can," Colonel Sevier directed.

"I want to change the seating arrangements," Bonny Kate said.

"You can't do that," John cautioned.

"I need to be able to see everyone's face, so I'm moving my blanket up here to the end and make a horseshoe," she declared.

Jacob Brown reached out to physically restrain her, but he was too late. As the chiefs and commissioners took their seats, Bonny Kate walked to her blanket, picked it up, and moved it to the near end of the council ground and spread it before her and waited. Nancy Ward was quick to follow her example and moved her blanket over to the top of the horseshoe next to Bonny Kate. John moved his blanket next to Bonny Kate's and the horseshoe began to take shape. Instead of two opposing parallel lines, the council now was horseshoe shaped, with the two sides meeting at the spiritual focus where the Beloved Woman of the Cherokees sat beside the Beloved Woman of the Hunakas. The dynamics of the talks were altered, and the chiefs were prepared to speak about things that really irritated them.

"Hellooo, Chief Little John," cooed Nancy Ward leaning forward to see around Bonny Kate.

"Hello, Nancy," John replied. "Good of you to join us here."

"It's the spirit," Nancy replied. "Today we will hear the Beloved Woman speak to the chiefs, no?"

"No," John replied. "The Beloved Woman has already done her part to help move the talks forward. Tomorrow I will take the Beloved Woman home."

"Does the Beloved Woman live in the house of Chief Little John?"

"Certainly not!" Bonny Kate answered. "I live in my father's house."

"Your father is a great chief of the Hunakas?"

"Her father is a great medicine man of the horse warriors," John bragged a bit on his neighbor.

"Have you known the hot breath of love?" Nancy Ward asked.

"What?" Bonny Kate asked.

"I think she means are you married?" John interpreted.

"No, of course not," Bonny Kate declared. "I have never been married."

"Then your father has great medicine, and the spirit has saved you for his own purposes. Is that the secret of your power?"

"I wish that would remain my secret," she answered, glancing at an amused Chief Little John. As she turned her head, she noticed the mysterious Indian woman again seated beside Jacob Brown. Bonny Kate leaned over to John. "Who's that woman next to Mr. Brown?"

"Nan Henderson," he replied without looking.

"Is she a Beloved Woman too?"

"Only Mr. Brown would know, and I'm too much of a gentleman to ask about it."

"Should I make an effort to befriend her?"

"No," John warned. "Leave her be. You need to concentrate on the business."

Chief Oconostota rose to speak, and Jacob Brown interpreted for Bonny Kate from his seat behind her. "There are a great many thieves among the white people. They come to steal our sacred hunting lands. They come to steal the sacred places where our ancestors are buried. They come to steal our sacred meeting places. And now they have stolen our beloved sons who chose the warrior's path as their fathers did before them. Old men talk peace with these trespassers while our young men go into the mountains to keep the war fires burning. Our divided nation cannot stand. We must not give these thieves what they demand. I want my brothers to search the teachings of the Great Spirit to understand why the medicine of the white people has overpowered our medicine. There are a great many thieves among the white people." Chief Oconostota sat as his words sank in to his fellow chiefs. The commissioners of Virginia conversed among themselves to develop some kind of response.

"He has a good point," John appreciated. "We have to get the land office set up so the new people settle where they are supposed to and not cross the line into Indian Territory."

Bonny Kate's feelings and observations had moved her to speak. She rose as if in a trance and stepped into the center of the council ground as all parties to the conference watched. Jacob Brown was horrified. "Stop her, Jack, you have to stop her!"

"It's the spirit, Jacob," John said solemnly. "There's no stopping the spirit!"

Nancy Ward looked into John's eyes and recognized a sincere belief in Bonny Kate's medicine. As if to confirm the message came from a divine source, a shaft of morning sun broke through the overcast and illuminated the council ground as the Beloved Woman of the Hunakas opened her mouth to speak.

"Among the Cherokees there are a great many woman killers!" She pointed to the war lances standing behind the chiefs. The hair that adorned them did not dance merrily in the breeze as it had the previous day, but hung lifeless, drenched by the night rain. "These are not the trophies of great warriors but symbols of sadness for the motherless child and the lonely husband and the parents who lovingly raised these dear daughters." Bonny Kate stopped and allowed the translators to deliver her chilling message. The words had their effect, as rage built in the eyes of some of the chiefs. "The Great Spirit is greatly offended by woman killers. Woman is the sacred vessel of life, the teacher of the children, the keeper of the fire, and the bearer of the water. She tends the garden, grinds the corn, and prepares the meals. She is the light in the darkness, the delight of her husband, and a comfort to the old ones. The Great Spirit says you shall not kill the woman. It is wrong, and if you continue in this, his judgment will fall upon your nation." Bonny Kate returned to her place and sat down.

"Miss Sherrill, you said a mouthful," John marveled. "Where did all that come from?"

"It's been building up in me for a couple of days," she answered.

Chief Oconostota stood again and spoke a tirade against the Beloved Woman of the Hunakas. She sat quietly, nobly, and listened intently; but Jacob Brown did not translate completely word for word, sparing her the sting of many a sharp barb. Nancy Ward stood in protest and defended Bonny Kate during his most vicious attacks and took a full measure of his rage upon her own exalted person. Bonny Kate remained calm despite the apparent rage of the old warrior. When Oconostota stopped, at long last and sat down, Nancy Ward turned to Bonny Kate.

"The war chief has said before the entire council that you are a liar, a trickster, and a fraud. He says that there is no medicine in you at all. He claims the medicine you showed to the chiefs is all in the rifle you used," Nancy Ward explained.

"Colonel Sevier," Bonny Kate spoke calmly. "Do you have Sweet Lips?"

"You know that I do, Beloved Woman." He grinned.

"Get me the rifle," she said with steely determination.

"Jacob, go get my rifle from Lieutenant Lenoir," John directed.

"What's she going to do, shoot the bully?" Jacob wondered.

"No," John answered. "I think we are going to see another display of divinely inspired shooting."

When Bonny Kate received the rifle, she refused the powder and shot. "All I need is this here rifle." She marched across the council ground toward Oconostota, followed by Jacob Brown. The old warrior rose at her approach and stood a little taller than she. Bonny Kate looked into his eyes, and he could not look away despite the affront.

"Oconostota, war chief of the Cherokee, I came here to ask for peace. The Spirit Warrior has given me the words, and I spoke them faithfully. If you believe my medicine is in this rifle, then take it as my gift to you. May you enjoy the blessings of peace," she said smiling up at him.

He grabbed the rifle from her hands and tossed it behind him on his blanket. He walked over to Chief Attacullaculla and snatched away the treasured lion skin. He returned to Bonny Kate and shoved the gift into her hands.

Jacob Brown explained quickly. "When you give a gift, he has to give you something of equal or greater value in return."

Oconostota, gathered his things and left the council ground for that day. Bonny Kate stroked the soft fur of her lion skin. Then she walked over and presented it again to old Chief Attacullaculla with a smile.

"I have no gift to give you in return, Beloved Woman," the old chief said.

"I want only peace between our peoples," she requested.

"That is not mine to give," he replied indicating to her that the decision of the council could not be influenced by one man's opinion.

She returned to the center of the council ground and spoke one last time. The Cherokee interpreter for Attacullaculla followed her and translated her words to the chiefs. "It is the wish of my people that we can live together as neighbors in peace, prosperity, trust, and love." As soon as the translator finished her statement, the Cherokee side erupted in laughter, that kind of hilarious, unexpected, sidesplitting laughter. It continued in waves. Bonny Kate was bewildered. Nancy Ward and John Sevier were at her side in a moment escorting her from the council circle. Some of the more adept translators among the commissioners explained that the Cherokee translator had bungled the translation and rapidly the laughter spread to the white party as well. Bonny Kate's handlers soon had her among the armed escort of North Carolina rangers. Sam Sherrill was waiting with the horses as John and Bonny Kate joined him.

"Are we ready to travel?" John asked quickly.

"I've been ready all morning!" Sam replied.

Nancy Ward caught Bonny Kate and hugged her. Through tears of laughter, she shouted, "We are friends forever, you and I, Beloved Woman!"

"Yes, ma'am, I had a wonderful time, but why are they laughing?" Bonny Kate asked.

"Little John will tell you if he has the courage to talk of such things to the Beloved Woman," Nancy told her, looking at John's face.

"So long, Nancy." John laughed. "I'll be back tomorrow."

They spurred their horses homeward.

The laughing crowds could be heard for quite some time as the riders moved up the valley of the South Holston. Several times John laughed out and shook his head as he thought about the riotous scene. The soldiers were as clueless as Bonny Kate and her father.

Bonny Kate demanded to know the cause of the laughter that caused their rapid departure, but John refused to tell her in front of the soldiers.

"Wouldn't they enjoy a good laugh too?" she reasoned.

"Oh, they'll have it tonight around the campfires and in the barracks at Fort Patrick Henry," he assured her. "But I'm going to spare you the embarrassment."

"Was it something I said?" she wondered aloud, but John would give her no satisfaction.

When they reached the ridge that marked the divide between the Holston River valley and the Watauga Valley, the soldiers turned back after some sincere good-byes that endeared the young men to their lovely responsibility. She was quite taken with Lieutenant Lenoir and spoke of him at length until John became annoyed.

"Did Lieutenant Lenoir happen to mention Annie, the love of his life?" John inquired.

"Don't tell me he's married!" she reacted.

"Yes, Miss Sherrill, I'm afraid it's true."

Her face showed her disappointment and embarrassment at not realizing an important bit of information. "But he seemed so interested in me."

"Men of French blood are naturally interested in all sorts of women," John informed her. "I can understand how you might have become confused."

"Well, I'm still confused about why we left so suddenly," Sam interrupted to change a subject that was causing his daughter discomfort. "What caused the riot?"

"The Cherokee translator chose one of their words for love that more often applies to the physical act between man and wife," John explained and laughed again.

Bonny Kate felt even worse than before. "Oh, that's terrible! What a way to end such a beautiful speech! Oh, Father, those serious commissioners will never forgive me for breaking up the peace talks."

"I tried to tell you, John, taking Bonny Kate to the pow-wow would bring nothing but trouble," Sam told him.

"Say, what's the idea of giving away my rifle to that old picklepuss, anyway?" John demanded. "I'd have sooner seen the devil take it than that old hoot owl."

She laughed at his language but still felt the sting of reprimand. "I'm sorry Colonel Sevier. He was the holdout on every issue. If I could win him, I knew the talks could move forward. There was much more at stake than the value of one rifle."

"That rifle meant a great deal more to me than you will ever know," he scolded. John fell silent, and his attitude toward Bonny Kate cooled considerably the rest of the day. Bonny Kate knew that she had trespassed in his property and disappointed him by not asking permission to trade away his rifle for peace. The rifle meant a great deal to her as well. It had saved her life, drawn attention to her as a famed markswoman, and caused her to prosper when she bagged the lion with it.

Sweet Lips, the rifle, would not stay in the possession of Oconostota for long. He would find no medicine in it and trade it away to a white trader, and it would find greater fame still in the hands of another owner.

Three weeks after her return from the Long Island peace talks, Bonny Kate was visiting Sarah and working at her large spinning wheel, while Sarah sat weaving cloth at her loom.

"Thanks to you, I'll have enough thread to weave John two fine linen shirts," Sarah rejoiced.

"Will they have the lace ruffles?" Bonny Kate asked. "You know how he likes lace."

Sarah laughed. "Yes, with lace included! You, my dear friend, are an excellent spinster. Where did you learn to do such fine work?"

"Granny Sherrill taught me all I know about spinning," the tall girl answered.

"You always speak so fondly of your grandmother," Sarah exclaimed. "It would have been a pleasure to know her."

"Yes, ma'am, she was a real pioneer woman!" Bonny Kate agreed. "There was nothing she couldn't do. She raised eight sons who could all make their own way in the world. They were the first settlers at Sherrill's Ford on the Catawba. Her name was Elizabeth. I'd like to name a daughter after her if I ever get married."

"Speaking of marriage, what prospects did you discover up at Fort Patrick Henry?" Sarah asked. "Mr. Sevier told me the cream of the crop turned out for the peace talks."

"Oh, I met a very nice lieutenant in my honor guard. He was from the eastern waters at the head of the Catawba. I was very charmed with his manners and his bearing, but it turned out he was married. I didn't have much time to make acquaintances. Mr. Sevier and Mr. Brown managed all my time and all my activities."

"I'm sorry, it was such a short busy trip," Sarah empathized.

"Granny Sherrill always said I was destined to marry a man of quality, a great and powerful man, and I never knew her to say a false thing!" Bonny Kate declared.

The work continued at wheel and loom, but after a moment, Sarah spoke again.

"A great and powerful man . . . I'd say that's a mighty tall order. Most great and powerful men were made that way by a good wife! I know that's Mr. Sevier's secret." Sarah and Bonny Kate laughed together.

"Yes, ma'am, he's a great credit to you; but I believe he had a good start by being a Sevier."

"Yes, they are quite a family," Sarah agreed.

"Sarah, did you know Colonel Sevier's mother?"

"I sure did. Joanna was a great lady and loved her boys something powerful. It broke their hearts when she died. We were all still living in Augusta County when that happened. You might say the restlessness began when Joanna passed away. First it was John's brother Val who moved down here, then John, Robert, and big Val came with Joseph, Abraham, and two of John's sisters. Mr. Cawood was selling farms along the Holston, and we bought Holly Bottom."

"Holly what?" Bonny Kate mocked.

"Oh, stop it, you silly." Sarah laughed.

Bonny Kate grinned. "I couldn't resist." She changed the spindle on her spinning wheel having filled the one she was spinning. "When did big Val remarry?"

"It was after we moved to Cawood's," Sarah answered. "Papa Val was lonely, and Jemima was a lovely widow in need of a family."

"She sure landed a good one!" Bonny Kate enthused.

"That was one of my most brilliant matches," Sarah boasted. "It's a shame, you just missed Robert Sevier. Kesiah Robertson worked so hard to win him, but persistence pays off, I suppose. What about William Tatham? Don't you just love his dreamy English accent?"

"He's a fine gentleman," Bonny Kate affirmed. "But I found out, he wants to return to his home in England. He left a sweetheart there."

"Well, what about Isaac Shelby?" Sarah suggested. "He's a most eligible bachelor, and I believe, destined for greatness."

"He's a very forceful young man who speaks his mind, without regard to how it might offend a lady," Bonny Kate assessed. "But he is always away in Kentucky surveying or filing land claims or something. He's never shown me any interest in marriage."

"He's a traveler, but no man ever became great by staying home," Sarah said wistfully.

"Sarah, I have one more requirement that I hold most dearly," Bonny Kate intimated. "I'm going to marry only once, and it will be for true love. Life's too short to do it any other way."

"Oh my! This is a greater challenge than I imagined, my bonny girl." Sarah laughed, and Bonny Kate laughed too.

Bonny Kate had long wondered about the mysterious woman that sat next to Mr. Brown at the peace talks, and she chose now to change the subject.

"Sarah," she asked, "who is Nan Henderson?"

"Where did you hear about her?" Sarah demanded, her mood darkening.

"I saw her at the peace talks," Bonny Kate replied. "She is very beautiful."

"Was she anywhere near Mr. Brown?"

"She was always near Mr. Brown."

"Oh, that's not good!" Sarah moaned. "Don't you ever mention her to Ruth Brown, do you hear?"

"Thanks for warning me," Bonny Kate said. "What can you tell me about her?"

"Her mother was a Cherokee, her father was a Virginia trader, and she doesn't belong in either world," Sarah spoke sadly. "She took up with Mr. Brown when he first entered the country as a long hunter. She served as a useful interpreter for Mr. Brown in his dealings with the Indians, until Mr. Brown found her useful in other ways."

"Oh, I see," Bonny Kate felt a sad disappointment in Jacob Brown. She also felt sad for Ruth Brown as the injured wife. There was also sadness for the outcast Nan Henderson, whose only sin was finding a man she could love and serving him faithfully.

Sarah continued, "A few years back, Ruth swore she would kill the woman if she ever found her in the community, and Jacob swore the thing with Nan was over. Now you bring me the dreadful news that our good neighbors the Browns still have much unresolved trouble."

"I'm sorry, Sarah!" Bonny Kate regretted that her observations had become a burden to Sarah. She wondered what Sarah might do with the information—kindly protect a good friend from the hurtful truth or faithfully force a friend to face the hurtful truth. Sarah wisely chose protection, possessing at that time, only hearsay evidence.

"Bonny Kate, would you recognize Nan Henderson again if you saw her?"

"Oh, that face is unmistakably beautiful," Bonny Kate assured her.

"Even if she showed up around here dressed as a white woman?" Sarah asked.

"Yes, I think so."

"Then I want you to warn me if you ever see her at Carter's or Robertson's store or any other place around this community because I've never seen the woman," Sarah instructed. "The best thing we can do is keep her away from Ruth Brown. Can you do that for me?"

"Yes, ma'am."

Outside in the yard, where Betsy and the smaller children played, came the announcement. "It's Papa! Papa's coming up the lane."

Colonel Sevier rode into the yard and dismounted only to be surrounded by children. Sarah quickly put away her work.

"Oh my goodness, the man of the house is home much earlier than we expected!"

"I've got to get on home too," Bonny Kate declared.

Sarah's attention was focused on John as she moved through the door and into the yard. She rushed into his arms and hugged and kissed him passionately. Bonny Kate walked out to the porch and stood watching.

"Oh, I didn't notice we had company," John said. "Hello, Miss Sherrill."

"Good evening, Colonel Sevier, any good news from the peace talks?"

"The peace talks are adjourned for now. Oconostota and some of the other hardliners have accepted Colonel Christian's invitation to meet with Governor Henry in Williamsburg," John announced. "We think that is a very positive step until North Carolina appoints her commissioners and gets more actively involved. The peace talks will reconvene the first of June."

"John, are you home for a while?" Sarah asked hopefully.

"No, my dear," John said sadly. The General Assembly starts up again in a few days, and we have to get county status granted to Washington Territory; all of our land claims depend on this very important issue."

There was no hiding Sarah's disappointment, but she didn't cry. She was not going to spoil this homecoming. "We are going to prepare a feast for my glorious hero," she declared.

"I'd better get home now," Bonny Kate said, beginning down that well-worn path.

"Oh, Bonny Kate," Sarah stopped her. "Can I send down the children to visit with you for a few hours after we've had our dinner?"

Bonny Kate turned to see Sarah and John grinning at each other. "I would be honored and delighted to have them," she answered. She turned and ran barefoot down the lane toward the Sherrill house.

"It's always a pleasure to see you," John called after her.

"Thank you, good-bye, sir, good-bye, Mrs. Sevier."

"Good-bye, Bonny Kate," Sarah called. "And thank you for your help!"

Chapter 20

The Spring Gathering

April and May of 1777 passed as the farming folk along the Watauga and its tributaries completed their planting of corn, flax, wheat, barley, and the vegetable gardens they all loved so well. The Sherrills had worked especially hard, first ensuring the successful planting of Stony Creek farm then camping down at Daisy Fields, their new farm, along the Nolichucky River. There they cleared the land and planted several acres of corn and wheat to be left untended through the summer. Sam figured any yield would benefit the family when harvest time rolled around. The trees they felled were dressed and stacked for the cabin they would begin building later in the year on a defendable rise overlooking the big bend in the Nolichucky. In three weeks, they were back at Stony Creek tending the Sevier Farm.

State Senator John Carter and State Representative John Sevier were gone the entire spring since the reconvening of the North Carolina General Assembly. They worked hard to get the land claims recognized for all the citizens of the overmountain settlements. Peace with the Cherokees had eluded them earlier in the year, but a resumption of the peace talks in the summer promised better results when North Carolina commissioners would attend. On the Cherokee side, the friendly chiefs had been very impressed with their visit to Williamsburg. They were inclined to believe that a policy of Cherokee neutrality might better serve them than the alliance with Great Britain. They were most concerned about their young warriors that Oconostota had grieved over losing, who remained hostile in a breakaway tribe, at Chickamauga Creek, beyond the reach of the Wataugans. By mid-May, the leading ladies of the Watauga community could postpone the spring gathering no longer. They would have to proceed without the leading men who remained tied to their business at the General Assembly, hundreds of miles to the east.

Sarah Sevier poured her energy into making the gathering a success as they planned it for the last week in May. The most exciting aspect of the coming event to the young unmarried women was the fact that Watauga Fort had been officially renamed Fort Caswell and designated a military post by the North Carolina State Assembly. A company of rangers was stationed there including the dashing Lieutenant Lenoir.

One morning, two weeks before the gathering, Sarah proposed a ride down to Sycamore Shoals to consult with Charlotte Robertson about the details of the event. She invited the Sherrill women to accompany her. Sam Sherrill and Leroy Taylor would escort them and do some trading while there. Sarah's children were left in the capable care of Adam, John, and George Sherrill at Stony Creek. The sunshine made the day a hot one. Ruth and Jacob Brown were there, and so was Susan Carter. Mary Jane and Bonny Kate kept a sharp lookout up toward Fort Caswell hoping to see some young soldiers, but Charlotte told them that most of the young men were out on patrol.

Sam Sherrill, Leroy Taylor, and Jacob Brown lounged about in the shade of a Sycamore discussing land deals and other subjects related to the gathering.

"I think it will hurt our Virginia business because of Bonny Kate's demonstration at the peace talks," Jacob Brown predicted. "Most of the rich fellows were there and saw what she could do. It will be hard to find any takers who will bet against her shooting."

"What about the footracing?" Leroy asked.

"We won't do any good at footracing either," Jacob complained. "She finished so far ahead of Jack Sevier she made him look like he was running lame. With Jack at General Assembly, we have no close contender for the rich men to bet on. Naw, we have to find something else that girl can do."

"What about the horse race?" Sam suggested. "She sure can cut a fast track on her black stallion. I think you'll have some takers there, because a man's pride is wrapped up in his horse's ability, without considering the skill of a good rider."

"Can she ride well enough?" Jacob asked.

"She was born to ride," Sam affirmed. "And she's easy on the horse too. She's light as a feather."

"She would be the only girl rider," Leroy pointed out. "I think these North Carolina horse soldiers would bet their entire month's pay against her, as a matter of pride."

"That settles it, we will enter her in all three events and take what winnings we can get," Jacob decided. "Can you have her ready in two weeks?"

"If she rides Blackie, she's ready now!" Sam promised.

"Gentlemen, let's keep this thing secret," Jacob advised. "We'll bring her out the morning of the race as a surprise entry and run up the betting in the heat of the moment and strike while the iron is hot!"

Inside the trading post the ladies were busy planning too. "Are you girls ready for the contest?" Charlotte asked.

"What contest?" Bonny Kate responded.

"Why, the dancing contest, of course," Charlotte replied. "What other contests are there?"

"We are fairly good dancers," Mary Jane answered modestly.

"Their party dresses will make them winners for sure!" Sarah declared. "Half the contest is looking good doing it."

"Take it from one who knows, girls," Ruth told them. "Sarah always wins when she and Colonel Sevier enter!"

"But poor little Sarah has no partner this time," Charlotte observed. "So it's a wide open field of opportunity!"

Sarah smiled. "That's why I have invested so much in my Sherrill girls. I'm counting on these two young ladies to still bring home the honors to Stony Creek!"

Mary Jane and Bonny Kate were radiant with enthusiasm. The ladies worked hard that morning to plan events for the children, develop menus for the cooking, make assignments for handiwork demonstrations, find musicians, and of course plan the dancing program.

Just before noon, Waightstill Avery—a North Carolina attorney and commissioner to the approaching peace talks—arrived at Robertson's store to buy some supplies for his associates who were staying at Fort Caswell with the soldiers. He walked into as fine a gathering of females as he had seen in his visit to the west, and Charlotte performed the introductions. His study of the assembled ladies focused on the two unmarried ones, sisters as he discovered. His introduction to Bonny Kate was cordial and respectful but not as warm as the smiles and pleasantries he exchanged with Mary Jane. Bonny Kate noticed it even if no one else did. After trading, Mr. Avery tipped his hat politely, smiled especially wide for Mary Jane, and left.

The coming weeks would certainly provide an interesting measurement of how the social structures of the Watauga community were managed by the ladies in power. Sarah Sevier and Susan Carter were missing their husbands at the General Assembly. Charlotte Robertson and Ruth Brown had their powerful husbands and that gave them the ability to play their normal parts without having to adjust to the absence of a loved one. The females of lesser families and those unmarried had to forge alliances and friendships where they could be found. Bonny Kate's allegiance and unwavering loyalty was to Sarah Sevier her mentor and sponsor.

That afternoon the horse soldiers returned to the fort and descended on the trading post on news that there were some fine-looking ladies gathered there. Their captain introduced himself as William Alexander, and this time it was Bonny Kate that enjoyed the attentions of a fine-looking young officer with excellent prospects. That left seventeen-year-old Mary Jane with the attentions of no fewer than ten private soldiers who admired her beauty and charming speech.

Sam Sherrill and Leroy Taylor finally came in to suggest to Sarah and Mary that they begin their trip home so as to arrive before dark. The Sevier-Sherrill party soon said their good-byes and made their way home escorting Susan Carter to her home on the way. The day had been a good preparation to the coming gathering.

The next two weeks were filled with frantic activities in preparation for the spring gathering. Mary Sherrill and her three daughters spent many long hours finishing handiwork to trade at the gathering, and as the gathering day approached, they baked cherry pies and many loaves of wheat bread and barley bread. Sam Sherrill's herd of sheep and cattle had increased with the spring births and he was looking to trade down the numbers to keep from overrunning Stony Creek Farm. He was anxious to move to the Nolichucky, even irritable, with his impatience to be running his own show. He frequently called Bonny Kate away from her work among the women, and had her running messages by horseback, down to Mr. Brown at Sycamore Shoals.

"Can't you go any faster?" Mr. Brown complained to her. "I've got some men here that want to buy your father's horses. I don't want to see your father lose out on this deal! Here, give him this." He gave her a piece of paper with a number written on it."

She rode back to Stony Creek at a fast pace and delivered the message to Sam Sherrill. "Tell Mr. Brown that's not good enough. Go fast, girl!" He slapped Blackie's flank, and the horse took off. She rode him hard back to Sycamore Shoals.

Mr. Brown seemed pleased to see her arrive and looked at his timepiece. Mr. Brown was the only man she knew who owned a timepiece. They were rare items on the frontier.

"Papa says that's not good enough," she reported faithfully.

"Oh, I beg to differ with him, my dear." Mr. Brown smiled. "Step down and rest your horse while I mull this over." He walked into Robertson's store while she watered Blackie at the banks of the Watauga. About fifteen minutes later, Mr. Brown returned with another piece of paper. "Give your father this, and get me an answer as quick as you possibly can. These horse traders are very impatient!"

Bonny Kate urged Blackie to full speed, and let him run as free as he liked. Blackie loved to run, and she loved the thrill of riding a horse at racing speed. At Stony Creek, Sam Sherrill was waiting for her and looked at the number on the paper.

"Tell Mr. Brown that's better but still not good enough."

"Don't you want to send a counter offer?" she suggested, hoping to make the negotiations go more smoothly.

"Tell him what I said and ride faster!" Sam snapped. He again slapped Blackie's rump, and the horse sprang into action.

This is a crazy way to negotiate a horse deal, she thought as she rode back to Sycamore Shoals. Mr. Brown again looked at his timepiece and seemed very pleased as she rode up.

"Papa says the offer is better, but still not good enough," she told him.

Mr. Brown smiled. "Take another rest, my dear."

Bonny Kate accompanied Mr. Brown into the trading post. She wanted to see these mysterious horse traders and determine what sort of men they were. As they entered the store Charlotte smiled and greeted her, but there were no men in the store.

"Where are the horse traders, Mr. Brown?" she asked.

"I told you they are very impatient men," he replied. "They'll be back tomorrow, at midday. Could you come again and run messages?"

"Midday?"

"Yes, midday, Miss Sherrill, and ride the same horse that you rode today. Brush him down good, and give him extra feed this evening."

"Mr. Brown, I think I know how best to care for my horses."

"Of course you do, my dear, but take very good care of this one!"

"Why doesn't Papa come down here tomorrow and meet with the horse traders directly?"

"I'm brokering this deal," Mr. Brown reacted. "What are you suggesting, Miss Sherrill? Are you trying to cut me out of my own deal?"

"No, sir," she reassured him. "I just thought it might help the process along."

"Your father and I know what we are doing," he explained. "You just need to trust us. Are you ready for the shooting match and footrace?"

"I think so, and Sarah has high hopes on me to show well at the dance contest."

"I certainly wish you well, Miss Sherrill, but don't lose focus on the important things, my dear!"

Captain Alexander entered the store at that moment and her focus shifted to him. "Good afternoon, Captain Alexander," she spoke. "It's a pretty day, isn't it?"

"It just got prettier!" he responded as he walked over to her.

Bonny Kate became suddenly aware she might not look her best with hair wild and tangled by the wind and her face blushed from wind and sun, but still, there was a fresh wholesome beauty that could attract the right sort of man. Her next concern as he drew near was how she might smell to a man. Horse lather and saddle leather mixed with her working woman odor might repel a gentleman but not a horse soldier like Captain Alexander. He was man enough to stand close and admire the beauty.

"You have more than one admirer over at the fort, Miss Sherrill," he informed her.

"Do I?" she asked almost nonchalantly, making an attempt to smooth out her hair.

"Yes, ma'am, so I want to be the first to ask you to the dance," he stated his case.

"I wouldn't want to disappoint my other admirers," she replied. "I thought I would just go and play the field. You see, Captain, I'm looking to place well in the dance contest so I want to look around and pick a partner who has the best chance of helping me win it. Do you dance, Captain Alexander?"

"The Alexanders come from the highlands of the old country, Miss Sherrill," the captain advanced his case. "We are the most elegant dancers in the world. I would be delighted to help you win the dance contest. Would you have any time to practice this week?"

"Oh," she responded, impressed with his confidence. "I'm awfully busy helping the program committee put together all the activities."

"Yes, she's awfully busy, Captain," Mr. Brown cut in. "In fact, she was just about to carry another message up to Stony Creek."

"I hope you are not expecting it to get it there as fast as the others, Mr. Brown," she cautioned. "Blackie has already run twenty miles today."

"No hurry, Miss Sherrill," Mr. Brown agreed. "Just walk him home and give him a nice reward."

"I should very much like to accompany you, Miss Sherrill," Captain Alexander volunteered. She accepted and made ready to leave. The way home was slow and easy and Bonny Kate basked in the afternoon sun and enjoyed the exercise of her womanly charms as a result of pleasant flirting with an ardent, attentive man like Captain Alexander. He possessed a dash and charm that attracted her curiosity. Bonny Kate lost track of the time as they dawdled up the Watauga Valley, and about the time they reached the Sherrill cabin, she realized she would have to rush through her evening chores to finish before dark. The likeable Captain Alexander lingered longer than she thought he should have discussing state politics and the weather conditions with her father. She didn't want him getting too close to her family yet, because families are prone to jump to conclusions and see relationships that are not there. When the captain had gone, she applied herself to the long list of evening chores, beginning with the care and feeding of Blackie, the racehorse.

About the middle of the following day, Bonny Kate figured out that her horse was being prepared for a race and confronted her father about it.

"You are going to enter Blackie in the horse race at the gathering, aren't you?" she questioned.

"Yes," Sam admitted.

"And who is going to ride him in the race?" she demanded.

"I was thinking you might, if you thought we could win it." Sam challenged her.

Bonny Kate's competitive nature was stirred by the idea of adding more accomplishments to her past honors. "I know nothing about how Blackie compares to the competition he will face," she contemplated.

"Mr. Brown thinks we have a good chance," Sam said. "Just imagine what a win would do for our horse-breeding business."

"Why did you keep this from me yesterday?" she asked.

"I wasn't sure you would want to do it with all the other events you are involved with," he baited her.

"Of course I'll do it!" she exclaimed. "I don't believe anyone else in the family can get Blackie to do for them what he will do for me!"

"Then it's settled," Sam declared with satisfaction. "The Sherrill Family Horse Company will have an excellent chance to win an important race!"

"I'm so excited!"

"I would appreciate your complete silence about this, even with other members of the family," he cautioned. "I'm keeping our entry a surprise until the morning of the race."

Bonny Kate appreciated that strategy. Many times in the past, she had been excluded from competition because of her gender. It always worked better to just show up at the starting line before anyone could formulate a judgment about her eligibility to enter a race.

When the big day finally rolled around, people came from all over the valley of the Watauga, the Nolichucky Valley, and the more settled lands of the Holston River area. Bonny Kate's competitions and the time in between them allowed her to meet many interesting people. Of course, Captain Alexander showered her with attention, but there were others showing interest. Sarah Sevier introduced her to Joseph McDowell, another young officer from the Catawba River district in North Carolina. Bonny Kate had heard of the McDowells from her youth and respected the family greatly. She met Isaac Taylor, a young surveyor newly arrived in the district to sort out the various issues of land ownership and registration. He was handsome, ambitious, and carried himself well. Next, Sarah brought her William Tatham, the young Englishman who worked so diligently in Colonel Carter's trading company. Even though Bonny Kate already knew him, Sarah was trying to show him all the female attractions of the overmountain communities to keep him from returning to his native England. Bonny Kate Sherrill was definitely a "must see" attraction for young unmarried men on the frontier, at least in Sarah's opinion.

In the morning, Bonny Kate won the footrace. It wasn't as easy as she thought it would be, but she reached deep within herself to force the win, so her recovery took longer. After the race, she took a dip in the cold waters of the Watauga to freshen up and cool down. She changed out of her wet clothes in the Sherrill wagon and made ready for the turkey shoot. She won that too. She enjoyed the midday meal with Sarah and the other ladies of Stony Creek. As they relaxed on blankets spread in the shade of the sycamores after lunch, the rumors reached them that Bonny Kate Sherrill would be entering the horse race late that afternoon.

"Is this true?" Mary Sherrill asked her daughter, completely surprised.

"Yes, ma'am." She smiled. "Papa entered Blackie and asked me to ride."

"Didn't he understand that you should be making yourself presentable for the dance at the time that race is run?"

"I'll have time," she assured her. "I'll skip supper if I have to."

"That won't do you any good," her mother scolded. "You are trying to do too much and trying to please too many people, young lady. It's going to all come crashing down on you if you are not careful!"

"I'll be careful, Mama," she promised, trying to calm her. She laid back and languorously closed her eyes as though entering a deep state of relaxation.

"You'd better be careful!"

Bonny Kate wasn't quite sure how one becomes careful in a horse race. When horses are running flat out, like their tails are on fire, the best care she might hope for was to hold on for dear life. She knew the risks, but she also knew the confidence she had in her finely bred and finely conditioned horse. The exhaustion of the morning's activities and the heat of a sunny May day allowed her to drift into a long restful nap on the blanket under the sycamores.

Mr. Brown was in the middle of a betting frenzy all that afternoon. It was easy for most of the men to take a bet from the boastful Brown who outrageously claimed that an unknown horse ridden by a girl who had never raced before could win, place, or show against the finest horses and riders in the country of western waters. The soldiers had just been paid and many sought to double or triple their money in this popular frontier sport.

Sam Sherrill watched nervously as Mr. Brown amassed a fortune in promises if Bonny Kate could just make a good race of it. When Mr. Brown reached his limit an hour before the race, he excused himself from the throng and found Sam Sherrill with Leroy Taylor warming up the horse.

"Can you cover?" Sam asked.

"I did better than expected in both the turkey shoot and footrace, and I can always sell more land," he told him confidently. "Where's Bonny Kate?"

"She over there amongst the women," Leroy answered. "She's taking a nap."

"Oh, she's a cool one, Sam," marveled Jacob Brown. "How does she do it?"

"She is completely unaware that anyone she knows, and cares about, is betting on the outcome of this race; and I would prefer she remained unaware," Sam explained.

"She doesn't know? Good Lord, Sam, how do you keep her from it?"

"She trusts people, too much I'm afraid," Sam said sadly. "She would be very disappointed in us if she found out we were involved in this."

"Well, she won't find out from me!" Jacob declared. "My lips are sealed."

"I appreciate that, Jacob," Sam said. "But she'll figure it out soon enough. She's not stupid."

Leroy looked over at Sam. "Better wake her up now, Mr. Sherrill; she'll need to be alert at race time."

"I reckon so." Sam left to wake the sleeping girl and prepare her for another great adventure.

The horse race began as a dangerous melee, open to all sorts of horses and riders many of whom had done nothing in preparation except drink too much of the corn spirits. The serious riders soon outdistanced the rabble, and Bonny Kate led them all the way up the Watauga to the turn post at Carter's mansion. Blackie ran a route familiar to his training regimen but at the turn post, that nearly proved disastrous. Rather than obey Bonny Kate's guidance to turn around and head back for the finish, he thought that he was running the usual route all the way to Stony Creek. She struggled to turn him well past the post screaming and pulling at his bit to get his attention. When she finally had him turned and heading the right way, two horses had slipped around the post ahead of her. It was all she could do to get him back up to speed, but the black horse was no slacker. He finished strong, thanks to his conditioning, and regained the lead in the last hundred yards amidst the wildly cheering crowds.

Bonny Kate walked her horse to cool him down and settle him after the excitement of the race. She received many accolades for an excellent race, especially the efforts she had expended at the post to turn her spirited animal around. Mr. Sherrill was exceedingly proud, and so was Mr. Brown.

After all the praise had died down, Captain Alexander found her. "Congratulations on an excellent ride, Miss Sherrill." His charm and dash were strangely missing, and there was no happiness in his demeanor. "I wish you had warned me about your conspiracy. I had assumed your friendliness towards me was genuine."

"What's wrong?" she asked innocently.

"I lost a month's pay to that hillbilly Brown, and you never told me you were involved in this great fraud."

"What fraud?" she asked. "I entered this race on my own horse and won fair and square. How is that a fraud?"

"Brown was taking bets like a drunkard, bragging about how an unknown girl on an unknown horse could beat the best horses of the mounted rangers and all the horses of this territory. I, like many others, took the old fool to task; and he made fools out of all of us. I regret the day I ever met you!"

"I had nothing to do with any fraud!" she defended herself.

"Do you deny that you have any connection with this Brown?"

"He's a friend of my father's," she admitted.

"There you are Miss Sherrill. I call that guilt by association."

"I'm sorry you lost your money," she responded. "I am very much opposed to wagering. How can I compensate you for the loss?"

Captain Alexander laughed. "Just stay the ████ away from me."

"What about the dance tonight?" she despaired.

"I'm sorry, Miss Sherrill, I don't much feel like dancing with you or anybody else tonight." He left her, and she never saw him again. Her rage was building against Mr. Brown and her own father if the captain's charges were true. She went to confront her father about it, and he had a long hard hour trying to get her to calm down and wise up to the ways of the world of men in all of its complex facets. He never did accomplish his purpose. She felt her father's complicity in the matter was tantamount to betrayal.

Sarah was beautifully adorned in her party dress when found Bonny Kate sitting outside the family wagon in a controlled rage.

"Here you are, my dear," Sarah said sweetly. "We have to hurry to get you all dressed up for the party. I have lined up a dance program for you with the finest men in the west."

"I'm not going," she snapped. "I don't care anything about the finest men in the west."

"Oh," Sarah reacted. "We'll have to work on that attitude. Hurry now we don't have much time."

"Sarah, I've just been betrayed by the one man I loved the best in the entire world!" she declared. "Will you please knock me upside the head if I ever again show any interest in the ways of the world of men?"

"I'm afraid I'll never do you much good there," Sarah answered. "I'm intensely interested in the ways of the world of men."

"Lucky you!"

"Do you want to talk about it? I'm a great listener," Sarah offered.

"No, I'd only spoil the party for you," Bonny Kate told her. "Go on, I'll be all right in an hour or two."

"Join us later then?"

"Sure," she lied.

Sarah left her and worried all night. The community worried all the next day as search parties went up and down the river looking for the lost girl. The concern of a caring community has no equal when searching for a lost loved one. And there is no relief like that experienced by a family that finds a lost child safely at home the next day. Likewise, there is no embarrassment equal to that of a family trying to explain to friends the behavior of a hurt and confused child. And perhaps that is all we should say about the spring gathering of '77.

Chapter 21

Plum Grove

Sarah Sevier believed that community was like an intricately woven fabric and always felt a great need to mend it when the fabric was ripped. That's why she sought so earnestly to make things right again for her friend Bonny Kate. Her only problem was Bonny Kate wouldn't talk about her betrayal. Sarah felt bad she hadn't paid attention to who Bonny Kate was spending time with in the weeks leading up to the gathering. If the girl had fallen in love and then been betrayed, Sarah missed the whole thing. How could it have all happened so fast?

A week later Colonel John Sevier, Colonel John Carter, Mr. John Haile, and Mr. Charles Robertson came home to Washington County. They had managed to get the County officially established with courts, land office, and all. James Robertson was appointed by the state to be the Indian agent. He and Charlotte made ready to move to Big Creek on the Holston to live closer to the Cherokee capital.

John Sevier was no sooner welcomed home in the usual way, and unpacked; than Sarah sent him down to inquire among the soldiers at Fort Caswell about what happened to Bonny Kate and who was involved in her betrayal. John went reluctantly, knowing that Sarah was reaching into other people's business where she didn't belong, but his own curiosity about the strange developments and the chance to make some political connections were strong incentives to do his wife's bidding. John renewed a friendship with the commander of the fort, Captain Benjamin Cleveland. He was a heavy good-natured man with a deep love for independence and an implacable hatred of Tories. John's half day among the soldiers of the garrison turned up nothing of romantic significance in regard to Bonny Kate. Many admitted an admiration for the girl but none had any opportunity to develop a relationship. Most were angry that she won the horse race and they lost their money betting against her. His discussion with Captain Alexander was the most interesting.

"Sarah, I found several soldiers who had very strong opinions about Bonny Kate," John reported.

"I knew it!" Sarah exclaimed. "Give me their names, and let's investigate each one."

"Well, actually, they all complained about the same thing," John explained. "They believe she was part of a conspiracy to cheat them out of their money. William Alexander went so far as to accuse her of betraying him!"

"Did he say what happened?"

"Oh yes, he was very clear about it," John answered. "Jacob Brown made all the bets, and Bonny Kate won the race. Alexander called it a fraud and confronted her about it, but she denied any involvement. Some of those soldiers lost an entire month's pay."

"I'm shocked by this," Sarah said sadly. "I can't imagine her being involved in a deliberate fraud."

"I think Jacob Brown got her to enter the race without her knowing about the betting," John guessed. "There's no law against wagering."

"Well, what about her being betrayed by the man she loved best in the entire world?" Sarah asked.

"There's no law against that either," John joked.

"Silly boy." Sarah laughed. "You know what I'm asking."

"Yes, but that part remains the mystery," John admitted. "You'll have to dig a little deeper to solve that one. Ask Bonny Kate."

"Don't think I haven't tried," Sarah said. "She refuses to tell me anything."

"If she won't confide in you, I reckon you ought to leave it alone," John advised.

"I want her to be happy," Sarah sighed. "She deserves to marry the man of her dreams."

"Her own choices are going to determine that, along with the workings of Divine Providence," John pointed out.

Sarah looked at her husband and marveled at the wisdom of his private advice. This side of his nature was usually hidden beneath his "life of the party" public image. Any man who ever spent time with John Sevier felt he had developed a new best friend. It was his most amazing natural ability. This capacity to make friends, combined with his warmth and generosity toward all kinds of people, produced deep and abiding loyalties that would not diminish over time.

"Don't plan to go anywhere tonight." Sarah grinned at John. "I'm sending the children down to Bonny Kate's for a visit."

"I'm sure we'll all enjoy that!"

Some weeks later Sarah confided to Bonny Kate that she was pretty sure she was expecting her ninth child. She was hoping for another girl. Bonny Kate rejoiced with her in the news because Sarah seemed very pleased with herself and described how delighted John had been with the announcement before he left for the peace talks that were reconvening at the Long Island.

Sarah wanted to share the news with her friends so she proposed a trip to Robertson's store. Her other purpose was to get Bonny Kate out and about and seen by folks in the community. Sarah always believed that a person's presence was the best countermeasure to the effects of wild rumors and malicious gossip that flew around when a person was absent. They found Ruth Brown at the store buying up a large order of goods with cash that she had received from her husband's winnings. They had a nice visit with the prosperous Mrs. Brown and with Charlotte Robertson who informed them that she would be moving with her husband farther west to take up his post as Indian agent.

"It's important that a woman stay close to her husband in all circumstances of life to comfort and support him in his many ventures," Charlotte opined. "To do otherwise, invites disaster."

Bonny Kate was wise enough now about community dynamics to see that Charlotte was slinging hurtful arrows at Mrs. Brown. Before Mrs. Brown could react, a strange woman strolled into the yard leading a packhorse loaded with possessions. She traveled alone, on foot, dressed as any other pioneer woman.

"I wonder who that could be," Charlotte said. "Lord, a day hardly passes that we fail to see a new customer come in here." All four women watched as the stranger tied her pack animal and approached the store. Ruth Brown was the first to move. She backed away from the front entrance of the store and slipped out the back way.

"A pretty woman," Charlotte observed. "Graceful too, walks like an Indian."

The stranger stepped into the store and waited at the threshold as her eyes adjusted from the bright sunlight to the darker store.

"Good morning, madam," Charlotte greeted her. "Are you here to do some trading?"

Bonny Kate recognized her. "Nan Henderson!" The woman was surprised to hear her name as she turned to face Bonny Kate and Sarah.

"Where's Ruth Brown?" Sarah reacted.

Bonny Kate saw the open back door and turned to the yard. She saw Ruth drawing a rifle from her saddle horse. "She's fetching her rifle!" She looked again at Nan Henderson and saw the terror on her face.

"I'll stop her," Sarah bravely volunteered. "Find a safe place for Miss Henderson!" She ran out the door.

Ruth was cocking the rifle when Sarah grabbed onto it and tried to take it away from the enraged woman. Nan Henderson saw Sarah's efforts on her behalf and used the opportunity to escape. She ran out the door, headed for the river, and splashed across the Watauga. Little Sarah was no match for Mrs. Brown as the older, bigger woman jerked at the contested firearm. Sarah went down to the ground but never let go. She held on like a bulldog on a rag.

"████████, Sarah," Ruth growled. "I've got a clean shot at her. Let go of my gun!"

Sarah never answered and never let go. As Ruth's target completed her river crossing and turned with greater speed toward the sycamores, Ruth left Sarah lying in the dust with complete control of the rifle and grabbed the reins of her horse. Bonny Kate and Charlotte rushed over to help.

Sarah sprang up and shoved the rifle at Charlotte. "Hold this!" she ordered. As Ruth Brown mounted her horse, Sarah threw herself at the horse's head and latched onto the bridle. Her weight bowed the horse's head toward the ground.

"████████, Sarah," Ruth screamed. "I don't want to hurt you, but you are obstructing justice!" She slid off the horse having found a tomahawk hanging from her well-equipped saddle.

Sarah saw the weapon and warned her companions. "Stay back girls, she's got a tomahawk, and I believe she'll use it." Bonny Kate and Charlotte heeded the warning and made no interference.

"You have no idea what that little half-breed ██████ has done to me!" Ruth bellowed. "Let go of that horse, Sarah."

Sarah was lying on her back in the dust under the muzzle of the horse with a firm hold on the bridle. Bonny Kate watched a string of horse slobber drip on Sarah's best trading dress. "No," shouted game little Sarah. "It's wrong to kill her without a fair trial!"

"Then let it be trial by contest!" Ruth answered brandishing the tomahawk. She ran to the river and waded across as Nan Henderson had and ran after the defendant.

"You reckon she'll catch her?" Charlotte asked.

Sarah sat up and released the horse, pushing its head to the side. "No, she's wearing the wrong kind of shoes for a footrace." Charlotte and Bonny Kate laughed as they helped Sarah to her feet.

"My goodness, Sarah, you were heroic," marveled Bonny Kate. "Are you all right?"

"No, but I will be when I dust off and clean this horse slobber off my new dress" she replied. "Bonny Kate, take your horse and stay with Mrs. Brown. Just trail along after her and make sure she doesn't hurt anybody. Don't try to stop her, just let her run the rage out."

Bonny Kate kept Ruth Brown in sight, but it was quite some time before Ruth ran the rage out. Somewhere in the third mile, Ruth looked back and saw Bonny Kate drawing up to her. "Are you coming to help me or coming to stop me?" she panted.

"How can I help?" Bonny Kate asked.

"You knock her down, and I'll finish her off!" Ruth replied.

Bonny Kate searched the thick June foliage on the trail ahead as they ascended the forested banks of the Doe River. "Where is she?"

Ruth stopped and gasped for air that blistering hot morning. "I don't know. I lost sight of her some time ago. Maybe you can track her like you tracked the mountain lion."

Bonny Kate stopped her horse and corrected Ruth's version of the story. "I never tracked that mountain lion. He was tracking me, and the only reason I killed him was self-defense."

"Bonny Kate, I don't want to go through the whole sordid story again telling you why I'm acting so crazy."

"You don't have to, Mrs. Brown, unless it makes you feel better to talk about it."

"No, I won't feel any better, one way or the other," she sighed.

"Let's go home," Bonny Kate suggested. "Do you want to ride up here behind me?"

"Please," Ruth replied. "These shoes are killing my feet!" Bonny Kate helped her up on the horse, and they rode back down the forest trail. Ruth continued, "I gave her a good scare, didn't I?"

"That you did," Bonny Kate answered. "You gave me a good scare too. You shouldn't have treated Sarah so roughly. She came down to tell everyone she's expecting again, but she never got the chance."

"Oh, dear," Ruth fretted. "I would be absolutely mortified if my bad behavior was responsible for her losing that baby! How bad was she hurt?"

"She seemed all right when I left her, but you never know with babies. The damage may not show up for days or weeks," Bonny Kate expressed her concern.

As they made their way back down the wilder parts of the Doe River, Bonny Kate made out a menacing presence beside the trail, and she reined in her horse. "Give me that tomahawk," she ordered tersely. Ruth handed over the weapon quickly, unsure why she wanted it. Bonny Kate slipped off her horse and handed the reins to Ruth. "Hold him tight, Mrs. Brown." She walked toward the danger a few steps and threw the tomahawk with great force. There was still movement on the ground in front of Bonny Kate as the girl crept closer and closer. Ruth Brown urged the horse ahead to follow Bonny Kate. Into view, through the thick grass, appeared the scaly body of a writhing serpent.

"Ugh!" Mrs. Brown recoiled at the sight of the biggest copperhead she had ever seen. The head of the snake was cloven by the tomahawk and pinned against the root of a pin oak. The coils of the beast moved in reflex, unaware yet that life had ended.

"It's safe to pass by now." Bonny Kate breathed a sigh of relief. She moved closer to that denizen of death.

"What are you doing?" Ruth demanded.

"Retrieving your tomahawk," Bonny Kate answered.

"Oh, leave it!" Ruth said, disgusted by the thought of snake blood on her tool.

Bonny Kate lifted the weapon and walked quickly after the squeamish Mrs. Brown. "It's strange that you would run out here in this wilderness with blood lust in your heart for a poor fellow human being and can't stand to watch me dispatch a cold-blooded killer."

"There's a lesson for me, Bonny Kate," Ruth admitted. "I never meant to kill that woman, and I don't reckon I ever will, but I'll never give her the satisfaction of knowing that."

Bonny Kate smiled and remounted her horse in front of Mrs. Brown. She resumed their progress back toward civilization.

"I was always afraid you would do to Sarah what Nan Henderson did to me," Ruth said.

"Whatever do you mean?"

"Oh, the women were watching you every minute at Watauga Fort," she told her. "John Sevier is a strong man, but a woman like you could have worn him down in time. I really believe he might have fallen for you if the siege had gone on another month."

"What a horrible mess that would have been, had I been so tempted!" Bonny Kate declared haughtily.

"Are you saying you weren't?" Ruth asked. "What makes you any better than that Nan Henderson?"

"Jesus makes me better than I could ever be on my own," she declared. "Every morning I pray that the Holy Spirit lead me not into temptation but deliver me from evil, and so far, God has been merciful."

"Why Bonny Kate Sherrill, I never knew you had taken up the religion. What are you, a Quaker?"

"No, ma'am, Presbyterian," she answered.

"My grandfather Gordon was a Presbyterian," Ruth informed her.

"I sure wish we had a church at Sycamore Shoals," Bonny Kate sighed. "That would tame the wild nature in men."

"And in women," Ruth added with a grin.

"A church is a good place to meet every week and keep up with what's going on in the world."

"We rarely see a good preacher in this country," Ruth said. "Last time I remember one was shortly after I came out here to join Jacob. Charlotte Robertson and Becky Boone had all their children baptized in the river. That was the year the Boones lived here and made a crop."

"If I had known you were going to run so far, I would have packed us a lunch," Bonny Kate complained.

"Thank you for coming to help me," Ruth said. "You saved me from that copperhead."

"Be sure to thank Sarah too," Bonny Kate advised. "She saved you from the gallows!"

Ruth let the conversation drop as she contemplated the consequences that may have occurred from her uncontrolled anger. Bonny Kate carried Ruth Brown as far as Mrs. Carter's and left her there for a visit and several draughts of cool spring water as she recovered from her run. Bonny Kate rode alone the remaining two miles to Sycamore Shoals and retrieved Sarah. Then they rode up the Watauga, picked up Mrs. Brown, and carried her back to Stony Creek for an extended visit. Sarah's influence and John's involvement resulted in reconciliation between Mr. and Mrs. Brown. Nan Henderson made her way back to Robertson's sometime during the night after the disturbance, recovered her packhorse and possessions, and slipped out of the neighborhood presumably headed for Indian country.

After a month more of peace talks, Charlotte and James Robertson were moving to Big Creek on the Holston. The move greatly affected John Sevier. For all their joking and political maneuvering at each other's expense, the two had always been deeply loyal friends. Their opposite personalities had complemented each other perfectly. Robertson the peace chief and Sevier the war chief were a frontier force to be reckoned with. John and James had a long visionary talk before parting and explored some great concepts.

"I'm taking civilization across the country to be a blessing to all mankind," James Robertson declared. "I see that as my mission in life. Self-determination, self-control, and self-government under the rule of law, these are my principles."

"I agree with you, James," John said. "But I also believe in building up a community, to share one and all in the prosperity of human enterprise, in commonwealth with one another. All men should be free but sensitive to neighbors in need."

"That is a noble ambition, John, but difficult to instill in the hearts of other men," James observed. "At least, you practice that in your own dealings with others. Take care, you don't impoverish yourself."

"It is a delicate balance," John agreed. "I couldn't accomplish much without the excellent management my wife brings to my affairs, and of course we both trust to Divine Providence."

"I'm going to miss you, John," Robertson said sadly.

"You'll be back," John predicted. "These political appointments never last very long."

"No, John," James declared. "I'm going on west to settle beyond the Cumberland Mountain. I'll be opening up new lands for settlement just like we accomplished here."

"I wish I could talk Sarah into that!" John said excitedly. "I'd love to be right there with you."

"As my lieutenant?" James joked.

"No, as Colonel of the militia," John corrected him.

"Sorry, John." His friend Robertson smiled. "I'm going to be the colonel this time. Nobody is going to steal that honor from me again."

"I didn't steal that from you!" John protested.

"Of course you did, when you rescued your little girlfriend," he charged. "You became the biggest hero this community has ever seen!"

"She's not my girlfriend," John argued.

"Took her home to live on your farm, didn't you?" he teased. "I wonder how Sarah excellently manages that."

"See here, James, why are you making this into a scandal?" John asked indignantly.

"You stole my colonelcy," he complained.

"I did not!"

"Did too!" James stood up threatening to fight. John laughed at him, and James laughed at John. The friendship remained as strong as ever, but they had both reached an understanding of why James had to move on and why John couldn't go with him.

Summer rains and sunny days produced such an abundance of growing crops that even the gloomiest souls predicted a great harvest. Peace brought prosperity to both Wataugans and Cherokees. But other parts of the continent suffered from the continuing war. The British having secured New York City hatched a three-pronged campaign that was designed to subdue the rebellion in the settled valleys of the state of New York and isolate New England from the middle and southern states. The British governor in Canada worked tirelessly for the Crown to stir up resentments among the Indians and encourage attacks on the settlers of the western frontier.

Near the end of July, Captain William Bailey Smith came in from Kentucky with alarming news. Boonesborough, a settlement named for its founder Daniel Boone was under siege by northern Indians. They needed help desperately. Captain Smith and his small party were directed to Stony Creek to the home of Lieutenant Colonel Sevier when they reached the Watauga community.

Sarah sat at a small table on her porch making journal entries and feeling the effects of mild morning sickness when the Kentuckians came into view. She watched them ride up the hill to her house.

"Good morning, gentlemen," she greeted them.

"Good morning, ma'am. I'm Captain William Bailey Smith from Boonesborough on the Kentucky River, and I'm looking for Colonel Sevier on a matter of great urgency."

"Colonel Sevier is posted with his company down at Fort Williams on the Nolichucky," Sarah replied. "It's twenty-five miles from here."

The information seemed a crushing blow to the weary men who looked well nigh exhausted already from hard travel.

"How do we find this Fort Williams?" Captain Smith inquired.

Sarah had an idea. "Why not rest here while I send for Colonel Sevier? Your men and horses look as though they could use a good breakfast and a day's rest."

"Ma'am, the worry is that our families may be massacred before we can bring the help to save them," Captain Smith explained. "Every hour counts in our life-or-death struggle."

Sarah understood. "Betsy?"

"Yes, ma'am?" The little girl appeared in the cabin's doorway.

"Tell Bonny Kate to come up here dressed as the man, with her fastest horse and packed for a full day's ride. I need her as fast as she can get here. Now run!"

Sarah invited the weary soldiers to unsaddle their horses and come in for a breakfast. In a quarter hour, Bonny Kate reported, ready to ride, and was soon informed about the situation in Kentucky.

"Boonesborough Fort has been surrounded by hostile Shawnees since the fourth of July," Captain Smith explained. "The first rescue attempt by forty men from the Holston failed when the Holston men made it into the fort and became trapped as well. Supplies of shot, powder, and food were dangerously low when we slipped out five nights ago. There's no telling how bad it is now."

"So you see, Bonny Kate, every hour counts," Sarah told her.

"If Colonel Sevier could just spare forty men and resupply our stores, we might stand a chance," Captain Smith pleaded.

"Forty men didn't work the first time," Sarah pointed out. "I think it's going to take a hundred!"

"Mrs. Sevier!" Captain Smith exclaimed. "If a hundred mounted rangers showed up suddenly, those Indians would hightail it for the Ohio, without a fight, and leave us in peace for a long time!"

"There we are!" Sarah declared. "It's the perfect plan. Bonny Kate, tell Colonel Sevier we need a hundred volunteers for a quick expedition to Boonesborough!"

Bonny Kate swung into the saddle and was gone in an instant, pushing her black stallion at racing speed down the valley of the Watauga.

"If you can make this happen, Mrs. Sevier, this is the first time I've had any reason to hope since this thing began," Captain Smith sighed wearily.

"Rest your men, Captain Smith," Sarah said. "They'll soon be going home to save their wives and children!"

Bonny Kate made the trip to Fort Williams in less than four hours. She found Colonel Sevier discussing supply problems with his quartermaster, William Tatham. After a polite greeting and some curious looks at her attire, Mr. Tatham excused himself to conduct a supply inventory. Bonny Kate explained to Colonel Sevier everything about the troubles in Kentucky and requested the hundred men.

"A hundred men!" John exclaimed. "Where does Captain Smith think I'm going to find a hundred men this close to harvest time?"

"Well actually, Captain Smith only asked for a force of forty men, but Sarah thought a hundred would do the job quicker and better," Bonny Kate told him.

"My little Sarah is a military planner now." John laughed. "I'd hate to let her down after she's gone to so much trouble sending you down here. Give me an hour to plan this thing out. Have you had anything to eat?"

"Not since breakfast," Bonny Kate replied.

"Join me then," he invited. John looked at the slender girl dressed in her father's hunting clothes. "I thought you were a man as you rode in."

"I often travel this way, Colonel Sevier, so I draw less attention."

"The look of it works for you, Miss Sherrill." He grinned.

As they ate, John wrote dispatches for his soldiers to carry to various parts of the county. After completing half a dozen messages, he put aside his writing and made conversation. "What do you think of Fort Williams?"

She looked at the single blockhouse and hastily constructed palisade. "Not much to it," she answered enjoying a plum from a bowl of plums he had provided.

"This is going to be my new home on the Nolichucky." He smiled.

She looked at the bowl of plums. "This is it? This is Plum Grove Plantation? Oh, it's wonderful!"

"Of course the ramshackle fort has to go, but the house will be on the high ground there, facing east, and I guess I can convert the blockhouse into a horse barn with plenty of storage space on the upper floor."

"What a beautiful view of the mountains!" she exclaimed. "So where is the Nolichucky?"

"At the bottom of the hill," he replied. "Do you see that small cabin on the other side? That was Mr. Brown's first store when he came down here, living among the Indians all by himself."

"Where was Nan Henderson?"

John laughed. "What do you know about that?"

"More than I ever wanted to," she assured him.

"Well, I guess she was there too."

"If the walls of that little cabin could talk, I reckon Ruth Brown would want that place burned to the ground," she observed.

"I was going to fix it up and use it as a guest cabin, so please don't tell Ruth Brown what you know about it."

"I promise not to." She smiled. "Has Sarah been here yet?"

"No, she hasn't seen the place except in her mind's eye. I've told her all about it in great detail."

"She's going to love it," Bonny Kate assured him. "I imagine she's going to give birth to that new little baby right here on this hill."

"I reckon she will," he agreed.

"Colonel Sevier, do you know what day today is?"

"Today is the twenty-first of July," he replied.

"Do you know what happened one year ago today?"

"I saved your life," he declared.

"Yes, sir, and this has been the best year of my life!"

"I've had a year of remarkably good fortune as well," he responded. She thought about kissing him again for another year of good luck but decided she'd better not having dressed as the man for the day's journey. How would Colonel Sevier explain that to his soldiers, and how would she explain such reckless behavior to Sarah?

"Well, I'm glad everything turned out the way it did," he took a deep breath and exhaled slowly. "I reckon we have to travel fast. People are being killed in Kentucky."

They left Plum Grove on fresh horses and made it to Stony Creek before dark. Colonel Sevier had dispatched riders in all directions from Fort Williams gathering in the volunteers. Many of the settlers of Boonesborough and Harrodsborough had once been citizens of Watauga, and there were friendships and relationships that could be counted on to motivate men to answer the call. The North Carolina rangers could not be used to assist settlers in another territory, but they could be relied upon to protect the homes of the volunteers who went.

The next morning forty-eight mounted and fully equipped volunteers assembled in the field before John Carter's store. Captain William Bailey Smith was amazed at the rapid response so close to harvest time. He and Colonel Sevier reviewed the troops and Colonel Sevier although unable to go himself, made many helpful suggestions on how best to use the remarkable abilities of the irregular force he had called together.

"I know you asked for a hundred men, Captain Smith, so you can put on a show of force, but let me make a suggestion," John said. "The last day of your ride, have each man fill his extra clothing with straw, like a scarecrow. Make it look like each horse is carrying two men riding double. Indian braves ride double all the time and from a distance I believe that will fool them."

"That just might work." Captain Smith laughed. "I believe we'll give it a try."

"Good luck, Bill," John said. "Our prayers are with you and the folks of Kentucky."

"Thanks, John," Captain Smith said. "Please express my thanks again to your wife and to that fellow that rode down to fetch you back yesterday."

"Fellow?" John laughed. "That was no fellow. That was Bonny Kate Sherrill. She's kind of a legend in these parts."

"She sure looked like a feller to me." Captain Smith laughed. "Well, thank her just the same!"

"I'll do it!" John promised.

The volunteers of Watauga rode forth to the rescue, noble knights, mighty warriors, men of the rough edge, sinewy, grizzly-bearded fellows of the frontier. Every community needs such heroes.

Chapter 22

Daisy Fields

The Kentucky campaign brought a respite from the violence for the citizens of Boonesborough and Harrodsborough. The appearance of the ninety-six Watauga horsemen riding double into Fort Boonesborough prompted the troublesome northern Indians to quit the community and return to their homes along the Ohio. The Watauga volunteers came home soon after Virginia sent a hundred soldiers to Kentucky to keep the peace and protect the frontier families.

The summer peace conference settled the issue with the Cherokees and opened the way for the Sherrills and Seviers to move to the Nolichucky. The North Carolina soldiers had returned to their home counties, but having seen the beauty of the west and the opportunity offered by western migration, many made plans to come west again as settlers.

The harvest was a great success for everyone. John Sevier was very pleased with the yields of Stony Creek farm and planned to give the farm to his father, Valentine Sevier Sr., as a well-established operation and comfortable home for his father and stepmother to enjoy.

Colonel Carter hosted the fall gathering; and this time Bonny Kate chose not to concern herself with the ways of the world of men and stayed away from the footrace, the horse race, and the turkey shoot. Instead, she concentrated her focus on the dance. She had a party dress she wanted to show off, and Sarah set her up with William Tatham as her dance partner. When all was said and done, Bonny Kate and her partner turned in an average performance that won them no accolades. She learned a great deal about Mr. Tatham's sweetheart he left behind in England and how miserable he was without her. She also learned how miserable she was without the thrill of the competitions at which she had always excelled in the past. Colonel Sevier won every competition as he had in his days of glory. He and Sarah even won the dance contest. Bonny Kate's boycott of the daytime competitions didn't change a thing. The men still wagered on the outcomes of the events whether she competed or not. There was a lesson to be learned and for that lesson, Bonny Kate went to her father.

The day after the gathering at Carter's, Bonny Kate went out to help her father at the horse barn. After some discussion about the move to the Nolichucky, she turned the discussion to the affairs closest to her heart. "Father, forgive me for the way I've treated you this summer. I blamed you for all the wagering that went on at the spring gathering."

"I'm sorry that hurt you," he replied. "I knew what Mr. Brown was doing and should have told you."

"I was miserable yesterday," she admitted. "I wanted to be in that horse race so bad, but I was stubborn."

"Adam rode pretty well, I thought" Sam declared. "The experience was good for him."

"He held back on the turn, and let Sevier get past," she criticized. "I wouldn't have let that happen. And I wouldn't have let Landon Carter beat us in the stretch."

"Third place is not a bad showing," Sam insisted.

"But we had the horse that should have finished first," she declared.

"Well, that's all in the hands of Providence," Sam concluded. "Did you enjoy the dance?"

"No, Mr. Tatham and I were not well matched," she told him. "I missed my best chance when the soldiers were here last spring. Once again it seems the best men are all married or have sweethearts or are too young for me."

"It's going to get worse when we move to Daisy Fields," Sam warned. "The Nolichucky is thinly settled, and the only single men are likely to be Indians or Tories."

"How will I avoid living a wasted life?" she worried.

Sam laughed gently. "You have never lived a wasted life," he assured her. "You have always been useful and especially helpful to the family. Mrs. Sevier sees how useful you are and frequently relies on your help when her husband is away."

"I've let her down too," Bonny Kate admitted. "I have trouble presenting myself the way she expects me to when she introduces me to new prospects."

"There's your problem," Sam discovered. "Did you listen to your own words? You are trying to present yourself the way Sarah expects. You have to be yourself. You will never meet anyone else's expectations, and no matter how hard you try, you will never be Sarah Sevier!"

"I should have entered those races and contests yesterday."

"And not because anyone else expects it," Sam explained. "You have to use the gifts that the good Lord gave you. That's how you glorify God, and that's the only way to live the useful and happy life."

"And perhaps the single life," she said sadly.

"Have you asked God for the useful and happy single life?" Sam challenged her.

"No, of course not," she replied.

"There is nothing wrong with the useful and happy single life if that is where you feel closest to God," Sam advised.

"I want to be married with all my heart!" she declared fiercely. "That's what I pray for day and night. That is where I know God is leading me."

"Then do not doubt that our God will give it to you," Sam warned. "It is sin to doubt the power and mercy of God just because you are a spoiled and impatient child!"

She was stunned by the way he put that, and she realized her father was right. She was pulled into a fatherly embrace that said everything would be all right, and she hugged him tightly in response. Sometime later, she prayed about her situation as she applied her gifts to cleaning out the horse barn.

"When you have finished shoveling out the manure, brush down the horses and turn them out to pasture," Sam told her. "We won't need them for anything else today."

"Yes, sir," she complied.

Moving day for the Sherrills came quickly and the good old Sherrill wagon was once more loaded to capacity for the trip to Daisy Fields. The Seviers came down to see them on their way. Many close friendships had developed between the two families, and it surprised Bonny Kate how closely interwoven they had become. She also realized how much she would miss Sarah and the Sevier children. There were many hugs and kisses and sad good-byes, but the Seviers would soon move too and become their nearest neighbors, only five miles up the Nolichucky from Daisy Fields.

The meadows along the Nolichucky looked different in the autumn than they had in the spring. The trees were brushed with colors, and the wild daisies that had flourished in every sunny spot last May were now replaced with red sumac. The cabin at Daisy Fields went up quickly because the logs were well seasoned having been dressed the previous spring. Sam Sherrill and his sons were talented builders as was Leroy Taylor. The rush to get a warm dry cabin built before the really cold weather was good reason to work fast. But quality was also important to the Sherrills because they never did anything halfway. They were safely moved in before the first snow.

November of the year 1777 closed with news that Philadelphia had been surrendered to the British invasion. The frontier Tories received the news with the idea that it was just a matter of time before the British crown repossessed the American colonies. That made the Tory partisans bolder than ever and affected places even as remote as Daisy Fields. Sometimes war can show up on your doorstep when you least expect it.

One December morning, Mr. Brown rode down the river and called at Daisy Fields. He admired the neat cabin and surveyed the progress the Sherrills were making on their horse barn. He found Bonny Kate churning butter on the porch.

"What news do you have concerning the Seviers?" Bonny Kate asked.

"Old Colonel Jack went back to the General Assembly for the fall session," Mr. Brown informed her. "Sarah and the children are still living at Stony Creek, but Jack's parents are there to help her."

"Are they moving anytime soon?" Bonny Kate asked.

"Not likely," Mr. Brown answered. "Last year it was late December before General Assembly let out."

"I was hoping they could get their cabin built, and she could have the baby in their new home," Bonny Kate said idealistically.

"Not likely," repeated Mr. Brown. "Maybe they'll move down in March and get their fields plowed in time to put in a crop. Where's your father?"

"He's down at the corral with some of the boys," she replied.

Jacob Brown rode down to the corral. Bonny Kate, so hungry for news, left her butter churn and followed him.

Sam Sherrill greeted Jacob Brown as he stepped down from his horse, but the pleasantries were dispensed with quickly.

"Sam, I've heard some very distressing news," Jacob began. "And I think you ought to act on it. There is a band of Tories hereabouts that have become very strong by adding to their numbers several notorious horse thieves and highwaymen that have drifted in from the east."

"That's not good," Sam agreed.

Jacob continued. "They descended on poor Mr. McAneny and forced him to sign over his property at gunpoint. They threatened to kill his family if they ever came back to the farm. Sarah Sevier took in the McAnenys at Stony Creek where they sought refuge."

"Where is this McAneny's farm?" Sam asked.

"On Little Cherokee Creek up against the mountain. It's up beyond my place, but not far. I think the gang intends to use it as a base of operations to threaten and prey upon the settlers. Robert Sevier's Light Horse Company is on the way up there this morning, but he thought you ought to be warned."

"Thanks for letting me know, Jacob. And thank Robert when you see him again," Sam said.

"Robert thinks you ought to take your horses and your family up to Stony Creek until this thing is over," Jacob advised. "You are in a very exposed situation here and we think your horses would be a very desirable target for the outlaws."

Sam scanned his half-developed farm and admitted to himself that too short a distance separated his defensible house from the cleared edge of the forest. "That may be the best thing I could do."

"How many horses do you have now?" Jacob asked.

"Thirty that are already promised to the Washington County Safety Committee," Sam responded. "Then I have a dozen more family mounts and breeders that are not for sale."

"That's enough for an entire company of rangers! You'd better leave immediately," Jacob urged.

"Bonny Kate, tell your mother and sisters that we are moving all the horses to Stony Creek today," Sam ordered. "The county horses are leaving as soon as we can get them rounded up. We are crossing the Nolichucky here and taking Big Limestone Creek towards Watauga. The family will follow within the hour."

"Excellent plan," approved Mr. Brown. "I'll ride with the horse wranglers."

Mr. Brown, Leroy Taylor, Sam Junior, John Sherrill, and William Sherrill prepared to leave immediately. They rounded up the horses and drove them to the crossing of the Nolichucky.

Bonny Kate was thrilled with the prospect of a trip to Stony Creek and quickly informed her mother, Susan and Mary Jane about the plans.

"Why are we going to Stony Creek?" Mary asked.

"To keep a band of Tories from stealing our horses," she told her mother. "The men are taking the horses now, and we are to leave within the hour."

Mary rushed her girls to begin the preparations for the journey.

"Bonny Kate," Mary said worriedly, "Adam went out hunting rabbits this morning. Somebody needs to find him and tell him what's going on."

"I'll go, Mama," she volunteered. She lifted her favorite rifle from its cradle on the wall and took a powder horn and shot pouch. "I might get me a rabbit or two while I'm out there."

After the horses for Washington County were safely across the river, Sam went to see about his womenfolk. He saddled the family horses and brought them up to the cabin to be packed with necessary goods as fast as the women could prepare the bundles.

Adam Sherrill returned from his morning hunt having walked a large circle around the farm. Sam quickly explained the situation and put him right to work packing the horses. At last, Mary and her girls were ready to travel and came out of the cabin to the horses.

"Where's Bonny Kate?" Mary asked.

"Wasn't she in there helping you pack?" Sam asked.

"No, I sent her out to fetch Adam," Mary replied.

"I didn't see her," Adam explained. "I came back on my own."

"Thunderation!" Sam stormed. "It's always Bonny Kate. That girl is giving me gray hairs!"

A distant volley of rifle shots cut short his tirade and replaced his anger with the deepest worry a father holds for his dearest daughter.

"What do you suppose that was, Sam?" Mary knew as much as he did but asked anyway.

"That's a report from Bonny Kate," he told his wife. "She just warned us that trouble is nearby. Adam, leave me two horses, and the rest of you cross the river and ride hard to catch up with Junior." Sam took the reins of the horses.

"Sam!" Mary cried. "Don't leave me!"

"I've got to go, Mary, she will need my help."

"Sam, please don't blame me. I was the one who sent her." Mary burst out crying. Susan and Mary Jane joined her.

"We are not blaming anybody," Sam said gently. "I'll just go retrieve Bonny Kate, and we will rejoin you at Stony Creek. Adam, move out and don't stop until you catch up with Junior."

"Yes, sir," Adam Sherrill, the serious, forthright, obedient son led the weeping women toward the river crossing. The realization that the loss of his sister was due to his zeal for rabbit hunting was his heaviest burden for the journey ahead.

Bonny Kate had never shot a man before, but her choice of twelve Tories now presented her the opportunity to kill one or two and warn her family at the same time. They had conveniently dismounted their horses and tied them to some low hanging tree branches not very far from her hiding place in a canebrake. Then they crept forward to reconnoiter and plan their attack on her home and family. The cabin was still about two hundred yards away, safely out of range of the bandits, so she had time to consider carefully her options. When the bandits were a good distance past her, she made a quick decision and slipped out of her hiding place while a December breeze rustled the cane and the leaves of the forest floor, effectively covering the sound of her movements. She was among the horses quickly untying them and gathering the reins to tie together to a lead horse she chose to ride herself. She was hoping her theft of the horses would create enough of a ruckus to warn her family of the danger. She climbed up on the lead horse and kicked its sides and slapped its rump to get it moving, pulling the others along. What started slowly, gained momentum. A rifle shot sounded, then several others, as she lay against the horse's neck praying the bad men would consider shooting high for fear of injuring their own horses. The gunfire motivated the laggard horses, and she soon found herself amongst a sort of stampede. The horses left behind such shouting and cursing as she had never heard. She knew she had discovered some very bad men.

Bonny Kate's intention was to draw the outlaws away from Daisy Fields. After a short run, she drew the horses in and stopped them just in the woods at the far side of a natural meadow. She slipped off the horse, knelt behind a small holly, primed the pan of her hunting rifle and waited. She was surprised when a single young strong outlaw came running into the meadow stripped down to his shirt and breeches for speed. He carried only a tomahawk. She stood shouldering her rifle and fired at the man's right knee. He fell immediately among the briars and long meadow grass, cursing at her in pain. She reloaded quickly and made ready to ride.

"Tell your friends it will take more than a boy with a tomahawk to recover their horses!" she shouted. "We demand a ransom in blood!"

"Who are you?" the outlaw demanded.

"Blackbeard the Pirate and the Princess of Pain!" she shouted back. The man continued cursing at her and threatening her with all sorts of horrible things they would do to her when they caught up with her. Bonny Kate worked hard to get the horses moving again along the wooded trail. She and her brothers had hunted up this way and she knew the trail led up the valley toward the location of the deserted Fort Williams, a place someday to be called Plum Grove Plantation. She was looking for another place she could get a long-range shot at the outlaws from ambush, when she remembered the advantage the river might afford her. She turned the horses due north leaving the trail and sought the banks of the Nolichucky.

Sam Sherrill heard another rifle report farther up the valley, one shot and no answering fire. The tracks of a dozen horses had come nearly to the clearing at Daisy Fields and then turned suddenly around and gone back the way they had come. Over the tracks of the horses were the tracks of about a dozen men, running after their horses. He guessed his daughter was involved in a dangerous game of cat and mouse. As long as she had their horses, she was the cat. He knew the Tories were well armed and too dangerous for him to vigorously pursue, so he followed the outlaws cautiously hoping that Bonny Kate would stay ahead of them well out of range. Near the edge of the Sherrill's property, he arrived at the natural meadow and saw a young man sitting alone, deserted by his fellows. Sam primed his rifle and approached the man carefully, noting that the man was armed only with a tomahawk.

"Hello, friend," Sam greeted him. "What happened to you?"

"I'm shot in the knee."

"Hunting accident?"

"No, that ▓▓▓ deliberately shot me from ambush, and she stole our horses."

"A woman did this?" Sam acted surprised. "Who was she?"

"She called herself the Princess of Pain."

"Oh, her," Sam said knowingly. "She's crazy like that."

"You know her?"

"I'm scared to death of her," Sam answered. "Have you ever heard of Ute Perkins?"

"Sure, I heard stories about him when I was growing up. He ran the biggest gang of horse thieves Virginia ever saw."

"She's a member of his gang, one of the meanest."

"I thought Ute Perkins was dead."

"Not hardly," Sam said. "In fact, his western hideout is very close by. You can't sneak up on Ute Perkins."

"We were trying to find a man named Sherrill. The king's government has need of his horses."

"Don't you fellows know anything?" Sam laughed. "Old man Sherrill is a cousin to Ute Perkins! You must have stumbled into his pickets."

"I didn't see nobody, then this girl is making away with our horses before we know it."

"Ain't that just like horse thieves," Sam marveled. "Nobody is safe these days! Are your friends coming back for you?"

"As soon as they catch her," he replied.

"How many went after her?"

"Eleven," answered the Tory

"That won't be enough," Sam told him. "Ute will pitch a fit when he sobers up enough to find out she's gone on another rampage. He and his forty thieves are drinking up old man Sherrill's whiskey. When they realize she's run off again, they'll be in an ugly mood."

"Did I miss a part of your story?" the Tory asked.

"You better hope you miss it all," Sam advised. "You and your friends had better go back where you came from, and don't ever come back."

The man eyed Sam's extra horse. "Can you help me up on your horse?"

"Nope," Sam replied. "My job is to collect and bury the dead ones. It looks like you'll live. Better not move around too much and try to stop that bleeding. Some of the boys will come out to get you later. I've got to try to stop that crazy female."

Another rifle shot from the direction of the river captured Sam's attention. It was followed by several shots close together. He urged his horse forward praying that his daughter was not getting careless in her deadly game.

Bonny Kate found a good crossing of the Nolichucky and swam the horses across. She guided the horses up a dry wash that ascended a bluff on the north side of the river that commanded a view of the crossing. A game trail followed the trend of the bluff and she planned that as her escape route. She tied the horses securely out of sight and crept to the crest of the hill. She primed her rifle and waited.

Bonny Kate counted eleven outlaws when they emerged warily from the cane and waded into the cold river. She stopped her first target in midstream, and he fell into the rapids losing his rifle. She quickly reloaded beneath the crest of the hill, and she moved to a new position. When she peered around a tree trunk, she saw two men trying to help the wounded man up the bank, and she wounded another just above the right knee. Her pursuers took refuge in the cane where she couldn't see them. She reloaded and wondered if any of the bandits had made it across the river.

"Hey you, girl!" shouted one of the men. "You better give up now and give us those horses. We'll let you go free if you do. What do you say?" She scanned the cane trying to locate the position of the speaker. She knew they were trying to locate her too. She didn't answer and didn't move a muscle. After some time of silent waiting, one of the Tories parted the cane and stepped out presenting her a target. She tagged him in the knee and ducked the wild shots that whistled all around her in response. She ran for the horses while the Tories reloaded and got the herd moving again. While in the saddle, she reloaded her rifle and breathed a prayer of thanksgiving for another successful encounter with some very desperate men.

Sam Sherrill counted eight men running single file along the top of the bluff on the opposite side of the Nolichucky. He welcomed that sight as a sign that Bonny Kate was still in control of the game. He went looking for the wounded men she'd left in her wake. Sam got the drop on the three men washing their wounds beside the river. He disarmed them and tossed their rifles into the deepest channel of the Nolichucky. He entertained them with stories about Ute Perkins, king of the horse thieves, and his deranged accomplice, the Princess of Pain. He warned them not to mess with old man Sherrill and his forty thieves or they would suffer the direst consequences.

"The Princess is in a generous mood today," Sam explained. "You all have the right knee wound. She could just as easily have hit you between the eyes like she usually does."

"We'll get even with her," threatened one man.

"I'd let it drop, friend," Sam advised. "You're lucky to be alive. Take your good fortune and go back where you came from. This territory belongs to the Perkins gang."

"Who are you in all this?" another man asked.

"I'm just the cleanup man," Sam answered. "I usually bury the dead ones, but like I said before, the Princess is in a generous mood today."

Sam Sherrill mounted his horse and rode off following the south bank of the Nolichucky. He figured he'd keep the river between him and the remaining bandits and maybe even overtake them. The game trail following the south side of the river ascended steeply to a hill four times the height of the sixty-foot bluff Bonny Kate had defended at the crossing of the river. Sam had a spectacular view of the river and the floodplain on the river's north side where he could see the Tory outlaws pursuing their stolen horses. Bonny Kate was nowhere to be seen from his lofty vantage point. He pressed forward with the idea that if he could get close enough to the bandits, he might be able to help thin their numbers. Another fifteen minutes of ridge riding the game trail brought him to an overlook where the Nolichucky twisted suddenly north to make a horseshoe bend. The overlook commanded a crossing at the turn of the river, creating a perfect place for an ambush. Sam found the stolen horses hidden behind the crest of the hill.

"Bonny Kate," he called in a hushed voice as he scanned the boulders at the crest of the hill. Her head popped up.

"Over here, Papa," she called, and then she ducked down again. Sam climbed up to join her and approved of her choice of spots.

"I saw you when you came down the ridge," she greeted him. "I'm so glad to see you. I've had a very lonely and stressful day. These fellows have called threats and insults at me like you wouldn't believe. They're starting to make me mad."

"Well, let's put a stop to their insolence right now." Sam pulled out a brass telescope he had gained recently in a trade with Mr. Brown and extended it to focus on the crossing of the river.

"What's that?" she asked.

"It's a telescope like the artillery officers use to view distant targets," he explained. He showed her how to use it.

"Where did you get it?" she asked.

"Mr. Brown," Sam replied. "He likes these new fangled things."

"Oh, there they come following my trail, step for step."

They prepared their rifles and aimed as the outlaws emerged from the cane and stepped out on the sand bar at the river crossing.

"Take the lead, man," Sam directed. "I'll take the second."

Father and daughter squeezed their triggers at almost the same time and two bad men buckled on the sand. The six others scampered back into the cane. Sam watched them through the telescope. It was clear the men had no idea where the shots had come from.

"We have them pinned down now," Sam observed.

"I see you didn't kill your fellow," she whispered.

"I'm playing along with your game," he answered. "I don't know why you chose to do it this way. Judge Carter is just going to hang them anyway once Captain Robert Sevier catches them."

"I wasn't sure they were the same fellows that robbed Mr. McAneny," she explained.

"I'm pretty sure they are the same ones," Sam told her. "One of them admitted that they were on their way to rob me."

"Thank you, Papa." She breathed a sigh of relief. "I've been feeling bad about this all day, until now."

The wounded men on the sand bar crawled back into the cane and hid with the others. Using his telescope, Sam studied the problem of persuading the eight men to give up the fight.

"Bonny Kate, I see one fellow hiding there and I want you to place a shot where I tell you," her father directed. She aimed her rifle at the riverbank. "Do you see that patch of cane behind the birch tree?"

"Yes, sir," she replied.

"There's a fellow with a rifle in there just behind the first fork on the right side of the birch. Place your shot right in the fork, and you should hit something."

The shot rang out and a man screamed in pain from his place of concealment; there was a lot of cursing, and Bonny Kate hoped it was a wound the poor man could recover from.

"Hold your fire!" shouted the injured man's companion. "We want to parley!"

"I don't think we can trust them, Papa," advised the Princess of Pain. Sam let a period of silence pass.

"Who's up there?" the voice persisted.

"Blackbeard the Pirate," Sam roared in his deepest most commanding voice. He grinned at Bonny Kate.

A white rag was hoisted on one of the men's rifles and waved vigorously above the cane. "Parley," the voice pleaded.

"Surrender or die," boomed Blackbeard the Pirate.

"We surrender!" the answer came.

"Papa, there's more men coming over here on the right," Bonny Kate warned.

Sam swung his telescope in the direction she pointed and identified Captain Robert Sevier and his rangers riding in from upriver.

"It's Sevier's company!" he told her. "Run down there and explain what's happening."

"Yes, sir." Bonny Kate ran to get a horse and rode down the hill to greet the rangers.

"Drop your rifles in the river and surrender to the horsemen!" Blackbeard ordered. The outlaws moved to carry out the terms of their surrender and the capture of the Tory horse thieves was accomplished without additional bloodshed.

Sevier's rangers covered the distances rapidly, collecting all the wounded Tories strewn across the landscape by the Princess of Pain. They were gathered in to Fort Williams where their wounds could be properly treated. Bonny Kate accompanied the company horse doctor in his rounds to care for the wounded. His name was James Cozby, and he was a fun-loving sort of fellow who liked to joke around with his patients. She introduced herself as Bonny Kate and was immediately attracted to him.

"Strange business this is to have all these wounds so similar," Dr. Cozby observed.

"A woman shot me from ambush," one of the Tories claimed. "She stole our horses, and she called herself the Princess of Pain, but she was the devil, I tell you."

"Did you get a look at her?" the doctor asked.

"Never got close enough," the Tory said. "But the old man said she was a member of the Ute Perkins gang."

"Ute Perkins?" marveled Dr. Cozby. "I thought he was dead."

"Not hardly," insisted the Tory. "You soldier boys have your work cut out for you in this territory with Ute Perkins on the loose. And watch out for Blackbeard the Pirate!"

"Oh, I certainly will." The doctor turned to his pretty assistant. "I'm new to these parts, Bonny Kate," Dr. Cozby admitted. "What can you tell me about these wild stories of Ute Perkins, the Princess of Pain, and Blackbeard?"

Bonny Kate shrugged. "It sounds like an overactive imagination to me. I've heard stories about Ute Perkins from my childhood, but before today, I've never heard of the Princess of Pain. As for Blackbeard, I thought he was dead."

"Not hardly," enjoined the Tory.

Dr. Cozby considered the young woman and was taken with her engaging smile and sparkling eyes. He watched her all evening as she assisted with cooking for the soldiers and cleaning up afterward. The end of the evening found her reclining on a blanket beside a cozy fire in the blockhouse. Sam Sherrill and Robert Sevier sat nearby and caught up on all the news of the overmountain community. Bonny Kate fell asleep in the warm glow of the fire, and Sam covered her with a blanket.

"She's had a very busy day," Sam explained.

"I would certainly agree." Captain Sevier laughed.

In the morning, a cold wind from the northwest made snow likely. Nevertheless, Sam and Bonny Kate set out on horseback hoping to arrive at Stony Creek before dark to relieve the family of terrible anxiety about their well-being.

"Father," Bonny Kate inquired. "Why were those Tories talking about Ute Perkins last night?"

"He was a very important figure in his day," Sam answered. "He helped make horse thieving the occupation that it is today with his innovations and marketing skills!"

"I thought we were to never mention Cousin Ute to anyone outside the family."

"Yes, that's a rule your mother and I insist on."

"Then why did you?" she asked.

"My dear," Sam explained. "Yesterday's emergency presented many challenges for you and me. You were forced to shoot a human being for the first time in your life. How did that make you feel?"

"I felt terrible," she admitted, "sad and sick all at the same time."

"That's the way I felt when I found myself telling those Tories that our lands were protected by the greatest horse thief there ever was," he explained. "I was hoping they would show us a little respect and avoid Daisy Fields in the future."

Bonny Kate laughed. "Good idea!"

"Listen," Sam warned. "For our own good at home, let's not tell anyone what happened yesterday. We can talk about taking the horses from the Tories and turning over the gang to Captain Sevier, but the business of you shooting people and the whole Ute Perkins thing, we need to keep that to ourselves. Understand?"

"Yes, sir," she promised.

The visit to Stony Creek was short but happy. Sarah glowed in her expectation of her ninth child, and the women talked for two days of every important thing under the sun while the snow blew, drifted, glistened, and melted. After a week, the Sherrills returned to Daisy Fields to wait through many lonely but active days for the coming of spring.

Chapter 23

Liberty and Justice for All

One day in February 1778, before the convening of the Washington County Court, Sheriff Valentine Sevier called upon the Sherrills at their Daisy Fields home. He brought along a company of thirty dragoons, one of the new light horse companies that John Sevier had organized to patrol the county and prevent outbreaks of violence from Indians and Tories. Sheriff Sevier looked a lot like his elder brother John, but heavier and less graceful. He had a keen intelligence about the world and tended to judge men according to their darker motives. His personality was well suited for the office of sheriff. He was suspicious of strangers and well acquainted with the flaws common to the human condition. He had been the first of his family to move to the Watauga territory and had built a successful cattle business. His wife Naomi, known to family and close friends as Amy, brought a delightful balance to her husband's gravity. She was light and cheerful, never complaining and was admired as a hardworking woman who could make cattle farming pay handsomely.

Sheriff Sevier was investigating reports or perhaps rumors of organized gangs of horse thieves or land pirates operating on the lower Nolichucky. When he arrived at Daisy Fields, he found a neat well-ordered cabin, a completed horse barn, some recently cleared pastureland, and in his judgment the beginnings of a successful horse-breeding operation. The two elder sons of Sam Sherrill were out making money with their Conestoga freight wagon. The younger sons were across the river, clearing land on Big Limestone Creek for Sister Susan's husband Leroy Taylor. Leroy was preparing his land for a large corn crop that year. Sam Sherrill and his daughter Bonny Kate were working around the horse barn, while Mary and daughter Mary Jane were up at the house cooking, cleaning, and sewing. Pioneer families had to be ready for anything. You never could tell when someone might drop by for a visit. And you never knew whether they were coming for a friendly, neighborly visit, or coming to do the family harm. Sam

Sherrill had seen the horsemen when they first emerged from the forest on the north side of the Nolichucky and recognized the sheriff using his telescope and assumed they were in for a friendly visit.

The entire company dismounted when they arrived at Daisy Fields and most of the men went up to visit with Mrs. Sherrill and Mary Jane. The Sheriff walked over to the horse barn to greet Sam.

"Hello, Val." Sam smiled.

"Good morning, Mr. Sherrill. Hello, Miss Bonny Kate," he tipped his hat.

"Good morning, Mr. Sevier." She curtsied.

"I have a matter of some gravity to discuss with you, Mr. Sherrill," The Sheriff began. Bonny Kate read the seriousness of his approach and guessed she ought to excuse herself.

"I'll just go help Mama entertain. She was baking some apple pies this morning, so you picked a good day to visit," Bonny Kate said.

"No, Miss Sherrill, you should stay here," ordered the lawman. "Some of this concerns you." She became concerned at that moment.

"Mr. Sherrill, I'm here on official business of the court inquiring about some reports we have received about suspicious activities."

"You have my attention, sir," Sam responded.

"Last December my brother captured a gang of Tories who had robbed and threatened Mr. McAneny and his family. Robert reported that you and your daughter were involved in the apprehension of those outlaws, is that correct?"

"Yes, sir. Mr. Brown warned us that the gang was out to steal our horses," Sam explained. "Bonny Kate discovered their approach, and we prevented them from carrying out their mischief. Whatever happened to those fellows?"

"There were outstanding warrants for their arrest from the court in Morganton, so we took them back east," Val said. "But they made certain statements that implicated you in ill practices of harboring and abetting disorderly persons who are prejudicial and inimical to the common cause of liberty and frequently disturbing our public tranquility in general."

Bonny Kate laughed at the high-sounding words, but the sheriff did not share her amusement, and neither did her father. He looked at her in all seriousness.

"Those are the words of the court," Val informed them. "The Committee of Safety has sent me to investigate the allegations, and if probable cause can be found, I am authorized to arrest both you and your daughter and any other persons that may be involved."

Sam knew he was in serious trouble and hoped Bonny Kate would have sense enough to keep her mouth shut and let him do the talking. "Sheriff, I believe I can clear up those misunderstandings, but I suppose you have prepared some questions for me."

"Yes," Val proceeded. "First, there is the matter of the forty thieves. It does not appear to me that you are harboring a gang of forty thieves."

"You are correct," Sam assured him. "There never was, and I hope there will never be any gang of forty thieves at Daisy Fields. I made up that story and told it to several of the outlaws to frighten them away from ever attacking my farm again."

"When did you have the opportunity to tell that to the outlaws?" Val wanted to know.

"Well, sir, Bonny Kate discovered them some distance from the house and watched them from a hiding place in the canebrake. When they left their horses to attack us on foot, she took their horses and diverted their attention away from their intended mischief. I heard the shooting that resulted and followed the action up the valley. I found several outlaws wounded and left behind. It was those men that I told about the forty thieves."

"So you made up the forty thieves," Val confirmed.

"It was not my original idea, but the outlaws apparently accepted it."

"They certainly did," Val agreed. "My next concern is your apparent connection to the legendary horse thief Ute Perkins. Would you be willing to tell me what you know about him?"

"I told the outlaws that Daisy Fields is his hideout and headquarters. Once again I was trying to scare them away. If they have no respect for the law, then perhaps they might have some respect for the greatest horse thief who ever lived."

Val laughed. "You can't explain this one away so easily, Mr. Sherrill. I grew up in Augusta County and was able to ask some men who remember the Ute Perkins connection to the Sherrill family."

Bonny Kate looked at her father in shock, and the sheriff noticed, then he continued. "Charles Robertson suggested that you yourself might be Ute Perkins living under an assumed name." Sam laughed despite the seriousness of the charge.

"It's a lie!" Bonny Kate defended her family's honor.

"It wouldn't be the first lie told around here, Miss Sherrill!" the sheriff said. "Or should I call you Miss Perkins?"

"This is ridiculous!" she declared.

"I can explain," Sam said calmly. "I'm willing to tell the whole story."

"Good, you can tell it to the Committee of Safety," the sheriff said. "Get your coat, Mr. Sherrill. You are coming with me."

"No, this is outrageous!" Bonny Kate exploded. "Sam Sherrill is the best friend of Colonel John Sevier. You can't treat him like a common criminal!"

"My brother John makes friends easily and trusts people too readily," Val stated. "He's the county clerk, an officer of the court, and therefore not qualified to act as a character witness."

"These charges are arbitrary and completely unfounded," she declared. "Colonel Sevier will not allow such a miscarriage of justice to go forward."

"Miss Perkins—"

"Don't call me that," she snapped. "You'll never prove your case!"

"Miss Sherrill," Val continued. "The law makes no allowance for family connections, wealth, or privilege of office. Yesterday, I had to arrest my own brother on assault charges. Do you suppose that I'm enjoying my duties as sheriff?"

"Which brother?" she asked.

"Robert," he replied. "Elijah Robertson accused him of assault, just because the two of them had a little scuffle over some disagreement."

"I never imagined that law and order could be so messy!" she empathized.

"Bonny Kate," Sam said. "Tell your mother to gather some things for my trip to county court."

"Yes, sir," she obeyed sadly. She started for the house.

"Oh, Miss Sherrill, could you tell Captain Walton it's time to go?" Val requested.

"Yes, sir."

She walked slowly to the cabin.

"The other allegations are so ridiculous they are not worth pursuing, Mr. Sherrill," Val said. "The Tories claimed you were Blackbeard the Pirate, and your accomplice was a deranged killer known as the Princess of Pain."

"Imagine that, why don't you?" Sam marveled. "That is ridiculous! It's true my little princess has caused me considerable pain, but no one can accuse her of being a deranged killer."

Captain Walton appeared on the porch a few minutes later and called out to the sheriff, "Hey, Val, what's the hurry? Mrs. Sherrill has the best hot apple pie in the world!"

"Jesse, tell the boys it's time to go," Val told him. "The committee is waiting for us at Charles Robertson's at noon today. Let's move!"

The Sherrill women traveled along with the sheriff, his suspect, and his horsemen once the men had eaten their fill of hot apple pie. Mary Sherrill regretted her hospitality when she discovered the nature of the business that had brought the sheriff out to Daisy Fields. Mary Jane complained of the cold wind and longed for the fireside at Daisy Fields. Her mother had plenty of fire in her temper to keep her from feeling the cold. She roundly scolded Bonny Kate.

"None of this would have happened if you hadn't taken the law into your own hands the day those Tories showed up," Mary charged. "You worried me terribly at the time, and now you have brought down this trouble on your poor innocent father!"

"I'm truly ashamed of myself, Mother," she replied. "I thought that I could keep those horrible men from attacking our house, so that's what I did. I worked all day to take the fight out of them and discourage them at every turn until they surrendered. I turned them over to Robert Sevier's rangers without loss of life, never knowing the shame and humiliation that would result from trying to do the right thing."

"Don't sass me with that haughty attitude!" Mary warned.

"Now, Mary," Sam tried to settle her down. "Let's not be unkind. I take full responsibility for this episode. I broke my own rule about never mentioning my kinship to cousin Ute. I broke the rule, and this is the result. I'll clear up this misunderstanding when I present my case."

"I'll testify!" Mary offered. "There is no way Sam Sherrill and Ute Perkins are one and the same. I married this man when he was but a lad of twenty; and in thirty-two years of marriage, I have never let him out of my sight long enough for him to pursue a single skirt, let alone a life of crime. Oh, there was the year he rode with Hugh Waddell's rangers in the French and Indian War, but the Waddells all know him and will vouch for his useful service! I'll swear that on a stack of Bibles he never took anything that wasn't his. We have the bill of sale and receipt of payment on every horse he's ever owned!"

"Thank you for the excellent testimony, Mrs. Sherrill," Val said. "But the law does not admit the testimony of a wife on behalf of her own husband."

"If the law has no use for the gospel truth, then I have very little use for the law!" she declared.

Jesse Walton spoke up, "You don't need the law, Mrs. Sherrill. Just bake the judge one of your hot apple pies, and you'll win the case every time!" The men laughed.

Mary smiled and returned the compliment. "Thank you, Captain Walton. Please convey my compliments to your wife. No woman alive can match her blackberry cobbler!"

John Sevier looked better than ever to Bonny Kate when she saw him that afternoon with the Committee of Safety at Charles Robertson's house. It was worth the trip just to see the man, even under such dire circumstances. She wanted to speak with him and seek his advice about her father's predicament, but there was no opportunity. The men talked business in their tight little clusters where no woman was welcomed. No formal charges had been entered against her father yet, so they waited outside in the cold for the Committee of Safety to call Sam Sherrill's case.

Kesiah Robertson Sevier found Mrs. Sherrill and her daughters and invited them to join the other ladies at the cookhouse. A cheerful fire burned in the fireplace of the warm cozy cookhouse. Susannah Robertson, Kesiah's mother greeted the Sherrills.

"This is an unexpected pleasure." Susannah smiled.

"Unexpected, yes," Mary replied, "but hardly a pleasure."

"I'm sorry to hear that Mrs. Sherrill," Susannah empathized. "I suppose the men have their reasons for trying to sort things out in court, but it does create inconveniences for us ladies. What is the charge against Mr. Sherrill?"

"They suspect him of being Ute Perkins, the horse thief."

"Oh, that's impossible!" Susannah laughed. "What a waste of time for the court!"

"I know," Mary agreed.

"What kind of trouble is Robert Sevier in?" Bonny Kate asked Kesiah.

"He punched Elijah Robertson, and they are calling it assault," Kesiah answered. "I'm sure cousin Elijah was so drunk; he never felt it and probably doesn't remember it, but Waightstill Avery was there to see it and offered to take the case. It's just lawyers looking for work."

"Another waste of time for the court," Bonny Kate decided.

"What is this world coming to?" Mary said sadly. "I remember my own experience with a court and it's nothing but bitter memories."

"You can't leave that one laying on the table, Mrs. Sherrill," Susannah prompted. "Tell us the rest of the story."

"I was born in Belfast. My sister Polly and I lost our mother as very young girls. Father was a well-to-do merchant who gave us a good education and a strong connection to the Presbyterian Church. When I was thirteen, my father's political leanings got him in trouble with the law. The experience broke his health, consumed his wealth, and he died leaving us orphans. A court confiscated and disposed of Father's estate, with no explanation or justification to his two frightened dispossessed daughters. We shipped out to Virginia to live with our uncle John in Augusta County. So you see I have very little trust in the workings of a court of law."

"That's a sad story, Mrs. Sherrill," Susannah empathized. "I hope your present trouble can be easily resolved."

"Robert's trouble too," Bonny Kate added.

"Thanks, Bonny Kate. I don't need another worry just know," Kesiah shared. "I'm expecting a baby."

"Kesiah, that's wonderful!" Bonny Kate exclaimed.

"Congratulations, Kesiah!" Mary said. The attention pleased Kesiah, and her mother was obviously proud of her.

"If only the court can work through their problems as easily as we women do," Susannah wished.

"Perhaps it can," Mary said. "I suppose it has fallen to you, Mrs. Robertson to feed the members of the court."

"Naturally," Susannah replied. "Charles is responsible for being a good host, extending hospitality even to the criminals."

"What next?" Bonny Kate exclaimed. "Soon we shall have to extend the same hospitality to the lawyers!" The women laughed uproariously, and it did them good.

"Mrs. Robertson," Mary offered. "I should like to bake some pies. Do you have any apples?"

"Of course," Susannah replied. "I'm sure we can find whatever you need. That should put the men in a goodly humor and allow them to make wise decisions."

The matter of Samuel Sherrill came before the Committee of Safety late that afternoon, and Sam had the opportunity to tell his story.

"My father Adam Sherrill had a sister named Margery who married a man named Elisha Perkins. It was not a happy marriage. One of their sons was Ute Perkins who gained some notoriety for himself as a horse thief, escape artist, gang leader, and master of disguises. My father helped Aunt Margery to escape her violent husband, but the outlaw son came to visit his mother at my father's house at a time when the Augusta County sheriff was in hot pursuit of Ute and his gang. They arrested my father and charged him with harboring and abetting a fugitive from the law. He was fined a hundred pounds. That's when my father made the decision to quit Augusta County and move to North Carolina. I haven't seen or heard from Ute Perkins for thirty years, and I don't know what ever happened to him."

"So you are a first cousin to the notorious Ute Perkins?" Charles Robertson asked.

"Yes, sir," Sam affirmed. "I have always cautioned my family not to mention the fact. It does not look good for a legitimate horse breeder to have such family connections even though my father and the rest of the Sherrills have disowned and disassociated ourselves from him for close to thirty years."

"How is it that this matter has come before the Committee of Safety accompanied by reports that Ute Perkins is hiding out and actively pursuing his profession on the south Nolichuky?" John Sevier asked.

"Well, John, I started the rumors myself when that gang of Tory horse thieves attacked our community last December. I told the fellows we captured to never come back to the Nolichucky, because it was territory under the protection of the Ute Perkins gang. I wanted to scare them off for good."

John laughed. "That's a good reason but the wrong way to go about it, Sam. I would rather have the outlaws come to fear the Committee of Safety and stay out of our community because of our strong militia and our efficient County Court. Mister Chairman, I move that we dismiss this matter with a warning to Mr. Sherrill to stop spreading rumors of outlaw activity that does not exist."

"The motion is out of order," Judge Carter ruled. "We have no satisfaction that Mr. Sherrill and Ute Perkins are not one and the same. He admits the family connection; he's about the same age, pursues the profession of horse trading, and obviously has enjoyed great prosperity."

"Prosperity does not indicate criminal activity," John defended. "If it did, we might examine the past careers of every man on this committee. Any one of us might be Ute Perkins!"

"Don't be ridiculous, John," Judge Carter answered. "I think the committee ought to recommend this matter to the next session of the county court and bring formal charges against Samuel Sherrill alias Ute Perkins."

"The docket is too full already with a year's worth of backlog," John objected. "I know a man who knew Samuel Sherrill at the time that Ute Perkins was captured and held for several days in Augusta County. If I bring him to tomorrow's committee meeting can we dismiss the matter then without the expense of going to court?"

"Unless I hear an objection to that, I will allow it," Judge Carter agreed. "The suspect will remain in custody until tomorrow's inquest. Who's your witness, John?"

"My father, Valentine Sevier Sr.," answered John.

The Committee of Safety, the Sherrills, and the Robertsons had a delicious dinner and were treated to some hot apple pie on that cold February night. After dinner, John sat by the fire in the great room and visited with the Sherrills.

"I'm going up to Stony Creek tomorrow to fetch back my Papa. He can testify that Sam is not the same person as Ute Perkins."

"Thank you, John," Sam said. "I appreciate everything you have done to help me, especially traveling all those miles to bring back your father."

"That's what friends do." John smiled. "I was wondering if I could ask a favor of you in return."

"Ask away," Sam replied.

"Sarah will have that baby this week whether I'm there or not," John said. There was concern in his voice and sadness for missing an important date in the family experience. "I was wondering if Mrs. Sherrill and her daughters could go up to Stony Creek with me tomorrow to help Sarah with the delivery."

"Oh yes!" Bonny Kate exclaimed. "We would love to be there." Mary Jane and her mother exchanged smiles and expressed their excitement at the prospect as well. So it was that Sarah Sevier had the most loving and caring assistance with the birth of her beautiful daughter Rebecca Sevier.

Sam Sherrill was soon a free man and returned to Daisy Fields to the work he loved best. His womenfolk rejoined him two weeks later, and Sam and Bonny Kate recapped the events of the month. They considered things they might have done differently in dealing with the outlaws.

"There's a lesson for us, my girl," Sam said. "Even our best intentions are sometimes misunderstood."

"Amen," she agreed with a sigh.

The rhythm of farm life with the changing of the seasons and the harmony of the various activities that all members of a large family accomplish toward the success of the enterprise can scarcely be described. Chop wood, carry water, cook food, wash dishes, clean house, shear sheep, wash wool, card the wool, and spin the yarn. Plant flax, harvest flax, brake flax, spin linen, weave cloth, cut and sew. Plow and plant, hoe weeds, feed hogs, herd cattle, milk cows, help birth, run horses, care for flocks, feed chickens, collect eggs. Harvest time; busy time; mend clothes; pick peas; dry beans; crib corn; pick apples, peaches, cherries, plums, pears; bake pies; make preserves; cut tobacco. Render tallow, make candles, make lye soap, catch fish, clean fish, fry fish, dig potatoes, string beans, snap beans, shell peas, pick watermelons, pick pumpkins, collect maple sap, boil down syrup, find honey tree, collect honeycomb. There's so much to do and only half done. Brush horses, shoot skunk, wash dog, sharpen ax, make wooden tools, make wooden toys, split rails, build fences, hunt rabbits, hunt turkey, hunt pheasant, hunt deer, skin game, tan hides, grind corn, kill hog, make sausage, dress hams, sweep cabin, shovel manure, plant cabbage, sing praises, listen to the word of God, pray long and hard. That should do it for one week! Let's get up the next day and start it all again.

The John and Sarah Sevier family finally moved to the Nolichucky in April and Sarah settled her big family into the small cabin that Mr. Brown once lived in all alone, or perhaps not as much alone as the story goes. Plum Grove house was not finished. It wasn't even started, because John had been so busy building a community.

It was the community that finally gathered to help build the colonel's new house. In a month, Sarah had a fine home where Fort Williams had once stood. Bonny Kate could travel from Daisy Fields to Plum Grove in less than half an hour if she took the southern route that did not require a river crossing until the trail came up to Sevier's Ford, beside the old Brown cabin.

Colonel Sevier was allowed to stay home more during the year 1778. Other men were elected to serve in the State Assembly, and the war did not plague the southern states as it did the northern states. The frontier was disturbed more often by the Tories than by Indians, but the light horse companies organized the previous winter, did a good job keeping the peace.

That summer, Mary Sherrill had a special secret to share with her daughters. It was a delicate secret for a forty-nine-year-old woman, who had a twenty-six-year-old married daughter who was still childless, a twenty-four-year-old spinster daughter who had no prospects, and an eighteen-year-old daughter in the prime of life with several good prospects.

"Girls, your father and I have a little surprise," Mary told them. "This may come as a bit of a shock to you, but I'm going to have a baby."

"Mother, are you sure?" Susan reacted.

"Yes," Mary replied. "There is no doubt."

"When will it come?" Bonny Kate asked.

"In the early spring." Mary smiled.

"How did it happen?" asked a shocked Mary Jane.

"I'm not answering that!" Mary exclaimed

"Mary Jane!" Bonny Kate admonished her. "You shouldn't ask such a thing."

"How am I going to learn anything, unless I ask?"

"You watch the animals like the rest of us did." Bonny Kate laughed.

"Girls, please, don't make this more difficult for me than it already is," Mary said. "When we go to gatherings, people are going to assume I'm the baby's grandmother."

"They will think it is Susan's baby," Bonny Kate declared.

"Or Bonny Kate's," Susan returned. "Oh, Mother, what a delicious scandal we could create!"

"I'm not taking part in any make-believe scandal," Bonny Kate declared. "It's hard enough for me to deal with the genuine scandals of my life!"

Harvest came and another community gathering was celebrated, this time at Plum Grove. Mary Jane and Bonny Kate were once again put on display in their finest. Bonny Kate won more races and the turkey shoot but struggled to find the right partner for the dance contest. The dance of life seemed to be passing her by, so she prayed day after day for divine guidance. The Spirit was always there saying "In time my child, in the fullness of time!"

Chapter 24

Never a Dull Moment

In March of 1779, Bonny Kate Sherrill led a string of a half dozen horses from Daisy Fields to Plum Grove. The horses were trained and ready for Colonel Sevier's militia company. She left the horses in the colonel's corral as she had so many times before when making deliveries and then walked her own horse up to the house. She found Sarah sitting at her small desk on the porch reading one of John's letters.

"Hello, Bonny Kate," Sarah said without lifting her eyes from the page.

"Hello, Sarah. I brought six more horses that Colonel Sevier ordered for the militia. Is he here?"

"Not yet," Sarah said, putting down the letter. "He's due home any day from Fort Patrick Henry. Something big is about to happen, but nobody is allowed to say what it is."

"Is it something to do with the war?" Bonny Kate asked.

"No doubt," Sarah answered. "When he comes home, he'll be up in Jonesborough every day at some sort of political meeting."

"So they named the new village Jonesborough?" Bonny Kate asked. "Why didn't they name it Sevierborough?"

"As much time as he's given the project, you would think that's the least they could do." Sarah laughed. "He needs to be helping me plan the spring community gathering and the muster of the Washington County Volunteers."

"He sure is busy," Bonny Kate declared. "Papa says he's the most useful man in the whole country!"

Sarah laughed. "Oh, he's pretty handy when you can get on his docket, but he's away so much his own children hardly know him."

"Has he seen how well little Becky can walk?"

"Not yet," Sarah said sadly. "He's missed so many precious moments, the poor man!"

"He's not to be envied, that's for sure," Bonny Kate empathized. "And what about you, Sarah? You're left alone so much, with all these small children. How do you bear the weeks of separation?"

Sarah smiled dreamily. "He writes such beautiful letters, and then those heavenly homecomings. Mmm . . ."

Bonny Kate blushed and regretted soliciting such an intimate response. She quickly changed the subject. "It's mighty quiet around here. Are the children napping?"

"Only little Becky," Sarah replied. "Johnny and Betsy took the rest of them down to wade in the river. It's the first pretty day of spring. I thought they would all enjoy an outing."

Betsy Sevier came running up the hill from the river. Her golden hair was loose and flying. "Mama, Mama, help! Dicky is drowning. He slipped and fell!"

"Oh my goodness!" Sarah reacted. She jumped out of her chair and raced toward the river following Betsy. Bonny Kate sprang to her horse and quickly outpaced them.

The Nolichucky River was high and rough from the spring melt in the mountains. The turbulent white waters were a spectacle to behold, but close observation could be fatal to overadventurous children. When Bonny Kate arrived at the river's edge, she raced down the river trail and caught up with the other Sevier children where they helplessly watched four-year-old Dicky struggling to keep his head above water. He was caught in a snag of branches of a fallen tree in the middle of the river.

"Hold on, Dicky," Bonny Kate shouted over the roar of the rapids. "I'm coming to get you!"

Bonny Kate threw a lasso over her horse's head, slipped off his back, and left him standing on the bank of the river. She charged into the water tying the end of the coiled rope around her ribcage as she went. She fought her way through the swift current. The children watched anxiously as Bonny Kate half-waded, half-swam against the white water.

Little Dicky was terrified. "I can't hold on!"

"Don't go anywhere! You stay right there!" she shouted, dodging a large piece of driftwood in the channel. In the deepest part of the channel, she swam furiously against the current. On the bank behind her, Johnny waded out to take the horse's reins to steady him. Bonny Kate reached the snag downstream of Dicky and found a boulder that afforded her a place to gain her footing.

"Can you move toward me?" she shouted.

"No, my foot is caught!" the poor little fellow answered.

Bonny Kate entered the branches of the snag fighting her way to where she could reach Dicky. She dove below the surging waters to feel for his trapped foot and found it snared in a web of crisscrossed branches. She pulled violently to break away the submerged branches that held his little ankle. Suddenly he was free. His body slammed into her, and she lost her footing but her arms held fast to the precious little boy. Together they were swept back into the swift channel. While she held his head up, she quickly looped the rope around them both as they tumbled through the rough water. The rope tightened as Johnny reeled them in from the bank of the river. Johnny had help from the other children and soon they were dragged into the shallows at the river's edge. Sarah charged into the water and picked up little Dicky as Betsy and Johnny helped Bonny Kate to her feet. They climbed the bank and breathless Bonny Kate collapsed on the grass.

"Oh, darling, are you all right?" Sarah cried, clutching her littlest boy tightly.

"Yes, ma'am." He shivered. "I was scared until Miss Bonny Kate came. After that it was fun."

"Well, I was scared the whole time!" Bonny Kate declared, also shivering from the shock of the cold water.

"Let's go to the house and get everyone dried out," Sarah directed. "You'll feel much better sitting in front of a good warm fire."

As they made their way up the hill to the house, Bonny Kate let little Dicky sit up in the saddle of her tall horse. He felt a special thrill at the honor. "That's for being such a brave boy," she told him.

"It was the hand of Providence that led you here today, Bonny Kate!" Sarah declared.

"Oh, I think you would have saved him if I hadn't been here," Bonny Kate replied modestly.

"I would have died trying," Sarah stated seriously. "You see, Bonny Kate, I have never been able to swim."

"Oh, don't be so dramatic," Bonny Kate tried to lighten the moment.

"You saved two lives today, possibly three," Sarah told her.

"Three?" Bonny Kate asked.

"Yes, I want another baby, if I can get my husband to stay home long enough to oblige me," Sarah announced.

Bonny Kate laughed. "There's never a dull moment at Plum Grove!"

As they approached the house, they saw two horses tied up at the porch. Dashingly handsome Colonel John Sevier came out of the house carrying little Becky. He was followed by a young man, dressed as a Quaker, in somber clothing and a broad brimmed hat. Bonny Kate had seen many Quakers back in North Carolina.

"Sarah, honey, you gave me quite a scare," John said. "I come home to a deserted house, except for little Becky here, and can't tell if it was Indians or Tories that carried y'all off!"

"I'm sorry, John," she said as she slid into his embrace. A long kiss followed, and the young Quaker fellow smiled at Bonny Kate, eyeing curiously the wet hair and clothes.

"Where was everybody?" John asked.

"Down at the river, Father," answered Johnny.

"Hello, Miss Bonny Kate," the colonel acknowledged the girl. "What happened to you?"

"I went fishing, the hard way," she said wryly.

John laughed. "Catch anything?"

"She caught me," Dicky declared honestly. "And she saved me from drowning!"

The colonel got serious in a heartbeat. "She did?"

"Yes, sir, and it was fun!" the child declared.

John looked to Sarah for an explanation, "How did it happen?"

"I let them go wading and Dicky slipped and fell into the current," she told her husband. "Bonny Kate had just arrived for a visit when we heard the cries. She rode down there and saved him. We were so blessed she came along when she did!"

John reached up, took Dicky off the horse, and held his son close. He turned to his neighbor, a girl he had known and admired for almost three years. "Thank you, Bonny Kate! And thank the Lord for great rescues."

"Amen!" the Quaker lad exclaimed. Sarah and Bonny Kate looked at the newcomer with curiosity.

"Oh, Sarah, this is Mr. Thomas Embree, a new business partner of mine," John announced. "He's going to help us build the mill."

"How do you do, Mr. Embree?" Sarah greeted him.

"Very well, thank you, ma'am," Thomas replied.

"Mr. Embree," Sarah continued the introductions. "I'd like to introduce our good friend and neighbor, Miss Bonny Kate Sherrill."

"Miss Sherrill, it is a pleasure to meet you." The young man took off his hat in a sweeping motion and politely bowed.

Bonny Kate smiled and curtsied, the best she could manage in her drenched clothing. "Likewise, sir."

Sarah began immediately to deepen the relationship. "Mr. Embree, my husband has always been fascinated with water mills. As a lad, he slipped and fell into a mill race and would have been crushed under the wheel if the miller's daughter hadn't pulled him to safety."

"I've never heard that story," Bonny Kate marveled. "Mr. Sevier saved me from certain death when he pulled me to safety over the wall at Watauga Fort the morning the Indians attacked."

"And today Bonny Kate pulled little Dicky to safety from the raging river!" Sarah declared.

"That's quite a chain of rescues, don't you think?" John said.

"It's the hand of Providence!" Sarah affirmed.

"The hand of Providence, indeed!" agreed Mr. Embree.

"Mr. Embree, I want Mr. Sevier to show you the guest quarters while I prepare our supper. John dear, the room in the old blockhouse would suit Mr. Embree in grand style."

"What about the guest cabin?" John suggested.

"No, dear, the guest cabin has been reserved for someone else," Sarah winked at him. "Bonny Kate, won't you join us for dinner?"

"Thank you, Mrs. Sevier." She smiled. "I'd enjoy that, but my clothes are soaked."

"No excuses now," Sarah insisted. "Come change into something of mine." She looked at the youthful good looks and charming politeness of Mr. Thomas Embree and then at Bonny Kate. "I'm thinking of something very special. We'll get you all fixed up for the evening!" She prodded the bedraggled Bonny Kate into the cabin.

Inside the cabin where the men could not hear them, Bonny Kate expressed her reservations. "Sarah, aren't you rushing this thing a little? I don't want to appear too obvious."

"Don't question an expert, my dear," Sarah said. "I saw interest."

"I looked like something the cat dragged in, all soaking wet." She laughed.

"He could see your figure mighty clearly, and I think he liked what he saw."

"Oh." She realized the water had made her clothing cling in awkward embarrassing places. She had already appeared too obvious. She wondered if both men had noticed. Had they been staring?

"Get out of those wet things, right now!" Sarah ordered as she helped little Dicky get changed into dry clothes. "Bonny Kate Sherrill, I'm going to get you matched up and married off if it's the last thing I ever do," Sarah promised, and she meant it.

Sarah was an excellent hostess, who could manage and direct conversation so as to feature her guests in the most favorable light. The soft spring air and a full-rising moon over the eastern mountains cooperated to make a remarkably memorable evening. After dinner, Bonny Kate and Thomas Embree stepped out on the porch.

"I love the fragrance of spring night air. It reminds me of the nights in Watauga Fort, when we sat up all hours with the night watch," she reminisced.

"I heard it was dreadful," Mr. Embree empathized, "helplessly surrounded by hostile Indians . . ."

"It was delightful," she continued. "Captain Sevier and Captain Robertson told every funny story they ever knew to keep our spirits up. We laughed and laughed."

"Out of food, out of ammunition," Mr. Embree marveled. "You might have easily despaired."

"How I would love to do that all over again . . ."

"With never a hope of rescue from the civilized world!" he exclaimed.

"What wonderful feelings we shared!"

"Day after day the never-ending threat of disease, starvation, and death stalked every man woman and child."

"How I miss that!"

"Miss Sherrill, you are certainly different from other women."

"I am?"

"Oh yes," he affirmed. "You speak as though you enjoyed openly courting danger, ignoring disaster, and laughing in the face of death! What sort of life are you living?"

"Actually, except for a few remarkable events, my life has been rather dull," she admitted. "It's just life on the farm. How long will you be staying in these parts, Mr. Embree?"

"Colonel Sevier has several projects in mind," he informed her. "First, we'll build a saw mill, then a gristmill, a powder mill, and maybe even a lead mine. He wants me to look at his property to see what metals are there."

"Tell me, Mr. Embree, where would you locate a mill on the Nolichucky?" she asked.

"The Nolichucky is too big and prone to flooding. I recommended the creek north of here closer to the new town of Jonesborough. Once a mill and a store are established, a thriving community will spring up with nice houses, churches, schools, and a forge. How would you like living in a town like that?"

"Not much!" she said. "I've got to have room to run, feel the freedom of the open meadows, and enjoy the cool green freshness of the deep forest. I love hunting and farming too much to ever be a town girl."

"Don't you ever get lonely?"

"Not with family and neighbors," she replied. "My goodness, a week doesn't go by without some kind of visit or even a big gathering! Colonel and Mrs. Sevier host the biggest and best gatherings. In fact, the next one is just a month or two away. Everyone is invited."

"I shall most definitely be there," Mr. Embree promised.

"Good." She smiled.

"Mrs. Sevier asked me to see you home. Which way do we go?"

"The best way to enjoy the moonlight is through the back pasture," she advised. The cabin door opened and out stepped Sarah leading John by the hand.

"Oh, are you still here?" Sarah seemed surprised. She and John had cleaned up the great room at Plum Grove and put the children to bed.

"Yes, ma'am," Bonny Kate replied. "I could stay a little longer and visit, but my folks will miss me and likely send out a search party."

"Yes, it's time you were getting on home." Sarah grinned. "John and I were just going to take a stroll before bed. We have a lot of catching up to do."

"I enjoyed the dinner and thanks so much for having me," Bonny Kate said.

Sarah hugged her. "Thanks for being here today! Have a wonderful ride home." Bonny Kate and Mr. Embree walked toward the horses and were soon saddled up and on their way down the hill to the ford.

John turned to Sarah. "Do you think she'll be all right alone with Mr. Embree?"

"John, I never worry about a girl who packs a rifle, a tomahawk, and a bullwhip everywhere she goes."

"I don't know much about Mr. Embree yet, except that he's very adept at building things."

"Let's hope he knows how to build a relationship," Sarah giggled.

When Bonny Kate and her escort arrived on the opposite side of the river and ascended the hill, she looked over her shoulder and what she saw made her stop and turn her horse around. In the light of the moon, she saw Sarah and John, not strolling, but running down the hill to the river. He swept her up in his arms and waded across the shallow ford. He set her safely on the other side, and they ran up the bank to their guest cabin, where Mr. Brown once lived "alone" when he first came to the territory. They entered the cabin and closed the door.

"Is that what they call their guesthouse?" asked Mr. Embree.

"Yes." Bonny Kate laughed, somewhat embarrassed by what she was thinking.

"What do you suppose they will do in there?" He grinned impishly.

"I believe Sarah was trying to oblige him to schedule some family time on his docket," she replied with a smile.

"Mighty nice folks, the Seviers," Thomas observed. "I will truly enjoy working for them to get their businesses started."

"Yes, I've never had a better friend than Sarah Sevier," Bonny Kate said turning her horse back onto the trail.

By the end of March, the soldiers rode west to rendezvous at Big Creek. Colonel Sevier called out all the militia including Bonny Kate's brothers Junior and Adam. Leroy Taylor also went. It was a sixty-day enlistment, so Sarah was right, something big was happening. Thomas Embree, objecting to military service as a faithful Quaker, did not volunteer to go on the campaign. He stayed and progressed on Colonel Sevier's business projects. Sarah tried her best to make Bonny Kate available to Mr. Embree, but both young people stayed so busy. It was difficult to schedule.

The first week of April, Sam Sherrill got a request that the militia needed as large a group of horse wranglers as he could gather to pick up a herd of horses and return them to the homes of their owners. It was a strange request, but Sam managed to pull together old men, women and boys enough to manage the horses and set out for Big Creek. Bonny Kate was excited to be going down to camp and very curious about a military expedition that needed no horses.

Big Creek was the home of Charlotte and James Robertson, and when Charlotte saw there were women among the horse wranglers, she naturally invited the women to stay at her place for the night. Bonny Kate enjoyed the visit at Charlotte's home, but the next day, she was out early visiting the troops. Her brothers showed her around the camp on the banks of the Holston River. She soon discovered why the soldiers would not need their horses. Keelboats, barges, and canoes lined the riverbank and the men worked feverishly to prepare them for launch.

John Sevier made a special effort to find Bonny Kate and personally thank her for helping with the horses. "Quite an operation, isn't it, Miss Sherrill?" he greeted her.

"Oh, hello, Colonel Sevier" She smiled. "I've never seen so many boats in all my life! Are you in command of all this?"

"No, ma'am" he replied. "This campaign belongs to Virginia. Colonel Evan Shelby is in charge, reporting directly to Governor Henry. We are just here to help out."

"Aren't we still at peace with the Cherokees?" Bonny Kate asked.

"Yes, but the Chickamaugas still cause a lot of trouble for everybody," John explained.

"So you are going after them by boat," she judged.

"Can't tell you, it's a military secret." He laughed. "But I did want to thank you for coming to get the horses."

"How will you get back home again after floating downriver?"

"Walk," he replied. "Or maybe we can recover the horses the Indians stole from us these past many years."

Colonel Sevier showed her more of the camp and introduced her to several good-looking officers. One was Colonel John Montgomery, of Virginia. He spoke very pleasantly with her, and she enjoyed his company briefly before he excused himself to return to his duties. It wasn't long before her father called for her to report to the horse corral to begin the trip home.

"Well, Colonel Sevier," Bonny Kate said. "I have enjoyed our little visit, and I bid you adieu. Good luck on your campaign."

"Thank you, Bonny Kate," Colonel Sevier answered. "Will you deliver a letter to Sarah for me?"

"Of course I will," she replied, taking the letter he held out to her.

"Thank you." He smiled and returned to his duties around the boats of the expedition.

Bonny Kate contemplated the activities of the soldiers and their gallantry, bravery, and sacrifice so their families and neighbors could live in peace and freedom. Her admiration and attraction to such men of valor was so strong, she knew then that a relationship with the peaceful Mr. Embree would never bear fruit. The desire to be free was so strong in her that she would make the necessary sacrifices and bear the hardships of the citizen soldier's wife as Sarah was doing.

Sam Sherrill and his horse wranglers returned to Daisy Fields to pasture the horses they had collected until one by one they could be returned to the farmsteads of their owners. It would be a big job and a great responsibility for the Sherrill family, but it was another instance where the Sherrills could provide useful service according to their many and diverse talents. As Sam and his daughter arrived home, they recognized Sarah Sevier's favorite horse in their corral. Sarah came out on the porch to meet them holding a newborn baby.

"Congratulations, Mr. Sherrill," Sarah greeted him. "It's another boy!" Sam paused only long enough to look at the angelic face of his infant son and rushed into the cabin to the bedside of his beloved Mary.

"How's Mama?" Bonny Kate asked the first of many questions about the labor, the delivery, and the health of her mother and new little brother.

"She's fine," Sarah answered. "She's strong as a horse. I never saw an easier delivery. It's hard to believe she's fifty this year."

Bonny Kate took the baby and held him expertly as she had done so many times before when helping her mother raise her younger brothers and helping Sarah with little Becky. "This is the greatest miracle of life!" Bonny Kate marveled.

Sarah looked at her friend and felt sad for Bonny Kate. "It's time you were more directly involved in miracles such as these. Bonny Kate, why don't you marry?"

Bonny Kate looked up at Sarah. "I've had no offers. I'm looking for just the right sort of fellow, and I need not settle for less."

"You'll never find the perfect man," Sarah cautioned.

"You did," Bonny Kate countered. Sarah could not argue with that, so she changed the subject.

"Your mother named the baby Aquilla," Sarah told her.

"He's named after my father's younger brother," Bonny Kate explained. "Aquilla means 'eagle' in Latin. Uncle Quillar and his family are moving out here soon to help us with the horse farm. He has a big family too."

"That's wonderful news," Sarah declared. "Now I have some news to tell you. I'm not letting your mother get ahead of me in the baby business. I'm expecting my tenth child come January!"

"Another snow baby," Bonny Kate exclaimed. "You did it just like you wanted. I'm so happy for you."

"Thank you, my friend." Sarah smiled. "I can't wait to tell my dear John, but he's run off again to play soldier."

"Oh," Bonny Kate remembered. "He sent you a letter." She cradled the baby in one arm to search for the letter with her other hand. She found it in the pocket of her hunting shirt and presented it to Sarah.

"Thank you!" Sarah said excitedly opening the letter and reading it immediately. A broad smile spread across her lips, and a dreamy glaze in her eyes seemed to transport her away to her lover's side as she read his written words. Bonny Kate thought it best to leave her alone for a while so she could enjoy reading and rereading her love letter. Bonny Kate stepped into the cabin with her new little brother to celebrate the miracle with her parents.

The spring gathering was cancelled because so many men were away, but the campaign was a great success. The Chickamaugans were not home when the expeditionary forces arrived, so there was very little loss of life. The Chickamauga towns were burned, horses recovered, and food stocks seized. Some of the younger Watauga militiamen volunteered to go on down the river with Colonel Montgomery to join Colonel George Rogers Clark. Greater victories than the one at Chickamauga awaited them in the northwest. In the next year of service, Clark's forces would capture several British outposts and disrupt the enemy's ability to use the Indians to carry on the war against the settlers. John Sevier and the Sherrill men had responsibilities at home and did not go out to join Colonel Clark. Instead, they returned from the campaign by early summer and strengthened the defenses in their home community.

The Chickamaugans retaliated by attacking the homesteads of isolated settlers. Mr. Boydston's station near the French Broad River was attacked, killing Mr. Hardin and Mr. Williams. Colonel Sevier and his light horse company flew to the defense and remained active those summer months to prevent the violence where they could.

Whenever John Sevier could manage it, he left the military patrols in command of his majors Charles Robertson and Jonathan Tipton, and he slipped away to spend time with Sarah and his children at Plum Grove. He loved conversations with Sarah. She was as articulate, as energetic, and as witty as he was; and even on the most serious topics, the two of them could find the humor in the human condition. One afternoon in late September, Sarah and John were engaged in conversation about matters of the community. He was cleaning and waxing all the leather articles he owned, while Sarah attended to some mending.

"I think there's hope yet for Bonny Kate," Sarah remarked. "I saw a spark of interest between her and Mr. Embree, even though I know that's not going to work."

"Why not?" John asked.

"She loves the farm life too much," Sarah explained. "She wouldn't be happy moving place to place watching Mr. Embree building his mills. She will only be happy as the wife of a cattleman or planter and the mistress of a large farm. So I have a new prospect in mind for Bonny Kate."

"Sarah, my dear, we have spent almost an hour of our conversation on Bonny Kate!" John exclaimed. "Can't we talk about something else, sweetheart?"

"Like what?"

"I don't know," he answered. "What about the details of the fall gathering?"

"That's all planned, dear," Sarah told him. "Besides, Bonny Kate's happiness is important to me. We can't have our good friend marry a bad man. She deserves the same kind of happiness we have."

"Well, if it's important to you, go ahead with it," John conceded.

"Thank you." Sarah smiled. "Yes, so we have a new prospect. He's the new traveling preacher that has been staying with the Browns."

"A traveling preacher?" John asked.

"He's a Presbyterian just like Bonny Kate and about the same age. Isn't that perfect?"

"Won't a traveling preacher be moving from place to place the same way Mr. Embree would?"

"Not if we give him a good reason to stay and settle down," Sarah replied. "Suppose he were to start a church in our community?"

"A church would strengthen the community and promote growth," John declared.

"And what about Bonny Kate as his wife?" Sarah proposed.

"That wild thing, a preacher's wife?" John laughed. "He would have to be a mighty powerful preacher to keep his own wife out of trouble!"

"They say he's big, strong, and very intelligent," Sarah defended her idea.

"And still unmarried?" John wondered.

"I don't know yet," she answered. "The Browns are bringing him to the gathering. We'll know more about him then."

"That would be an interesting match," John chuckled. "By the way, I've been appointed to another commission by the state assembly."

"What is it this time?" Sarah responded.

"A new county is being established to our north," John explained. "They are calling it Sullivan County. It will take some of the land from Washington County so I won't have to patrol up beyond the Holston River anymore. I'm on the survey commission with Isaac Shelby and John Chisholm that will establish the county line."

"Will it take you very long?" Sarah asked. "I don't want you gone when our baby is born."

"It will take about a month," he replied. "I should be back long before the baby comes."

Sarah sighed, "Suddenly I feel tired. I need a little rest before supper." Sarah began to rise from her chair with the difficulty of having sat too long in one position, but John stepped over and pulled her up easily.

"How is our little fellow?" he asked stroking her extended tummy gently.

Sarah smiled. "He's still kicking."

"That's a good sign!" he said, escorting her into the house.

The Harvest Gathering, a week away, was anticipated with the greatest excitement and interest ever generated. There were so many new settlers and strangers coming that no one could predict the outcomes of the sporting events. The Sherrills arrived in advance to help Sarah with the preparations.

"Welcome neighbors!" John greeted them. "Sam, you can park your wagon wherever you choose." John helped the ladies down and greeted them one by one. "Hello, Mrs. Sherrill, Miss Catharine, Miss Mary Jane, Mrs. Taylor. I'm so glad to see y'all."

"Not half as glad as I am," Sarah called out from the porch. "I can sure use the help."

"I'm sure you can," Mary Sherrill agreed. She received little Aquilla back from Susan once she was safely down from the wagon. Motherhood was a delight that seemed to agree with Mary Sherrill. It made her feel young again, but she also enjoyed the relief of having Bonny Kate and Mary Jane in her household who could take care of the baby when she was in great need of a few hours of rest.

Sarah hugged all her friends in welcome and invited them in.

"How are you feeling, Sarah dear?" Mary inquired.

"I'm finding I can't do like I used to," Sarah replied.

"With the tenth child, we all slow down a little," Mary empathized.

Sarah laughed. "But I'll love this one as much as any of them," she declared cheerfully. "Come in, ladies. Let's start our visit with a little refreshment."

John helped Sam unhitch the horses.

"I hope hosting this gathering isn't too much strain on Sarah," Sam remarked, having heard much about the topic from his womenfolk on the way upriver from Daisy Fields.

"We've hosted some kind of gathering every year," John replied. "It's traditional, but you know Sarah, she wants everything perfect and will wear herself out trying to make it that way."

"I wish she could just relax and enjoy herself this time," Sam said.

"I'm hoping that she can. She has been really excited about having Mary and your girls staying over this week to help, and I appreciate having you here too, Sam."

"We are happy to do it," Sam assured him.

The ladies spent the afternoon in Sarah's well-equipped cookhouse, rolling out piecrusts and baking pies for the party.

"I heard the Robertsons are moving farther west again," Mary reported.

"Yes," Sarah confirmed. "John says they are setting out this fall after the harvest."

"Where are they going?" Mary asked.

"Hundreds of miles to the west, beyond the mountains where the Cumberland River flows to a place called the French Lick," Sarah replied.

"That's a name with possibilities!" Bonny Kate quipped.

"Oh, Bonny Kate." Sarah laughed. "You are a naughty girl."

"Don't talk like that around the children, Bonny Kate," Mary scolded.

"I sent the children out to wash more apples, Mama, they won't hear me," she replied with a mischievous smile.

"You are just too careless, my girl, much too careless," Mary admonished. "Now why would Mr. Robertson want to move so far and why would Mrs. Robertson allow it?"

"James Robertson has a vision of being the one to bring settlements and civilization to the west," Sarah explained. "John was all set to go with the Robertsons, but I told him that the community here needed him more."

"Well, of course, we couldn't afford to lose our colonel of the Washington County Riflemen, while the whole country is at war!" exclaimed Mary.

"Another thing that kept John from going is all these new businesses he is developing with the help of Mr. Embree," Sarah shared.

"John is becoming quite a businessman with the gristmill, the store, and the plantation," Mary observed.

"And did I tell you he's discovered a lead deposit just over the mountain? He and Mr. Embree are digging a mine, and building a shot mill."

"Sarah, you don't fool us," Bonny Kate interjected. "We know who runs the family businesses. You are the real brains behind the enterprises!"

"Why, Bonny Kate!" Mary tried to restrain her.

"It's true," Bonny Kate insisted. "Every venture means more work for Sarah. I can just hear the colonel saying, 'Sarah, this country needs a gristmill, here it is, Sarah, you run it. This country needs a lead mine. Here, Sarah, you run it. We need a lumber mill, Sarah, run that too. We need a gold mine, a tannery, an iron forge! Now, Sarah, we need a baby mill. You run it!'"

"A baby mill!" Sarah began laughing. She laughed so hard she had to sit down.

"Bonny Kate, that's enough!" Mary ordered.

Sarah continued to laugh hysterically. "Oh, I can't stop . . . Bonny Kate, do I really look like a baby mill?" Mary Jane and Bonny Kate laughed with her. Even Mary had to grin at Sarah's reaction. Betsy Sevier entered with a basket of washed apples.

"What's so funny?" Betsy asked. She was greeted with another round of laughter as she watched bewildered.

Outside the cookhouse, John and Sam walked past on their way to the corral and heard the women laughing.

"I wonder what set them off like that," John said.

"You can be sure that Bonny Kate had something to do with it," Sam remarked.

"She's a wild one, Sam," John observed.

"It worries me that I just can't get her married off."

"Well, maybe she'll find the right young man this week," John said optimistically. "The gatherings have sparked quite a few romances in years past."

"I'm afraid Bonny Kate will focus more on the competitive events," Sam predicted. "She loves to show off her many skills."

"One of these years I'm going to beat her at something," John declared. "Wrestling is the only event I have a chance at, because she never enters that one."

"I won't allow any daughter of mine to take part in a wrestling match," Sam assured him.

"By the way, Sam, what horse is she entering this year?"

"I can't tell you, John. It's Bonny Kate's surprise. It's not a horse you've ever seen race before."

"Not that it matters," John admitted. "I suspect that her success at horse racing is more the skills of the rider than the quality of the horses."

Sam beamed with parental pride. "I'll never bet against her!"

Chapter 25

Game Day

The pastures and meadows of Plum Grove Plantation were dotted with wagons and tents where families from all over the community had camped for the night. Crowds of men, women, and children milled about in a festive mood, visiting and catching up on the news. Bonny Kate walked purposefully to Sarah's cookhouse. She entered, put on an apron, and busied herself among the other women. She could not escape the notice of Sarah however.

"Oh no, you don't," Sarah reacted. "Get out of my kitchen!" The other women were surprised at her tone but amused as Sarah pushed Bonny Kate toward the door.

"Come on Sarah, let me help," Bonny Kate protested.

"No! You worked like a horse all week helping me prepare. Now that I have plenty of married women to do the work, your job is to get out there and socialize." Outside in the yard Sarah untied Bonny Kate's apron and took it from her. "Oh, look at those clothes. Don't you have anything better?"

"I dressed for the footrace today. I'm not wearing my best clothes for that!"

"No matter," Sarah sighed. "I don't want you wasting time changing your outfit. The important thing is to get out there and make yourself available. I'm sure young Mr. Embree will be looking for you."

"That won't do," Bonny Kate resisted. "He'd want me to live in a town. Can you see me living in a town?"

"Nevermind him then, there are plenty of others," Sarah encouraged. "Oh, have you seen the new minister? He's a Presbyterian just like you and mighty fine looking. I met him this morning when he arrived with Mr. Brown. Now get out there and find him."

"Yes, ma'am." Bonny Kate turned and walked toward the horse corral. She passed a group of children playing a game called Old Maid, which was played with a blindfolded subject trying to catch another child to be the Old Maid. Seven-year-old Mary Ann Sevier was the blindfolded player and the other children called out to her.

"Old maid, old maid, try to catch me, old maid!" The children darted behind Bonny Kate to escape Mary Ann's pursuit, and the little girl stumbled into Bonny Kate and held fast to her skirt.

"You're it! You're the old maid," Mary Ann shouted triumphantly, pulling up the blindfold. "Oh, Bonny Kate, can you play with us?"

"Of course, my darling," answered Bonny Kate. She put on the blindfold; and the children began again to shout playfully, "Old maid, old maid . . . old maid, old maid!"

Sarah watched from the door of the cookhouse and shook her head disapprovingly. At that moment, a tall handsome powerful man approached Sarah.

"Hello again, Mrs. Sevier," Samuel Doak greeted her, removing his hat respectfully.

"Hello, Reverend Doak," Sarah responded. "Are you getting a chance to meet everyone this morning?"

"Yes, ma'am, this is a most excellent place to get to know folks. Mr. Brown was telling me about the woman who raises horses to sell and travels all over the county making deliveries. Could you point her out to me?"

Sarah pointed at Bonny Kate. "She's the one with the blindfold, playing the Old Maid."

"Do you think she would be willing to help me learn the layout of the community and introduce me to some of the leading families?"

"I think she would be more than willing to help you get your church started," Sarah encouraged him. "She is a Presbyterian too."

"Excellent! Thank you, Mrs. Sevier." Reverend Doak nodded and turned to walk to the playground. He watched the game until Bonny Kate lunged at one of the children and ran into his arms.

Bonny Kate removed the blindfold and saw she was in the arms of a handsome stranger. "Oh, excuse me, sir!"

"So you are the old maid?" Reverend Doak asked.

"Yes, sir, I suppose I am." She laughed.

"That's rather an unkind game, don't you think?"

"I didn't think it so when I taught them how to play it some years back," she answered. "But the truth of it has come back to haunt me. I have never been married."

"I would be pleased to marry you when you are ready," offered the parson.

"Sir?" she reacted. "I'm quite sure I don't understand. We have never been properly introduced, so I couldn't possibly entertain such a proposal."

"I will perform the ceremony." He smiled. "I'm a minister. That's what I do."

Bonny Kate laughed. "Oh, for a moment, I thought . . ."

"Oh no . . . no, no!" Reverend Doak laughed. "But I'd be happy to officiate when your day arrives."

She continued laughing as the children chose another "old maid" and the game resumed. "We should be introduced. I'm Bonny Kate Sherrill." She offered her hand.

He took her hand in a warm handshake. "And I am the Reverend Samuel Doak."

"It's a pleasure, sir."

"The pleasure is mine, but I admit this is no chance meeting," he said. "I was searching for someone who knows all the families in the Nolichucky Valley to help me get oriented to my new parish. Mrs. Sevier recommended you."

"Oh, she did?" Bonny Kate was never surprised at Sarah's efforts to pair her up with any new gentleman in the community, but she could pretend.

"Yes, and Mr. Brown was telling me your horse-trading business has taken you all over Washington County, and you know almost as many people as Colonel Sevier."

"I've met nearly all of them, traveling about with my father and brothers."

"I understand you are Presbyterian also," he said.

"Yes, sir, I was baptized in the Catawba River at Sherrill's Ford, North Carolina. That's where we came from. My mother was raised Presbyterian, and she taught me to read the Bible. I know my catechisms by heart, and I helped teach them to my younger brothers and sister."

"Teaching is an important part of our faith. I plan to start a school as well as the church," Reverend Doak shared.

"Wonderful!" she enthused. "What about books? Other than the family Bible, there are precious few books in this part of the world."

"My horse was so loaded with books, I had to walk the whole way from Philadelphia," he declared.

Bonny Kate could hardly contain her excitement. "Oh, how I would love to see your books. I yearn to read about people and places I've never seen! Tell me, Reverend Doak, do you have any Shakespeare?"

"I have a good collection of his plays," he replied.

"What about poetry?" she asked.

"I have several volumes of classical as well as romantic verse."

The lady from Daisy Fields found a new friend in the Princeton educated Minister of the Word and Sacrament. They strolled about and talked a long time until she had to prepare for the footrace. A young man with a mission from God to establish churches and schools would indeed become a great and powerful man in the frontier communities.

The best runners in the community lined up for the footrace, including John Sevier and Bonny Kate. Judge Carter fired a rifle to begin the three-mile race. Bonny Kate got a fast start and took an early lead across the meadow, through the forest, and beside the beautiful brooks of white water. She ran as gracefully as a deer, with moccasin-clad feet, streaming hair, and flowing skirt. In the glen, her approach startled a small herd of deer that bolted for the safety of the deeper reaches of the forest. Bonny Kate raced along the forest path with John and a host of other men in hot pursuit of the swift, graceful girl. At last, the finish line came into view for the runners and people cheered as they saw Bonny Kate emerge from the forest across the meadow still in the lead. The other racers struggled to overtake her but in vain. There was much celebrating as she crossed the finish line.

The next event of the day was the horse race. Bonny Kate surprised everyone by entering the race on a tall, powerful mare, the new pride of the Sherrill stables. The horses bolted at the sound of the starting gun. Bonny Kate pulled out in front crouching low. John and the other riders rode after her through fields, across brooks, over hills, and through forests. Bonny Kate thundered across the finish line as betters rushed to collect their winnings. John dismounted grinning and joined the adoring crowd that surrounded Bonny Kate. They took her from her horse and bore her on their shoulders in victory. John and some friends took the leading places of those carrying her, and on his signal, they headed for the river. Her triumph turned to indignation as she saw them steering for the water. The cheering of the crowd turned to laughing. She struggled in vain to get free, and at the water's edge, she fell into the arms of John alone. She placed her arms around his neck; she stopped struggling and watched his face in fascination as he waded into the river and dropped her into the water. She came up quickly, grabbed John, and pulled him all the way into the water too. They splashed each other like children as the crowd laughed and cheered. Finally John retreated up the bank and turned to his victim and gallantly extended his hand to help her out. She looked at him reproachfully as she took his hand and climbed up the bank. She shook the water from her hair and clothing.

Later in the day, Jacob Brown looked everywhere for John Sevier, before finding him supervising the pig roast.

"John, we got us a wrestling match all set up!" he said excitedly. "We found you a likely challenger, and the bets are made!"

"That's fine Jacob as long as it's not Bonny Kate Sherrill."

Jacob laughed. "No, it's not Bonny Kate. John, all you got to do is whip that new preacher."

"The preacher?" John asked in surprise.

"Yes, this will be so easy!"

"Now see here, Jacob," John protested. "Is this any way to welcome a new fellow into our community?"

"It will work out fine, you'll see," Jacob assured him.

At the center of a crowd of spectators, Colonel John Sevier and the Reverend Sam Doak prepared to wrestle.

"Colonel, why don't we make a small wager on the outcome?" the minister offered.

"What do have in mind, Reverend Doak?"

"I need a church built for my new congregation, and you command the resources to do it!"

"So you get a church built if you win. What if I win?" John asked.

"What would you have me do for you?"

"I'd like all my children baptized, and a new Bible for my wife," John requested.

"More than fair," agreed the parson. The two strong men shook hands.

Judge Carter gave the signal to begin the match and they squared off for a long difficult contest. The crowd of onlookers cheered and shouted encouragement to their champions. After a tough match, the Presbyterian Parson pinned the Washington County Colonel. John admitted defeat graciously and yielded.

"I give," John said breathlessly. Both men were near exhaustion. As they rested and cooled off, John looked at the parson and admired his strength and engaging personality. "I reckon we'll build you a church. I'd have helped you anyway."

"Thank you, Colonel," Sam Doak responded. "I'll baptize your children anyway; and as for the Bible, I'll gladly order one from Philadelphia, special for Mrs. Sevier."

"Thanks, Reverend." John smiled. The two men stood up and breathed deeply. "I can't call a man who wrestles that good anything but friend." John held out his hand with a grin.

Sam Doak smiled and took his hand in a warm handshake. "Your friendship means a great deal in this community as many have already told me."

Bonny Kate walked up to the men in a fresh-linen dress and sunbonnet that created for her a stunning appearance. She took Sam Doak by the arm. "That was magnificent, Reverend! You're so big and strong! I think we have a new hero." She flashed a vindictive smile at Colonel Sevier as she walked away with her champion. "The colonel is a poor loser, Reverend Doak. Take care he doesn't chuck you in the river."

"I'll be the one who chucks people in the river." The pastor laughed. "Whoever desires to know the Lord can be baptized!" They walked away.

Jacob Brown walked over to John Sevier grinning, counting his winnings. "How'd you make out Jacob?" John asked him.

"Like a bandit," Jacob assured him. "I'd have won either way, but odds are always better on the unknown side of the deal."

"Miss Bonny Kate seems to have found a likely prospect," John observed.

"Don't bet on it." Jacob laughed. "Just enjoy the show."

"What do you mean?"

"She's going to make a fool of herself with a married man, again," Jacob predicted.

"Somebody ought to warn her," John said.

"Don't spoil the fun," Jacob advised. "If it weren't for Bonny Kate this world would be such a dull place!"

The turkey shoot was always a favorite competition and scheduled in the late afternoon so the men would have plenty of time to place their bets on their favorite shooter. Judge John Carter conferred with other officials as they tabulated the results of the semifinal round. Then the Judge signaled for the crowd to be quiet for the announcement. "The results are all in folks! It's time for the winner's round! Last year's champion, Miss Bonny Kate Sherrill has once again qualified. And her worthy opponent is, once again, Colonel John Sevier!" The crowd cheered their approval and the betting continued.

"Every year it's the same old thing," Major Charles Robertson complained to his wife. "I reckon she'll whip him again!"

"His luck's bound to change." The perky Susannah Robertson smiled. "I'm going for the colonel!"

Jacob Brown found Sam Sherrill standing with Bonny Kate in the crowd. "Sam, Sam Sherrill! Is she ready?" Jacob asked enthusiastically. "I have a sizable wager riding on our girl. Do you think she can do it again?"

"She'll do!" Sam answered. "She's practiced more this year than I've ever seen. She can't miss."

John Sevier, for all his popularity, occasionally had his detractors, small jealous men who believed that getting ahead in life and politics meant tearing down the accomplishments and reputations of others. John Tipton, one such politician, strolled over to where Bonny Kate waited with her father and Mr. Brown for the contest to begin.

"Whip him soundly, Miss Sherrill." Tipton grinned.

"I'll do my best, Mr. Tipton."

"When the governor hears about the great John Sevier losing to a girl, he'll have to appoint a new Colonel. Old Sevier is obviously unfit to command. I wouldn't be surprised if he proved to be an irresponsible drunkard. He should be removed from office." Tipton strutted away as abruptly as he had arrived. Bonny Kate was surprised and confused at his remarks.

"Father, what did he mean by that?" she asked. "Could Colonel Sevier lose his office if I win?"

"Don't pay Tipton any mind," Sam answered. "He's just stirring up trouble like he always does. It's only politics, Bonny Kate."

Bonny Kate didn't care for that brand of politics, and she felt some indignation on behalf of her neighbor. "But he lied. Colonel Sevier is no drunkard!"

"Now, Bonny Kate, don't get riled up before the shooting match," Sam warned. "Just settle down and concentrate on winning. Bonny Kate?"

Bonny Kate left her father and strode through the crowd to the firing line.

"Confound it!" Sam swore.

"What's wrong?" Mr. Brown asked.

"Tipton got her riled up," Sam advised. "She's likely to do most anything in that state of mind."

The crowd continued to rumble with excitement, but Bonny Kate stood tall, looking cool, confident, and focused at the shooting line. She knew she controlled the outcome, but wasn't sure yet what outcome she desired. John stepped up to the line, and they smiled at each other.

"Well, Miss Sherrill," John addressed her. "Here we are again."

"Yes, sir, here we are," she agreed. "I suppose you had your fun throwing me in the river?"

"I suppose the fun got out of hand," he admitted. "Mrs. Sevier called it undignified. I'm sorry I treated you that way. I regret it now."

"Not the way you will regret it, if I win this match," she warned. The crowd took her statement as a boast and rumbled with anticipation as more last minute wagers were placed.

"Let the shooting match begin!" declared Judge Carter.

"Hey, Colonel, don't you miss old Sweet Lips?" Major Robertson asked. The crowd laughed at memories from Watauga Fort.

"I sure do," he said, leveling his gaze at his opponent. Bonny Kate smiled back at him, but there were multiple meanings in his words and expressions that unsettled her. She wondered what old Chief Oconostota had done with Sweet Lips.

The first round at short yardage was a tie as both shooters were right on the mark. The second round at middle range was a tie as well. At long range, they played for points and their shots wandered off dead center. The runners delivered the results to Judge Carter who indicated Bonny Kate was clearly leading. She remained cool and confident while the colonel's face showed his determined resolve.

"The targets will be moved twenty-five paces farther," Judge Carter announced.

"She's good at that range," Sam Sherrill declared confidently. "It's all but over."

The shooters fired three shots each, and the runners brought in the target sheets. Judge Carter examined them carefully on his official table and stood to announce the winner. A hush fell over the crowd. "The winner of this year's shooting match, decided on points scored from the last group of shots is . . . Colonel John Sevier!"

The crowd cheered. John turned to Bonny Kate and offered his hand; and she took it gracefully, felt its warmth, and responded with a smile. John's friends quickly gathered around him, while Bonny Kate slipped away from the cheering crowd. Sam Sherrill confronted her immediately.

"Bonny Kate, you lost!" Sam exclaimed incredulously. "I've seen you make shots at that range hundreds of times. How could you possibly miss?"

"I never miss what I aim at," she declared.

"Well, what in thunderation were you aiming at?" he bellowed.

"My freedom!" she snapped. "I'm tired of constantly beating him. I'm tired of the bragging, the betting, the bruised feelings, and the infernal politics!"

Sam was clearly angry with her. "Your freedom cost me a great deal of money, my girl."

"Forgive me, Father," she begged, trying to come to grips with her strong feelings. "But winning is no longer enough. Life is passing me by. I'm sorry about your money. I'll make it up to you somehow. Excuse me now. I have some women's business to attend to." She winked at him and smiled mysteriously and left her bewildered father.

John in his jubilation was also confronted by an unhappy father. "I'm mighty disappointed in you, son," old Val Sevier said sternly.

"But, Papa, I just won the turkey shoot!"

"You cost me a considerable amount of money."

"Don't tell me you were betting on Bonny Kate!"

Val nodded sadly. "She's always been such a sure thing."

"You bet against your own son?"

"Sorry, John," Val said. "I bet on you in the wrestling match, and I lost there too."

"Well, I'm sorry about that, Papa," John comforted him. "I'll try to make it up to you somehow. What about a pair of foxhounds, all raised up and trained for hunting?"

"Foxhounds?" Val brightened. "Are they here at Plum Grove?"

"Yes, sir," John replied. "I'll show you." Val put his arm around his son's broad shoulders, and they walked toward John's dog kennel.

Bonny Kate found Sarah Sevier on the porch resting a few minutes before the big push to coordinate the serving of the big dinner. She stepped up and sat in a chair beside her ever-encouraging friend.

"You're having a big day," observed Sarah.

"Am I?" Bonny Kate sighed dejectedly.

"What's wrong now?" Sarah asked.

The Reverend Samuel Doak approached them.

"I'll tell you later," Bonny Kate replied quickly.

"Mrs. Sevier and Miss Sherrill," he bowed politely. "I've had the most wonderful time. Thank you for your hospitality and personal attention. I'll be leaving right after dinner."

"You're not staying for the dance?" Sarah asked. "I know a fair lady that will be so disappointed." Bonny Kate glanced at her smiling friend, trying to signal Sarah to leave the topic alone.

"Please offer my regrets to the fair lady, but I have a sermon to write and letters from home that I need to answer," he replied politely.

"It was truly a pleasure getting to know you Pastor Doak," Sarah continued. "I'm very happy to hear that you are joining our community."

"Thank you, ma'am," he replied. "The Lord has clearly called me to minister among you."

"My husband believes that the church should be at the center of the community, right beside his store, his gristmill, his iron forge, his tavern . . ." Sarah and the pastor laughed. The thought of Colonel Sevier trying to run all those diverse businesses even gave Bonny Kate reason enough to smile. She knew Sarah was the secret ingredient in every one of those ventures.

"Where is the colonel?" asked Pastor Doak.

"He went down to the roasting pits to check on the dinner," Sarah answered.

"Thank you again, Mrs. Sevier. Good evening, Miss Sherrill." The reverend walked out to the roasting pits, a short distance beyond the cookhouse.

As soon as Pastor Doak was beyond earshot, Bonny Kate spoke her mind. "He's married. Her name is Esther. She's expecting their first baby, and she's moving here from Virginia in the spring."

"Yes, Ruth Brown told me. Mrs. Doak is a Montgomery. That's a mighty fine Virginia family from Augusta County."

"I just found out," Bonny Kate said sadly. "I suppose I was the last to know, and there I was, flirting and laughing and chattering all day."

"Nonsense," Sarah said soothingly. "A young woman needs to practice her social arts. Don't let this spoil your day. There's still the dance contest."

"I was hoping he would be my partner."

"Why didn't you speak up and encourage him?"

"He's married that's why!"

"So what?" Sarah asked. "It's just a dance, not a life commitment."

"I know. It's good practice, that's what you always tell me," Bonny Kate said thoughtfully. "Sarah, there has been too much attention focused on me today. The concerns of this community are much bigger than me. I just sense that something is going on with you that you haven't told me. Is the baby all right?"

"The baby is fine," Sarah assured her. "All the children are fine."

"Then what am I sensing?" Bonny Kate asked.

"Bonny Kate, your senses never fail you," Sarah confided. "Yesterday, John decided to move our family to Limestone Creek."

"Why would he do a thing like that?"

"So we can live near his new gristmill, and be closer to Jonesborough where he's a county clerk," Sarah explained.

"Who will manage Plum Grove?"

Sarah shrugged. "There are still a lot of details to work out."

"Are you going to live in the cottage near the mill?"

"Yes," Sarah answered. "It's too small a place for a family our size, but John has promised to build on and make it a real showplace. Will you still be able to come and visit me?"

"Not as frequently," Bonny Kate said sadly. "Father won't let me ride up Limestone Creek without an escort. Some rough-looking Tories have settled along the north side of it. I'm afraid a visit from me would be a rare event."

"Oh, what will I do without my dearest friend?" Sarah lamented. "The children adore you, and when you are entertaining them, I can accomplish so much business!"

"I'm sure you'll manage well enough with a new collection of friends," Bonny Kate said. "But I sure will be lonely."

"I had thought I would have found you a husband by now, so you could live happily ever after," Sarah wished. "But I won't stop trying!"

"I told you, I would be your greatest challenge. And now I don't even have a partner for the dance tonight."

Sarah gave that problem some thought and came up with a brilliant idea.

"I can fix that!" she exclaimed. "Why not enter the contest with last year's champion?"

"Colonel Sevier?" Bonny Kate asked in surprise. "But he's your partner!"

Sarah laughed and pointed to her pregnant condition. "Not this year! Poor John will need to find a substitute."

"Oh, I forgot." Bonny Kate laughed.

"Bonny Kate, he loves to dance, and I hate to disappoint him. Can't you help us?"

"But I'm not the dancer you are, Sarah," she said. "And besides that, I behaved badly towards him in the competition today."

"John Sevier has never been a man who holds grudges," Sarah countered. "And if he thought he could win the dance contest with you, wild horses couldn't hold him back!"

"Well, all right," Bonny Kate agreed. "I'll do it if he asks me."

"Thank you, Bonny Kate." Sarah brightened. "I'll set it up. Don't worry. Just go and have a good time tonight. What do you need to get ready?"

"Thanks to your husband, I've had my bath in the river!" she replied.

"Did you bring your party dress?"

"Yes, ma'am, it's out in the wagon."

"Go get it and I'll help you get ready," Sarah offered. "A big part of winning the dance contest is looking good doing it!"

"Yes, ma'am," she obeyed. She rose from the chair and went out to the Sherrill wagon for her dress.

The evening was delightfully cool, and the air was clear and crisp. It was the perfect night for a dance. The musicians tuned up their instruments on the porch and displayed considerable talent for such a backwater community. Torches and candle lanterns lit the scene. John, Sarah, and the elder Sevier children, down through Betsy, emerged from their cabin and walked to the row of chairs that surrounded the dance area. The Sherrills made their way into the dance area stopping to speak to friends, new and old.

"Just look at Miss Bonny Kate all dressed up!" Sarah exclaimed to John.

"She looks mighty fine," he remarked.

"Yes, but there's still one problem," Sarah confided to him. "She has no partner for the dance contest. Why don't you ask her?"

John had not considered taking part in the dance contest because of Sarah's condition. He looked at Sarah, and she smiled at him.

"I would rather spend the time with my own dear lady," he replied.

"It would seem a shame to waste such good music and not enjoy something you dearly love to do," Sarah reasoned. "There's a lady who would love dancing with you." John looked at Bonny Kate across the dance circle and saw her approaching. She smiled as she arrived before the colonel and his wife.

"Good evening, Miss Sherrill," John greeted her with a bow of the head.

"Good evening, Colonel." She curtsied. "Good evening, Mrs. Sevier."

"Bonny Kate, you look divine!" Sarah declared. "John dear, doesn't she look divine?"

"Absolutely divine!" he agreed.

"Thank you, sir."

"Miss Sherrill, we were just discussing the dance contest later tonight," John said. "We were wondering if you would honor us by standing in for Sarah. You see, she's temporarily unable to perform." Bonny Kate and Sarah exchanged smiles.

"I'm not sure I can measure up to the talent to which you are accustomed," Bonny Kate answered.

"Sure you can," Sarah encouraged. "Just practice together before the contest."

"Yes, I'll help you," John assured her. "This time we'll be cooperating instead of competing."

"I'm willing to try." Bonny Kate smiled.

"Thank you, Bonny Kate," Sarah said. "Have fun!"

The music began and John and Bonny Kate moved to the center of the dance area. Sarah admired the romantic picture she had painted. Her husband at five feet eleven inches was perfectly matched to a woman five feet eight inches tall. Sarah had wanted to grow tall like that and thought she might when she married at fifteen. John had continued growing after their marriage; she hadn't. Sarah noted that John and Bonny Kate were both slender and graceful in their movements. Her black hair contrasted with his blond hair. Sarah imagined that Bonny Kate had the look of a proud, hot-blooded Spanish princess; and John might have been a French marquise actively involved in complicated court intrigues, as the romantic stories and fairy tales go. Sarah felt blessed to have such a loving devoted husband as her dearest John, and such a loyal, trustworthy friend as her dear Bonny Kate. Sarah loved creating such romantic images and turned her attention to making more matches among the wallflowers and shy boys of the community.

The dancing couples formed up the cotillions or square dance groups. They made lines for the lively reels. They danced in circles and in the French style, directed by experienced callers and talented musicians. All night the judges watched the couples and took notes on what they observed. At the end of the evening when most dancers were all danced out, and the judges had turned in their results to Judge Carter; the crowd awaited the announcement of the winners of the dance contest. There were several categories of winners for different parts of the contest, and the third place and second place winners had been announced with Bonny Kate and John coming up empty handed. A hush fell over the crowd as Judge Carter announced the first place winner.

"The winning couple of this year's Harvest Dance Contest has been selected for their great originality, charm, grace, and presentation—couple number seven, Miss Bonny Kate Sherrill and her partner, Colonel John Sevier."

The crowd cheered, and in her excitement, she jumped up and down several times before throwing herself into the arms of her partner. He received her and wrapped her up in a tight embrace, warm against the cool of the night. Familiar feelings swept over her, and she pressed tighter; he responded. The people applauded. She held tightly to the embrace she had so long desired. The people cheered. The lonely heart could not be torn easily from its present sensation of completeness. Other dancers came near to congratulate the winners. Her conscience screamed at her to let go and stop being so obvious, but her muscles would not obey. These powerful feelings would betray all her guarded secrets if she could not let go immediately. That's when John released her to stand on her own tired legs and weak knees. Judge Carter presented ribbons to Bonny Kate and John. Their smiles communicated the joy of the moment, but she very shortly left his side and went in search of Sarah.

She found Sarah praising her daughter Betsy's first attempt at the dance contest where she had learned much by being paired up with Georgy Sherrill. Sarah encouraged Betsy with suggestions on how to improve for next time. Sarah hugged Betsy with pride and gave her leave to go join the other children.

"Betsy, don't let the children have any fruit punch," Sarah warned. "Somebody has mixed in some corn liquor, and it's quite strong."

"What can we drink then?" Betsy asked.

"Granny Jemima has some hot-spiced cider ready in the cookhouse. You and the little ones can have some of that before bedtime."

Sarah turned to Bonny Kate and saw tears in her eyes that she assumed were tears of joy. "You won! Congratulations! Isn't it wonderful?"

"No," Bonny Kate shook her head. "The prize is yours for a brilliant strategy." She took the ribbon from her own neck and draped it around Sarah's.

Bonny Kate leaned toward Sarah and embraced the shorter woman. In a low and serious voice, she said, "Don't ask me to stand in for you again."

"Why not?" Sarah asked.

"I enjoyed it far too much," she confessed.

Sarah laughed and hugged her tighter. "That's the Sevier effect. Thank you for making him happy. He loves to win."

Bonny Kate pulled away from Sarah as John walked over to join them. She could not look him in the eye. She ran from the lighted circle seeking the cover of darkness.

"Where's Bonny Kate going?" John asked. "There's always one more dance after the contest."

"Woman's business, my dear." Sarah smiled. "You really looked good out there tonight."

"Shall we dance?" he asked, bowing politely.

"I'd love to." She curtsied.

John led Sarah out for the last dance of the night, a romantic slow dance most popular with wives and their husbands.

A struggle ensued in the darkness beside the Sherrill wagon. Four men had overpowered the exhausted girl and muffled her cries with a gag. She was bound hand and foot and rolled in a blanket so tight she couldn't move. They tied her over one of her own horses like a sack of grain and led her away, up the Jonesborough road at an easy walk. They left the main road and took the Onion Creek trail before any of her captors spoke.

"Are you sure this is the right one?" a man asked.

"She's the one who danced with Sevier all night."

"She sure made it easy wandering out into the dark like that."

"Where are the local boys?"

"They will be along later, covering our trail."

The men spurred their horses to a faster gait, and Bonny Kate was bounced around roughly lying across the back of the horse on her stomach. She was so uncomfortable and downright scared she couldn't do anything but endure hour after hour of punishment to her stomach and ribcage.

Finally, relief came when the men stopped and removed her from the horse and carried her into a building, still trussed up tightly. The room where she was left smelled like a smokehouse, but in the quiet and the stillness, she managed to fall asleep.

Chapter 26

The Dreaded Pox

Before dawn, the kidnappers were moving again. They roused Bonny Kate roughly, unbound her ankles, and allowed her to sit properly on her horse. She was blindfolded, gagged, and her wrists were still tied; but she traveled much more comfortably than before. She learned from their scant conversation they were Tories of the worst kind, outsiders from Georgia and the Carolinas who would have been outlaws anywhere had not the king of Great Britain offered them amnesty and land grants in exchange for doing the king's dirty work. After an hour or two in the saddle, the men stopped for breakfast. They pulled her off her horse and sat her down on a blanket.

"Take the gag off her, boys, the blindfold too," the outlaw leader said. "Let's see what she looks like."

Bonny Kate was greatly relieved to have the gag out of her mouth and to be able to see again. She studied her captors trying to figure out who the leader was and how she might talk her way out of this jam. Five desperate men studied her too, and she suddenly felt overdressed for the occasion.

"Would you like something to eat?" asked the authoritative leader.

"What do you have?" she asked.

"Parched corn and dried beef."

"I suppose that will do," she accepted. "Can you untie my hands?"

The leader nodded to one of his men who then untied her hands. "Tie up her feet again while you're down there," he directed. "I don't want her to eat and run." They handed her a tin plate of food, which she ate slowly.

"Is it too much to ask what possible purpose could you have for carrying me away from my home and family?"

"The king's men need horses," answered the leader. "I reckon Colonel Sevier would trade us a whole herd to get his wife back."

"I'm sure he would," she replied, "but he wouldn't trade a single old nag for little old me."

"Don't pretend you're not Mrs. Sevier," warned the outlaw leader. "We saw you dancing with him all last night."

"That doesn't mean I'm married to him," she said. "I was the colonel's dance partner because Mrs. Sevier is too pregnant to dance."

"You acted like somebody special in your fancy dress," the Tory said scornfully. "What's your name?"

"Bonny Kate," she replied.

"Who's your husband?"

"I have no husband," she answered. "And you can forget about the horses. No one will ever pay a ransom for me!"

"Damn you!" he swore angrily. "If you're not Mrs. Sevier, we'll have to kill you right here and now!" The man kicked the plate of food out of her hands, drew his pistol, and pointed it at her face. Her heart was racing, and she wanted to be able to run free, but her feet were tied so tightly. Why this fate? What purpose could such a death serve?

"Wait, don't shoot!" she pleaded. "I confess I've long wanted to be Mrs. Sevier. Doesn't that count for anything?"

"Hold on, Henry," spoke up one of the other Tories. "Don't be hasty. She's too fine a gal to waste like that. Let's have some fun with her before we leave her to the buzzards."

"I'd rather be shot and have you all hanged for murder!" she declared defiantly.

"Don't shoot her, Henry," warned an older and wiser Tory. "You'll give away our position to one of Sevier's light horse companies. I'm sure they are trailing us by now, and I've heard they always move fast. Use the tomahawk. Make it look like an Indian killing."

"Please let me say my prayers before you kill me!" she shouted, deliberately loud enough to be heard within rifle shot of the Tory camp.

A sixth Tory suddenly stepped into the clearing. He was tall, muscular, and right handsome in buckskins, like a long hunter.

"Who are we killing this morning?"

The five Tories whirled about and found the man in their midst.

"Damn it, Dyckes!" the leader wheezed. "Don't sneak up on us like that."

"I'm sorry," he replied. "I didn't know there was any other way. Why didn't you post your pickets? Sevier's men could ride right in here and shoot you all to hell."

"Bates, go down the creek to that open meadow and keep watch, but stay out of sight," the leader ordered. The man left reluctantly.

The Tory known as Jacob Dyckes was a local man. Bonny Kate knew his wife and even considered her a friend. She had no idea that Mary Dyckes's husband would be mixed up in such a messy business as kidnapping and murder.

"So who are we killing here?" Dyckes repeated.

"He's going to kill me because I'm not Mrs. Sevier," Bonny Kate cried.

"Mrs. Sevier is not cooperating," charged the Tory leader. "She's lying about who she is, and I'm just trying to scare the truth out of her."

"She's not lying," Dyckes acknowledged. "That is not Mrs. Sevier. She's Bonny Kate Sherrill, my wife knows her."

"Are you Jacob Dyckes?" Bonny Kate asked.

"My wife appreciates your kindness to her."

"All she wants, Jacob, is for you to stay home and provide for her like a proper husband."

"Sevier's rebel militia makes that quite impossible for a loyal subject of His Majesty King George."

The Tory leader put away his pistol. "All right, Dyckes, where are the rest of your men?"

"We never wanted any part of this," Jacob told him. "Messing with the Seviers is too dangerous. If you killed the colonel's wife and stole all his horses, it wouldn't be just him to deal with, no, sir. His brothers hate the king even more than he does, and they would track you down to the ends of the earth! And now it seems you didn't even get the right woman!"

"So we took the wrong woman. Is this one worth trading?"

"She's not worth a damn," Jacob pronounced. "Even the rebels consider her a pain in the ass. Sevier once saved her life, but now I think he hates her."

"Why is that?"

"She can outrun and outshoot him," he explained. "Every year, she publicly humiliates him at the races and shooting matches."

"Well, I'll be!" the Tory leader was amazed. "We have a girl who can whip the great John Sevier. You ought to be working for the king."

"My king is the Prince of Peace!" she affirmed. "Your king is the lapdog of the devil." The Tory leader scowled at her.

"So what will you do with her?" Jacob asked.

"Give her to me, Henry," said a wicked Tory. "After I'm done with her in the canebrake, she'll never insult His Majesty again."

"Don't threaten me, you nasty boot licker," she raged. "I'll cut out your filthy tongue and hang it up to wag in the wind until the crows come for it!"

The angered Tory glared at her menacingly and sprang at her like an enraged bear. He gagged her roughly, and when she resisted, he tied her hands behind her back while the other men laughed. "There, she's ready to go," the wicked Tory huffed and puffed as he stood over her. "Just give me the word, Henry, and I'll finish her!"

"Simmer down, Jimmy!" Henry restrained him. He was weighing their options. "We can't take her along to Indian territory. She's obviously a troublemaker. We can't let her go either, she'd set the militia on our trail."

"Tell you what I'll do," Jacob offered. "I'll take her to another settlement north of here and let the militia come after me. That will keep her from causing you trouble while you get a head start on the Seviers. They'll be out like hornets when they find your ransom letter."

"Dyckes, she's your problem then," the Tory leader decided. "I'm sorry, we didn't get the horses we came for, but we'd best be moving on quick."

The Tories collected their gear, mounted up, and rode away. Jacob cut the ropes that bound Bonny Kate's hands and feet and helped her up. He removed the gag, and she breathed in the air of freedom.

"Who were they, Jacob? I never saw them before."

"Eastern loyalists, lowland men, it was a stupid plan," he judged. "They should have talked to us before blundering their way through our territory. They were expecting me to arrange that trade. I'm glad you spoiled their scheme!"

"I'm glad you came along to save me. Thank you so much," she hugged him, but he did not respond. "And I know you didn't mean all those unkind things you said about me." He pushed her away abruptly.

"Miss Sherrill, do not delude yourself," he warned. "I only stepped in because you were kind to my wife. Do not consider me your friend. I know you are a dangerous rebel and an enemy of the king. I will deliver you as I promised to a nearby settlement. Now let's go."

"Oh, Jacob, they took my horse," she realized.

"That's right, they did," Jacob agreed. "Six horses came into this camp, and six horses left. That's what I want Sevier's trackers to read."

"Where is your horse?"

"I left him out in the woods some distance," Jacob explained. "I don't want the militia tracking me."

"Oh, but you told those men you would lead the militia after you."

"Oh, come on, Miss Sherrill, do I look as stupid as those jackasses?"

She wasn't sure. Jacob Dyckes was not as friendly as she would have liked. She wasn't sure she could trust him even after the risks he had already taken on her behalf.

"Maybe I should just wait here for the militia," she reasoned.

"Why do you think the militia is out looking for you?" Jacob asked.

"Because of the ransom letter," she guessed. "Didn't you say they left a ransom letter?"

"I assumed they did, but do I know for certain those idiots did? Certainly not!" he concluded.

"I'm coming with you," she decided. She followed him out of the clearing and began the next stage of her descent into purgatory.

Sunrise at Plum Grove promised a beautiful October day as the community awoke from pleasant dreams and treasured memories of the Harvest Gathering.

At the Sherrill wagon, Sam was the first to rise. He climbed to the ground and looked around at his sleeping children in the usual familiar arrangement, two beautiful black-haired daughters under the wagon and the boys under their blankets surrounding the freighter to protect the ladies in case of night marauders. Sam poured cold water into a basin from their water bucket and washed his face. He was eager to begin his day.

"Bonny Kate, Mary Jane," he called. "It's time to get up and be about your chores. Dancing the night away is no excuse to sleep the day away."

Mary Jane's head popped up from her pillow, and she looked around. She crawled out over her sister and gave her a sharp slap on the rump. "Let's go lazy bones!"

"Mary Jane, you disrespectful pup," Susan Sherrill Taylor complained. "Is that any way to treat your eldest sister? I ought to tan your hide!"

Sam's attention was drawn quickly to his playful daughters. "Susan, I thought you were going home with Leroy last night."

"I volunteered to help Sarah in the cookhouse this morning," Susan explained. "It's the big farewell breakfast."

"Where's Bonny Kate?" Sam demanded.

"She never came back to the wagon last night," Mary Jane reported. "She's so tight with the Seviers I just figured she slept up at the big house with Betsy and the other children."

"Thunderation," Sam growled. He walked toward the manor house muttering. "It's always Bonny Kate! I swear that girl scares the living daylights out of me. A man is blessed with three beautiful daughters: one that don't know nothing, one that don't do nothing, and one that don't tell me nothing!" That morning Sam Sherrill was not being fair to his lovely daughters. Mary Jane knew far more than she ever let people see. That air of mystery was one of her most charming features. Susan Sherrill Taylor did almost no work on her father's farm now that she and Leroy had their own farm to clear, plant, and harvest; but she wasn't lazy. And Bonny Kate was an excellent communicator except in times of emergency when communication was impossible.

John Sevier was fully dressed and pacing his porch. He was extremely alert for so early an hour of the day. He held a piece of paper in his hand, the contents of which had greatly agitated him.

"Good day, Colonel Sevier," Sam greeted him. "I'm missing a girl this morning. Have you seen my Bonny Kate?"

"Bonny Kate is missing?" John sounded surprised. "Did you look in the cookhouse?"

"That's where she must be," Sam reasoned.

"Let's go see," John said, quickly and decisively. He led the way around to Sarah's well-stocked and well-equipped cookhouse behind the main house.

Sarah Sevier was blissfully directing her helpers in preparing one of her famous farewell breakfasts for the guests at the gathering. Mary Sherrill was already there expecting her daughters to arrive shortly, but Sam saw no Bonny Kate. "Good morning, my darling," Sarah called cheerfully when she saw John in the doorway. "Bring a hearty appetite to breakfast now. It will be my best one ever!"

"Sarah, have you seen Bonny Kate this morning?" John asked.

"No, dear," she answered. "She's probably sleeping like a princess after winning the dance contest last night." The ladies laughed at Sarah's joyful giddiness and missed the look of consternation on John's face. John and Sam strode quickly toward the corral and met Sam Junior coming from that direction.

"One of our horses is missing, saddle and all," Junior reported to Senior.

"That careless, irresponsible girl," Sam Sherrill fumed. "She's probably sleeping like a baby in her own warm little bed in the loft at Daisy Fields."

"It's not the first time she's done this, Pop," observed Sam Junior. "At the spring gathering two years ago, we searched the banks of the Watauga all day before we found her at home safe and sound. This is probably the same deal."

"I need confirmation of that immediately," the colonel ordered sternly as though the issue of Bonny Kate's disappearance were the business of the Washington County militia instead of a Sherrill family matter.

"I'll go," Junior volunteered.

"Report back to me as soon as you can," Colonel Sevier directed.

"Yes, sir." Junior saluted and rushed to do his colonel's bidding. In old Washington County, family matters, civil matters, and military matters blended together in a sort of indistinguishable continuum. For that reason, the behaviors of the officers and men often shifted seamlessly from informal family interactions to strict conventional military conduct depending upon the nature of the emergency.

Colonel Sevier took a deep breath, forced a charming smile, and clapped his hand on the shoulder of his friend. "Here we are again, Mr. Sherrill, two old soldiers of the night watch looking for a good breakfast. Come, sir. Let us fortify ourselves for the demands of the day." They walked toward the yard where the guests were assembling for the morning blessing and a festive breakfast that met all expectations as the best one ever.

Every family was breaking camp and scattering in all directions after breakfast. The activity would erase the recorded history of the comings and goings around Plum Grove the night before. That's why John sent out his best trackers, Isaac Thomas and Andrew Greer, to learn what he could about the fate of Bonny Kate before the breakfast was over. John soon had the information he needed. Sam Sherrill was with John when Thomas and Greer made their report. Mr. Greer went first. "One rider went upriver last night before the frost settled in. He was headed in the direction of Brown's."

"That would be the Reverend Doak," John decided.

"One took the river road towards Daisy Fields, also before the frost," Greer reported.

"Leroy Taylor," Sam guessed. "He went home to feed our livestock."

"I also saw where the oldest Sherrill boy forded the Nolichucky this morning and took the fast route to Daisy Fields. That was all I saw," Greer finished his report.

Isaac Thomas went next. "John, I found six riders heading up the Jonesborough road last night, and one of them was a Sherrill racehorse."

"How do you know that?" John asked.

Isaac Thomas grinned at Sam Sherrill. "Mr. Sherrill files grooves into the shoes of his racing horses. I guess that helps his horses run better on a muddy field."

"That's a family secret," Sam bristled. "Where did you get that information?"

"You are too friendly with Jacob Brown." Isaac laughed. "Jacob never could keep a secret." The men laughed as John pulled out the piece of paper that had disturbed him so much that morning.

"Gentlemen, I have a secret that needs telling also," John announced. "I found a letter tacked to my washstand on the porch this morning. At first it didn't make any sense, but now the threats are all too clear."

John was interrupted by the arrival of Junior Sherrill reporting from Daisy Fields. He rode up to where Colonel Sevier was conferring with Sam and the trackers and dismounted.

"There's no sign of Bonny Kate anywhere at Daisy Fields," Junior confirmed. "I talked to Leroy, and he hasn't seen her either."

"God be merciful," Sam breathed. All his hopes were dashed by the news, now he wanted answers. "What does that letter say, John?"

John read the chilling words. "To the rebel Colonel John Sevier, sir, we have your wife. You can gain her release by delivering one hundred head of horses to the king's commissary at Chickamauga Town on or before the thirty-first day of October. Failure to meet this demand or the display of any hostile show of force on your part will result in her untimely death. Understand that the king's allies show no mercy in carrying out the most painful and degrading treatments on women captives that you can imagine. It's signed, king's agent, Henry Grimes."

"Damn, Tories," Isaac Thomas swore.

"They were after my Sarah and took your Bonny Kate by mistake," John assessed.

"Somebody has to tell the women," Sam said sadly.

"Go with me, Sam," John requested. "They'll likely take the news with great hysteria." The other men stepped back to make way for the two. "Isaac, did you say they were on the Jonesborough road?"

"Yes, sir, but they turned off west through Onion Creek Gap."
"So it's likely we could pick up their trail on Onion Creek?"
"More than likely," Mr. Thomas assured him.
"Good," John said. "Call up Company B. We ride within the half hour."
"Yes, sir," Isaac responded. "I'll have the boys ready."

The news was delivered to the women, and they reacted as expected, Mary Sherrill weeping with worry while hoping for a miracle and Sarah with loud lamentations.

"It should have been me," Sarah wailed. "It should have been me! She sacrificed her own life to save me. What can I do? Oh, what can I do to save her?"

John knew what must be done to save Bonny Kate, and he struggled to separate himself from Sarah who really needed his shoulder to cry on just at that moment. More than thirty minutes passed occupied with the women's business of dealing with the calamitous news. When he managed to extricate himself from his wife and daughters and the wife and daughters of Sam Sherrill, he flew to his horse and led his gallant horsemen into action. The Tories must not be allowed to leave Washington County. Their eight-hour head start seemed insurmountable, but John knew his strike force was the best equipped and fleetest force in the west. If anyone could affect a rescue, it was him.

Jacob Dyckes was not good company for Bonny Kate as she rode double behind him. He probably hadn't bathed since leaving home some time last season. He had nothing good to say about any of her friends and even spoke disparagingly about his own wife. She couldn't engage him in conversation about people, politics, religion, history, geography, Shakespeare, domestic industry, or any useful topic. Not even the weather was satisfactory in his opinion. What could possibly satisfy him if his king were to win the conflict? How would a man like him be any happier under royal authority? At long last, he stopped his horse beside a small creek.

"This is as far as I go," he announced. "I can't be seen around these rebel settlements. Do you need any help getting off?"

"I can manage well enough, thank you." Bonny Kate slid off the horse and landed nimbly on the soft creek bank. "I don't see any settlement."

"Just follow this creek down to where it runs into the river. The people there will help you get home."

"Jacob, I won't forget this," she declared. "Thank you so much!"

"Don't thank me," he responded coldly. "You will all suffer the consequences for your rebellion." He rode away without another word. She turned and followed the stream. Fifteen minutes of wilderness walking rewarded her with a whiff of campfire smoke. Soon she heard the distant sounds of human communication and picked up her pace. She breathed a prayer of thanksgiving that Jacob had not betrayed her and left her stranded in the wilderness. Her salvation from her enemies was at hand. When she reached the clearing, she stepped out of the wilderness and right into purgatory. Bonny Kate had arrived at the lowest point in her human experience.

"Damnation!" howled the voice of a suffering man.

"Just shoot him and give him some relief!" a voice answered. "We are all dying here, and nobody gives a damn!"

Bonny Kate winced at that reception. She wasn't accustomed to language like that even around horse camps and regular soldiers. She was again aware she was overdressed as she scanned a tent city surrounding a small farmstead of a main cabin, smokehouse, and a two horse stable barn. There wasn't enough cleared land to support a small family, let alone a settlement of this size. Then she noticed the graveyard.

James Cozby, a horse doctor become frontier doctor, was the man in charge. He was exhausted, haggard, stressed beyond human capacity, yet still making his rounds among the sick and dying. He looked up from tending a patient at the approach of a beautiful woman in a fine linen party dress, though quite soiled and disheveled, and thought how odd it was.

"You look a little used. Must have been some party," he remarked brusquely.

"Oh my!" she answered. "I do look frightful."

"You don't look sick though," he observed. "What makes you think you have the smallpox?"

"I don't think I have the smallpox," she answered.

"Then why the hell are you here?" he demanded angrily.

"I was attending a dance party at Colonel Sevier's when Tory outlaws captured me and carried me off thinking they were abducting Mrs. Sevier. When they discovered their mistake, they were about to shoot me, but one of them rescued me and kindly delivered me here."

"Kindly delivered you here?" he mocked her. "Lady, he as good as murdered you if you've never had the smallpox!" He unloaded a fair measure of his frustration on the hapless victim of a case of mistaken identity.

"No, I never have," she admitted.

"Well, you have been exposed now!" he judged. "I'm ordering you into quarantine until this epidemic is over."

"How long will that be?"

"Two months, if no more cases come in after you."

"What about my farm work, my horses, my sheep, my cattle, my spinning and sewing, my family, my friends, Sarah, and the baby . . ."

"You gave it all up when you walked into my camp," his words hammered her without mercy. "You might as well understand from the beginning that patients as old as you rarely survive."

"I'm not old," she protested, "and I've never been very patient."

"Well, make yourself useful, and don't cause me any trouble. Can you cook?"

"Yes, sir," she responded, fighting back a flood of tears. A proud woman never gave a bully the satisfaction of seeing her cry.

"We'll see," he promised. "I can't seem to keep a good cook. The woman over there will show you what to do." He pointed to a cabin where an exhausted woman sat, apparently unconcerned about the suffering all around her.

When Bonny Kate reached the cabin, she saw up close a pox-scarred older woman bitterly judged and judging bitterly those around her. Her voice had the same bitter edge as her look.

"You're a pretty one," she squinted. "Where did you come from?"

"Nolichucky settlement in Washington County," Bonny Kate answered.

"Has the pox spread there too?"

"No. I was brought here by mistake."

"I'd call that a fatal mistake," the old woman cackled. "I can tell by looking at you, you've never had the pox."

"No, ma'am, I haven't," she admitted again. "Is that man always so gruff and rude?"

"Dr. Cozby is a good man," the woman explained, "but this pestilence has worn him down. He just hates to see another one take the pox and die. He will never learn your name. He can't stand to think that these hopeless dying people have names or families or even feelings. Do you have a name?"

"Bonny Kate," she replied.

"All right, Bonny Kate, I'll remember that for your grave marker."

"I'm not staying here, and I'm certainly not going to die," Bonny Kate insisted.

"You can't leave," the woman warned. "Colonel Shelby posted sentries with orders to shoot anyone who tries to leave this camp. And they won't bury you either. That's my job. I also burn the clothes and bedding of the dead. It'll be a shame to burn that pretty dress."

"You won't have to," Bonny Kate snapped.

"We'll see. Did Dr. Cozby give you a job?"

"Cooking," she answered.

"I tried that one," the old woman crowed. "But the doctor didn't care for the way I was doing it. He said it wasn't healthy!"

"He doesn't play favorites," Bonny Kate observed. "He was just as ugly to you as he was to me."

The old woman released a shrill, cackling laugh. "Say, I'm going to like you, Bonny Kate. You're a girl who says what she thinks."

"Where are the provisions?" Bonny Kate asked. "I'll get started right away."

"I'll show you," the old woman rose and led the way into a filthy, dark, smoky cabin.

When night fell on the smallpox camp, something had changed. People were talking about the change, and the tired doctor wanted to see for himself what it was about. He arrived at the cabin and in the yard was a pot of boiling water. He peered into it. Bonny Kate watched from the door of the cabin awaiting his arrival. He glanced up and saw her.

"What kind of stew is this that the patients were so excited about?" he asked.

"That's wash water for the dishes," she told him. "Your stew is in here, hot and ready."

He straightened up and stepped away from the washpot, stumbling a little. "Yes, of course! I know the difference between wash water and stew. Of course I do." He followed her into the cabin, and as he came close to her, she smelled the unmistakable odor of distilled spirits. Inside the table was set for him on a linen tablecloth. The inside of the cabin was scoured and spotlessly clean. He removed his hat politely and sat at the place prepared for him.

"Cook, you were too generous with the portions tonight. We will soon run out of food at the rate you give it away."

"Maybe you should more closely guard the liquor supplies," she suggested.

"What do you mean by that?" he demanded.

"A doctor with the responsibility for dozens of lives out here should be clear-headed and alert in his decision making. I distinctly smelled the spirits on you, Dr. Cozby and you must not repeat that performance again," she warned him.

"I am not a drinking man," he insisted. "But a persnickety woman like you could easily drive a man to it!"

"Why thank you, Dr. Cozby that is the kindest compliment I've received all day! I shall try to think of one for you."

"Cook, I want to caution you about the provisions," he said.

"My name is Bonny Kate, and I have already inventoried your provisions," she informed him. "I counted the people in this station, and I made out a list of our needs for the next two months. Where do you get your provisions?"

"Colonel Shelby sent them," he replied. "But there was never a plan to resupply us."

"Then it's time to make a plan," she decided. "I'll write a letter to Colonel Shelby with our needs and a similar letter to Colonel Sevier. Will those sentries carry messages for us?"

"Perhaps they will."

"I'll take care of it," she promised. "I hope Colonel Shelby had the good sense to choose sentries who have already had the smallpox."

"I know for a fact he did. I insisted on it."

"Good, then the sentries will dine with us as members of your staff. With my cooking, we'll literally have them eating out of our hands!"

"What's the purpose of that?"

"They can hunt and bring in fresh meat, carry letters to the outside world, and fetch us more provisions."

"Good thinking, Bonny Kate!" the old woman encouraged her.

Dr. Cozby finally looked Bonny Kate in the face. "Do I know you? I think we have met before somewhere."

"Fort Williams," she reminded him. "It was almost two years ago. You were treating some Tories with knee wounds."

"Yes, that's it," he remembered. "You're the girl who brought in that gang. What did they call you? Ah, now I have it, the Princess of Pain."

"But my friends just call me Bonny Kate Sherrill."

"Bonny Kate Sherrill," he repeated slowly. "I bet you never thought you would die like this," he added sadly.

"I'm not dying. I'm living in the mercy of God and for the purposes of Divine Providence!" she affirmed.

"Don't get your hopes up," he warned. "In three weeks, you'll be suffering horribly, maybe even dead."

"I'm not going to take the smallpox," she argued. "I've been a milkmaid all my life, and I've had the cowpox."

"You ignorant girl, cowpox is not the same thing as the smallpox."

"My Granny Sherrill always said she never heard of a milkmaid taking the smallpox," she explained.

"That's an old wives' tale," he discounted.

"It is not!" she reacted angrily. "Granny Sherrill never once said a false thing! It must be true!"

"Suit yourself," he shrugged.

"You better eat, Doctor," she advised. "Get something on your stomach to clear your head and improve your humor. I'm going out to wash the dishes." She left the cabin.

Dr. Cozby tried a spoonful of the stew and chewed thoughtfully. "Cook is stubborn, but she sure makes a fine stew."

"Bonny Kate is one to watch out for," the old woman asserted. "And you better start calling her Bonny Kate. She won't stand for you ignoring our names."

"Go away and give me some peace, gravedigger," the doctor ordered.

"My name is Glenda Person," she declared. "And don't you ever forget it!" She climbed up into the loft intending to go to bed and remembered Bonny Kate had thoroughly cleaned the cabin before fixing dinner. "Doctor, do you know what Miss Goody-Goody has done? She burned all my bedding and scrubbed down the floorboards of the loft with lye soap. She said she was removing the vermin."

"Maybe tomorrow she'll give you a bath!" called up Dr. Cozby.

"How am I going to sleep without some straw and my quilt still hanging out to dry?"

"You'll manage," he replied, really enjoying his stew.

"You better hope I do," she railed. "If I can't get any sleep and work myself to death around here, who's going to dig my grave?"

"We'll manage," he chuckled.

"If I'm not here to look after you and protect you from that girl, she's likely to turn your life upside down. She's a whip-cracker, I tell you, and she ain't never been married."

"How do you know that?"

"I asked her," Glenda replied. "If you ask her anything about John and Sarah Sevier, she'll talk your ears off. It's enough to make a body sick."

"Sarah Sevier?" the doctor asked.

"Yes, have you ever heard of her?" Glenda asked.

"I met her three years ago at John Shelby's fort." He smiled at the memories. "She introduced me to the girl I'm going to marry."

"Why, Doctor, I never knew you was promised for marriage."

"There's a lot you don't know, Glenda."

"You said my name." She leaned over the edge of the loft to look at him.

"So what?" he said and brought out his journal to make the day's entries.

"Things are changing around here, all because of Miss Bonny Kate," she cackled. "She is going to change everything."

"She'll manage," he agreed sadly. "I'll give her three, maybe four weeks. We know so little about the disease, but its progress is very predictable."

Bonny Kate sat exhausted at the fire where the frothy washpot boiled the tin plates and spoons collected from the patients. She still had to rinse and dry the utensils and plan a breakfast for about forty folks. There were thirty-five patients, two sentries, Glenda the gravedigger, Dr. Cozby, and herself. She watched the smoke float up to the starry sky. "Are you smiling tonight, God? Is there joy in heaven? There isn't any joy down here, no, sir. I'm feeling mighty blue. I wish Pastor Doak was here to explain this crazy day to me."

Bonny Kate had good reason to be discouraged. In one day, she had descended from the queen of the dance and the partner of the handsomest man in the west to become a lost condemned soul and intended victim of a dread disease. Where had Divine Providence been while all of this was happening to her? She had looked up the barrel of a pistol, pleaded for her life, behaved less than courageously when faced with death, been cast away into a hellish purgatory where death was imminent, even expected for her, and now in doubt about her faith. It sure is easy to be a Christian when you make the right decisions, uphold your standards, and life holds out so many rewards to the gifted, the articulate, the intelligent, the witty, the beautiful, the confident, and the successful. But strip it all away and gaze upon the battered, bruised, and bleeding raw meat of humanity and all that's left is the spirit.

"Oh, Jesus, I'm right there with you tonight. I was crucified today in place of Sarah Sevier. The things those evil men did to me on the journey last night would have killed that dear little pregnant woman, but I went in her place.

Did the same thing happen to you when you went in my place? If God would let such a thing happen to you, his own son, what hope do any of us ordinary sinners have?"

Bonny Kate started the task of rinsing and drying the plates and spoons. Thoughts came to her as divine answers, thoughts that were not her own; but they entered her head just the same, quicker and clearer than her own thoughts. That was just how the Holy Spirit worked with her and how she had learned to listen for the Word of God.

"I am glorified in Jesus Christ. I will be glorified in you," the message came.

"What am I supposed to do now?" she prayed.

"Take up your cross and follow me." She imagined Jesus talking directly to her.

Bonny Kate took a deep breath, raised her eyes to the stars again, and waited quite a while for more but enough had been said. Finally she spoke, "Thank you, dear Lord." A meteor flashed across the sky as quick as a wink. She took it as a sign that the conversation was over.

Taking up her cross, shouldering the burden, and following Christ would be easy in the middle of a smallpox camp. So many needs presented themselves almost immediately. Names are important. She resolved to learn every patient's name and encourage the doctor to use their names during treatment. She would teach them all the name of Jesus and show them the power that comes from calling on the name of Jesus. She would clean up the patients, feed them well, and bring back the spirit of life, love, hope, and faith in them. She was going to put Glenda the gravedigger out of business!

Chapter 27

The Attack at Sherrill's Station

The Sherrills and the Seviers sat quietly in the parlor at Plum Grove as John described the days of searching for Bonny Kate.

"We tracked them all the way to the river but couldn't catch them before they crossed into Indian Territory," John said.

"Why stop there?" Sam asked.

"An armed force invading Indian Territory would have inflamed another frontier war," John explained. "I sent Isaac Thomas to Chota and on to Chickamauga Town if necessary to learn of her whereabouts. I hope to hear his report soon."

"What can we do now?" Sam asked.

"Start collecting the horses to pay the ransom," John suggested.

"Jacob Brown told me he'd pay the whole amount to get her back," Sarah shared. "He said the girl was worth her weight in gold! I certainly agree with his assessment."

"Jacob's offer is mighty generous, but I think we can do it just fine without him," John insisted. "After all, it was my fault for dancing with her the night of the abduction."

"It was my fault for setting that up," Sarah admitted.

"Bonny Kate is still my responsibility," Sam declared. "A Sherrill girl ought to be redeemed with Sherrill horses."

"Now hold on, Sam," John argued.

"No, sir, I insist on this. It's the right of a father."

"Stop this!" Mary Sherrill shouted. There was the thunder of authority in her Scots-Irish pronouncement harkening back to the Celtic warrior queens in her bloodline. They all watched as she dug into her husband's shot pouch and pulled out five lead balls. Holding them up above the table in Sarah's parlor, she let the balls drop one by one. "Here's the ransom payment they deserve for all the suffering and heartache they caused our family! Do you think Bonny

Kate will ever be the same when those savages are done with her? Will she be able to sleep without the nightmares, go outside on a dark night, ride anywhere without an escort, make love to a husband, or ever trust another man? This is the only ransom they'll get from us. Where is a man bold enough to deliver payment in full and bring my baby home?"

The two men scrambled to pick up the rifle balls. Sam was able to get two while John got three.

"There," Mary said with grim satisfaction. "The matter of ransom is settled."

"We will know where to retrieve her when Mr. Thomas gets back from Chota," John said. Sam nodded.

The news from Chota was not helpful. Reliable Indians had seen the five Tories posing as traders pass through the Cherokee lands and move on to Chickamauga Town. They led an extra horse with an empty saddle. The outlaws had no woman with them. John and Sam struggled to understand what that meant. Five days were gone without a sign of the missing girl and even the brightest optimists had doubts.

Sarah collected the ingredients for a vat of black dye. When John questioned her about the expense to the house account, she explained, "I'm dyeing everything I wear black. I shall be in mourning for a year."

"Don't you think you ought to wait until we get some news?" John cautioned. Sarah answered with another outburst of tears and wailing that tore at John's heart.

"It should have been me! They were after me, John. Why, oh why couldn't they have gotten it right and taken me?"

"They shouldn't have taken anybody!" John declared. "We'll find them and deliver Mary Sherrill's ransom. You just hold on to that hope, and I'll get it done. I promise!"

Rumors flew through the community and persisted that Bonny Kate Sherrill—the frontier legend, champion horse racer, prize-winning sharpshooter, and dancing queen—had been murdered by Indians, Tories, or perhaps a combination of both. Speculation ran high about how many it had taken to accomplish the crime. Estimates ran as high as fifty. One enterprising long hunter offered a tour of the battlefield featuring the bloodstained ground where she supposedly ran out of ammunition and hewed down her remaining adversaries with her tomahawk. The fellow could even quote the heroine's last words for the entertainment of his excursionists. Business was good until Sam Junior and Adam Sherrill found the entrepreneur and beat him soundly for spreading lies about their sister.

At the smallpox camp, improvements went forward at a rapid pace. The sentries went out hunting daily for fresh meat, there was fish from the river that some of the stronger recovering patients could provide, and the vegetables and breads that Bonny Kate prepared were first rate. But she was very concerned about supply levels. After a week, there was still no response to her letters appealing for help from the authorities of Washington County and the Holston establishment. She had also written a letter to Pastor Doak that had gone unanswered. She went out to discuss the matter with the trusted sentries who loved her for the meals she prepared and the entertainment she provided.

"Caleb, why haven't we heard from Colonel Sevier?" she asked the sentry on duty.

"It's not time yet," he answered.

"What do you mean exactly when you say it's not time yet?" she persisted.

"The letter hasn't gone yet," he answered.

"Where is my letter?"

"In my saddlebag," he explained. "That's how the doctor wanted it done."

"Why in the world are you holding my letters?" she asked with rising anger.

"Doctor says the little bugs that make people sick will die in two weeks, and then we can deliver the letters, and they can be handled without spreading the disease," Caleb explained. He was proud of his ability to share his advanced knowledge in the science of contagion.

"That's ridiculous," she argued. "Caleb, please deliver those letters; I thought they went out last week. My parents will be worried sick about me if you don't deliver them now. And my supply requests are in those letters too. The whole camp is going to starve if you don't deliver those messages!"

"Sorry, Miss Bonny Kate," he stalled. "One more week and they can go. The doctor told me just how to do it, and you can't argue with a man of science."

"Just watch!" she fumed. "Come with me."

Caleb followed her quick march to where they found Dr. Cozby, relating amazingly well to one of the critical care patients. She waited until he looked up.

"Dr. Cozby," she snapped her words to communicate her displeasure. "Caleb is holding up my supply requests while this camp is close to starvation."

"Standard procedure for outgoing mail," Caleb explained.

"Caleb is correct," Dr. Cozby told her. "The last thing we want to do is send Colonel Sevier and his family the smallpox infection in a letter. It's probably not warranted, but I'm taking every precaution."

"I appreciate that, sir, but why couldn't Caleb just take the letter and read it to Colonel Sevier."

"I don't know how to read, and neither does Joshua," Caleb admitted.

Bonny Kate looked at the sentry. "Colonel Shelby was not very generous with the human resources he provided, and I shall take him to task about the conditions under which we are forced to operate this camp."

"Is she talking about me?" Caleb asked.

"That's all right, Caleb," Dr. Cozby praised the lad. "I'm proud of your conduct. You may return to your post."

"Wait," Bonny Kate stopped him. "Suppose Caleb takes the letter and holds it up for Colonel Sevier to read without ever letting him actually touch it. Would that work?"

"What do you think, Caleb?" Dr. Cozby asked.

"I could do that," he affirmed.

"Good man," Dr. Cozby said. "Bonny Kate will tell you where to find the recipients."

"The what?" Caleb asked.

"The people you are supposed to deliver the letters to," the doctor clarified.

"Oh yes, sir."

"And don't spare the horses," she directed. "Don't come back empty handed, wait for the colonel to write a response. I want to know what he says the minute you return. I'll go fix you some food for your journey. You go saddle your horse."

When she was gone, Caleb turned to Dr. Cozby and said, "She's like a tornado, ain't she."

"Yes, Caleb." The doctor laughed. "That's what she's like."

Another week passed, and Glenda ran into camp raising the alarm, "Dr. Cozby, the supplies are here! The colonel himself brought 'em. He's out there with another colonel. They are asking for you and Bonny Kate!"

Dr. Cozby stepped out from a tent where he had been tending patients. Bonny Kate ran out of the cook's cabin and outpaced the others to the sentry post. Dr. Cozby and Glenda walked with more decorum.

"I wouldn't have believed it if I hadn't seen her do it myself," marveled the good doctor.

"What's that, Doctor?" Glenda asked.

"The way she commands these militia colonels and makes them jump to obey."

"I told you she is one to watch out for," Glenda reminded him.

They hurried toward the road where the colonels waited beyond the sentry post. The two sentries were reporting on camp conditions to Colonels Isaac Shelby and John Sevier attended by other mounted men including Sam Sherrill. There were two wagons of supplies, blankets, a milk cow, and crates of chickens. Bonny Kate reached the clearing first. She stopped beside a tree beyond which no smallpox patient could go.

"Hello, Father! Hello, Colonel Sevier and Colonel Shelby. Thank you for making the trip." The colonels removed their hats.

"Are you all right, my dear?" Sam inquired.

"Yes, sir, completely unharmed, but I'm not allowed to come past this tree. My goodness! Look at all the supplies."

"We could tell from your letter how desperate the situation is," John remarked.

"Mother and the children send their love to you," Sam called to her. "We sure do miss you."

"Tell them I love them too," she replied.

Dr. Cozby arrived beside Bonny Kate.

"Good day, sir, I'm John Sevier. You must be Dr. Cozby."

"Your servant, sir," the doctor bowed. "Thank you, gentlemen, for bringing the supplies. We are saving lives because of the improved conditions in the camp."

"Dr. Cozby, is there anything else you need?" John asked.

"I don't believe so," the doctor answered.

"Colonel Sevier, is Mrs. Sevier doing well?" Bonny Kate inquired.

"Sarah is much better now that we know you're alive, but she still worries for you," John said. "It was clear from the ransom letter that the Tories were after her but took you instead. We are so sorry."

"Tell her not to worry," Bonny Kate advised. "I'm fine, and I will be home in a few weeks."

"Take care of yourself, daughter," Sam said. "Reverend Doak is coming later in the week. Watch for him on Thursday."

"I will. Good-bye, Father. I love you. Good-bye, Colonel Shelby. Good-bye, Colonel Sevier."

Bonny Kate and Dr. Cozby turned and walked back toward the camp. The sentries drove the wagons to the camp. The visitors turned their horses to leave.

"Mr. Sherrill, I'm so sorry this happened to your daughter," Isaac Shelby empathized. "She's a brave soul, and she'll do a lot of good in the time she has left."

"She'll do fine," Sam answered.

"Sarah and I will always feel responsible for Bonny Kate's tragedy," John told the victim's father.

"Don't worry, she'll pull through," Sam said confidently. "We have faith."

The colonels, John, and Isaac exchanged glances that communicated the reality of the grave situation that Sam Sherrill was apparently not prepared to face.

Rumors flew through the community and persisted that Bonny Kate Sherrill—the frontier legend, expert spinster, markswoman, and escape artist—had defeated a host of perhaps as many as one hundred renegades before wandering into a smallpox camp. She had probably died there when her luck finally ran out. Minstrels wrote sad songs about the remarkable feats that were accomplished during her lifetime and the most extraordinary accounts of her last days. One long hunter, undaunted by his past experience as a tour guide, offered to show excursionists the place where she was supposedly buried. The offer included a lock of the heroine's hair for the first one hundred to sign up for the tour. The entrepreneur's business quickly folded when he heard that the Sherrill boys were looking for him again.

The reality of Bonny Kate's existence would have disappointed the romantics that had made so much of her character. She would be the first to admit that her twenty-five years of life had been filled with the tedium of routine farm life, missed opportunities, unfulfilled aspirations, and shattered dreams. The only events that lifted her above the ordinary were a few perilous misadventures brought on by her own poor judgment. Yet she was open to the leading of Divine Providence, and her faith always kept her hopefully optimistic about the days to come.

Another day found Bonny Kate carrying a water bucket to patients under a large canvas tent where they rested on makeshift beds in the hay. She stopped beside a little girl. "Would you like some water, sweetheart?"

"Yes, ma'am, please," the girl replied with a soft little voice as thin as a reed.

The life in her was delicate and fairylike, and could have easily fluttered away like a butterfly on a gentle breeze. Bonny Kate dipped a tin cup in the bucket and handed it to the girl.

"Drink as much as you like," Bonny Kate said gently. "I have plenty. I want you to know, Karen, I'm praying for you. I want you to get well so you can help me at the cookhouse. I need a good helper like you."

"Yes, ma'am," the frail girl lay back on her straw mat and sighed.

Dr. Cozby had told Bonny Kate that Karen's mother's status had been upgraded to probable survivor. She sat beside her daughter, feeling stronger and smiled at Bonny Kate. "Thank you, miss, you've been so kind to us."

"I'll be back later to serve your lunch," Bonny Kate comforted the lady. "Today we are having hot chicken soup!" Bonny Kate moved on to another tent.

"Mama, I like that lady," said the small girl. "Who is she?"

"I don't know, baby," the mother said. "But she's been like an angel."

"Haw, haw, haw!" laughed an old man lying on the other side of the tent. "I reckon I've heard it all! Ma'am, that wild thing you called an angel is Bonny Kate Sherrill. She can outride, outshoot, and outrun any man in these mountains."

"That's Bonny Kate Sherrill?" she asked in amazement.

"Sure is. I see her all the time at races and shootin' matches."

"I wonder what moved her to come to a place like this and do all that she has done?" the mother said.

"Mama?" the weak little voice spoke up.

"Yes, dear," her mother answered.

"Maybe she could teach me to shoot when I get better!"

"That's something to look forward to, dear child, something to look forward to." The mother turned her head as her tears welled up.

Dr. Cozby tracked the days in his journal and planned accordingly. While Bonny Kate was distributing hot soup among the patients, he shared his concerns with Glenda.

"She'll have her own tent, with all the comforts we can provide," he announced.

"Put her in your bed, Doctor, right beside the warm fire," Glenda proposed. "It's the least you can do. You can sleep in the horse barn with Caleb and Josh. How long do you think she'll suffer?"

"It's hard to say. She has a very strong constitution, but with the cold weather coming on, the pox will likely weaken her for the pneumonia to set in. After that they go pretty quick, and there's very little I can do for them."

"Damn our luck!" Glenda cursed. "Finally somebody comes along who treats me like a close friend, almost like a sister, and this has to happen."

"I regret this as much as you do, but her days were numbered the hour she walked into this camp."

"I would have given this story another ending," Glenda declared. "I would have dressed her up in the finest wedding gown in the country and married her off to the handsomest doctor, and the two of you could have lived happily ever after!"

"You silly dreamer!" he scoffed. "That would never happen if we all lived to be a hundred!"

"Why not?" Glenda asked. "Bonny Kate is so sweet on you, she drips honey. You're just too big a flunk-head to see it."

"I'm already engaged, remember?" Dr. Cozby declared.

"That's a cold trail," Glenda charged. "If you haven't married that little Hawkins girl in these past three years, it's never going to happen."

"Oh yes, it will!" the doctor insisted. "We have continued to write. And Bonny Kate has made me realize how much I love my precious girl, with all her talk about the perfect married couple, John and Sarah Sevier."

"Why would that have anything to do with you?"

"My Miss Hawkins is Sarah Sevier's first cousin," he declared. "I'm joining the family, just as soon as we can close this place down."

"That seems like a poor excuse to marry a girl you barely know," Glenda mused.

"But I do know her, and I love her," the doctor declared earnestly. "And it took getting to know someone like Bonny Kate to teach me how to live in the presence of God and letting him work through my hands to help others. A physician is just an instrument in the hands of a loving, healing God, and I personally no longer have to bear the responsibility for whether a patient lives or dies. I'm free to live a full life now, and I'm not waiting any longer to court my Miss Hawkins."

"Praise the Lord," Glenda exclaimed. "I'm happy for you, Doctor. So are you going to give Bonny Kate your bed when she starts to show signs?"

"It's the least I can do," he agreed sadly. "About midday tomorrow, you'll see the sores begin to develop on her face and neck. She'll slow down and begin to feel like ▓▓, after that it just gets worse."

Three days later, Dr. Cozby went into the sick tent chasing down Bonny Kate among the other patients. "There you are," he huffed. "Spending a lot of time and energy on one little patient, aren't we?"

Bonny Kate smiled at him, bravely prepared to take another scolding. "She's worth every bit of it!"

"Bonny Kate is going to give me shooting lessons," declared the little girl, her voice gaining strength each day.

"And when the doctor says it's all right, I'll teach you to handle a spirited horse," Bonny Kate added.

"The day is coming soon for you, Karen, when you are going to be completely well," he predicted. He turned to the child's mother and continued, "Her young skin will rapidly minimize the scarring. She's going to make a beautiful bride."

"Thank you, Doctor." Karen's mother hugged him. "You have all been so good to us. We are so blessed."

"Some cases turn out to be miracles," he said kindly. "Excuse me while I attend to my other patients." Dr. Cozby walked over to Bonny Kate. "Pull up your hair and let me look at your neck."

"Why, Dr. Cozby, is this a personal interest or a professional interest?" she flirted as she pulled up the hair from the nape of her neck. The surrounding patients were enjoying the show.

"A little of both," he said, taking a closer look down her collar.

"Your hands are cold, Doctor," she complained. "Cold hands mean a warm heart. That is what my Granny Sherrill used to say!"

"She was a wise woman, Bonny Kate," the doctor said. "Have you felt any fever or aches?"

"I'm sorry, Doctor, but men never have that effect on me," she teased. "Dr. Cozby, are you getting sweet on me?" The patients laughed.

"Why would you ask that?" He grinned.

"You have been giving me a lot of attention these last couple of days, and Glenda said you were trying to get me into your bed!"

The patients laughed long and hard at her little play as Dr. Cozby turned red with embarrassment.

"Go for it, Doctor," shouted the old man. "We need some good entertainment around here!"

"It will never happen!" the doctor shouted back with a broad grin. "I already have a sweetheart!" Dr. Cozby stepped out of the tent, placed his tri-corn hat jauntily on his head, and strolled away.

"Don't let the good doctor get away that easy," the old man shouted. "Go for it, Bonny Kate!" She ran out of the tent to the laughter, whistles, and cat calls of the rowdy patients who really seemed to be enjoying themselves. She had enjoyed herself too but felt an apology was owed to her friend, the good doctor.

Two more weeks passed and many patients had recovered and left the camp. Bonny Kate missed her family and friends terribly and deeply yearned to go home.

"How long does this quarantine go on?" she challenged Dr. Cozby. "Winter is coming on, and we usually have the hog killing about now and make sausage, ham, and bacon. I miss my family so much, and I'd really like to be there when Sarah has her baby. I've got mares that are delivering too. I hate to miss the new colts. Please, couldn't I go home?"

"I counted the days in my journal and watched you like a hawk for every day I thought the symptoms would appear; and, Bonny Kate, you have completely baffled me."

"I often have that effect on men." She smiled. "You never did get me into your bed though. Any regrets?"

"Like I said, that will never happen." He grinned. "When Sarah Sevier makes a match, it's permanent. I got another letter from my sweetie this morning."

"I wish you all the happiness in the world," she said. "We will probably see you frequently at the Sevier Gatherings, now that you are becoming part of the family."

"Most likely," he agreed. "Anyway, I was going to tell you that you apparently have the same resistance to smallpox that any recovered victim has."

"So Granny Sherrill was right about the cowpox!" she exclaimed.

"Or maybe you had a light case of it as a child and nobody recognized it," he theorized. "For whatever reason, if you haven't taken the pox by now, you're not going to get it. That means you are free to go home."

"Thank you, Doctor. My faith in the Lord was my salvation. I also have great faith in the sayings of Granny Sherrill."

They laughed together as they had so many times during her weeks of quarantine.

"Thank you so much for helping the patients," he said. "The good food and the cleanliness have prevented other diseases and saved many a life. Now that's a fact!"

"I did my duty," she declared. "I wanted so badly to overcome this deadly plague."

"And overcome it we did!" the doctor agreed.

Homecoming for Bonny Kate was not a time for rejoicing and hugging or family gathering. She was moved into the new guesthouse at Daisy Fields, and her parents watched carefully for signs of disease. Mary Sherrill wasn't taking any chances for her baby Aquilla. No visitors came to see her except for Pastor

Doak, and all he wanted to do was talk about the opportunities for evangelism in the community. Still, she enjoyed his visits because he always brought her books to read from his extensive collection. Her period of family quarantine at the homeplace did not exempt her from farm chores however, and it was a particular joy to once again herd and hunt the meadows and woods around her beloved Daisy Fields. Finally her confinement ended, and she was again welcomed into the bosom of the family.

The Sevier family had moved from Plum Grove to the Mill House on Little Limestone Creek early in November at the time John had gone out to survey the new county line between Sullivan County and Washington County. Bonny Kate learned from her mother that Sarah's life had been one party after another between the activity in the new community at Little Limestone and the bustling county center a few miles away in Jonesborough. Well-connected women sought favors and advantages for their husbands by association with the wives of established men of influence like Colonel Sevier. Mary Sherrill complained that such political foolishness distracted mothers from their proper responsibilities of homemaking and child caring.

"You wouldn't know Sarah Sevier," Mary said sadly. "Since you went away, Bonny Kate, she's a changed woman. I think it's that Jonesborough crowd. I wouldn't give two cents for the whole flock of them."

On a cold January night in the year 1780, Sam Sherrill and his sons Adam, John, George, and Sam Junior entered the door of their cabin. Mrs. Sherrill, Bonny Kate, and Mary Jane were preparing supper. Bonny Kate met the men at the door and helped them out of their cloaks.

"It's another cold night," Sam declared. "Katie, bar that door. Robert Sevier came by today with the patrol. He said the Chickamaugas are sending out raiding parties again. Settlers with horses are their favorite targets. We ought to move up to the fort in the next day or two."

"Blast the Chickamaugas!" Mary exclaimed. "We want news about Sarah and the baby!"

"Oh yes," Sam remembered. "The baby was born the day before yesterday. I think he said it was another girl."

"Are mother and daughter well?" asked Bonny Kate.

"I guess they are," Sam said. "Robert didn't say much about it."

"Men!" Mary said with frustration. "They never ask the right questions."

"I wish the Seviers had not moved away to Little Limestone Creek. If they had stayed at Plum Grove, we could have been there to help. Mother, when can we go up to see them?"

"It's not safe to travel these days," Sam cautioned. "You can see Sarah when we all go into the fort. Now let's eat!"

The family gathered at the table, and Sam led them in prayer. "Gracious Heavenly Father, grant all families thy protection in these troubled times, and watch over Sarah Sevier and her new baby. Bless this food to our use and us to thy service. Amen." They began eating.

"Bonny Kate, whatever happened to that Dr. Cozby you were so fond of down at the sick camp?"

"He's been up to the Holston for medical supplies. Colonel Sevier keeps him mighty busy."

"Is he too busy for courting?" Sam asked.

"Father, Dr. Cozby and I have never been anything more than friends," she explained. "Besides Mrs. Sevier introduced him to her cousin, and I believe they are engaged to be married."

"You let a fine looking, unmarried doctor get away?"

"Now, Sam, don't go into that again," Mary tried to soothe him.

"Thunderation, Mary!" Sam pursued the topic. "Did you understand that our girl lived in the same cabin with this doctor fellow for almost two months, assisted him caring for his patients, ordered all the supplies, did all the cooking, cleaning, sewing, and washing, and all she got was another friend?"

"I'm sorry, Father, but there wasn't time for romance."

"Then how did the good doctor find time for Sarah Sevier's cousin who wasn't even present those two months!" he stormed. "What's this generation coming to?"

"Hush, Sam," Mary stopped him. "Listen now, you've stirred up the dogs." The dogs outside barked ferociously and something was also alarming the horses. Sam cocked his head to listen. He rose from his chair.

"That wasn't me, Mary," Sam announced. "Only Indians worry the livestock like that. Get your rifles! Take your posts!"

Everyone old enough to shoot grabbed a rifle, shot pouch, and powder horn from hooks around the walls of the room. They scattered to different vantage points in the house. Young Aquilla was shoved under a bed in the corner. Mary blew out the candles on the table. Bonny Kate kicked the washpot over into the fireplace to douse the fire. Tense moments passed as their eyes adjusted to the dark.

"I see shadows by the corral," Sam observed. "Pick your targets carefully after I start shooting. Don't hit the horses!" Sam aimed and fired. Bonny Kate fired next, and the firing became rapid and steady as all the Sherrills joined in.

Chapter 28

An Angel Flies Home

The Sevier family arrived about noon at Fort Nolichucky on a cold gray overcast day. It required two wagons to carry them all, one driven by seventeen-year-old Joseph and another by fifteen-year-old James. Sarah and the smaller children rode in the back of the first wagon. The second wagon carried the supplies and household goods they might need for a siege. John rode his horse beside Sarah's wagon. The Sherrills were there to greet them.

"It's Bonny Kate!" Mary Ann shouted excitedly.

"Bonny Kate!" Dicky took up the call as the children greeted their old friend. They clambered out of the wagon and ran to her for a hug.

"Hello, everyone!" Bonny Kate greeted them with her usual enthusiasm. "Oh, how I've missed you, and look how you've all grown! How does it feel to have a new baby sister?"

The children fell silent as Bonny Kate walked to the back of the wagon and saw Sarah lying on a pallet, weak, and pale but cradling her infant in her arms.

"Hello, dear friend," Sarah greeted her softly, without making any effort to rise. "I have so much to say to you. Please stay with me."

"Sarah, what's wrong?" Bonny Kate asked with great concern. There was no answer. She looked to Colonel Sevier's face and saw a worried man. He dismounted and climbed into the wagon kneeling beside Sarah.

"Sarah's not well," he explained. "Is Dr. Cozby here?"

"Yes, sir," Bonny Kate answered. "Dr. Cozby is set up in the blockhouse across the way." The colonel gently picked up the baby and handed her over to Betsy. Then he slid the pallet over to the back edge of the wagon bed and jumped to the ground. When John lifted Sarah from the wagon, she winced in pain.

"We prepared the northeast blockhouse for your family, Colonel," Bonny Kate directed. "There's a bed in the same room as the fireplace." She led the colonel to the commander's blockhouse.

Inside John carefully laid Sarah on the bed in the great room. Betsy followed with the baby. They arranged the linen bedding to make her as comfortable as they could.

"It's so cold." Sarah shivered.

"I'll stir up the fire," Bonny Kate offered helpfully. She went to the fireplace to build up the fire. At that moment, Sam and Mary Sherrill entered.

"Sarah dear, it's the Sherrills," John announced. "I told you those Indians were no match for the Sherrill family rifles!"

Sarah greeted them weakly, "Hello, Mary, hello, Sam. We heard about the Indian attack and worried about you all morning."

"It was a small group, after horses, I reckon," Sam assessed the situation. "The only thing we lost the other night was sleep."

"Sarah hasn't been well since the baby came," John said. "Where's Dr. Cozby?"

"I'll show you," Sam volunteered. The men walked out as the Sevier boys and Sherrill boys began bringing in the furniture and supplies from the wagons.

"Where is Bonny Kate?" Sarah asked.

"I'm here, Sarah." Bonny Kate crossed the room from the fireplace.

"Dear, sweet friend, would you see that little Nancy has everything she needs?"

"It will be my pleasure," she answered. "So you named her Nancy, let me see the little darling." Bonny Kate received the tiny baby from Betsy. "Oh, she's adorable!"

"Thank you, Bonny Kate," Sarah sighed with relief. "I'll rest much easier with you here."

That evening the fire still blazed cheerfully. Bonny Kate sat in a chair, gently rocking Baby Nancy while she told another story to the children who still listened intently. Across the room, Sarah lay quietly attended by Dr. James Cozby, Mr. Sevier, Esther and Samuel Doak and Mary and Sam Sherrill. Bonny Kate had seen enough to know that Sarah's condition was very serious. Mary crossed the room to the fireplace.

"It's time for you children to go to bed," Mary announced. "Your mother wants to hear your prayers now. Come along!" The children made their way slowly over to their mother's bed. Mary continued, "Bonny Kate, the doctor wants to speak with us outside for a moment."

"Yes, ma'am," Bonny Kate responded. She rose carefully but woke little Nancy anyway. She laid Nancy in the arms of her twelve-year-old sister Betsy.

The Sherrills and Doaks met with Dr. Cozby outside the blockhouse.

"Folks, it's not good," Dr. Cozby began. "She's bleeding, and the fever indicates infection. The best we can do is to keep her comfortable and hope she finds the strength to fight back. We agreed that someone should sit up with her through the night. She asked for you, Bonny Kate."

"Me? Shouldn't the colonel be the one?"

"The colonel is occupied with the defense of the community. Sarah knows his restless state of mind, and she knows her own needs. That's why she asked for you."

"I'll do my best for her," Bonny Kate promised.

"Thank you, my dear," the doctor said. "Call for me if anything changes, Bonny Kate. You know I'm a light sleeper."

"Yes, Doctor."

Dr. Cozby looked at the faces around him and thought about his new friend Colonel Sevier. He felt a deep sense of remorse that he hadn't been available for Nancy's birth when the midwives from Jonesborough had encountered something they couldn't handle. Now with the poison of infection already in the blood, he couldn't do any more for the lady. "Good night, folks," he said sadly. He walked toward his blockhouse on the opposite side of the fort.

"Thank you, dear," Mary Sherrill hugged her daughter. "Call me if you need anything. Your papa will be on the night watch, and I'll be sleeping in the wagon."

"Good night, Mama." Bonny Kate shivered in the cold wind and turned back toward the blockhouse.

In the darkest moments before the dawn of day, Sarah opened her eyes and observed an apparition approaching, silhouetted in the glow of the firelight. "Are you an angel?" she asked.

"I'm no angel, Sarah, I'm just Bonny Kate."

"There were angels here a moment ago. Did you see them?"

"I'm sorry, I startled you. I wanted to see if the fever had come down any." Bonny Kate touched Sarah's face and it was quite warm. "Can I get you anything?"

Sarah looked into her eyes and answered, "Water." Bonny Kate poured a cup of water from a pitcher and elevated Sarah to drink. After her drink, Sarah laid back and grasped Bonny Kate's hand. She looked again into her friend's eyes and spoke. "You are my dearest and most constant friend. Make me a promise."

"What can I do?"

"Care for my children until John remarries."

Bonny Kate looked at Sarah in shocked surprise. "Should I go get the doctor?"

"No, he's done with me," Sarah told her. "The angels will come for me soon. I need your promise."

"Sarah, I can't . . ." Bonny Kate fought back the tears.

"Why not?" Sarah challenged. "Are you running off to get yourself married?"

"No, of course not," Bonny Kate assured her.

"Then what will become of my precious children?" she asked. "John, alone, can't do for them properly. The little ones need their minds and souls nurtured by a good Christian woman."

"The mill house is too far. I can't make that trip every day."

"I have already persuaded John to move the children home to Plum Grove," Sarah declared.

"But you know how busy I am," Bonny Kate insisted.

"I know how you love them. Stop by once a day to look in on them, just until John remarries. That won't be long. Please, Bonny Kate, for a dying friend?"

"I don't want you to die," Bonny Kate cried.

"We have no choice, you and I." Sarah smiled. "Death gives me no choice, and love gives you no choice. Please do it for me and my children."

"I will do it," Bonny Kate promised.

"Thank you, dear friend. You are a blessing to me. I love you."

Bonny Kate's tears rolled down her cheeks. "I love you too."

"I'm glad you could sit with me tonight," Sarah said. The room fell silent except for the crackling fire. "Bonny Kate?"

"Ma'am?" Bonny Kate answered.

"You had better call Mr. Sevier now," Sarah requested.

Bonny Kate rushed to put on her cloak and hurried out. The cold wind met her full in the face, but she could see the winter sky beginning to lighten despite the snow-laden overcast. She searched for Colonel Sevier along the palisade walls with great urgency.

When John entered the great room of the blockhouse, Bonny Kate waited outside trying to shelter herself from the wind. She knew John and Sarah needed their time alone. John hung up his cloak and sat beside Sarah.

"Good morning, my dear."

"Hello, sweetheart," Sarah greeted him. "I dreamed of angels standing around me. I feel such peace."

"What can we get you this morning?"

"John, I need you to promise you will remarry quickly," she said seriously.

"Sarah, don't talk like that!" he gently admonished.

"I have to get this settled, John," she declared. "I know our family needs a good woman to hold it together."

"I can't think about that," he replied.

"Then hold it in your heart and consider it when you can," she instructed. "You won't have to look far for that good woman."

John grasped her hand. "I have the perfect woman, and I'm not letting go!"

"Thank you for being the perfect husband. My life has been so blessed. I love you for all time!"

"I love you!"

Nancy began to cry. Bonny Kate was prepared for that and entered the blockhouse when she heard it. She rushed over to the cradle in a dark corner of the room to tend her. When Nancy was changed, dry and happy, Bonny Kate delivered her to her mother's bed.

"Nancy, say good morning to Mama." She placed the baby in Sarah's arms.

"God bless you, my poor little darling," Sarah cried. "You will never know me."

Both Bonny Kate and Mr. Sevier were deeply stricken by her words.

"Sarah, please," Bonny Kate reacted. "Nancy and all the others will know your great love, and they will rise up and call you blessed. This I promise!"

"Thank you for taking care of her. I want her to have my good Bible and grow up to be a great lady."

"Yes, ma'am," Bonny Kate acknowledged. She resigned herself to the inevitable outcome that Sarah understood was coming.

Sarah passed the baby back to Bonny Kate who took her to a chair by the fire to feed her a breakfast of warm goat's milk.

Pastor Samuel Doak entered next.

"Hello! Is Mrs. Sevier receiving visitors?"

"Come in, Pastor Doak," John answered.

"Good morning, Mrs. Sevier. How are you feeling this morning?"

"Pastor Doak, I saw angels standing beside me last night. Will you pray with me?"

"I will indeed." Pastor Doak took off his cloak and hat and knelt beside her bed for prayer. John knelt on the other side of the bed and each great man held a hand as they began a prayer, the first of many that morning.

In the early hours of the day, the great lady gathered all her loved ones and expressed many a beautiful good-bye. Friends and family poured out their expressions of love for her, and she did the same for them. No one harbored any unexpressed sentiments when the moment arrived.

Chapter 29

The Night of Lamentations

Bonny Kate walked out of the Sevier family blockhouse, exhausted and numbed, without any coat, into the teeth of an icy wind. She leaned back against the exterior wall, and through a flood of tears, gave full expression to her anguish.

"Oh, Heavenly Father, why?" she prayed. "Why? Oh, Lord, why?" The brisk wind mournfully joined her lament as it moaned in passing through the palisade walls of the stockade. The tears rolled down her pale cheeks, stinging her face in the freezing wind as sorrow ripped at her heart.

Sam Sherrill came out looking for her, chasing her with her wool cloak, until he found her, and wrapped her up in it.

"Papa, I can't stand the depths of this sorrow!" she cried.

Sam pulled her into his tight embrace. "There, there, bonny lass," he comforted. "Let it all go. You haven't slept. You're completely worn out."

She sobbed uncontrollably while he held her for quite a while.

"Why don't you go over to Dr. Cozby's and get some rest?" he advised. She nodded, turned, and walked toward the blockhouse on the other side of the fort. A sentry paced nearby. Sam turned to speak to the lad. "Are the scouts back, yet?"

"No, sir, all is quiet. I heard the girl crying, what's the news?"

"The colonel's wife just died."

"I'm mighty sorry," the young sentry said sadly. "There's not a soul in this fort that won't be sorely grieved to hear it."

Sam nodded his agreement. Pastor Doak stepped out of the blockhouse to find and speak with Sam Sherrill.

"Mr. Sherrill, the colonel has decided he wants the funeral at midnight on that forested hill up yonder," Pastor Doak explained. "Can you build a coffin by then?"

"Yes, Pastor. What does he want on the marker?"

"No marker," the pastor directed. "We're hiding the grave to keep the Indians from desecrating the body."

"It's a shame the children can't be there for the funeral of their mother," Sam Sherrill said sadly.

"Oh, they will all be there," Pastor Doak replied. "The colonel insisted they all go out of respect for their mother, even the baby."

"By the saints!" Sam exclaimed. "He's beside himself with grief. It's too dangerous to take all those children so far away from the fort with Indians skulking around."

"I can't dissuade him," Pastor Doak said.

"I'll get started on the preparations right away."

"Thank you, Mr. Sherrill."

That night the silent funeral procession passed through the gates of the fort and moved across the open ground toward a distant forested hill. Colonel John Sevier and Rev. Samuel Doak cautiously led the way followed by the pall bearers carrying Sarah's coffin. The Sevier children followed, with Bonny Kate carrying Baby Nancy. The Sherrills, the Browns, the Charles Robertsons, and several other families followed, accompanied by an armed escort of militia men. The procession moved beyond rifle range of the fort and into the silent forest. A sudden flash of lightning followed by distant thunder announced an approaching storm. Baby Nancy cried out, and Bonny Kate rocked her gently, trying to quiet her. Colonel Sevier and the soldiers looked around anxiously.

A detail of soldiers had prepared a grave in a small clearing on the forested hilltop. In any other season, it would have been a beautiful, peaceful setting; but at midnight in midwinter with an oncoming thunderstorm, it resembled a frightening nightmare. Sarah's family and friends arranged themselves in a solemn circle around the open grave as the wind rose and whipped at their clothing.

Thunder rumbled as Rev. Samuel Doak began the memorial. "The Lord is my shepherd; I shall not want. He maketh me to lie down in green pastures: he leadeth me beside the still waters. He restoreth my soul: he leadeth me in the paths of righteousness for his name's sake. Yea, though I walk through the valley of the shadow of death, I will fear no evil: for thou art with me; thy rod and thy staff they comfort me. Thou preparest a table before me in the presence of mine enemies: thou anointest my head with oil; my cup runneth over. Surely goodness and mercy shall follow me all the days of my life: and I will dwell in the house of the Lord for ever. Amen."

Another flash of lightning illuminated the faces or the mourners, and the rolling thunder boomed over the hills and valleys.

Samuel Doak continued. "Friends and beloved family of Sarah Hawkins Sevier, we celebrate the life of our dear sister in Christ. Her many virtues and kind deeds in a life of useful service are well remembered. She was a beautiful spirit, a perfect wife, and a loving mother of ten fine children. She was a constant friend to her community and was a blessing to the less fortunate. How then can even the angels in heaven not shed a tear as we mourn this dear woman's departure from our midst. Our only comfort in life and in death is that we belong—body and soul—not to ourselves but to our faithful Savior, Jesus Christ, who at the cost of his own blood has fully paid for our sins and by his Holy Spirit assures us of eternal life! Let us pray. Merciful God, Lord of life, we thank you for the gift of Sarah's life. We commend her soul to thy care until our blessed reunion at the resurrection. Comfort us as we grieve. Let us say together the prayer the Lord taught us to pray saying."

The entire assembly joined the pastor in saying those familiar and comforting words. "Our Father, which art in heaven, hallowed be thy name. Thy kingdom come. Thy will be done in earth, as it is in heaven. Give us this day our daily bread. And forgive us our debts, as we forgive our debtors. And lead us not into temptation, but deliver us from evil: For thine is the kingdom, and the power, and the glory, for ever. Amen."

The rain began as though the heavens were indeed shedding tears for Sarah, but there is no sorrow in heaven so they must have been tears of joy that no human heart can yet understand. Colonel Sevier signaled the soldiers, and they lowered the coffin into the grave and rapidly shoveled earth over it.

Reverend Doak concluded the service, unhurried by the coming storm. "May the peace of God, which passeth all understanding, keep your hearts and minds in the knowledge and love of God and of His Son, Jesus Christ, our Lord, and the blessing of God Almighty, the Father, the Son, and the Holy Spirit, be among you and remain with you always. Amen."

The rain came heavy and the people turned toward the safety and shelter of the fort. Many broke into a run. Eight-year-old Mary Ann Sevier fell to the ground in front of Bonny Kate and Mrs. Sherrill. While most of the mourners hurried away, Mary Ann lay weeping on the forest floor.

"Mary Ann, honey, we have to go." Bonny Kate urged her.

Mary Ann cried hysterically, "No, I cannot leave my mama!"

Bonny Kate handed Baby Nancy over to Mary Sherrill who hurried after the others. Bonny Kate knelt beside Mary Ann. "Oh, sweetheart, I'm sorry, but we have to get you out of this cold rain."

"No! I want my mama!" she wailed.

"Come now, sweetheart!"

"Go away!"

"I will not leave you," Bonny Kate promised. "Look, you are getting your pretty white mitts all muddy. Come on, get up. I'll carry you."

Lightning illuminated the soldiers covering the grave with brush and leaves. As they finished they picked up their rifles and shovels and ran for the fort.

"No, I can't go," Mary Ann insisted.

A young woman ran over to Bonny Kate and placed her hand on Bonny Kate's shoulder. A familiar voice asked, "What's the trouble?"

"It's Mary Ann," Bonny Kate responded. "She's too frightened to move."

"You better hurry," the young woman told her. "You're all alone. The soldiers are gone."

"I'll have to carry her," Bonny Kate decided. "Can you help me get her on my back?" The young woman picked up Mary Ann and moved her to Bonny Kate's back. Bonny Kate stood up with her little burden and began her journey toward warmth and safety.

"Come quickly!" the young woman urged, dashing ahead of Bonny Kate, who glanced up in time to see her helper in a white gown. The young woman, already far ahead, vanished in the gloom. Bonny Kate meant to overtake her and wondered who owned that familiar voice, and who in the world would wear white to a night funeral? Bonny Kate ran through the chilling driving rain, plunging through forest undergrowth. She stopped a moment to look around and listen. A flash of lightning illuminated the form of a man, a powerful warrior, with a rifle in one hand and a tomahawk in the other, running after her. She turned and ran as fast as she could, burdened with her precious load. The sound of the pursuer drew closer, louder than either her labored breathing or her pounding heart.

"Is that my Bonny Kate?" sounded another familiar voice.

"Oh, Colonel, thank God it's you! I thought everyone had left us."

"I'm the last," he said, at last drawing near to her.

Bonny Kate looked at the hand she thought was carrying the tomahawk and saw it was not what she imagined. "It's your hat!" she exclaimed.

Colonel Sevier looked at the crumpled hat clutched in his hand wondering why the shallow female mind would be so concerned about so minor an accessory at a time like this. "Oh yes, the rain has rather ruined it. What's wrong with Mary Ann?"

"She's overcome with grief and fright," Bonny Kate informed him.

"I'll take her," he offered.

"You have burdens enough, good sir," she turned and continued her run, feeling safe now, but desiring the comfort of the fireside. "Keep your rifle ready, and your powder dry!"

They jogged along silently, leaving the dark woods behind, and crossing the open ground approaching the fort.

"Who goes there?" The lookout on the wall challenged them.

"Colonel Sevier," John answered. "And with me is the last of the funeral party."

"Come on in, Colonel Sevier," the sentry called.

Samuel Doak and Samuel Sherrill met the stragglers at the gate.

"The last shall be first and the first shall be last," quoted Pastor Doak as he lifted Mary Ann from Bonny Kate's back and carried her into the blockhouse. Samuel Sherrill barred the gate and also headed for the blockhouse. Bonny Kate leaned against the palisade wall to catch her breath. John stood beside her. He had so much in his heavy heart to say in gratitude to Sarah's best friend.

"Bonny Kate, thank you for your kindness," his voice wavered and either rain or tears were streaming down his face.

She answered breathlessly, "I loved Sarah. This hurts so bad . . . for the children . . . and for you!" She sobbed uncontrollably. "I'm sorry! I'm so sorry for you!" She turned and rushed toward the blockhouse. Pausing in the light of the open door, she turned her lovely head and looked at the man still clutching his bedraggled hat, standing forlornly, bareheaded in the rain. Baby Nancy, good as gold throughout the funeral, now cried hungrily. Bonny Kate disappeared into the blockhouse.

Inside the blockhouse, the Sevier children were helped out of their wet clothes, dressed for bed, wrapped in warm wool blankets, and seated near the cheerful fire. They were surrounded by caregivers who ministered to them or simply sat with them in brooding silence.

"Who wore the white gown to the funeral?" Bonny Kate asked out loud, hoping to discover the identity of the young woman who helped her retrieve Mary Ann.

"Nobody but Sarah," Sam Sherrill answered the strange question.

"You were resting when we prepared the body," her mother told her. "We dressed her in her finest white gown, washed and fixed her hair, and we gently lowered her onto her finest quilt lining the box. She was beautiful in death as she was in life."

Ruth Brown spoke next, "John placed her silver cross, the one she was always so fond of wearing, right over her heart and folded her hands across her breast, first the right, and then the left. He sweetly kissed her on the lips, and dropped the veil over her face. Ah, he bade her so tender, the sad good-bye."

"And peace she found at last, until the day of resurrection!" Sam Doak finished the conversation.

Bonny Kate would ask no more questions about the woman in white. The lightning must have blinded her in the instant she looked at the helpful lady. Nevertheless, a chill ran up and down her spine, and she scooted closer to the fire.

Chapter 30

The Days of Mourning

When the sun came up, John, unshaven, cold, weary, and hungry, entered the blockhouse to find Bonny Kate reading Bible stories to his children. "Good day, Colonel Sevier," Bonny Kate greeted him from the circle of children at the fireside. John closed the door and looked around the room. He was surprised to see all the children still awake.

"I'm afraid it is not a good day, Miss Sherrill," he sighed.

"Please sit here by the fire, sir." She stood offering her chair. He approached slowly, and she met him, taking his cloak and hanging it on a wall peg.

John eased himself onto the chair she had vacated, and the children all turned to look at him in silence. He looked at each face in turn, searching for that part of his Sarah in each one. He studied fair Betsy the longest, for she at age twelve resembled her mother the most, just three years shy of the age Sarah had married him. His gaze finally fixed away on the glowing embers, and none of them said anything.

"A bowl of hot porridge will set you right," Bonny Kate volunteered. She moved lightly, entering the family circle with a bowl and spoon and opened the pot hanging in the fireplace. She ladled a helping into the bowl and served it to their father.

"Thank you, Miss Sherrill. You are most kind." He was a man undone, weathered and beaten, wrecked on the rocks of life, and lashed by the winds of misfortune; but his politeness never failed. He ate, slowly, all the while gazing into the fire.

"Excuse me, Colonel," she broke the silence. "I'll fetch some more firewood." She pulled on a heavy cloak and stepped out into the icy wind that nearly took her breath away. "North wind," she thought out loud, "that will drop the temperature." The cold air cleared her head, too long occupied with the melancholy. She breathed deeply to clear her lungs clouded with the smoke of cook fires. "I must be strong for the children," she told herself.

The fort was quiet. Many folks, including her own, were still soundly asleep. She paused in the rare solitude and sat on the stump they used for splitting firewood. "Be strong for the children," she repeated, but it was no use. In the early morning stillness in the midst of the woodpile, she gave herself up to another good cry and wept like a motherless child.

Sometime later she became aware of a man standing nearby. She looked up into the tear-streamed face of the colonel. She stood and curtsied and he bowed politely, making an effort to wipe away his own tears.

"I have shed no tears since the midnight service, but the effect of your demonstration has moved me again to do likewise," he explained.

"Forgive me, Colonel Sevier, I had hoped not to be observed," she replied. "I never had a more constant and loving friend than your dear Sarah, and I suffer great pain in the loss of her. So I beg your forgiveness."

"There is no offense to forgive," he spoke gently. "It is natural for us both to express what we feel."

From his words, Bonny Kate thought he might now actually express his feelings, a rare thing in a great and powerful man. If so, she resolved to stand and take it, right now here in the woodpile, whatever he chose to unload.

"Thank you for comforting my children this morning," he began. "Lord knows they need it." He paused a moment thinking. "When you left to gather the firewood, they all looked at me with the same thought in their eyes. 'What now, Papa?' And for the first time in my life I had no answer!" He turned from her and looked at the door of the blockhouse. "What shall I tell them, Miss Sherrill? What words of wisdom, hope, comfort, or love will do at a time like this?"

Bonny Kate, who had prepared herself to listen, could not think of a thing to say. She was totally unprepared with any kind of response.

Inside the blockhouse, Baby Nancy began to cry. "That's Nancy," Bonny Kate observed.

"What shall I say to them?" he repeated.

"I know she is not hungry, she must be wet," Bonny Kate said as she stepped toward the blockhouse. John took her hand to help her step over the firewood scattered about, but retained his hold on it, and asked his question again.

"What now, Papa? How would you answer that?" he persisted.

Before Bonny Kate could say anything to excuse herself, the sergeant of the guard approached and saluted smartly. "Colonel, the morning patrol has returned and awaits your pleasure."

"My pleasure?" John asked.

"To hear their report, sir. You wanted to be called when they reported in."

"Oh yes, their report." John's fatigue manifested itself as distraction.

The baby's crying became more insistent. Bonny Kate pulled gently on his hand so that she might free herself, and he turned his head to face her. "I'm hearing Nancy's report," she said. "By your leave, Colonel, I must go to her." John released her hand.

"Carry on, Miss Sherrill, by all means, carry on."

Bonny Kate was struck by his words and quickly turned about. "There's your answer, Colonel Sevier," she said. "As good an answer as any."

"What?" His thoughts had not followed hers.

"Carry on, sir."

"Carry on, Miss Sherrill?"

"Carry on," she repeated. "Tell your children to carry on."

"Are you ready for the morning report, Colonel?" The sergeant again captured John's attention.

"Yes, carry on sergeant. I'll collect my cloak and join you." John turned again to Bonny Kate who had arrived at the blockhouse door. "Oh, Miss Sherrill, could I trouble you for my cloak, when you have done with it?"

"Oh, am I wearing your cloak? So I am!" She removed it quickly and handed it to him. "Forgive me, Colonel. It seems I am always trespassing among your possessions."

"For the life of me, I cannot understand what that means." His bewilderment was perhaps tinged with genuine annoyance.

Bonny Kate laughed, entered the warm blockhouse, and closed the door. She immediately regretted laughing and feared the impulse had been inappropriate. She had indeed trespassed among his possessions ever since he rescued her, and her own mouth had just now confessed it, without herself realizing what it really meant. She rushed to Nancy's cradle.

Bonny Kate had correctly guessed little Nancy had wet her diaper and her gown and her bedding. As she busied herself with the baby's needs, her thoughts returned to the encounter at the woodpile. The only man in the world she respected so highly, and admired so frequently, had come to her for help to find the right words. She had failed him, in an awkward, unprepared moment, failed him miserably. No, it was worse than failure. His needs were deeper than the words he sought. He had leaned on her, emotionally leaned on her, placing his fragile trust, and the uncertain health of his family relationships into her hands for a moment; and she had proved unuseful. Oh, what a difference a few hours of sleep might have made! She could have thought of something profound and important to say. She needed time to search the Psalms and Proverbs, but the moment was gone, the colonel annoyed with her and other experienced women readily available on which he could lean. Ruth Brown, Kesiah Sevier, Susannah Robertson, Esther Doak, and Mary Sherrill would all have served him better than she did.

Bonny Kate rejoined the children at the fireside with Baby Nancy in her warm embrace. Betsy and Mary Ann were sobbing softly, Rebecca and Little Val were napping on a blanket, Dolly, and Dicky sat still, lost in their thoughts.

"I thought you were getting firewood," Dicky reminded her. "Couldn't you find any?"

"Oh, Dicky," Bonny Kate replied. "I completely forgot."

"Papa, followed you out there and made you forget, didn't he?" Betsy observed. "What were you talking about?"

"Well, Betsy," she began carefully, choosing not to confide the whole sorry story of her recent encounter. "He is very concerned about each and every one of you. He loves you so much and wants what is best for you."

"They are going to divide us up and send us away, are they not?" Betsy charged. "You and he were discussing that, weren't you?"

"No, Betsy," Bonny Kate denied vigorously. "Where did you get such an idea as that?"

"Aunt Kesiah told me," Betsy replied. "She has already spoken for me and Mary Ann. We will live with them in Jonesborough and be put to work taking care of her babies and working in Uncle Robert's tavern."

The idea of Sarah's sweet girls made to serve as barmaids to the rough characters of Jonesborough's taverns shocked Bonny Kate. Surely, Colonel Sevier would never have been a party to such a plan for his own daughters. But then again, he himself had grown up in his father's tavern in Augusta County, Virginia, and thrived on the experience. Bonny Kate was faced with a fateful decision at that moment. Should she risk trespassing again in Sevier family business by advocating for keeping the children together, or should she stay away from the issue and seem to be a part of the adult conspiracy to break the family apart? She followed her heart.

"There has been a misunderstanding," she stalled. "Let's try to clear it up with your father when he returns. I don't believe he would agree to any such thing, especially when your mother's wishes were so well known."

"I knew Bonny Kate would take up the fight and declare for our side!" Betsy exclaimed dramatically, throwing her arms around Bonny Kate's neck and hugging. It started a parade of young Seviers each giving her a hug, including those who had appeared to be napping. "We heard you promise Mother to care for us until Papa marries again," Betsy continued. "And a deathbed promise is sacred. You must remind Papa of that."

Bonny Kate immediately had misgivings. She found herself not only trespassing in Colonel Sevier's family business again, but as the ringleader of an insurrection in his immediate family. She was sure his military powers as a wartime Colonel would allow him to hang her for the crime of high treason. She yearned for someone to take over at that moment, and let her get some sleep. She needed someone to arrive that could give these children hope, faith, and patient love. As soon as she thought it, the door opened, and in walked Reverend and Mrs. Doak.

"Oh, Pastor Doak, thank God you're here!" Bonny Kate spoke with such deep feeling the Doaks were a little surprised. "I am so done in!"

"Well, you go rest, dear. We will take over from here," Esther Doak reassured her. "My, my, do I see some smiles this morning?"

The gloom that had prevailed the entire morning had lifted; and Bonny Kate, the revolutionary leader, knew the reason why. The children now had the hope of staying together as a family, and maybe someday as their beloved mother had wished, they would once again know a mother's love. Bonny Kate was satisfied that she had done all she could for now. Even a false hope is better than no hope at all.

The exhausted girl repaired to her corner of Dr. Cozby's blockhouse and collapsed on her cot. The noise of midday activities in the crowded fort might have kept her awake, but it was her thoughts that forestalled sleep. She thought about the grieving children and their strong desire to stay together as a family. She resented Kesiah Sevier's ill-timed offer to take away the two elder girls so they could be made useful in Robert's Jonesborough tavern. She struggled to understand Colonel Sevier's priorities as he labored under the pressures of public service and duty to country. How much of that could he or would he give up now? In a military emergency, he might well consider options as strange as Kesiah's plan to take the two elder girls. She decided she must seek another interview with the colonel and clear up the whole mess without the appearance of trespassing.

She drifted into a troubled sleep. Unbeknownst to the sleeping beauty, "carry on" became a sort of Sevier family motto that day, expressing both the burden of sorrow they must carry and the hope of moving on to eventual healing. She had accomplished more than she knew.

Chapter 31

The Childcare Problem

At dawn the next morning, Bonny Kate awoke and realized she had slept all afternoon and through the night. She prepared herself for the day, and joined Dr. Cozby at the fireside. She busied herself cooking breakfast for the doctor and some of the garrison just relieved from the night watch. After breakfast, the soldiers bedded down on the upper floor of the blockhouse, and Bonny Kate had some time with the good doctor to learn some of the news.

"I am glad to see you alive," Dr. Cozby said. "I have rarely seen a person sleep so soundly amidst so much activity."

"What activity?" she asked indulging her curiosity.

"The Committee of Safety met here last night to consider allowing families to return to their homes. Then there were the callers who came by to inquire of your whereabouts and well-being." Dr. Cozby smiled.

"Who called?" she asked.

"Reverend and Mrs. Doak, your parents, your sister Susan, a delegation of young Seviers, Mr. and Mrs. Brown, Kesiah Sevier, and Colonel Sevier himself," he replied. "They all appreciate the care you provided to the Sevier family."

"I managed to wear myself out, without doing anybody much good," she sighed.

"That's not the general opinion among those you assisted," Dr. Cozby assured her. "Anyway, the rangers have been all the way downstream to the French Broad, and there are no signs of Indian activity. The harsh weather has worked a hardship on the Indians, as it has on us. The committee decided last night to let families on the upper Nolichucky return to their homes."

"That does not include my family, does it?" she contemplated.

"Which family is that?" Dr. Cozby asked.

"That's a silly question. I most certainly do have a family!" she exclaimed.

"Of course you do, perhaps more than one. There is some speculation that you may move in with the Seviers because of a certain promise you made." Dr. Cozby was probing for a reaction.

"That is pure speculation. There have been no discussions with me about it and certainly no invitation from the head of the family," she declared.

"I don't suppose you could explain why some members of the community attach great meaning to the fact that you and he were seen holding hands in the woodpile yesterday morning, just hours after the funeral of his wife." Dr. Cozby grinned.

"Oh, for goodness' sake, there was no meaning to it at all! He was just helping me step over some rough ground." Under Sarah's influence, Bonny Kate had become very sensitive to appearances. "James Cozby, don't you go starting rumors and making up scandals," she scolded. "You know Colonel Sevier is the most honorable man in the country, and he may very well die of a broken heart before he ever again courts another woman. So, Doctor, broken hearts are your problem, not mine."

Dr. Cozby sat in a chair beside the fire. "I suppose you are right; but when I treat his case, if I determine it to be in his best interests that he should marry again, could I impose upon you?"

"You may not! I want no part of any of your harebrained schemes." She sat in another chair beside the mischievous doctor, tired of his game and continued almost sadly. "Besides, what have the colonel and I ever really had in common?"

"Hot blood," Dr. Cozby replied quickly.

"Hot blood, indeed?" she raged playfully. "I'll show you hot blood." She jumped up and seized a tomahawk from the mantle above the fireplace and menaced him with it. "Come now, Doctor, I'll only bleed you a little. This won't hurt a bit."

Dr. Cozby jumped up and made for the door with the savage girl on his heels. As he threw open the door, Pastor Doak blocked the way with his impressive frame.

"Excuse me, Doctor, I'm calling for Miss Sherrill, but it appears that I have stumbled into a domestic squabble."

"Good morning, Pastor Doak. Actually we were just now considering the medical uses of the tomahawk. Miss Sherrill seems to have developed a technique that may revolutionize the art of modern medicine," explained the doctor.

Bonny Kate dropped the tomahawk on the doctor's table and blushed as red as the rose. "Yes, Doctor, perhaps we could postpone the demonstration until Pastor Doak has concluded his business here."

"You appear much rested since last we saw you, Miss Sherrill," the pastor observed. "And there is much color in your cheeks."

"It's my hot blood," she replied sarcastically, with a withering glance at the highly amused doctor.

"Well, fetch your cloak, we have been summoned by Colonel Sevier to attend to some business for him concerning his family," explained the Pastor.

"I cannot imagine why he would involve me in his family business." Bonny Kate was reluctant to return to the emotional turmoil and brooding sadness and silent oppressiveness of the grieving Seviers, but return she must. Pastor Doak was a good companion for such a mission. He always had a sense of the appropriate that might steer her clear of trouble this time.

The day was overcast and cold enough to snow. On the commons, there were family groups huddled around their morning cook fires. The eyes of the community followed her as she crossed over to the colonel's blockhouse. She was curious as to what they knew and what they might be thinking. She thought she might like to stop and visit some of the friendlier families, but Pastor Doak's pace communicated the urgency and perhaps the importance of his business.

Sam Sherrill approached them halfway across the commons. "Hold up there, Pastor, I'd like a word with my daughter."

"Certainly, Mr. Sherrill, but be brief. Colonel Sevier is waiting for us."

"Listen, Kate, I had a talk with the colonel yesterday; and he's being pulled in so many directions he's not thinking straight. Don't agree to anything long term or long distance. I won't have you moving off."

"Father, I'm sure I don't know what this is about," she replied.

"Remember, you may be twenty-five, but you still have some good prospects. Don't throw it away by getting mixed up in the colonel's business," he warned.

"But he's our friend," she protested.

"Don't ever mix friendship with business. If they offer money, don't take it!"

"Mr. Sherrill, we are only discussing Colonel Sevier's plan for the care and education of his children. I'm sure you can trust your daughter to give him good advice," Pastor Doak reassured him. They left Sam Sherrill and continued their way to the opposite blockhouse.

"What is the plan?" she wanted to know.

"There is no plan," he answered. "I think the problem is too many planners. All John's folks have their ideas, and Sarah's folks arrived yesterday evening with more suggestions. It is a mess."

Inside the blockhouse, the whole extended family had gathered; John's father Val and stepmother Jemima, Sarah's parents Joseph and Sarah Hawkins, Robert Sevier and Kesiah, Kesiah's parents, Charles and Susannah Robertson and Sheriff Val Sevier and his wife Naomi. Waightstill Avery, the Jonesborough lawyer was also there. The lawyer, Bonny Kate, and Samuel Doak were the only ones not related to the family.

Mrs. Hawkins eyed Bonny Kate and asked, "Is this the young woman?"

"This is Bonny Kate Sherrill, Sarah's best friend among the neighboring families," Pastor Doak introduced her. Bonny Kate curtsied respectfully.

"Miss Sherrill," Mrs. Hawkins spoke with a sharp edge. "Did my daughter instruct you to care for her children?"

"Yes, ma'am. That last night, I was asked to attend her and she understood the urgency of putting her affairs in order better than any of us."

"Under what circumstances were you to care for the children?"

"Sarah asked me to ride to Plum Grove every day and make sure they had proper meals and the attentions of a Christian woman. She charged me with the especial care of bringing up Baby Nancy in the Christian faith," Bonny Kate answered clearly. "Sarah assured me that this arrangement was only to last until Colonel Sevier remarried, and she thought the event would take place soon. With those assurances, she made me promise to carry out her wishes. I am willing and able to keep my promise for the sake of the children and because of my devotion to the best friend I ever knew."

Everybody turned to look at John. He was shocked at Bonny Kate's confidence in a speedy remarriage. "Miss Sherrill, I do not understand where you got the idea that I will remarry soon, for I grieve long and deep these days, and I see no end in sight."

"Mr. Avery did you write down everything she said?" Mrs. Hawkins asked.

"Yes, I believe I have it all. Miss Sherrill, is there anything else the late Mrs. Sevier told you pertaining to her wishes?" Mr. Avery asked.

"Why yes," she responded. "Sarah told me she wanted Nancy to have her good Bible as an inheritance. She also said that Colonel Sevier had already promised her he would move the family back to Plum Grove so I could more conveniently care for the children."

Everybody again turned to John, and he looked surprised. "Sarah talked about that, but I gave no promise."

"What do we know about this young woman?" asked Mrs. Hawkins.

"She comes from a good North Carolina family," Pastor Doak replied.

"Her grandfather was Adam Sherrill," spoke up Val Sevier. "I served with him in the Augusta County militia years ago. Joe, you probably traded with 'Honest Will' Sherrill."

"Sure I did!" responded Mr. Hawkins. "Is she related to Honest Will?"

"He was my great uncle," Bonny Kate answered. "I can read, write, figure, and teach the children to do the same."

"Her mother was a Preston," Val Sevier continued.

"How is she related to Colonel William Preston?" Mr. Hawkins asked.

"He is a cousin of my mother," Bonny Kate replied. "I can sing, read the Bible, and recite my catechisms."

"She breeds horses," Robert Sevier contributed.

"She can outrun and outjump any Indian!" Betsy exclaimed.

"And she shoots fairly straight," Colonel Sevier added with a smile, which brought a smile to Bonny Kate's face.

Kesiah Sevier spoke up. "We have learned that she is related to the notorious Ute Perkins and his gang of horse thieves!"

"That is true," Bonny Kate spoke in defense of her family's honor. "Ute Perkins was my grandfather's nephew, but all that happened before I was born. On the Sherrill side of the family there has never been anything but honest trading and fair prices."

"Enough about her character and breeding," Jemima Sevier interrupted. "What will she cost us?" She turned to Bonny Kate. "Young woman, you must certainly know that my stepson is exceedingly rich with trunks full of money all over the house, and in a few short weeks, women like you will be as thick as flies after his fortune."

Bonny Kate smiled and suppressed a laugh. "Mrs. Sevier, I cannot accept money for care of the children. It is for love of Sarah and her children that I am prepared to keep my promise. Besides, Sarah showed me the trunks of state notes and continental money, and I know that unless the cause of liberty is won, the money is not worth the paper it's printed on. Even then, Congress will have a hard time backing that currency while meeting the financial obligations it incurred to fund the war. No, Mrs. Sevier, the colonel's wealth lies not in trunks of money but in the friendships he has made in the cause of liberty, and in the people he has helped by taking their worthless continental notes in exchange for hard silver and rights to land."

John smiled and bowed in acknowledgment. She returned the smile.

Charles Robertson stood up to speak. "Miss Sherrill, that was a fair demonstration of an advanced knowledge of the economic and the politick."

"Thank you, Major Robertson," she replied. "Now why must I stand trial to be allowed to help my best friend's family through a very difficult time?"

"Because we have other plans," Kesiah cut in sharply. "And we don't need outsiders to direct our family business."

"I will do what I promised to do if Colonel Sevier directs me to, but don't forget to listen to what the children themselves want."

"Miss Sherrill, would you take the children to Dr. Cozby's and keep them there while we discuss the matter further?" John directed.

"But at least listen to what the children want," she pleaded.

"Carry on, Miss Sherrill," John ordered impatiently.

"Yes, sir," she conceded. "Come along children fetch your cloaks and bundle up. We must obey the colonel's orders." Betsy brought Baby Nancy to Bonny Kate and herded the others out the door.

"Pastor Doak, please present your education plan for the older boys," John was heard saying as they left the blockhouse.

Outside Bonny Kate drew a deep breath of cold air and looked at Betsy and the others. *What brave little children*, she thought. *They don't even understand what is happening and yet here they are, going along with whatever the colonel orders, and what Betsy directs them to do. Sarah would be so proud of them. Oh, Sarah, the joys you will miss by not seeing them carry on and grow up!*

"You were magnificent!" Betsy exclaimed.

"Betsy, the object is to keep your family together at Plum Grove as your mother wanted. In that, I accomplished very little," Bonny Kate replied.

"The men were enchanted with you, and the women were jealous of you. That is the measure of great womanhood," Betsy observed.

"No, Betsy, your mother was the model of great womanhood," Bonny Kate corrected her. "She enchanted the men to be sure, but she also converted the jealous women into loyal allies and dear friends. Now that is great womanhood!"

Back at Dr. Cozby's, the children played and napped, quite indifferent to the designs being debated concerning their future lives. Only Betsy showed any anxiety. Sam and Mary Sherrill came in to warm themselves by the fire and inquire of Bonny Kate, the results of the morning interview. There was little she could tell them.

About midday, Colonel Sevier emerged from the blockhouse with his brothers Robert and Val. The patrol assembled, mounted their horses, and rode out. Shortly after that, Kesiah Sevier called for the children to return to the family blockhouse.

"Kesiah," Bonny Kate inquired. "What decisions have been made?"

"John says he's not prepared to make a decision until the Indian trouble has been resolved. Men are so stubborn," she replied. "The advantages of society are found in Jonesborough, not on some isolated wilderness farm."

"Plum Grove is the finest plantation in Washington County!" Bonny Kate argued.

"Fine for horse people and dirt farmers, but John Sevier is no part of that," Kesiah declared. "He's destined for greater things. And here's some advice for you, Miss Sherrill. Do not covet those things to which you can never aspire. Come along children, your family is waiting for you."

Kesiah gathered the children, took up Nancy, and retreated across the commons. Bonny Kate felt her hot blood begin to rise and thought of Dr. Cozby's tomahawk over on the mantle, not that she would ever harm Sarah's dear sister-in-law. But what a scandal she would create brandishing that weapon and chasing the haughty bitch around the fort a few times giving her a proper fright, and a healthier respect for horse people and dirt farmers. Bonny Kate laughed out loud at the image and thought about what to prepare for lunch. The night watch was stirring on the floor above, awakened no doubt, by the rough nature of Kesiah's speech.

A break in the harsh winter weather and the evaporation of the Indian threats lifted spirits at Fort Nolichucky. Colonel Sevier was constantly busy organizing patrols and detailing troops to bring in fresh water, firewood, and food. His insistence on fresh water and his notions about boiling the drinking water, were widely credited and particularly praised by Dr. Cozby as the reason Fort Nolichucky had avoided the dreaded outbreaks of camp fever that invariably accompanied "forting the families." As a result of his activity, he was absent from the children most of the time.

Bonny Kate spent every day caring for the seven younger Sevier children. She noted that more and more cheerfulness was returning to their games and their conversations. She thought the grieving and healing process for the children might have progressed more steadily with more involvement from Colonel Sevier, but his service kept him away. The children spoke openly about returning to Plum Grove after Aunt Kesiah and Uncle Robert left to return to Jonesborough. Granny and Grandpa Hawkins had also left the fort and taken the lawyer with them. John's parents also left returning to their home on Stony Creek. Apparently, they all got tired of waiting for the colonel to make his decision.

Bonny Kate found opportunities to talk to Sarah's three elder boys to make sure they were healing as well. They seemed to be adjusting to life without a mother by staying busy. Joseph, nearly eighteen, rode with the rangers. James at fifteen wished he could ride with the rangers but served on the water and firewood details. John Junior was fourteen and busied himself around the horse corral. The boys usually ate with the soldiers for breakfast and lunch but always joined the rest of the family for dinner. Bonny Kate had recruited her mother to help with the cooking, so Seviers and Sherrills often ate together further improving the mood in the Sevier family.

The Robertsons and Browns had returned to their farms, on the upper Nolichucky, and all of Jonesborough was resettled. The day finally arrived when Colonel Sevier had determined it was safe for the downriver families to go home as well.

Bonny Kate made an excellent breakfast in the great stone fireplace of the blockhouse and was ready to serve the few remaining families. Betsy helped her and seemed very happy.

"Betsy, we are going home today; what did your father decide about your family?" Bonny Kate asked.

"I can't say," she replied. "But I think you will be pleased."

"What do you mean?"

"Father confided in me last night," she said with a smile.

"Then it's Plum Grove!"

"I can't tell you. Father needed to speak with you first." Betsy was guarding a family secret.

Bonny Kate thought about what Colonel Sevier might propose. He had not spoken to her since the family meeting where so much discussion had gone into the arrangement, so she wondered if she would be included in the plan at all.

All ten of Colonel Sevier's children came to the breakfast; and in addition, all the Sherrills were there with the Waddells, the Taylors, the Doaks, and Dr. Cozby. When everyone had eaten, Colonel Sevier stood and announced the resettlement plan for all those present, except for his own family. After the other families had left to pack their belongings, while Bonny Kate, her mother, and the young Seviers were washing the plates and pans from breakfast, Colonel Sevier stepped over to where she worked.

"Miss Sherrill, could I speak with you at your convenience?" John asked.

"Why yes, Colonel Sevier," she replied. "I'll be right there." She dried her hands and removed her apron. He escorted her outside to a bench beside the gate of the fort where they both sat down.

"Miss Sherrill," he began. "I am moving Joseph and James to the millhouse, so they can operate the business, and live within riding distance of Pastor Doak's Log College, where they will attend to their schooling. The younger children will move to Plum Grove with me, where I will maintain my headquarters. Plum Grove must become fully productive this year to support the family, supply the militia, and provide care for the needy families. I will need the help you so generously offered Sarah."

"A very good plan, Colonel Sevier," Bonny Kate responded. "I will be glad to help you out."

"That's fine, my Bonny Kate," he exclaimed. "I knew I could depend on your help, even though most of my family opposed the plan. I have decided to appoint you governess to my children, to oversee their care and nurture, their spiritual development, their discipline, their education, and their training to manage Plum Grove Plantation. In consideration for the responsibilities of this position, I will provide you room and board, pay you an annual salary, and set up a household account to spend as you see necessary. I have a contract here that spells out all the details."

Bonny Kate stared at the paper in his hand in stunned silence. She could not say a word, until she remembered her father's warning about receiving money for helping a friend in need.

"No . . . ," she stammered. "No, I couldn't do that." She stood up and walked a few paces away.

"But why not?" he asked. "What in my offer displeases you?"

"Well, first of all, it is the idea of this contract," she answered.

"That part was not my idea," he explained. "The family insisted on it."

"My father would never allow me to enter into a contract," she said.

"Why not?" he asked.

"Colonel Sevier, I am a freeborn woman of the wilderness. I won't be bound by any contract. I will perform according to the promise I made to Sarah, nothing more and nothing less," she declared. "I'm not living at Plum Grove, I want no salary, and I am not doing for your children those things that you yourself ought to do."

John stood and faced her with all his authority. "Miss Sherrill, you are known to drive a hard bargain. What is it you want?"

"I want you to know your children," she implored. "Spend time and be involved with them and listen to their thoughts and feelings. It is the best medicine you could ever give them to heal their young souls from the horrible hurt they have suffered."

"I wish I had the time," he replied regretfully.

"Take the time, Colonel," she urged. "I will only be present a few hours each day to help with meals and to reinforce the progress you make with them. They will be forced to rely on your wisdom and counsel, your steadfast devotion, and your loving discipline. If you do this, your children will recover quickly and completely, and so will you! Then, maybe in a year or two, you could begin to think about reintroducing a loving feminine presence that they could learn to love as 'stepmother,' and one with whom you could allow yourself to fall in love again."

"Stop, Miss Sherrill, stop . . ." Colonel Sevier was agitated. He seemed to be disturbed at what she said. Perhaps she had carried her vision of the process too far. Perhaps he was too pained to imagine ever finding a loving relationship again. She waited, not knowing what to say next.

He reached into his pocket and felt the paper of a secret letter from Governor Caswell, urgently calling the Washington County volunteers, to make ready for war. He wished he had never seen the letter.

"I suppose I could break up the family as Sarah's parents suggested, and place the children with family members. Then if something were to happen to me everything would already be arranged," he said sadly. "Thank you for your time, Miss Sherrill."

As he turned to walk away, she grabbed his arm firmly with both hands, arresting his progress. "Nothing is going to happen to you, do you hear me?" She reacted fiercely. He looked into the fire of her blue eyes. "I can't believe you would want such an arrangement for your children!"

"I don't," he replied calmly. "But what choice do I have? I may require more help from you than you are willing to give."

"Try me," she insisted. "We can make this work, without your silly contract!"

"What if I have to take a trip for a day or even a week?" he asked.

"The children can go home with me for a short stay at Daisy Fields. My mother would help too."

"Your horse business needs your attention. Would you be able to set aside your profession for the time you spend with my children?" he asked.

"Father and Adam can handle that," she replied.

"Nancy's care concerns me the most," John admitted. "Someone has to be there for her day and night."

"Mrs. Brown has offered to cover for me one day a week if the children are settled at Plum Grove, or I could take them up to Mrs. Doak's for a day visit." She was thinking fast. "I would even be willing to leave them with Aunt Kesiah for a day!"

"Miss Sherrill, you don't know what you are getting yourself into," he said.

"For the sake of the children, please try this my way!" she insisted.

He thought for a moment. "I will not require the contract."

"Thank you," she replied. "And I will be there each day, if you promise to be there for them every night!"

"I will do what I can," he said quietly. She released his arm from her iron grip as she realized Dr. Cozby was watching them.

Dr. Cozby had saddled his horse, mounted, and was leaving the fort to make his rounds when he approached them at the gate and stopped. "Colonel Sevier, she drives a hard bargain. If you wish to engage her, it will cost you a fortune."

"I think I will be able to afford the price." He smiled.

"So you have a deal?" Dr. Cozby asked.

John nodded, and Bonny Kate smiled.

"Did you get everything you wanted, Colonel?"

"No, of course not," John replied. "Everything is compromised."

Dr. Cozby laughed. "That's the way it is with her. Take good care of yourselves. I'll be up at Jonesborough, delivering babies, lots of babies!"

"Oh, the baby!" she exclaimed. "I have to prepare the baby's milk before she wakes!" She rushed toward the blockhouse. "Good day, Doctor! Good day, Colonel!"

Chapter 32

A State of Emergency

A meeting of the Washington County civil and military leaders convened in the log courthouse in Jonesborough at nine o'clock in the morning of March 19, 1780. A cold rain fell outside soaking the men as they made their way from the Tavern where they had their breakfast to the new courthouse. A roaring fire in the large fireplace welcomed them and removed the chill of the icy rain. Judge John Carter called the meeting to order and John Sevier, as clerk, took minutes. Major Charles Robertson, the next in command to Colonel Sevier, was present and the other commissioners included Jacob Brown, and William Bean. Major Jonathan Tipton, and the militia Captains, Joseph Wilson, John McNabb, Godfrey Isbell, William Trimble, James Stinson, Robert Sevier, and Lieutenant Landon Carter, had also been invited because of the military nature of the meeting. John Sevier was a distracted man as he sat at his clerk's desk, staring out the window, completely lost in melancholy thoughts.

The most important item on the agenda that day was a letter from the governor and a requisition from General Rutherford for militia to send to the aid of South Carolina. Judge Carter read the most chilling parts of the letter slowly and deliberately.

"The British are moving north out of Savannah, and an invasion fleet is being readied in New York. The target of all this activity is no doubt Charleston. The reason for the concern of the Assembly and the governor of this state is the alarming uprising of Tory militias throughout the Carolinas. These Tories are brutal, savage, and greedy riffraff motivated more by personal gain, than by allegiance to their king. The horrors of their atrocities are unparalleled in any other place or time."

Charles Robertson stood to speak. "Colonel Sevier showed us how to deal with Tories. He's brought peace to our settlements!"

"Thank you for that report, Major Robertson, but there's more required of us than just suppression of the Tories," continued Judge Carter. "The governor is requesting Colonel Sevier, to bring our men east and be available for action to defend Charleston as well. Our men may come up against professional British regulars, the finest soldiers on earth."

Charles Robertson stood again to be recognized.

"Yes, Major Robertson?" Judge Carter called on him.

"Mr. President, I move that Colonel Sevier and the Washington County militia be directed to answer the governor's call to arms, and we organize an expedition of one hundred men to the east for a period of sixty days."

"I second the motion," Jacob Brown called out.

"Is there any discussion?" Judge Carter saw John Sevier's raised hand. "Colonel Sevier?"

John stood up slowly and thoughtfully. "Mr. President." He stopped, and an uncomfortable silence filled the room. All eyes watched him and awaited him to continue. He stared into the fire and continued to speak. "I am grateful for the confidence placed in me as your Lieutenant Colonel, but I have reached the painful decision that I will not lead this expedition. I cannot leave my family at this time." He raised his eyes to meet the gaze of Judge Carter as silence again settled over the assembly. Many of the men knew that an expedition without their beloved Colonel Sevier at its head was likely to be poorly attended and more dangerous for those who did volunteer.

"John, you know the community will care for the children," Judge Carter promised. "The Sherrills are helping already, and many others are willing."

"I'm the only parent my children have left. I have resolved to stay behind regardless of today's vote. I'll turn over command of the militia to Major Robertson."

Jacob Brown spoke up, "With all due respect to the major, no one in this district has the same genius for leadership of the militia as John Sevier!" A rumble of side conversations and debates developed quickly.

"Order in the assembly!" Judge Carter ordered, and the room quieted. "Colonel Sevier, would you not reconsider?"

"No, sir," he answered sadly. "As always, I'll equip and provision the men for the expedition at my own expense. Major Robertson, I wish you Godspeed and pray for your success." Charles Robertson nodded his thanks.

John walked to the door and put on his cloak. He opened the door and paused to look around the silent room. He nodded to his friends, put on his hat, and stepped out into the rain. There was a moment of silence.

"The chair appoints Landon Carter as clerk to complete the recording of the minutes for the clerk who just left." Landon moved to the vacant desk and picked up the quill. "The chair rules that debate has ended," Judge Carter announced. "The motion states that we answer the governor's call to arms with a force of one hundred men for an enlistment period of sixty days. Major Robertson will command. All in favor say yea?"

"Yea!"

"Any opposed?"

There was silence.

"The motion carries," Judge Carter announced. "Having completed the stated business and there being no other matters to consider, I declare this meeting of the Washington County Assembly adjourned." Judge Carter tapped the gavel twice, and the men stood, talking and joking and delaying the trip home in the rain.

Kesiah Sevier, five months pregnant with her second child, waited upon her favorite brother-in-law in the tavern across the street from the courthouse.

"What do you mean you walked out?" she scolded John. "How does the clerk of the court just walk out during a special session of the county court?"

"I suppose it was poor form," John admitted, "but it passed for high drama, don't you think?"

She grinned. "Colonel Carter will fine you for contempt if you're not careful!"

"I'm sure he would, if he knew how contemptible I'm feeling right now," he moaned. "I announced I wasn't going to lead the eastern campaign next month."

"So they voted to go fight the Tories in North Carolina, did they?" she asked.

"Yes."

"And without you to lead them," Kesiah marveled. "That's crazy. Who will volunteer if you don't go? I'm definitely keeping my Robert home!"

"Robert has no choice." John laughed. "Your father will be in command, and what will people think if his own son-in-law refuses to serve with him?"

Kesiah laughed too. "That changes the complexion of things completely. Of course Robert will serve and proudly, even if I don't want him too. He will miss the birth of our baby."

"The campaign will very likely consume the whole summer," John predicted.

Kesiah pouted. "What excuse did you use to get out of it?"

"I'm the only parent my children have left," he explained. "I can't serve while the fate of my children is in question. They would have no legal standing even as heirs to my estates if something were to happen to me. Unfortunately for them, my estates are probably worth less than the sum total of my debts."

"Is it really that bad, my dear brother-in-law?" she empathized.

"Maybe worse than I realize," he admitted. "Sarah was the money handler, and it saddens me too greatly even to go near her neat, well-organized desk. Now I have promised to supply the militia with the provisions for the campaign."

"Why would you do that?" she demanded.

"Because I so deeply love the cause of freedom!" he declared. "I really wanted to go and serve, but it would be completely irresponsible and uncaring to do that before I find the children a new mother."

Kesiah sat down at the table across from him, her pretty face knit with concern. "John, it's only been two months. You can't possibly be thinking about marriage again, can you?"

"No, it's the farthest thing from my mind," he said sadly. "But I do worry about the children. They grow up so fast, and to do that without a loving mother is, to me, the saddest part of this family tragedy."

"I know," she said sympathetically. Several moments passed before she thought of a new direction for the conversation. "How are the children doing out there at Plum Grove?"

"Surprisingly well," he brightened.

"Is the Bonny Kate arrangement working out?"

"Yes, she has done far more than she agreed to do," he reported. "I have not kept my part of the commitment, so I avoid seeing her."

"She comes to your house every day, and you don't see her? How is that possible?"

"She never spends the night," he explained. "So I leave early before she arrives, and go home late after she leaves."

Kesiah laughed. "Good Lord, John! That's not fair. She's not going to last long doing it all herself. I thought you and she were working together!"

"Betsy tells me she's doing a good job."

"You placed all your trust in her and promised to help then deserted her?"

"I'm going to do better now that I have declined to lead the expedition," he declared. "I'll have more time to stay at the farm when court is not in session."

"Well, she sure didn't get what she expected out of this deal!" Kesiah crowed. "It serves her right for trespassing in the Sevier family business! My offer still stands, John. I'll take the two older girls when you decide it's time to farm them out and settle them here in Jonesborough."

"There are some thirsty customers, Kesiah. I'll buy the first round, and you can charge it to my account." The rain had let up and the rest of the county assemblymen repaired to the tavern. Surrounded again by his friends, John's state of mind improved temporarily to his old lively nature. He laughed at jokes and joined in the lusty songs the men sang at the fireside in the taproom that rainy afternoon.

One of John's debtors arrived at the tavern, a Mr. Anderson, and drew John aside for consultation. "Colonel Sevier, I know I owe you for the filing fee on the land I settled, but could you stake me for some seed money?"

John looked at him and recognized a truly needy man. Mr. Anderson was young, temperate, industrious, and shouldered responsibility for a wife and three children not yet to an age where they could be of much help. They had worked hard the previous year, and then suffered loss at the hands of a roving plundering band of Tories while Mr. Anderson was away with the county militia. Mrs. Anderson and the children had escaped injury by vigilance and having a secure place to hide. The Andersons were just the sort of people a community depends on for the general welfare of all.

"Mr. Anderson, have you figured out what you'll need for your acreage?" John asked him.

"Yes, sir, I have it all written out," the young man replied.

"Good," John said. "Go down to my gristmill on Limestone Creek and show that to my son Joseph. Tell him I said it was all right to give you whatever you need."

"What will I owe you?" Mr. Anderson asked.

"You paid in advance with your services to the Washington County militia last year. I hope and pray Divine Providence gives you a better year."

"Thank you, sir." Mr. Anderson smiled with relief. John invited Mr. Anderson to join the fellows at the fireside, but he politely declined. He was anxious to be on the road to Limestone Creek. John watched him go and admired the young man's ambition. He would no doubt have the horse in the field and the plow in the ground just as soon as the rain let up.

John thought about his own fields at Plum Grove and the need to begin planting for his own prosperous year, but the thought of doing it all without Sarah saddened him. He returned to the warmth of the fireside and rejoined the lively conversations of politics, real estate deals, and hunting. For a time, he pushed his cares and heavy responsibilities to the back of his mind.

Chapter 33

Something Needs to be Done

April came and with it warmer days, abundant wild flowers, and the work of planting the fertile fields along the Nolichucky. Rev. Samuel Doak had established the Salem Presbyterian Church and school on Little Limestone Creek and the Sherrills were devoted members. One morning Bonny Kate rode to the church and found the good reverend chopping wood in the yard of his cabin. His wife Esther was sitting on the porch sewing baby clothes. Pastor Doak put down his ax and greeted her.

"Hello there, Bonny Kate!"

"Good day, Pastor Doak." Bonny Kate dismounted and tied her horse to a tree. The good pastor walked over to meet her at the porch.

"Hello, Esther!" Bonny Kate greeted the pastor's wife.

"Hello, Bonny Kate. Can I get you some spicewood tea? I have it brewing."

"Yes, ma'am, I'd enjoy that," she answered. Esther rose from her chair and entered the cabin.

"What brings you out so early in the morning, Bonny Kate?"

"Pastor Doak, I need help. I've been going over to the Seviers every day to look in on the children as I promised, and my heart is breaking for those little ones . . . and for their father. I've never seen a man suffer so."

"It was a terrible loss for a family to suffer."

"Yes, sir, but now Colonel Sevier is struggling to manage all the business that Sarah used to do. They had a very cooperative partnership that allowed him the freedom to pursue positions of public service. He is a man of great mission and vision, but Sarah handled the details of his business. Without her contributions the man is failing!"

"What evidence have you seen?" Pastor Doak asked.

"It's no secret he has always generously supplied the county militia from his own resources whenever they mounted a campaign. I remember how Sarah struggled to collect debts owed to Colonel Sevier and even sold property so the money could be used to buy powder, shot, food, blankets, and horses. Now he has pledged to outfit the Carolina campaign, ordered the supplies, and now the suppliers are coming to his home seeking payment. I don't know what to tell them."

"Where is the colonel when these creditors come to call?"

"He's never home. He rides the frontier, a lonely sentinel, watching out for Indian trouble. Betsy tells me he comes home every night at suppertime, but he's gone again after breakfast. I rarely see him, and I know the children are worried about him."

"Is there anything else about his business that hints at trouble?"

"Mr. Embree who built the gristmill, the forge, and is now developing the lead mine came over recently looking for Colonel Sevier. He confided to me that all those businesses will likely fail if Colonel Sevier doesn't stop extending credit and neglecting to collect what is owed him. Mr. Embree believes Colonel Sevier is too nice a man to be in business. Everyone takes advantage of his generosity, even those who can well afford to pay!"

Esther Doak reappeared with three cups of tea on a tray. "I hope you enjoy this brew." She smiled.

"Oh, it smells wonderful!" Bonny Kate exclaimed.

"Thank you, Esther dear," Pastor Doak patted her on the back lovingly.

"You are welcome." She smiled, settling into her chair again. They all sipped the tea thoughtfully.

"The desk where Sarah kept up with all the amounts being paid and received is just the way she left it over there at the Mill House where she last lived. I visited Joseph and James Sevier the other day, and took a peek at the books. The last journal entry is in her hand, dated January 6."

"I see why you are concerned." Pastor Doak nodded.

"I realize I am trespassing in the family's business again, but on her dying day, Sarah made me promise to look after those children every day until he remarries. How will I fulfill my promise if the poor man's business crumbles around him, and he dies of a broken heart? What then, will I do with Sarah's children?"

"Have you discussed any of this with Colonel Sevier?"

"You would suppose I have access to Colonel Sevier's attentions, as the governess of his children, but that is not the case. He is disconnected from his children, his businesses, and life in general."

"That's a heavy burden for you, my dear," Pastor Doak empathized. "I see all his problems stemming from the same spiritual cause. The shock and grief of losing his wife has caused him to withdraw from those who care deeply enough to help him."

"I thought maybe you could pray a special prayer for Colonel Sevier tonight and go talk to him in the morning," Bonny Kate suggested.

"That is an excellent beginning. I can do that. As for the business problems, we can solve those as well."

"Oh, can you? I would be so grateful!"

"I'll tell you how we'll do it," Pastor Doak explained. "Joseph and James Sevier are my brightest students. With me as their teacher, they can easily learn to keep the books, collect on overdue accounts, and tighten their credit practices. That would make the gristmill and the iron forge profitable businesses, able to support the rest of the family enterprises, no matter how generous the good colonel wishes to be."

"Oh, thank you!" Bonny Kate brightened. "You know, Pastor, if it weren't for John Sevier, I wouldn't be on this good old earth. He saved me from certain death when the Indians attacked Watauga Fort."

"Yes, I've heard that story," he replied. "Don't you worry, Bonny Kate. I'll go see him tomorrow."

Bonny Kate stood to leave. "Thank you, Pastor Doak. Remember to visit him before breakfast, or he'll be gone."

"I'll be sure to start early," he promised.

"I'll be going now," she said. "I have more to do than ever with all my chores at home and caring for the Seviers. Thank you for the spicewood tea, Esther."

"You're welcome, Bonny Kate. Come see us again anytime."

"Yes, ma'am. Good day, Pastor Doak, and thank you again."

"God bless you, Bonny Kate. I'll see you on Sunday."

Bonny Kate mounted her horse and galloped away.

"Bonny Kate has a lot of faith in you, Sam," Esther observed. "What will you say to Colonel Sevier?"

"Her faith is in the Lord," he replied. "I have no idea what I'll say, but I'll pray for the right words to come from the Holy Spirit!"

That night John Sevier slept fitfully tossing and turning in his bed. He dreamed of Sarah in a beautiful gown, walking barefoot, along the other side of a river. He ran after her, to catch up with her, and hold her close to him again.

"Sarah, my love, wait there. I'll come to you!"

"No, John, do not cross the river."

"Then come here to me," he called.

"I cannot do that, but we can speak. Have you considered marriage?"

"Yes, dear heart, forgive me. I will put it out of my mind forever, if you just come back to me."

"I cannot do that. You must remarry."

"No one will have me! Sorrow has deadened all my senses."

"One lives, destined for you, but you must win her."

"Of whom do you speak?"

"The lady is not far. Find her, hold her." The apparition turned and floated away from him.

"Who, who, who," he shouted desperately trying to regain her attention. "Whoop, whoop, whoop," echoed back to him. War whoops drew his attention, and he turned around and found himself on the catwalk of Watauga Fort. Outside the wall, he saw a girl struggling to free herself from the clutches of a fierce warrior. He aimed and fired Sweet Lips then reached down and pulled the girl over the wall. When the girl looked up into his eyes, it was Sarah. The dream dissolved. He sat up in bed shaking.

"Sarah? Sarah, come back!" he shouted. The only answer to his cry was his own heavy breathing.

"Oh, Sarah, forgive me and come back," he sobbed.

Betsy stood at the foot of his bed. "Father? I heard you calling. Are you all right?"

"Betsy, my dear." He recognized her. "I just had a dream, a nightmare, that's all."

"Was it about Mother?"

"Yes," he answered. "She wanted me to remarry."

"That wouldn't be such a nightmare, Father," Betsy said gently. "I'm worried about you."

"Go back to bed, sweetheart, and don't worry," he tried to reassure her. "I'm sorry I woke you. Good night, dear."

"Good night, Father."

Early the next morning, Rev. Samuel Doak arrived at Plum Grove and found Colonel Sevier on the porch, pulling on his riding boots. Sam dismounted, tied his horse, and settled into a chair beside John.

"Good morning, Colonel Sevier."

"Hello, Reverend Doak."

"I love getting an early start to my day, especially in the springtime," Reverend Doak began. "Every breath is fragrant and sweet. The world is full of life, and the farmers are plowing their fields, but I notice no plow has touched your fields yet. Isn't it time to plant your oats or corn or what have you?"

"We are getting a late start," John admitted. "It was a hard winter."

"Especially hard for you, John," Sam consoled him. "Your friends and neighbors are concerned about you. In fact, yesterday a member of the congregation asked me to pray especially for you. So last night I did some serious praying!"

"Last night?" John asked. "You were praying for me last night?"

"I sure was," Sam Doak responded.

"What a strange coincidence," John marveled. "I had a dream last night. Does God ever send messages in dreams?"

"He sure does," Sam replied. "There are many examples of that in the Bible. Tell me about your dream."

"Well," John began, "Sarah was walking on the other side of a river. I called to her to come back, but she could not."

"Did she speak to you, John?" asked Sam.

"Yes, as clear as in life. She said I must marry again." John stopped, and several seconds passed. Somewhere in the barnyard, a rooster crowed.

"Anything else?" Sam prompted.

"Then the dream got kind of wild. I found myself back at Watauga Fort on the morning of the first attack. That's when I pulled Bonny Kate Sherrill over the wall."

In the distance, where the river road came up from the Nolichucky, Bonny Kate appeared, riding her horse into the lane leading to Plum Grove.

"There's another coincidence," John remarked. "I mention her name and there she is, as wild and free as the mountains." Bonny Kate slowed her horse to a walk as she approached. John's entire attention focused on the rider.

"Yes, there's a free spirit!" Reverend Doak agreed. "The story goes that you once held her in your arms."

"It was the day I rescued her, she held me so tight."

"What did you feel, John?"

"Her hands were powerful, grasping mine, and after I brought her over the wall, she latched on to the lapels of my coat."

"That kind of grip comes from milking cows," Sam explained with a grin.

"Oh, she was hot, wet . . . gasping for breath."

"They say she ran more than a mile on a hot July morning," Sam remarked.

"I felt her tension wound up like spring steel as I wrapped her in my arms. She was shaking like a leaf."

"I reckon she was downright angry at those savages. And who can blame her?" Sam asked.

"Then she released it all and went completely limp," John remembered. "Her gasping turned to sobbing as she realized she was safe. I tried to make light of that deadly ordeal. I told her she was a bonny lass for a footrace. That sure sounds like a silly thing to say now."

"John, you're hopelessly romantic," Pastor Doak declared.

"Yes, and I've said too much already. I'll thank you not to repeat a single word of it."

"Alas! What a great sermon could have been developed around that," Sam joked.

"Not a word!" John repeated more forcefully.

Bonny Kate arrived at the porch but stayed seated on her horse. "Good morning, sirs," she addressed them cheerfully. "I hope I'm not interrupting something important. I wanted to see about the children early today. It's soapmaking day at Daisy Fields, and I have to plant my flax this afternoon!"

"I was just about to leave," Pastor Doak announced. "John, it was certainly good to see you."

"Sam." John nodded. "Thanks for stopping by. Oh! What about my dream?"

"Hold on to it, John, it's a keeper," Sam advised him. "Oh, and another thing, John, it wouldn't hurt you and the children to come down to church on Sunday. More prayer and a heap of my preaching is what I recommend."

"Maybe when the planting is done, I'll come pray for rain," John procrastinated.

"Bonny Kate will be singing a new song on Sunday," Sam promised. "That's another good reason for you to be there, John."

"I'll consider that." John stepped off the porch and reached up to help Bonny Kate off her horse. She accepted the help and eagerly leaned into his arms. He set her down lightly, but she lingered in his arms, looking into his eyes. He returned her gaze.

"Thank you, sir," she spoke gently.

"My pleasure, miss," he responded.

"Good day, folks," Sam took his leave.

"See you, Sam," John said without taking his eyes off the smiling girl.

"Good day, Pastor Doak," she said with all her attention still focused on the colonel. Samuel Doak rode away unobserved. John released her and turned to take the reins of her horse.

"Did you have a nice visit with the pastor?" she asked.

"Sure did."

"What did y'all talk about?"

"Nothing much, I reckon just idle talk," he replied.

"He rode five miles down here this early in the morning for idle talk?" she asked.

"Oh," he remembered, "Pastor Doak advised me plow my fields and plant my oats."

Bonny Kate's eyes opened wide with surprise, and she blushed at what she thought that meant. Then she thought it best to change the subject.

"Have the children had their breakfast?" she asked.

Betsy appeared in the doorway looking exasperated. "No, we have not. Val won't fetch me water, and Mary Ann won't set the table. I asked Johnny three times to get some bacon from the smokehouse, and he left to feed the horses without doing it. I'm trying to roll these biscuits, and I can't keep the fire going because the woodbin is empty. Bonny Kate stepped up into the cabin. John examined Bonny Kate's horse with admiration and led it out for a walk up toward the Jonesborough road, fascinated with the movements of the powerful yet supple horseflesh.

Inside the great room of Plum Grove, there was the disorder of attempted biscuit making, the dying fire, the unmade beds, and the destruction caused by rough housing, bear cub wrestling, and thrown off clothing. Bonny Kate's hot blood began to rise, compounded by the embarrassment of her recent overly brief, possibly sensual encounter with Colonel Sevier.

"Oh, for goodness' sake!" she cried. "Look here everyone. We have to cooperate." She crossed to the fireplace and stirred what was left of the fire. She shouted out to John, but he had mounted her horse and walked it out of earshot. He was blissfully unaware of the storm brewing in the great room of his home. "Colonel, it's about time someone told you this, and I'm sorry it has to be me. But you are going to have to get yourself a wife! Are you listening? I can't keep doing this. It's wearing me out! You have to get out and meet some women. If you don't like what you see around here, and it's plain to me you don't, go on to Jonesborough. There are plenty of women there!"

Betsy burst into tears. "He's gone!" she shouted back.

Bonny Kate straightened up and turned to look out the open door to see John riding away down the lane. She walked to the door of the cabin.

"Oh, that was quick. One mention of the prospects in Jonesborough and he's gone and with my horse!" She sighed, turned around, and realized how much damage her words had done to the fragile young children crying in her presence.

"Don't you love us, Bonny Kate?" Betsy blurted out, the first to express her pain.

"Oh, darlings," Bonny Kate responded. "Of course I love you!"

"We don't want any other women. We want you."

"Betsy, honey, I'm sorry. I shouldn't have said such mean things."

"Why did you then?" Betsy demanded. There was rage to deal with in Sarah's daughter, as well as the hurt.

"I don't know," she admitted. "I'm frustrated, I guess. Your father seems no better. I come in here, and he's done nothing about your breakfast. Now he wanders off without telling anybody where he's going. There's no cooperation and no organization!"

"I'm sorry," Betsy sobbed.

"It's not your fault, honey," Bonny Kate tried to comfort her. "It's not anybody's fault. Come here everybody," Bonny Kate invited the children. "We all need a hug." She opened her arms wide and tenderly gathered in Sarah's children for a hug and a good long cry.

Chapter 34

The Horse Traders

There were precious few churches on the frontier but the Presbyterian parson, the Reverend Samuel Doak had managed to build one and fill it nearly every Sunday. John Sevier had given freely of his own resources to help establish the church but rarely had time to attend services. He had helped build a church in New Market too, because he felt very strongly about the civilizing influence of morality teachings, the educational advantages of Bible reading, and the community building of the ministries carried on by an active church. Sarah had always claimed John's life had been an instrument in the hand of Divine Providence, but since her death, he hadn't felt much connection to the divine. His heart ached from the emptiness, and he felt the need to be searching for answers. He thought maybe the dreams he had been having held significant messages, but he needed help understanding them.

One Sunday in April, John and his family traveled through the spring rains from Plum Grove by horseback, the four miles, to the little log church. The family filled up the back row, and John sat at the far right beside a window and stared out at the rain-soaked landscape, lost in memories. Samuel Doak delivered a rousing sermon about the resurrection of Christ, the salvation of mankind, and the joy of life everlasting. John's attention drifted frequently to images of Sarah walking in sunny fields on the other side of the river. How he longed to join her there.

"Today we will close with a new hymn that I received from a friend in Philadelphia," Reverend Doak announced. The choir filed up to the front of the church and arranged themselves with the taller folks to the back, and there was Bonny Kate Sherrill, scrubbed and dressed finer than he was used to seeing her on the days she would come to spend time with his children.

John noticed his children were intensely interested in what was happening. Dicky stood on the bench next him for a better view and whispered, "There's Bonny Kate."

John focused on her angelic face and considered the major role she had played in the lives of his children. She had been a solid fixture around his household for over three years as Sarah's best friend and faithful companion, during his long and frequent absences, and now as caregiver to the children. He remembered the care and attentions she had shown him at Watauga Fort after he rescued her. Her wild reputation and the rough life she led as a farm girl and horse trader made it hard for him to envision her as a choirgirl, but there she was, singing with the best of them. Mary and Sam Sherrill stood with their fiddles and played the introduction to the sweetest tune John had ever heard. The singers began.

> Amazing Grace how sweet the sound,
> That saved a wretch like me.
> I once was lost, but now am found,
> Was blind but now I see.
>
> 'Twas grace that taught my heart to fear,
> And grace my fears relieved;
> How precious did that grace appear,
> The hour I first believed.
>
> Through many dangers, toils and snares,
> I have already come;
> 'Tis grace hath brought me safe thus far,
> And grace will lead me home.
>
> The Lord has promised good to me,
> His word my hope secures;
> He will my shield and portion be,
> As long as life endures.

Many in the congregation were moved to tears, and John was among them. Reverend Doak rose slowly to deliver the Benediction. It was clear the music had moved him as well, but he managed to find his clear strong voice. "The Lord bless thee and keep thee; the Lord make his face shine upon thee and be gracious to thee; the Lord lift up his countenance upon thee, and give thee peace. Amen."

The rain outside had stopped. The people crowded the center aisle to leave and the line moved slowly as folks stopped to shake the Pastor's hand and make remarks about their experience in worship. When John reached the center aisle, he met Bonny Kate. Her face lit up with a friendly smile as she saw him.

"Hello, my Bonny Kate!"

"Hello, Colonel Sevier!"

"I enjoyed the song. It reminded me of the dangers, toils, and snares we faced at Watauga Fort. Do you remember the day you jumped into my arms?"

"I do, indeed, sir. And I would gladly endure that ordeal again to feel you hold me safe once more."

He was surprised at her directness, and it showed in his expressive face. She looked away, surprised a little at her own words, although they were not unfamiliar thoughts. John thought he might indulge her if she wanted to feel his touch again so he placed his right hand on the back of her upper arm as men will do when escorting a lady. He felt the warm firmness of an active lady. She thrilled at the touch of his warm hand and wanted more. As he stepped into the center aisle, she crossed in front of him and took his left arm as ladies will do when being escorted by a gentleman. She held firm as they stepped down the two steps out of the church and arrived before Pastor and Mrs. Doak. John shook hands with the Doaks as they passed, but her greeting was a nod and a smile, because she did not want to let go of his arm. They looked like a couple. Sam and Esther Doak exchanged glances, wondering at the meaning of their observations.

As Bonny Kate and John strolled through the crowded church yard, he looked at her and spoke. "Thank you for helping me with the children. Betsy tells me about all the kind things you do for them when I have to be away."

"They are adorable," she answered. "It has been a source of joy to spend time with them each day. I wish you could be there more often."

"I know I've disappointed you in that part of our arrangement, but there is great uncertainty in the country right now, concerning British intentions in the Carolinas. There is much work to do to prepare the militia for any emergency."

"I'm not happy about it, but Father has admonished me for troubling you with domestic details while you are occupied with the threats to our public safety. Did you complain to him about me?"

"No." John laughed. "I'm sure your wise father came up with that one on his own."

"Don't forget to tell your children, I'm taking tomorrow off. Mrs. Brown will be there bright and early."

"How do you spend those rare days off?" John asked.

"Training and grooming my horses," she replied.

"I've been admiring your horses. I need to buy some for the militia. Do you have any for sale?"

"We do. You should come see them tomorrow."

"I may just do that."

Irma Jenkins, the matchmaker, accompanied by Ruth Brown came rushing over excitedly to greet Colonel Sevier. Irma stood before them, and as she began to speak, she turned her back to Bonny Kate and wedged her body between them. Bonny Kate felt his arm slip away as the matchmakers guided him between the two of them with excited speech.

"Oh, Colonel Sevier, it's so good to see you in church," Irma gushed. "How we miss dear sweet Sarah!"

"Oh yes, what a loss!" Ruth exclaimed.

"Thank you, ladies," he replied politely. "It hasn't been easy."

"We know," Irma assured him. "It's been dreadful to lose a wife with so many small children. It won't be healthy for them, or for you, to wait too long before you once again consider matrimony. Why don't you let us hunt you up some lovely widows?"

"A man of your position in the community will naturally have the greatest selection of eligible and willing ladies," Ruth pointed out. "You have only to say the word, and we will arrange everything!"

"I was thinking of the widow Johnson, young, beautiful, with two adorable girls," Irma began.

"Or we could introduce you to Widow White," Ruth added. "She's a noble-looking woman, with classic features and a sunny disposition. She's not a bad cook."

"What about Widow Cole? She can cook." Irma was just warming up. "Oh my, how she cooks. You'd never go hungry again with a woman like that! And none of those nasty habits like tobacco use. Colonel, I don't believe I've ever seen you chew tobacco."

"No, I don't," he replied.

"There, now," Irma declared. "A match made in heaven, don't you think?"

"I'm sorry, ladies, I'm just not ready for this." John backed away slowly.

"We understand completely, but please find comfort in the fact that so many ladies of quality share your circumstances of loss, grief, and loneliness," Irma assured him.

"Yes, we understand. Just let us know when you are ready," Ruth chimed in.

"Thank you, ladies. Please excuse me." John looked around for Bonny Kate, but she was already visiting with the Waddells. He looked toward his horses and saw his children waiting for him and joined them for the ride back to Plum Grove. His journey home was filled with thoughts of Sarah.

Bonny Kate's journey home was filled with thoughts of John and her encounter with him. He touched her politely, but warmly, and allowed her the use of his arm for a long time. His decision to come to church that morning was an answered prayer for healing, comfort, and hope. Her appeal to Pastor Doak had worked. She didn't know if he was ready to deal with the matchmakers yet, but he was making amazing progress. The matchmakers had come on a little too strong she thought, and she was not sure about their choices either. They had presented widows. Could they not have presented an old maid or two? It was a complicated business she reasoned. Matchmakers would provide the next step in the colonel's progress. They could spark an interest, fan a flame, and ignite a passion in the man. There was no doubt that her involvement in his case would soon come to an end, but that thought disturbed her as much as his lack of progress had.

Monday morning, Esther Doak rocked her sleeping baby in a chair on the porch of their cabin. John Sevier rode into the yard. Esther motioned to John to be quiet and took the baby into the cabin. John dismounted, tied his horse, and waited at the foot of the steps to the porch. Esther came out and eased the cabin door shut.

"I just wanted to get the baby down for his morning nap," she explained. "How are you today, John?"

"Fine, Esther," John replied. "Is Sam here?"

"Monday he goes out visiting people new to the community. I'm sorry you missed him, but if you've got a burden, I'm a good listener. And as a pastor's wife, I've learned the importance of keeping a confidence."

"Sam and I were talking about dreams last week," John said. "I had another one last night. I wanted Sam to help me pray for understanding."

"Well, dreams and prayers are what Sam is better at," she deferred. "You'll need to wait for him."

John allowed a thoughtful silence. Esther studied him with compassion, without interrupting his thoughts.

"Esther, I'm thirty-five years old, and I haven't been courting in nearly twenty years," he declared. "I'm not sure how to start."

Esther knew she must treat this topic very gently. "First, John, you have to know you'll never find another Sarah."

"That's the gospel truth," he agreed. "But I have a deep yearning to love again as deeply as I loved Sarah!"

"All things are possible through Divine Providence!" she confessed. "But John, that's a pretty tall order even for the Lord."

"I suppose it is," he admitted. He took a deep breath and sighed.

"Is there someone special you are thinking about courting?"

"There might be, someday," he stalled.

"You know, you are quite a prize, Colonel Sevier," Esther observed. "I'd think single women and lonely widows will flock to Washington County to comfort and provide gentle companionship to our leading citizen."

"As flattering and tempting as you make that sound, I'd be in constant danger of blundering into a marriage of convenience! How would I ever find out if I could love one of those women the way I want to love a wife?"

"I see your problem. Love grows too slowly. If so many women chase you, there won't be enough time to develop a loving relationship with any one of them."

"That is my concern exactly," John confirmed. "Suppose I choose one to court. Then all my intentions would be much too clear. I could easily be rushed into a relationship where I would never know if the lady loved me for who I am or for what I can provide in comforts and security."

"So what do you intend to do?" she asked.

"I don't know. I was hoping Sam would have some ideas." They fell silent again, but Esther was thinking.

"What about Bonny Kate Sherrill?" Esther asked, watching for a reaction. "She's a treasure! Didn't I see you with her after church yesterday?"

"Yes," he replied. "She comes by the house every day to check on the children. She was one of Sarah's best friends."

"She's not married. Why do you suppose that is?"

"Sarah used to talk about her case all the time," John explained. "To her friends, she declares she will marry only once in her life, and it will be for true love. Only one man ever captured her heart, but she never married because he wouldn't love her."

"Oh, a bittersweet tragedy," Esther lamented. "That is a noble spirit that holds so tightly to the truth of her ideal love. Who was the man who wouldn't love her?"

"That's always been her secret, and many folks, including me, have learned the hard way not to disturb her about it."

"How romantic!" she exclaimed. There was another long silence. "You know, I think Pastor Doak might have been going down to see Mr. Sherrill this morning. Why don't you ride down there and see if you can catch up with him?"

"I believe I will," John declared. "It wouldn't hurt to visit with the Sherrills either. I wanted to look at some of their horses. Thank you, Esther, you've been a great comfort to me."

"God bless you, John! I pray you find whatever you're looking for."

John mounted, tipped his hat, and rode away. In the next moment, Samuel Doak rode into the yard from the opposite direction.

"Sweetheart," he addressed his wife. "Who was that leaving in such a hurry?"

"Colonel John Sevier," she answered. "I sent him down to the Sherrill's place looking for you."

"I never said I was going to the Sherrill's this morning."

"I know." She smiled.

"I'll ride after him," Sam offered.

"Don't you dare interfere, Sam Doak," she warned. "It's time for God's good providence to work in that poor man's life."

"Esther, what have you done?" he demanded.

"Step down, Pastor Doak." His wife laughed. "You need to hear my confession."

About midday, John Sevier arrived at Daisy Fields and dismounted in the yard. He tied his horse and saw Sam Sherrill working around the horse corral. Sam noticed his approach and greeted him. "Hello, John. How are you doing?"

"Fine, Sam," John answered.

"It was mighty good to see you at church yesterday," Sam told him. "Those young ones of yours are growing up fast!"

"They sure are," John agreed. "By the way, has Reverend Doak been by today? I was told he was coming this way."

"No, not today," he answered. "I haven't seen him."

"Well, would you mind if I hang around to see if he turns up?" John asked.

"Not at all," he replied.

"While I'm here, I wanted to pursue another matter," John continued. "I was talking to Bonny Kate yesterday about looking at some horses for the militia."

"Let me call her," Sam offered. "Her horses are the best on the farm. Bonny Kate, you have a visitor!" Sam returned to his work. Bonny Kate looked out the door of the cabin and saw Colonel Sevier. She quickly removed her apron, untied her hair, and let the soft tresses fall naturally. She took a drink of water dipped from the bucket they always kept by the door, took a few deep breaths, and walked across the yard. She smiled as their eyes met.

"Colonel Sevier, what a pleasure to see you!"

"The pleasure is mine, Miss Sherrill."

"Are the children all right?" she asked.

"The children are fine," he answered. "Mrs. Brown showed up as planned and will be with them all day."

"Forgive my appearance. I've been working in the cookhouse all morning. It's so close to noon, won't you eat with us?"

"I'd be delighted," he accepted. "I was hoping you would have time this afternoon to show me your horses."

"I look forward to that." She smiled. "I'll show you where to wash up for dinner."

Mary Sherrill, Bonny Kate, and Mary Jane served a big dinner in the middle of the day as the horse wranglers and field hands came in to take part. Daisy Fields had become a large operation, with the Waddells, the Taylors, and the Sherrills, all working for shares of the production. The dinner was loud with the voices of men dominating the conversation; and Bonny Kate and the other women moved around actively serving drinks, fresh biscuits, and second helpings. John liked to watch her in motion, active, graceful, alert, smiling, and responding sweetly to requests for food and drink. He lacked nothing in her attentions as she always seemed to be close by when he needed something.

In the warm early afternoon sun, the men relaxed and some napped after the big dinner. John and Sam found chairs on the porch and watched as Bonny Kate walked out to a sunny patch of grass and spread out a quilt. She lay down and stretched out.

"Is she taking a nap?" John asked with interest.

"She calls it her prayer time," Sam replied. "She won't be long. Now is the best time to talk horse trading with her."

"You think so?" John asked.

"She's less likely to cheat you after praying," Sam pointed out.

"Good idea, Sam," John rose and put on his hat. "Thanks."

John approached her and studied her beautiful form. As his shadow passed over her, she opened her eyes and looked up at him with a smile.

"This is such a beautiful day!" he declared, removing his hat.

"Yes, it's heavenly!" she agreed. "Sit down and make yourself comfortable." John sat beside her on the quilt. "Colonel Sevier?"

"Bonny Kate, when we are alone together, why don't you just call me John?"

"That's easier," she agreed. "John, I'm glad you came over today."

"I'm glad I did too."

Bonny Kate sat up and smiled mischievously. "I was afraid you wouldn't have time for horse trading. I thought you might have gone out widow hunting this morning."

"Irma and Ruth sure tried to sell me on that idea yesterday!" he exclaimed.

"It sounds like something that would appeal to most men." She laughed.

"Not me! Horse trading with you beats widow hunting any day of the week." They both laughed.

"I'm flattered you feel that way," she responded. "But don't you think you ought to accept help from experts like Irma and Ruth when it's offered?"

John became serious. "That won't be easy." There was a long silence. Bonny Kate studied his face as he continued. "I've done a lot of thinking about my home and family. I believe Sarah wanted me to marry again."

"I know it won't be easy for you," she said gently. "But it's the right thing for the children."

"I don't want to be pushed into a marriage of convenience. I want to take my time and a find a woman I can love, and one who can love both me and the children."

"Naturally," she agreed. "Love grows slowly over time. You can't let anyone rush you."

"Thank you for understanding," he said.

"Understanding what?" she asked.

"That our arrangement may require you to help me with my children a good while longer than you originally planned," he explained.

"Oh yes, well, I will do my best to remain . . . available," she replied.

"Just keep this in mind. I want to love again as deeply as I loved Sarah," he declared.

"Ah, true love!" she sighed. "Life is too short to do it any other way."

"Yes!" he reacted. "That's how I see it too."

John looked at her, and she seemed to be wrapped up in her own thoughts. "Sarah told me about your unfortunate experience with love."

"There wasn't much to tell," she said dreamily. "Once upon a time, I loved a man, and he didn't love me."

"And you never got over it?" he asked.

"I never even got around to it," she said sadly.

"That's exactly the way I feel sometimes," he empathized. "I can't get over it, because I can't even get around to it. We are noble spirits, you and I, forever true to the ideal of a lost love."

Bonny Kate's eyes met his, but she quickly looked away and rose to her feet walking a few steps away.

"Oh, good sir, how did we ever get so serious?" she asked.

"I believe you were trying to talk me into going widow hunting today," he joked.

"Nonsense! I could never talk you into anything you didn't already have a mind to do."

"But you sure have a knack for getting straight to the heart of the matter as well as to matters of the heart!"

Bonny Kate turned and looked at him again. "Forgive me, John. We won't speak of widow hunting again. Let's talk about horses! Do you have time for a ride?"

"I sure do!" he replied. John got up, picked up the quilt, and they walked toward the corral.

The rest of that April afternoon John and Bonny Kate rode horses, enjoying the beautiful sunshine, the rapidly greening mountains, the spectacular waterfalls, and the wildflower meadows of the Nolichucky Valley. Their childcare arrangement had led to an understanding that he would soon be ready to seek an appropriate lady to court for a new wife. He wouldn't be rushed, and she wasn't going to push him. They were both comfortable with that. With comfort came a relaxed familiarity and a friendship developed where more days were spent horse trading than were spent widow hunting.

Chapter 35

The Hunted Man

May gave way to June and one beautiful day, early that month, Bonny Kate rode up the hill to Plum Grove from the river crossing carrying Baby Nancy with her. She often took Nancy home to Daisy Fields with her overnight. She met Colonel Sevier on the front porch dressed for a day trip and obviously awaiting her arrival. His horse was already saddled.

"Good morning, Colonel Sevier," she greeted him as he took the baby so she could dismount.

"Good morning to you, Miss Sherrill." John spent a moment admiring Baby Nancy and kissing her. "Good morning, my dear Nancy. Ah, you are a pretty lass for a brisk morning ride and down to the Sherrills you went last night? How did you find those worthy folks?" He was bouncing her slightly, making her laugh with delight.

"Are you going out this morning, sir?" she asked.

He glanced up the Jonesborough road and quickly handed Nancy back to Bonny Kate. "I need to go down to the lead mine and survey the progress or go hunting on the mountain or be anywhere, but here, this morning," he replied.

"Why the hurry?" she asked.

"The widow, Mrs. White," he said anxiously.

"The one who cooks so magnificently?" she asked.

"That's the one," he replied. "Look up the road toward Jonesborough, but don't let on that I see her." As she looked away for a moment to see Widow White approaching with an escort, John removed his hat and quickly bent over and kissed Nancy again as Bonny Kate held the baby against her breast. Bonny Kate was surprised at his expression of affection so close to her own person.

"Oh!" she exclaimed in surprise and gave a start. Her heart leapt within her, and she felt her pulse quicken.

In a moment, Colonel Sevier vaulted to his horse and waved his hat to Bonny Kate. "Act like I didn't see them. Tell them I've gone hunting."

He charged his horse down to the Nolichucky and forded the river. Betsy came out of the cabin to see him leave. "There he goes again," she observed sadly.

"A hunting he will go," Bonny Kate watched him across the river. "Well, Betsy, we have company coming. Would you take Nancy in for her nap?"

"Yes, ma'am," she said as she received the baby, then she looked up the road. "Oh, it's Widow White. What does *she* want?"

"She's not here to borrow a cup of sugar, but I'll wager she wants something much sweeter," Bonny Kate remarked. Betsy laughed and took Nancy into the cabin. Bonny Kate then realized the children listened to everything she said. She shouldn't have spoken cynically about the most eligible, most prominent, and most available widow in Washington County. If John could be interested in such a candidate and a speedy marriage could be arranged, Bonny Kate could accomplish her promise to Sarah and regain her beloved liberty.

"Was that Colonel Sevier?" Widow White demanded as she arrived at the house.

"Yes, ma'am, he left on a hunting trip," Bonny Kate replied.

"Yoohoo! Colonel Sevier," Mrs. White bellowed.

"I don't think he can hear you," Bonny Kate said, less than helpfully.

"Go after him, James," she ordered her brother-in-law and escort.

"I've never seen the horse that can catch that black stallion of his," Captain White declared, smiling.

"Let me help," offered Bonny Kate, stepping into the cabin and lifting down John's rifle he kept over the door. "Try this," she handed the rifle to Mrs. White.

"What do I do with it?" she was perplexed.

"I just whistle a ball past his ear," Bonny Kate directed. "That always gets his attention. Here let me show you." She reached for the rifle, but Mrs. White wouldn't give it up.

"You might hurt him!" she protested.

"I would never hurt the man who rescued me from certain death among the savages," she declared. "But he sure gets angry when I signal him like that."

"Bonny Kate, I'm not taking any advice from you about getting a man's attention. You are so . . . so . . . uncivilized!" Widow White handed the firearm back to Bonny Kate.

"I reckon you are right, ma'am. I set a poor example of how to get a man's attention," she sighed and returned the rifle to its place in the cabin.

"Now, dear, I didn't mean that in a cruel way. You must know I didn't."

"I know, Mrs. White." She emerged from the cabin smiling and winked at Captain White. He smiled back at her, amused at her little joke.

311

"You just don't use good judgment," continued Mrs. White. "Your manner of dress, your attitude, your abilities, your helpfulness are all working against you. Today's woman should make herself beautiful and helplessly distressed. That's what men want!"

"I'm sorry, Mrs. White, I'm just naturally helpful. It's one of my most obvious faults."

"I know, dear," she sympathized. "But please work on it."

"Yes, ma'am," Bonny Kate answered. By now, Colonel Sevier had escaped into the trees on the far side of the valley.

"Oh, dear, he's gone," lamented Widow White.

"Yes, completely out of range, even for me," agreed Bonny Kate.

"I suppose I'll come back another day. Will he be here tomorrow?"

"We never know," Bonny Kate replied in all truthfulness.

"The poor children," Mrs. White empathized.

"I do wish he would spend more time with them here," Bonny Kate sighed.

"I'm sure you do," the widow replied coldly.

"Would you like to visit for the day and endear yourself to the children? Maybe you could cook us all a dinner," Bonny Kate offered.

"No, thank you," answered Mrs. White sweetly. "I couldn't impose upon you. With the master of the house gone, there's really no point in it."

The Whites, annoyed widow and bemused brother-in-law, mounted their horses. Captain White tipped his hat to Bonny Kate. "Miss Sherrill, it's always a pleasure."

"Likewise, Captain White." She curtsied. "Good day, sir, Mrs. White."

The noble widow, beautiful, but irritated at missing her chance to charm the lonely Colonel, turned her horse into the lane without another word to the spinster Miss Sherrill. She turned to her late husband's brother and remarked, "The colonel has a lovely location for a farm, but they would be so much better off in Jonesborough."

"Let's make breakfast, everyone!" Bonny Kate announced cheerfully and at once engaged herself with the business of life, directing the children to accomplish the preparation of good, wholesome food. The children peppered her with questions about the formidable Widow White, her history, her present circumstances, and her future prospects. It was reasonable for them to inquire, and Bonny Kate felt it her Christian obligation to fairly represent Widow White's case, and not damage her candidacy. The colonel could certainly do worse.

After breakfast, Bonny Kate went down to the spring to fetch the water for dishwashing. It gave her a moment to get away and think about her brief encounter with Colonel Sevier that morning. As he kissed his infant daughter, he came so close to her; it made her blush. Had he noticed her reaction, her pounding heart, or faster pulse? The affection he bestowed on his daughter was

312 | Mark Strength

so intense; she felt the power of it in her own heart, and dear Lord it was real. She ached with yearning to have such depth of feeling intended for her.

Warm summer days, thriving gardens, and meadows of wildflowers in June were a particular pleasure to Bonny Kate and the children of Plum Grove. Mornings of gardening were followed by picnic lunches in the meadow, naps at the house, reading and writing lessons, then domestic industries until the midafternoon swim at the river. Farm chores and dinner cooking rounded out their busy days, and Colonel Sevier never failed to make his appearance for dinner and the evening hours of fun with father that the children always looked forward to with great delight. When John arrived, Bonny Kate would take her leave so his children could have some relief from her rigid rules and routine and bond more freely with their loving father.

One morning during their gardening exercise, four horsemen came down the Jonesborough road. Bonny Kate took the usual precautions for the appearance of strangers and called to the children "Fortify!"

The children ran like rabbits for the house and closed all the door and windows. She and Johnny dropped their hoes and picked up their rifles, which they always took to the garden just like any other tool, and strolled to the front porch of the house to meet the visitors. "Johnny, I want you to stay here at the corner of the house and protect yourself, but don't start anything until I do. Go ahead and prime your pan," she directed.

"Good morning, ma'am," called a large man on a gray horse. He was dressed more like a gentleman than the usual visitor on farm business. "Is this the home of John Sevier?"

"Yes, sir, it is," she answered, looking to see how many guns the strangers were packing. Three of them had rifles but the big man carried only a brace of pistols.

"Is Mr. Sevier at home?" the man inquired.

"Colonel Sevier is not very far away," she answered warily. "He's on patrol with fifty rangers hunting Tories I reckon."

"That sure makes me feel safe." The big man laughed, and his companions laughed with him.

"State your business or move on," she ordered ignoring their laughter.

The big man looked at the tall confident young woman and judged her capable of defending the property with or without the fifty rangers. He stopped laughing.

"Sevier owes the Bank of Abington a considerable amount of money for cosigning a note with a Mister Gideon McNamara. Do you know anything about that, ma'am?"

"No, that's none of my business," she replied. "I'm just the housekeeper."

"Well, missy, if you want to keep this house, you better tell Mr. Sevier to pay the Bank of Abington the entire amount that McNamara borrowed with interest and penalties by the end of this month."

"Why would Colonel Sevier owe the bank for another man's debt?" she asked.

"That's none of your business," the bank agent snapped. "Just tell Sevier to pay up, or we will take the house and everything he has."

Bonny Kate cocked her rifle and aimed it at the big man. "I'll tell him, but the day you decide to take this house, you better bring a lot more men, all willing to die in the attempt."

"Don't make her mad, Mister Bank of Abington," called Johnny. "That's Bonny Kate Sherrill! I've seen her fire eight shots in a minute and never miss a moving target."

The riders raised their hands immediately as though they were facing a highwayman. The big man turned to the girl and apologized, "I'm sorry, Miss Sherrill. I'm a man of business, not violence. Sometimes we have to apply pressure to get people to honor their debts."

"Colonel Sevier is an honorable man," she insisted. "He always pays his debts, but you have no right to threaten and frighten his children like this."

"I believe we understand each other, Miss Sherrill," he replied. "I hope you will accept my apology."

She lowered her rifle and eyed the man of business. "You'll likely find the colonel in Jonesborough if you ask at the tavern across from the courthouse, but don't you threaten him with violence like you did here, or you'll have to answer to me!"

"Thank you, Miss Sherrill," the man answered. "We will be more careful."

The men tipped their hats and rode back the way they had come.

That evening Bonny Kate asked to speak with Colonel Sevier before she left to go home to Daisy Fields.

"Is this about the man from the Bank of Abington?" he guessed.

"Yes," she said. "Did he find you?"

"He did."

"Was it right for me to send him to Jonesborough like that?"

"Yes," John replied. "It was a matter that I settled some time ago directly with the president of the bank. This fellow had not received word of the settlement and pursued the matter in error."

"It nearly cost the rude fellow his life!" she exclaimed. "I never know if these people who constantly call at Plum Grove are Tory assassins or lawyers seeking to do you harm or British agents or old friends of yours, and I never know who to trust. Colonel Sevier, I know practically nothing about your business."

John looked at his governess, the trusted protector of his children, and decided she needed more information to perform her duties of protecting his interests on the home front. "Would you like to learn more about it?"

"Just enough to know where to send these people and exercise the proper care not to shoot them when they blunder in here unexpectedly," she pleaded.

"Can you stay for dinner?" he offered. "I'll explain it all this evening and see you home afterwards."

"Yes, sir," she agreed. "If you don't think I'm trespassing too much in your business. Don't tell me anything highly confidential or illegal you might be involved in."

John laughed. "All my business is completely legal and above board, Miss Sherrill. Sarah knew it all and approved of it, so I think I can trust you. I have to trust somebody to keep my affairs in order in case something happens to me."

"God forbid," she exclaimed. "No harm must ever come to you, good sir!"

"Yes, Miss Sherrill, I know I can trust you," he decided.

The children had to produce their own entertainment that night as the colonel and the governess discussed Sevier family business. It was complicated but in the end made much sense. A lot of people participated in the prosperity generated by John Sevier's businesses, and he seemed to place a higher value on trust and respect for people than on squeezing out higher rates of interest or cheating people for the sake of increasing profits. She gained even more respect for the man as a result of the two-hour lesson.

A violent storm rolled up the valley that evening and prevented Bonny Kate from going home that night. John gave her his soft bed in the main house where the children slept and took his quarters in the cookhouse.

Mr. Sam Sherrill appeared bright and early the next morning to locate a missing daughter and take issue with the gallant host over the appearances created by the overnight stay. Bonny Kate was already up and dressed when she saw her father ride into the yard but had not washed the bed linens she slept on. She answered the door and anticipated what her father might say.

Sam walked in, and she could sense his anger. He looked at the unmade bed. "Did you sleep there last night?"

"Yes, sir, because of the storm."

"Where is he?"

"Colonel Sevier slept in the cookhouse last night," she answered. "I reckon he's still there. Shall I wake him for you?"

"No, daughter." Sam breathed a sigh of relief. "I trust you wouldn't do anything unseemly, but the appearance of this might wag some powerful tongues in Jonesborough. Come take a walk with me." They walked out and strolled down the lane toward the river. Sam continued, "It's been five months since you took on this responsibility. First it was just take care of Sarah's infant, then you had to check in on the children every day, then you were cooking their breakfast, then lunch, and then every meal, and now suddenly it requires your nights too."

"I stayed because of the storm," she repeated. "I know it looks bad, but I won't let it happen again."

"Colonel Sevier is a man of great influence, powerful, wildly popular with his neighbors, the darling boy of the widows of Jonesborough; and if there were ever the breath of scandal, it would mean the ruin of his public life. Great and powerful men must live to a higher standard where even appearances are critically important."

"I understand that," she replied. "Sarah spoke to me about this very same thing on many occasions."

"As his Christian friend and his childcare provider, you must never be the stumbling block to lead him into temptation," Sam warned her. "I think you ought to call it quits."

"I can't," she replied. "I promised Sarah."

"Sarah will know you did your best," Sam reasoned. "I don't think she intended for you to waste the best years of your life. You ought to have a family of your own by now. You are nearly twenty-six."

"Father, the children are making real progress," she insisted. "The colonel is too. I would be dealing him a severe setback to withdraw my help now."

Sam looked at her. "I think he takes you for granted. The colonel should hire a servant or buy a slave to do the things you do."

"Nobody can do this job as well as I can. He trusts me. He said so last night."

Sam and his daughter had walked away from the house some distance. She saw Mary Ann, Dolly, Dicky, and Becky come out on the porch. When they saw Bonny Kate, they excitedly ran down toward her.

"Bonny Kate, Bonny Kate!" shouted the little ones joyfully. The beloved governess knelt, and they ran into her warm embrace.

"We missed our story time last night," Dicky declared. "Can you tell us a story this morning?"

"What story would you like to hear?" she asked.

"Noah and the whale," Dicky replied.

Bonny Kate laughed. "I think you mean Jonah and the whale."

Dicky nodded. "That's the one I want to hear."

"Then right after breakfast we will hear the story," she promised. "Let's fix some eggs and bacon." She turned again to her father. "Will you join us for breakfast, Father?"

"I rode five miles this morning worried sick about my missing daughter, I ought to get something out of the deal," he griped.

"Bonny Kate, you forgot to take Nancy home with you last night," Mary Ann observed. "Did you know you forgot her?"

"I didn't forget her. I would never forget my pretty little baby!"

"They watch every move you make, Bonny Kate," Sam pointed out. "Act responsibly in all you say and do."

"I'll do better, Father," she promised. "Please don't make me quit."

"One more month then you will have to walk away," he decreed. "You can't stay where you are forever." They all walked up to the house.

Chapter 36

Colonel Shelby Calls

Plum Grove was a beautiful, well built, easily defended cabin with all the modern conveniences common to homes in the year 1780. The cookhouse out back was one of the best-equipped kitchens in the community, and Sarah had always been proud of it. But Bonny Kate didn't like the isolation of going to a separate building to do the cooking. Being an old-fashioned girl, she preferred to cook in the family great room where she could watch sleeping babies and busy toddlers, keep an eye out for traffic in the lane, spin, weave, sew, and attend to multiple tasks at once while keeping the cooking going too. The problem with all Mr. Sevier's chimneys was the fact that he allowed them to be constructed of sticks and mud above the firebox. Bonny Kate preferred stone all the way up to prevent the accumulation of soot and creosote from someday starting a chimney fire. Stone chimneys were an unnecessary luxury on the frontier reasoned Colonel Sevier who had never lived in the same cabin for more than three consecutive years his whole life. Chimney fires had never been a source of concern for the restless pioneer. The differing philosophies between the colonel and the governess, soon led to disaster.

One morning in early July as the fire was boiling the water in the washpot, Bonny Kate walked in from feeding the chickens and noticed Rebecca standing near the fireplace pointing up the flue and saying "Hot, hot!" A draft was rushing into the fireplace and a roar as loud as a waterfall could be heard up the chimney.

"Fire in the flue!" Bonny Kate yelled. "Run, Becky, run outside!"

She gathered up Nancy and herded the children she could find out into the yard, and over to the shady oak. She made a quick count of the eight Sevier children she was responsible for keeping; she had six. Johnny and Betsy came running up from the barn where they had been doing their chores, and that made eight.

"What do we do?" Betsy screamed in panic.

"We lose the house," Johnny said matter of fact.

"Maybe not," Bonny Kate ventured. "Listen, everybody stay right here at the tree. Don't move from this spot. That chimney is going to fall, and I don't want anybody near it, understand?"

"Yes, ma'am," Betsy answered.

Bonny Kate raced into the cabin with a plan. She needed a tomahawk and a broomstick, both kept near the fireplace. The great room was already smoky but not so much where she couldn't breathe. The draft was going up the chimney like a tornado, sounded like a tornado too. She found the tomahawk on the mantle and the broom leaned against the wall to the side of the fireplace. The draft pulled at her skirt and apron. *Mustn't get too close to that and set my bloomers on fire*, she thought. With the tools in hand, she raced to the ladder and climbed to the loft. Upstairs the smoke was accumulating and she knew she had to work fast. The top of the gable was not a solid log. She would try to cut a hole with the tomahawk and gain access to the chimney there. She went to work desperately before the chimney burned through and caught the rest of the house on fire. In just a few tomahawk blows, she could see daylight. The burning chimney was inches away from the hole she made. She dropped the tomahawk and picked up the broomstick and shoved it out the hole in the gable into the side of the chimney. She stopped there to cough and clear her lungs. Then she gave a mighty push and felt the clay chinking give a bit. She pulled back a little to bear on one of the larger sticks in the chimney and gave another mighty shove. This time the broom handle kept moving as the chimney toppled out away from the cabin. A few moments later, she was down and out into the yard. The children were cheering at the amazing feat of quick thinking and fast action.

"Johnny, get a shovel," she directed. "Everyone else start bringing me buckets of water. And don't stop until we have this thing out for sure." Bonny Kate, still holding her broomstick, walked over to the glowing, smoking ruin of the chimney like a knight approaching a slain dragon. She looked up at the house for signs of burning embers on the cedar shakes. Johnny used the shovel to break up the chimney and move the burning parts away from the house. There was a lot of cleanup to do and rebuilding the chimney would be required. She wondered how Colonel Sevier would react to this, one more disaster in the poor man's life. She was pretty sure the finger of blame would point to her for not cooking in the cookhouse like she was supposed to, but it was doggone inconvenient to cook and attend to everything else at the same time. Men just don't understand all that is required. She resolved to defend herself vigorously when he brought the case against her and counter-attack with facts such as the need to hurry up and find a wife to run an operation as big as Plum Grove, and maybe hire a half-dozen servants to help.

Isaac Shelby rode up to Plum Grove and saw Bonny Kate drawing water from the spring. He dismounted and ran down to help her carry the buckets.

"Miss Bonny Kate Sherrill, I'm surprised to see you here," Isaac greeted, relieving her of her burden.

"No more surprised than I am to see you, Colonel Shelby. I thought you'd be leading your Sullivan County men through the high mountain passes by now, struggling to keep up with our Washington County heroes."

Supply problems caused me a delay. I thought I'd come down and give old Colonel Jack one more chance to join the fun."

"You wasted your time," she answered, pulling the hair back out of her eyes. "He's not going to leave his children."

"His country needs him, and I've never known Jack Sevier to shirk his duty."

"His family needs him so much more. I think he understands that his duty is here."

"It seems to be just a child-care problem, and that can be remedied with a convenient marriage if a suitable lady could be procured. Have you made any progress there, Miss Sherrill?"

"It seems we have our own supply problems around here. Colonel Sevier has so many choices he can't make up his mind. But I am not the one to ask. Ask the colonel."

"Is he here?"

"No, sir. He's in Jonesborough for the day."

"So Miss Sherrill, why do you appear to be the mistress of Plum Grove?"

"Sarah made me promise to look after the children until he remarries, and it's become a greater burden than I ever imagined."

"I admire your commitment," Isaac said. "And does he pay you well?"

"Oh no, sir, I could never ruin a friendship with a mercenary motive," she explained. "I'm just honoring the promise I made to Sarah."

Isaac Shelby was a keener judge of men than he was of women, but he still recognized relationships when he saw them. He grinned at her and spoke. "At least, that frees old Jack to go widow hunting. I've heard there are plenty of good ones in Jonesborough. I reckon he'll marry soon."

"He better not!" she exclaimed without remembering that she was speaking with one of the colonel's best friends. They had covered the distance from the spring to the cabin, and he put the buckets down on the porch. He studied her a moment.

"Why not marry?" he asked.

"He's not ready to love again. He's still hurting so much. We are all hurting."

"There's been enough time to heal these old wounds," he judged. "I'm thinking you could expedite matters if you would just go ahead and marry him yourself."

Bonny Kate lowered her voice and scolded the man angrily. "Colonel Shelby, how dare you speak such nonsense where the children can hear?"

"You love him, don't you?" Isaac guessed.

"I would never tell you!" she reacted. "What difference does it make anyway? He doesn't love me. The only reason I keep doing this is for love of these children."

Isaac noticed the damage to the cabin's chimney. "Did Indians do this or was it Tories?"

"No, sir, it was me," Bonny Kate admitted. "We had a little accident."

"How in the world did you create so much wreckage?"

"There was a fire in the flue."

"You could have lost the entire house. Damn lucky, it fell away like that."

"It wasn't luck," she explained. "I pushed it over with a broomstick."

"Whew-ee," Isaac exclaimed. "Old Jack's gonna throw a fit when he sees that! I'd better hurry on up to Jonesborough and tell him what a fine job you are doing wrecking his home."

"Why would you do that to me?" she complained.

"Because you are not being honest with my friend," Isaac charged.

"He needs more time," she insisted.

"There isn't any time!" he declared. "The British took Charleston more than a month ago, and we lost five thousand soldiers. Now they are marching through the Carolinas. Either we stop them there, or we fight them here on the porch of Plum Grove."

"Don't frighten my children!" she hissed. "Get off my place."

"It ain't yours yet, Miss Sherrill," he reminded her unnecessarily while mounting his horse. "I've got a war to win, and I'm going to need John Sevier's help to do it. The only thing in our way is this child-care problem, and that's going to require a willing little wife. Get the job done, Miss Sherrill, or get out of the way!"

Bonny Kate glared at him, and he knew his urgent words had not been kind. He judged correctly that he'd worn out his welcome.

"I'll catch up with Colonel Sevier in Jonesborough," Isaac said as he tipped his hat.

"Don't you dare meddle in his personal life," Bonny Kate warned him angrily. "I can't see where an old bachelor like you would be much help to a heartbroken man."

"True enough," he agreed. "I'd be no better use to him than a certain old maid I know. Good day, Miss Sherrill."

Isaac Shelby took the Jonesborough road, and Bonny Kate took the river road. Her anger was unresolved by her conversation with the insensitive Colonel Shelby. At the Nolichucky, she stripped down to her sheer petticoat and shift and waded into the cold water. She had a good long scream and unloaded all her frustrations and confessed all her dark thoughts. Then she dove into the cold rapidly flowing deep channel and swam against the powerful current until she wore herself out. She found a thick canebrake on the banks of the river and sat among the bulrushes. Her breathless gasping turned to uncontrolled sobbing, and she had herself a good cry. Following that, she had a good prayer dealing with everything she was involved with concerning the Seviers.

An hour later, she was back at Plum Grove, still wet, but smiling and acting like her usual self. Betsy found her some clothing to wear while her own clothes dried in the sun.

"We were worried about you," Betsy confessed. "We even prayed for you."

"Thank you, Betsy." Bonny Kate smiled. "The prayers certainly worked. I feel so much better now." Her heart swelled with pride to think that these adorable little children had prayed earnestly on her behalf. "My Granny Sherrill used to say, 'No greater faith is ever there than the faith expressed in a child's prayer.'" She remembered that little rhyme with fond thoughts of the many times Granny Sherrill had shared with her the secrets of life. Now she had the responsibility of sharing those same secrets with Sarah's little brood. The children seated themselves on the floor of the parlor at Plum Grove in a circle around their dear governess. She began by exploring, correcting, refuting, denying, and clarifying everything the children had overheard Colonel Isaac Shelby say to her at the porch that morning. Their questions provided her a measurement of how big a mess she had gotten herself into, how big a mess Colonel Sevier was mired in, and with the British now holding Charleston, how big a mess the country as a whole had gotten itself into by declaring its independence. She normally would not have included world events in a discussion of the family's problems, but since Colonel Shelby had brought up the British invasion, she felt she needed to discuss that as well to deal with all the fears of the children.

"It's a big, big, big, big mess!" declared little Dicky. "It's as big as a whale!"

"What do you know about a whale, Dicky?" Bonny Kate asked the cute little fellow.

"It's the biggest fish in the world," he answered. "Like the one that swallowed Jonah."

Bonny Kate was delighted that the children remembered the Bible stories she faithfully read to them.

Little Dicky had a gleam in his eye as he continued. "Bonny Kate, do you know how to eat a whale?"

"I'm not sure I know, Dicky." She smiled. "How do you eat a whale?"

"One bite at a time." Dicky laughed, and all the children laughed with him.

"So is that how you are going to fix this big, big, big as a whale mess?" asked Mary Ann sincerely.

"Me, fix the mess?" Bonny Kate clarified the request. "Oh, honey, if only I could."

"Sure you can," Betsy assured her, "one bite at a time!"

"Oh, dearest," Bonny Kate cried. "Thank you for your confidence, but . . ."

"You have never let us down yet," Betsy reminded her. "And like you always say, 'It's all in the hands of Divine Providence,' isn't that right?"

"Yes, there is no denying that. I always trust in Providence," she affirmed.

"Bonny Kate is going to fix the big mess, one bite at a time!" cheered Betsy. All the children cheered and felt better. The faith of children had overcome her objections and her practical considerations. Sarah would be so proud of their strength, courage, and will to make things right. How could Bonny Kate refuse them?

Even John Sevier Jr., a rapidly changing little man who was putting away childish things, believed in the prophecy. Later he confided to Bonny Kate, his friend and shooting instructor, "I don't know how you are going to stop the British invasion; but if anyone can do it, perhaps through prayer and influence in the spiritual realm, I believe it would be you." His belief was rewarded with a sisterly hug.

"I'll do whatever I can, one bite at a time."

Let the reader of this narrative search the scant histories of the Wataugans, the Franklinites, the Tennesseans, and the family traditions to discover how closely subsequent events paralleled the Plum Grove prophecies. A little known, little appreciated spinster enabled the nation nearly stillborn in the cradle of independence to rekindle the flame of liberty on the western waters and carry the tide of destiny east to crush the armies of the oppressive invader, in time, all in good time.

Chapter 37

Virginia Sends an Army

As Bonny Kate feared, Colonel Sevier was not happy to see the burned down chimney, but surprisingly assigned no blame. Instead, he was very appreciative for Bonny Kate's valorous action to save the rest of the house from burning to the ground. The colonel conceded to Bonny Kate's wisdom in having a completely stone chimney and commissioned young Mr. Thomas Embree to build the replacement. Bonny Kate had to use the fireplace in the cookhouse for a couple of weeks until the work was completed.

One morning during the reconstruction work at Plum Grove, Bonny Kate arrived on her horse carrying Baby Nancy after a night at Daisy Fields. She was delighted to find John's father and stepmother, Valentine and Jemima Sevier, relaxing on the porch. It would be a more interesting day and an easier day than the usual run-of-the-mill days.

"Hello, Bonny Kate," Jemima greeted her.

"Hello, Mrs. Sevier and Mr. Sevier," Bonny Kate responded. "See how much your granddaughter has grown? She's really doing well."

"She sure is," Val agreed. Bonny Kate gave Mr. Sevier the baby to hold and entertain.

"I wish I had known you were coming for a visit," Bonny Kate said. "I would have done a better job cleaning up the place and making up some special menus."

"The place looks fine," Jemima assured her. "And we won't be staying long. We are just taking a break from Kesiah's bedside for a day or two."

"We needed some peace and quiet, so here we are," Val added.

"How is Kesiah's new baby?"

"Baby is doing fine, but new little Mama is very demanding," Jemima declared. "And with Robert gone to the North Carolina campaign, Kesiah is very much on edge."

"Whoa," Val said, wrinkling his nose. "This little one just had an accident."

"I'll fix that," Bonny Kate volunteered cheerfully. "Come to Bonny Kate, little Nancy, I'll get you cleaned up."

When Bonny Kate took the baby inside to change the diaper, Val Sevier heaved a big sigh. "Quite a difference in the way things are running here compared to Kesiah's. I welcome the peace and efficient administration."

"John did the right thing, but it never would have worked without the kindness of that wonderful girl," Jemima agreed. "John's children seem very happy now. I wish he could settle down."

"I have an idea. Let's bring up the idea again of taking the children to Jonesborough," Val suggested. "I want to test the girl and see how she reacts."

"All right, Mr. Sevier, you lead, and I'll follow," Jemima agreed.

They enjoyed the peace of the morning until Bonny Kate returned.

"What's Nancy eating now, Bonny Kate?" Jemima asked.

"She's taking fruit and cereal and loving it."

"Already?" Jemima marveled. "What's her favorite fruit?"

"Plums from Plum Grove," she answered with a smile. "Nancy loves them."

Val laughed. "You know, seeing you with the baby in your arms, reminds me how much you favor your grandmother, Betsy Sherrill."

"You knew her?" Bonny Kate asked in surprise.

"Oh yes! Back in Virginia, we were neighbors."

"I never knew that," Bonny Kate exclaimed.

"It's true," Val declared. "I served in the Augusta County militia with your grandfather, Adam. And Betsy Sherrill served as midwife at John's birth."

"Oh my goodness!" Bonny Kate was astonished. "My dear Granny Sherrill who so often held me, also held him?"

"She rocked him to sleep his very first night."

"I'm amazed how Providence has thrown us together in such mysterious ways!"

"Yes, that was all before your time, my dear," Val said. "John was born in '45, and the Sherrills left the next year to settle the Yadkin country. They were always out on the edge of the frontier."

"Yes, sir," Bonny Kate agreed, "always the bait for Indian trouble. Just like the trouble I found at Watauga Fort." Everyone laughed, and even Nancy giggled without understanding the joke. "I reckon the colonel is gone again this morning," Bonny Kate concluded.

"He left early for business in Jonesborough," Val said.

"Yes," added Jemima, "he had to go to court today."

"That's the way it goes," Bonny Kate sighed. "Does he seem any better since the last time you saw him?"

"Not much," Jemima sighed. "He's very lonely."

Val winked at Jemima. "I don't understand why Sarah insisted that he move back to Plum Grove. I see no advantages being this far from Jonesborough."

"He's restless too," Jemima observed. "I've never seen a man so restless! Last night, he told me he wished with all his heart that he might love again. At least, he's thinking about it."

Bonny Kate smiled. "That's a good sign." She knew he was making progress and wanted others to see that he was.

Val stood up from his chair and spoke, "Now's the time to move to Jonesborough. Kesiah and Naomi, our sweet daughters-in-law, are there. The rest of the family is close, and we can all help John with the children while he looks for a new wife."

"Oh, oh no!" the words escaped Bonny Kate before she could stop herself.

"What's wrong?" Jemima asked.

Bonny Kate had to think fast. "These biting flies are terrible in July!" she said getting up. "Bad enough on the farm, but so much worse in Jonesborough, I'm told. Betsy, bring me out a flyflap. I've got to keep these biting flies off our baby!" Bonny Kate held precious Nancy close and paced the porch thinking desperately. Why had John's parents proposed Jonesborough again? Hadn't she proved she could make the children happy and provide the care they needed? Was John concerned about his children's well-being or perhaps somehow unhappy with her? Betsy delivered the flyflap, a clever device consisting of a piece of flexible leather attached to the end of a stick that proved lethal to flies. The device had given her time to formulate a defense.

"Jonesborough is so far away," Bonny Kate protested. "How will I care for Nancy and look in on the rest of them every day. I promised Sarah I would!"

"You've been a wonderful friend and neighbor, but in Jonesborough, the children would have family." Jemima wielded that word "family" like a tomahawk.

"Where would they stay? Who has room for them all?" Bonny Kate questioned.

"We will divide them up among the aunts and uncles," Val explained. "They would no longer be your burden."

"Oh, but I love taking care of them," Bonny Kate parried, feeling that old hot blood rising. "They have never been a burden. Please, don't divide them up. They need each other!"

"You've done more than you were ever expected to do, my dear girl," Jemima spoke gently. "I don't think John realizes how lucky he was to have your help."

"There's a lot he doesn't realize," Val observed. "There's a lot going on here that nobody realizes."

Jemima looked at her good old companion and partner in a happy second marriage. "What do you mean by that, Val?" He gave her a look but didn't answer and an uneasy silence fell over them.

Bonny Kate had reached the end of the porch and looked down the trail toward the river. The mountains beyond the river stood so peacefully, and she longed to be away running freely in some wild sport. But she was trapped in a snare, a dispute, and had trespassed again in Sevier family business. She knew there was a time when she would have to walk away from those she held so dear. She looked down at the beautiful baby in her arms. Maybe now was the time. The harsh words of Colonel Shelby still burned in her ears. "Get the job done, Miss Sherrill or get out of the way!"

"I'm sorry," she said softly. "I spoke foolishly. I've no right to interfere in family decisions. Excuse me while I fix dinner now." She turned and delivered Nancy to her grandmother's arms. "I'll fix something special in honor of your visit."

"Of course, dear," Jemima looked into her face, but Bonny Kate avoided her gaze. "Don't let us keep you from whatever you normally do." Bonny Kate left the porch and walked toward the chicken coup.

"Did you see that reaction?" Val crowed.

"You made her cry," Jemima marveled. "The idea of moving the family upsets her deeply."

"That's exactly what I saw," Val agreed excitedly. "It wasn't no biting flies that stirred her up. She has her cap set for our son."

"Not necessarily," Jemima cautioned. "Maybe she's just fond of the children."

"She's after the whole kit and caboodle," insisted Val. "I'd lay money on it!"

"The last time you bet on her you lost," Jemima pointed out.

"That was only one time," Val declared. "Every other time she was a sure thing!"

"If she wants John, she may be too late," Jemima declared. "John has his eye on the widow Johnson. That's where he is today."

"You told Bonny Kate he was in court," Val testified. "That was very sly of you, Jemima."

"Well, making time with the widow Johnson is the kind of court he needs to be attending to," she answered. From the chicken coup came sounds of upset chickens. Val walked to the end of the porch to see Bonny Kate carrying four chickens to the chopping block. He turned back to Jemima.

"She's cooking chickens for us!" Val couldn't contain his excitement. "I tell you, Jemima, she's a treasure! We ought to let the family stay here."

"You still think she has a chance?" Jemima asked.

"The horse race isn't over until someone crosses the finish line."

"Then the family stays at Plum Grove," Jemima agreed. "I never had it figured any other way." She rocked little Nancy as the grandparents exchanged smiles of satisfaction.

One afternoon a few days later, Bonny Kate and Betsy were hard at work cleaning, cooking, and taking care of the children at Plum Grove. Baby Nancy was napping on a quilt on the floor when a cat entered the cabin through the open door and approached Nancy. Bonny Kate saw it and reached down to pick it up.

"Here now, leave our baby alone," she told the cat. "Your job is to catch mice. Be on your way." She gently put the cat out on the porch and shut the door. She crossed the room to stir the pot in the fireplace. Little Valentine climbed in through the window from the porch.

"Bonny Kate, there's men in the smokehouse," he announced.

"What men?" she challenged.

"I don't know," he said. "Maybe they're Tories!"

Bonny Kate reacted quickly. "Betsy, get me your father's powder and shot." Bonny Kate lifted down John's new rifle from its familiar rack over the door and looked out toward the smokehouse. The smokehouse door was open, and she counted three strange horses. "Fortify," she told the children. The children knew that drill, and windows and doors were quickly closed and barred. Betsy brought the shot pouch and powder horn. Bonny Kate quickly loaded the rifle and primed the pan.

"Val, how many men did you see?

"Three."

"And did they all go into the smokehouse?

"Yes, ma'am, and they are all still there."

"Thank you, Val, good report." She turned to Betsy. "Betsy, listen carefully. Keep the young'uns in the house, doors and windows barred. Watch for me while I see what those men are up to. If I come running, let me back in, but only if I have a good lead; otherwise, keep it shut."

"Yes, ma'am. Be careful," she replied.

"I will." Bonny Kate took a deep breath. "But if this goes badly for me, clear out and get everyone to Daisy Fields. My folks will take care of you until your father comes home."

Bonny Kate slipped out and ran to the back of the smokehouse. She eased around the corner of the building with her gun ready before she saw the fourth horse. She hadn't bargained on that. There was nothing for her to do but play the hand she was dealt. Two Tories stood at the door peering inside, and she heard the voices of two more inside. She took a deep breath and bellowed out convincingly, "The first one that takes down a piece of meat is a dead man!"

The Tories at the door turned around slowly to face her and raised their hands. Their leader was a short stocky shifty-eyed man, and she knew not to trust anything he said. "Hold on, missus, don't shoot."

"Then come out of there slowly, with your hands up where I can see them," she ordered loudly enough so that even the children in the house heard her. "And latch that door!"

The Tories did as she commanded. "Don't get the wrong idea, ma'am," the short Tory continued. "We are friends of the colonel. Just making sure he has plenty of meat. I was thinking he might be a little short on bacon."

"Nonsense, we have plenty of bacon," she countered. "Now get off this place before I shoot you!" She had thrown down the challenge, but how would she back it up with one shot and only five yards between her and the nearest man? The Tories approached her menacingly, but she stood her ground. She aimed at the leader and shouted huskily. "Call them back or you're the dead man!" They stopped.

"Who the ▊▊▊ are you?" asked the leader.

"Ask the devil when you see him!" she shouted defiantly. "Get out of here now while you live and breathe or so help me I'll shoot!"

It was clear to them she wasn't backing down and she was no ordinary female. One of the Tories who had spent some time in the west guessed correctly whom they were facing. "Don't mess with her, Abner!" he warned. "I think that's Bonny Kate Sherrill. She's mean as a rattler! If she says she'll shoot you, she'll do it, and they say she never misses." The Tories froze in their tracks, and there was an awkward moment. In the distance, the sound of approaching horses drew the attention of the Tories. They backed slowly toward their horses hoping for a clean escape. Bonny Kate thought the approaching horsemen might be another group of Tories; so she bolted for the cabin, got inside, and slammed the door.

"Militia!" shouted the Tory leader. "Ride hard men!" The Tories quickly mounted their horses and rode away.

John Sevier, with his sons Joseph and James, rode up to the fortified house at the head of a troop of fifty mounted Virginia militiamen led by Colonel William Campbell. John sprang from his horse and called into the house. "Hello, my Bonny Kate, are you all right?"

The door opened wide and the tall slender black-haired girl flew out into his arms for an embrace as passionate as any he'd ever had. The children followed her example, and his arms couldn't hold all the welcoming bodies that flung themselves his way.

"Who were those men?" he demanded.

"Tories trying to plunder your smokehouse," Bonny Kate replied.

Colonel Campbell stood tall in his stirrups and turned, "Sergeant, give chase!" he ordered. The sergeant and his men rode in pursuit of the Tories. Colonel Campbell dismounted to observe the happy family scene.

"You saved my life again, and brought an army to do it!" Bonny Kate exclaimed.

John laughed. "Yes, and they came all the way from Virginia under Governor Jefferson's orders."

"The Lord certainly knows when I need help and makes long range plans to provide it!"

"Bonny Kate, I want you to meet Colonel William Campbell, commander of the Virginia expedition, and a personal friend of mine."

"Welcome, sir." She curtsied. "I'm honored you came to my rescue."

"Happy to oblige," he responded. "By the warmth of your welcome, I think you are closely related to Colonel Sevier."

Laughing and embarrassed, she stepped away from John. "Oh no, sir, it was the circumstances . . . I'm just a neighbor . . . I take care of the children for the colonel."

"I would wish for such a welcome when I go home!" Colonel Campbell smiled.

"Forgive me, Colonel Sevier." Bonny Kate blushed. "It was the circumstances."

"That's quite understandable, Miss Sherrill."

"Sherrill?" Colonel Campbell asked. "Would you be Bonny Kate Sherrill?"

"Yes, sir."

"Oh, the stories I've heard about you are amazing," he said. "You're a legend!"

"Don't believe everything you hear, sir." She smiled.

"Bonny Kate, the colonel and his officers are dining with us tonight, if you wouldn't mind staying and cooking us a meal. Could you please?" John requested.

"Yes, sir," she answered, "I'd be happy to. Betsy, open the shutters. Children, the danger has passed. Let's all work together and cook for our friends from Virginia." She turned to welcome Joseph and James home on a rare visit from their work at the mill and their studies at Pastor Doak's school. "Welcome home, boys. We have missed you."

Joseph smiled and gave her a brotherly hug, but James was cool to the welcome and walked past her into the cabin. Just then, Nancy began to cry, and Bonny Kate rushed into the cabin to pick her up. John freshened up at the washbasin at the end of the porch and invited Colonel Campbell to do likewise. Then they relaxed on the porch to discuss business.

"It's a good thing we came along when we did, Jack," Campbell said. "Miss Sherrill appeared to be outnumbered."

"Yes, but she showed great courage in the face of danger," John replied.

"I see now why you are reluctant to go on our campaign," Colonel Campbell said.

"Do you mean the danger or the woman?" John grinned.

"Both." Campbell smiled.

"Like I told you, Bill, the Tories are the bigger problem than the Indians these days. You are welcome to camp here until I can find you a reliable guide for your campaign."

Bonny Kate came out with Nancy. "Is this a good time for a visit, Papa?"

"It's always a good time for a visit with my little Nancy," John encouraged, taking the baby.

"Did I hear mention of a campaign?" Bonny Kate asked with great concern.

"Yes," John said. "Colonel Campbell has asked me to go on the Indian campaign."

"What are you going to do?" she asked.

"Don't worry, my Bonny Kate," John reassured her. "I haven't changed my mind. I have enough good reasons to stay right here." John bounced the baby on his knee gently and kissed the little one.

Bonny Kate was relieved, smiled at him, and went back into the cabin to work on the supper.

The soldiers returned from their pursuit of the Tories. The tired Virginia horses had not been able to overtake the fresher mounts of the king's men. The soldiers set up camp in the pasture at Plum Grove and began cooking their evening meal. The junior officers were invited to dine with the colonels. Soon the evening meal was ready and the officers gathered in the great room to eat with John's family.

John pulled out Sarah's empty chair as his family watched solemnly.

"Miss Sherrill, would you sit here please?"

"Oh no, I couldn't," she protested. "I never stay for dinner. I have to get home while there's still light to do my chores."

"Please stay," John requested. "I will escort you home and explain your late arrival to your father."

"Well, all right, but I can't sit there."

"Please?" he insisted.

"Is this important to you, Colonel Sevier?"

"Very important," he replied.

"Very well," she agreed, as she gracefully, but uneasily sat.

"Father, it's not right for her to sit in Mother's chair!" James Sevier protested.

"James, it is my wish," his father said firmly. James stalked out of the cabin.

Bonny Kate rose to go after him, but Colonel Sevier stopped her with the same stern tone that she knew must be obeyed. "Let him go, Miss Sherrill, he needs some time to himself." She settled back into the chair but felt bad for James.

Colonel Campbell and his officers sat next, and the children rushed to find their places around the table. All bowed their heads to pray.

After supper, John sat on the porch visiting with Colonel Campbell and the other officers.

"Betty and I were mighty sorry to hear about Sarah," Colonel Campbell said.

"It's nearly killed me, Bill. I loved her so deeply and so long. She was my whole life. Thank God for the children. They have been such a comfort to me."

"The children seem to be happy and well adjusted, with the exception of young James," Colonel Campbell observed.

"I have Bonny Kate to thank for that," John affirmed.

"She seems very capable and very fond of you. Is she married?"

"No," John spoke softly. "I don't think she would be interested."

"Could have fooled me," Campbell said.

Their conversation was interrupted when Bonny Kate stepped out on the porch carrying a basket. The men rose politely.

"I'm done with the dishes, and the children are all in bed," she announced cheerfully.

"Thank you, my Bonny Kate. The horses are waiting, and I will escort you home."

"If Colonel Campbell will excuse us." She smiled.

"Yes, of course," he replied.

"It was a pleasure meeting you today, Colonel Campbell," she said. "Thank you for the rescue. Take care on the Indian campaign. Good night, sir."

"Good night, ma'am."

John and Bonny Kate mounted the horses and rode away down the lane.

The moon rose over the mountains and illuminated the Nolichucky Valley. Bonny Kate and John rode slowly enough for conversation.

"Colonel Sevier, I'm worried that I offended James," Bonny Kate remarked.

"It was nothing you did, Miss Sherrill," John reassured her. "He's my sensitive one and took the death of his mother very hard. I'm very aware of what's going on with James so let me handle it."

"Yes, sir, I will," she replied. "I'm sorry to take you away from your guests tonight. Across the pasture is the quickest way."

"I'm in no hurry," John declared. "I just want to enjoy the moonlight on the river and the pleasure of your company."

Bonny Kate smiled. "Then, sir, let us go all that much slower!"

Chapter 38

An Important Conversation Interrupted

It was another one of those golden early August days when nature cooperates perfectly to produce an exquisite memory. Bonny Kate had gone to Plum Grove early that morning to make the children's breakfast but found that Betsy had it ready and waiting when she arrived. Betsy was getting quite good at fixing meals and had volunteered to keep the younger children that day and feed them lunch. The Virginia troops were gone, but a light horse company of the home guard was patrolling south of Plum Grove, and Joseph and James were home for a visit, so John felt he could give Bonny Kate the day off.

"I think the children are well cared for today with the older boys at home. And I know you need some time to yourself. May I escort you home?" John asked.

"Thank you, sir," she responded. "I would love to have your company."

The last thing she wanted was time to herself. She wanted his time. She had things to discuss with him about the children, and the progress the family had made in the healing process. She was so proud of John for resisting the temptation that Isaac Shelby had presented to go to the war in the east and then to turn down Colonel Campbell's offer to accompany the Virginians on the Indian campaign. To accomplish her purpose, she set a leisurely pace and suggested they take the longer route to her home through the upper pasture, instead of the river road.

"Somewhere on the upper reaches of Horse Creek there's a sizable waterfall with a large pool below. I sure would love to go swimming on such a hot day as this," she hinted.

"I know the place," he responded. "It is beautiful."

"Do you have time to go with me?"

"Sure," he said. He remembered that matchmaker Irma had sent him several requests for interviews with eligible widows, that, he had yet to answer. A day with Bonny Kate would allow him to put off that obligation a little while longer. And Bonny Kate's conversation, the sound of her voice, and her gentle laugh were all like music to his ears that brought him much pleasure. Then there was the appealing prospect of seeing her slender, well-shaped body in wet swimming clothes. He had seen her wet several times in the past but did not pay especially close attention at the time he was married. Things were different today. He thought about the dream he had about Sarah across the river. Why couldn't Bonny Kate have been the woman that Sarah had spoken of in the dream?

At the waterfall, they left their horses several yards to the east and walked over to the edge of the pool. Bonny Kate removed her day gown, cap, and moccasins and waded into the water wearing only her sheer petticoat and shift. When she eased into the cold water, air was trapped under the petticoat but came bubbling out as she glided through the water easily and dove her head under, wetting her sleek black hair. John was mesmerized by the grace and beauty of the woman who swam like an otter.

"Aren't you coming in, John?"

He quickly removed his boots, his shirt, and his socks and only wore his linen breeches. He dove in and swam in the waist-deep water. It was cold and refreshing, but his greatest pleasure was watching her enjoy it. Together they explored the waterfall and felt the relaxing force of the showering water on their bodies. They enjoyed the splendor of the place and the gentle companionship but observed a polite respect for each other's modesty. When the sun approached its zenith, she crawled out of the water onto a large sun-warmed rock to sit and watch John chasing some fish in the shallows like a little boy. From her rock, she could look across the pool and see the horses on the other side grazing.

"So, John, you were telling me the Virginians just turned around and headed home?" she asked.

"They were ordered home," he told her. "Colonel Campbell got word of a Tory uprising that threatened to take over the Virginia lead mines."

"Oh my! What about the Indian campaign?"

"Suddenly the Indians didn't seem so menacing," he said.

"Not so to the Virginians, but what about us?" she asked.

"It will be left for me to defend the southwest frontier for both Virginia and North Carolina," he declared. Suddenly she felt the family's security crumble under the weight of even heavier responsibilities for Colonel Sevier.

"What will you do?" she asked, fearful of greater periods of his absence than they had yet seen.

John smiled at her and waded over to the rock where she sat. He pulled himself out of the water and sat facing her. "Just what I'm doing now," he replied. "I see no need for action as long as the Indians don't cause us any trouble." He took her hands in his and looked into her eyes to reassure her. "Don't worry. I won't be going anywhere anytime soon." He looked down at her work-calloused hands. "My, you have such strong hands."

"From milking cows." She laughed.

"My Bonny Kate, there is something I wanted to ask you."

"What is it?"

"Well, it's about that man you once loved, and he did not return your love," he began.

Bonny Kate looked searchingly into his eyes and responded, "Yes, my first and only true love."

"I think he behaved foolishly," John judged.

"But he was not free to love me," she countered. "He behaved honorably, and so did I. Now, what did you want to ask me?"

John went on hesitantly. "Do you think . . . that . . . you could ever bring yourself . . . to love another man?"

Her answer was quick. "No, John, I don't think I ever could."

He released his hold on her hands and looked away from her steady gaze. "Oh . . . ," was all he said.

"What about you?" she asked. "Are you ready to love another woman?"

"I thought, perhaps I was," he replied. "But you know I want to love a woman who can love me with the same depth and passion I knew before."

The waterfall was the only sound in that place for several seconds. Then John turned and waded back into the cold water. A hunting party of Indians emerged silently from the woods behind Bonny Kate.

Her heart was racing. She had let slip an opportunity to declare her own feelings. She let it pass because she judged he was still not ready to take that step with her, but their words had left a terrible misunderstanding.

"John, please don't walk away," she pleaded. "There's more we need to say."

As John reached the opposite bank, he turned to look at Bonny Kate and spotted the hunting party approaching at some distance.

"Bonny Kate, be calm but get up and go to the horses as quick as you can. And stop looking so desirable." She smiled at what she thought was a compliment, but in the next instant, she saw that his intense gaze was not directed at her but up the hill behind her. She looked over her shoulder and saw the hunters. She jumped up, splashed across the creek, and ran to the horses.

John recognized the Indian leader as John Watts—an unpredictable, sometimes friend, sometimes enemy of the Wataugans—and watched him for signs of his intentions.

"Chucky Jack, war chief of the Hunakas, you know me?" Watts addressed him.

"John Watts, cousin to Dragging Canoe. Yours is a clan of chiefs and warriors." Colonel Sevier responded. John Watts seemed pleased to be so recognized.

Watts pointed at Bonny Kate. "This is your woman?"

"Yes," John declared. "She is my woman."

"We have seen her quickness. She is called by our people Swift Running Doe. Good squaw for a great chief. How do you catch her?"

Sevier laughed and responded. "My horses run faster." Watts repeated what had been said in Cherokee for the benefit of his companions and all the men laughed. It seemed to ease the tension. Bonny Kate led the horses to where John stood. She gathered their clothing from the ground quickly and made ready to ride. She had counted eight hunters and knew John was in trouble, unarmed, and wearing only his breeches. Even without a weapon, she understood that John would put up a 🔥 of a fight, all the more desperate, she imagined, to provide her a chance to escape.

"Would you trade Swift Running Doe for Cherokee horses?" Watts bartered.

Bonny Kate was sickened by the thought and angered that Watts would play such a game when he already possessed the advantage. She couldn't draw John's rifle any faster. She knew he kept it loaded but fumbled with the powder horn to get his gun primed, standing behind his horse so the hunters couldn't see what she was doing. John was still presenting a brave front with their time running out as some of the hunters moved slowly toward the creek on the downstream side. John then paid her a kind compliment she didn't have time to appreciate.

"You don't have enough horses in the entire nation to make that trade," John stated firmly but grinning widely. Watts turned to his braves and translated. While they still laughed, Bonny Kate stepped forward and pressed the rifle into John's right hand.

"Primed, cocked, and ready," she said in a low voice. She hung his shot pouch and powder horn in the positions he always liked them when dressed, and then stepped to her horse and prepared her own rifle. The Indians stopped laughing as her efforts shifted the balance of power.

"Swift Running Doe becomes impatient with talk," observed Watts. "We come to trade, and she prepares to fight."

Bonny Kate mounted her horse and leveled her rifle at the nearest hunter. She figured she would let John take down Watts, while she would buy him as much time as she could in dealing with the others. Her pounding heart told her she was not going to leave him.

But John had it figured another way. He laughed loudly. "Swift Running Doe is impatient for love! I must not keep her waiting."

The Indians joined him in a good laugh when Watts shared it in translation. The downstream hunters that Bonny Kate menaced with her rifle stepped back on a signal from their leader, opening the route of escape. John Sevier swung nimbly into his saddle.

"We will trade another day." John promised Watts with a smile, elevating his rifle skyward. John and Bonny Kate rode into the woods heading downstream as fast as the terrain allowed. After a good third of an hour, they broke out of the woods into the open meadows along Horse Creek, John slowed down and glanced back to make sure they were not followed by any mounted warriors.

"Thank you for moving so quickly." John breathed with relief. "I could tell he was trying to figure out a way to take my scalp."

"What are they doing so close to our homes?" Bonny Kate questioned.

"Hunting and spying," he replied. "The British keep pushing them to attack while our men are gone east to the war, but I'm glad they saw me. They will report that Chucky Jack still protects his home and neighbors. That will make them think twice."

Bonny Kate tried to remember all that had been said. "Why did you say I was your woman?"

"So they wouldn't mess with you. I thought they might show you greater respect," he explained.

"But you said it so easily, so naturally, you didn't even take time to think about it. Does that mean you'd like me to be your woman?"

"And supposing it did," he continued in the humorous vein. "How would I catch Swift Running Doe?"

"Your horses run faster." She laughed.

"I took liberties with your reputation when I mentioned your impatience for love. I hope you will forgive me. The circumstances required me to keep them laughing."

"What sort of reputation might I have among the Cherokees?" She laughed.

"You would be surprised at how often the tales of your exploits entertain travelers, soldiers, hunters, and even Indians around their campfires."

"That would make a girl blush!" she exclaimed with alarm.

"Oh no, Miss Sherrill, the boys always speak of you in glowing terms, with an uncommon reverence; and no one I know has ever related an unsavory tale attached to you," he assured her.

"Well, that's a mercy," she said, still shocked to learn of her widespread notoriety.

"I hope you were not offended," he said, quickening the pace of his horse.

Bonny Kate thought about his remark concerning her impatience for love and how they had so nearly gotten around to that important topic. Perhaps she could get it started again now. She urged her horse to catch up with John's.

"I take no offense at the truth," she declared, but it was a cold trail. John was silently preoccupied with Indian affairs as they continued riding. "John, did you understand my meaning, sir?" She waited for a response several moments before she continued, "No, of course you didn't, dear man."

"What's that again? I'm sorry, I was thinking about the Indians. This threat cannot go unanswered. What if they had harmed you? The home guard will muster at noon tomorrow for a campaign against the Overhill towns. Would you kindly convey that message to your brothers?"

"Yes, sir," Bonny Kate sighed, greatly disappointed that the progress John's family had made toward healing would now be cast aside in this present state of emergency. He urged his horse to a gallop.

"Colonel Sevier!" she called after him. "Wait, good sir!"

He reined in his horse and wheeled about. "What is it?"

"Don't you think we ought to get dressed before we present ourselves before my parents at Daisy Fields?" she reminded him. Sarah had taught her well about appearances.

"Oh yes," he agreed. "You look somewhat like a fish out of water."

"And you look like one of those savages as the sun begins to redden your shoulders," she observed.

"Did you per chance collect my shirt?" he asked, dismounting.

An air of formality and politeness of speech returned as they sorted out their belongings and redressed in the manner they had started the day. They traveled only a few miles from the Garden of Eden experience at the waterfall to the reality of her double life as daughter at Daisy Fields and governess of Plum Grove. She would always treasure those shared innocent intimate moments that endeared him to her as never before, but she worried about his feelings toward her. She had parried his approach to the subject, and what she said left a terrible misunderstanding in his mind. She longed to return to that interrupted conversation and correct the confusion she had created. She would have a great many days to stew about it as the Indian campaign unfolded, fearing she might never have the chance again to relate to Colonel Sevier in such a perfect setting.

Chapter 39

The Triumph of the Matchmakers

Bonny Kate heard the whole sorry story of the Indian campaign from her brother Sam Junior as she sat on the front porch at Daisy Fields watching the sunset and rocking little Nancy Sevier in her cradle. Colonel Sevier's home guard had gathered at Greasy Cove, a smaller company than expected. The first night some of the troops were hunting and encountered some Indians. Both parties fired and retreated. All night the soldiers lay upon their arms expecting an attack at any moment but nothing happened. In the morning, Major Tipton's company rode out to reconnoiter and found a trail of blood. One of the Indians had died of his wounds and was left behind. Major Tipton spent the day following the trail of the Indians leading deeper and deeper into Indian lands. By midafternoon, no more Indians were found so Major Tipton turned back and arrived in camp late that evening.

Colonel Sevier held a council of the officers and all advised against proceeding with the campaign. They had too few troops; they were undersupplied, and the best trained units had gone east to fight in the Carolinas with Major Robertson. The adventurous Colonel was the only one urging his men to vigorous action. The other officers prevailed and caution became the order of the day. Colonel Sevier kept a company of light horse patrolling and dismissed the rest of the men to their homes.

"Bonny Kate, the men don't know what to make of the colonel's strange behavior." Sam Junior told his sister as he finished telling the story of the campaign. "He is very agitated by something going on at home. What's got the man so distracted?"

"I am sure I don't know," she responded. "My responsibilities do not extend beyond the care of the children, and in that the colonel has not given his undivided attention."

"There is the problem," Sam Junior concluded. "Colonel Sevier has too many demands for his undivided attention. He would have preferred the hardships of an Indian campaign to what awaits him at home."

"What do you mean by that?" she demanded. "I have poured my heart and soul into restoring his home to the efficient operation and blessed shelter of love and nurture to his children that Sarah would have wanted! Nothing has been withheld from my devotion to that family!"

"No, my dear noble sister," Sam Junior spoke soothingly. "This is not about you or your service on behalf of the children. I think it's about the matchmakers. Irma and Ruth have worn him down to the point of making himself available to the wealthiest, the prettiest, and sweetest widows in Washington County."

"What foolishness is this?" she reacted.

"Oh, it's not foolishness. This is a deadly business to the soul of man," he said. "I know because I carried the message to Ruth Brown myself from the colonel's headquarters at Greasy Cove."

"What was the message?" Bonny Kate felt her hot blood rising, with great uneasiness.

"Whoa, Kate," he said. "I don't read the messages I'm entrusted to carry, but Mrs. Brown was very pleased with it. She said Colonel Sevier had finally come to his senses. She also said she would arrange everything this week. Now, knowing the business that Mrs. Brown enjoys most, I have put two and two together; and it's clear to me she's planning a widow party for the colonel."

Bonny Kate's disappointment was so evident that Sam Junior felt truly sorry for her. He tried gently to comfort her. "It's always been obvious to us that you were kind of sweet on Colonel Sevier. I don't understand why he never saw it. I think he's behaved foolishly."

"No, he behaved honorably," she insisted, but there was an undeniable sadness in her voice. She knew she had caused the misunderstanding that had prompted him to surrender himself to the matchmakers.

"Well, it will soon be all over for you," Sam Junior observed. "Once he marries, you never have to ride over to Plum Grove again. By the way, Colonel Sevier wants his daughter Nancy home by ten in the morning."

"Did he say why?" she asked.

"Nope, but have her there by ten." Sam Junior left her alone with her thoughts. The idea of it being all over, for her, was a new worry she'd never considered. She would most certainly be banished by John's new wife from ever again riding to Plum Grove, ever again caring for his children, ever again enjoying the close confidences of those precious children, ever again feeling the thrill of seeing John come home and discussing with him the needs of his children. There would be no more horse trading or flirting or joking with him or being needed and appreciated. She imagined losing all that and being left with the chilling emptiness of a void that could never be filled. She understood then what Colonel Sevier and his children meant to her. She hoped she would soon have the opportunity to speak privately with him and clear up the misunderstanding that stood in their way. The problem was how should she approach the subject?

A beautiful August morning rewarded the faithful Bonny Kate as she made her way to Plum Grove with her little companion Nancy Sevier. She found Colonel Sevier on the front porch impeccably dressed and handsome as ever, enjoying some family time with Betsy and his younger children. He rose to greet her.

"Bonny Kate, I sure am glad to see you!"

"I was glad to hear you returned safely from the Indian campaign," she responded.

"It wasn't much of a campaign. We trailed them for a day, but they were long gone. We considered the options, and decided to keep the home guard close to home. Can you stay awhile?"

"Well, I thought you'd never ask." She moved gracefully from the horse to the porch and settled lightly on a chair with Nancy in her lap. The children came to her and hugged her in greeting.

"My word, John, you are all fixed up today." She laughed. "If I didn't know better, I would have guessed you were planning to go out widow hunting."

"That's the problem. I don't even have to leave home for that anymore," he said a little sadly.

"You don't?"

"No, they're hunting me. Irma Jenkins and Ruth Brown are bringing over a wagonload of widows this morning."

"Oh, John, what a misery!" she exclaimed. "I know how you must hate that."

"You know how insistent Irma is," he explained. "You said yourself I should accept the help of experts. It got to where I couldn't say no to just one little spicewood tea party."

"Oh no, of course not," she agreed sarcastically.

The widow wagon turned into the lane with six well-dressed ladies, the driver was Irma, the matchmaker. Ruth Brown sat beside her and widows Coleman, White, Sparks, and Johnson rode behind.

"Here they come now," John said nervously.

"I need to be going," Bonny Kate said quickly.

"No, please stay," he invited her, with surprising urgency.

"I'm not dressed for a party," she objected.

"It doesn't matter," he insisted. "I want you to stay."

"I suppose I could help Betsy serve the refreshments, and keep the children entertained." Bonny Kate rose with Nancy in her arms and moved into the parlor as the wagon arrived at the porch.

"Good morning, Colonel Sevier!" Irma greeted with her usual enthusiasm.

"Welcome, ladies!" John said with a polite bow. He helped the ladies alight from the wagon and up onto the porch.

"Please step into my parlor and have some refreshments. It's getting warm, isn't it?" He began some polite conversation as they filed into the house.

Inside the parlor, Ruth Brown greeted Bonny Kate with a hug. Irma Jenkins was a little more formal. "Why Bonny Kate Sherrill, what brings you here?"

"My horse," she joked. "She needed the exercise." Nervous laughter filled the room, and Colonel Sevier smiled at her. "I really just stopped in to see about the children."

"That's so neighborly of you, dear," Irma said.

"Yes, so neighborly!" Mrs. Coleman agreed.

"Will you be joining our little tea party?" Irma offered.

"No, ma'am," Bonny Kate replied taking a couple of side steps closer to the door. "I'll just help Betsy serve the refreshments when the time comes."

"I see," said Irma. She watched Colonel Sevier watching Bonny Kate and read accurately what was there. She was so good at matchmaking that she knew that today's mission was good for nothing but practice. "Colonel Sevier, my son went with Major Robertson's expedition. Have you heard anything from the war?" she continued.

"No, ma'am," he replied. "I haven't received any reports. I'm mainly concerned these days with my duties as Colonel of the home guard."

"We understand how difficult these months have been for you, especially with your fatherly duties," Mrs. Johnson empathized. "Why only a Colonel could manage a family as large as this."

"Yes, ma'am," John responded. An awkward silence followed.

Bonny Kate broke the silence thinking he needed her help facilitating the conversation. "Colonel, why not introduce your children?" she suggested.

"Yes, Colonel," Mrs. Coleman agreed. "We need to learn all their names."

"Yes, ma'am," John responded. "This is Elizabeth, we call her Betsy, and over in the corner is Nancy, my youngest. Valentine here, is ten, Little Sarah whom we call Dolly, Dicky, Mary Ann, and Becky, she's three. The older boys Joseph, James, and John Junior are out this morning tending the farm."

"My, an impressive group and so fine looking," declared Mrs. Johnson.

"Yes, fine-looking children," agreed Irma. "Good looks naturally run in a family of quality."

Silence fell over the room again until John remembered the refreshments. "Ladies, I have a special treat, peaches chilled in the spring house. We should serve them now. Betsy, will you perform the service?"

"Yes, sir," she responded. Betsy and Bonny Kate left the room to go to the cookhouse. Again, John's eyes followed the light graceful movements of the lady from Daisy Fields.

"I'll go help," Ruth Brown volunteered, and she followed the others.

In the cookhouse out behind the main house, Betsy, Bonny Kate, and Ruth quickly prepared the peaches.

"Bonny Kate," Ruth began. "I must ask you a delicate question and please do not be offended. But are we trespassing on your claim?"

"What do you mean?" Bonny Kate stalled. "Betsy, please take these in to the ladies." Betsy Sevier knew Bonny Kate would not answer Mrs. Brown's question while she was present so she reluctantly did as she was told. She lifted the tray of peach bowls and walked out.

"By bringing these ladies here, are we trespassing on your claim?" Ruth repeated.

"I have no claim," she answered.

"How do you feel about today's tea party?"

"It's going so well, don't you think?"

"How would you feel if John married one of those fine ladies before the end of this month?"

"Oh, how could he? It would ruin the man to marry without the fullness of a deep passionate love!" Bonny Kate exclaimed.

"Bonny Kate, I think you know more than you are telling me," Ruth pried.

"It's just that in the last several weeks John . . . I mean, the colonel and I . . . have made considerable progress in the healing of his family."

"Does he ever spend time with just you, alone?" Ruth asked.

"Well, sometimes he will see me home after I've been here to care for the children, and we take our time. We look at horses in the pasture or go up to the waterfall, or one night it was really late, and there was a full moon to light our way." She smiled dreamily.

"Oh, Bonny Kate, that gives me goose bumps. Do you love him?"

"I . . . I shouldn't say until . . ." Bonny Kate stopped.

By then Betsy had returned unobserved to the door of the cookhouse and stood listening.

"Until when?" Ruth pressed her.

"Until he's ready to let go of Sarah and move on. That could take years." Bonny Kate admitted sadly.

"Bonny Kate Sherrill, do you love him or do you not?"

"Well, I suppose . . . Oh, what am I saying? Yes, of course I do, deeply . . . completely . . . hopelessly!"

Betsy ran from the doorway and into Bonny Kate's arms, tearfully, joyfully. "Oh, Bonny Kate, I just knew it would be you!"

Bonny Kate, surprised at Betsy's reaction, but sensitive to who should know her great secret and when it should be revealed, admonished her. "Betsy, no, you shouldn't have heard that!"

"But I did, and I'm so happy!" Betsy exclaimed.

"No, don't be," Bonny Kate warned. "You must never tell your father what you heard. It would ruin everything for me."

"Why?" Betsy asked.

"That is something I have to tell him myself when the time is right. I have to be sure he's ready to hear it and be sure that he has the same feelings for me. Do you understand?"

"I think so," Betsy replied.

"Then promise me," Bonny Kate demanded sternly. "You will never repeat what you heard me say when you came in."

"Yes, I promise," Betsy declared solemnly.

"Thank you, dear Betsy. Please keep my secret!"

"I will," Betsy affirmed. Another embrace sealed their alliance. Bonny Kate felt such pride in Betsy's maturity and her development over the past six months. She felt confident that Betsy would become a great woman, like her mother, sweet in disposition, and strong in character.

"Does he love you?" Ruth continued to work on the equation. She had only solved for one variable, and there was still no answer for the other.

"I don't know," Bonny Kate wondered. "He's so vulnerable. As close as we've become, he still doesn't share his deepest feelings very well. Sometimes I think he's just about to share something very important, and then . . . we are interrupted."

"Then it's time for a test!" Ruth exclaimed.

"What kind of test?" Bonny Kate asked.

"Well, let's see," Ruth said thoughtfully. "I know. You can leave in a huff."

"In a huff?" Bonny Kate questioned.

"Yes, huffs are very useful, it's time you had one," Ruth declared. "Just get on your horse and go home. Betsy and I will take care of the rest."

"Now, why am I leaving in a huff?" Bonny Kate wanted to know.

"To see what he'll do," Ruth explained. "If he follows you that's a good sign."

"A sign of what?" Bonny Kate was still not sure about this idea.

"Never you, mind. Just go!" Ruth insisted. "Right now, go" She pushed Bonny Kate toward the door.

"I'm going," Bonny Kate stopped resisting.

"Betsy, make sure she leaves in a huff, mind you," Ruth instructed. "I'll manage your father's reaction."

They all left the cookhouse. Bonny Kate and Betsy went around to the front porch where Bonny Kate left her horse.

"I don't see what good this will do," Bonny Kate protested.

"Look your best and be ready for anything," Betsy advised. "And remember, leave in a huff." Bonny Kate's actions were quick and deliberate, without a word, she gained the saddle and urged her horse to a gallop down the lane to the Nolichucky and out into the open fields beyond.

Ruth Brown rejoined the party as Bonny Kate rode away.

"My, my, what lovely peaches," Irma complimented her host.

"Excuse me, ladies, I heard a horse out in the lane." John was always alert to the comings and goings of traffic out in his lane. He stepped out in the yard and found Betsy standing under the shade of an oak tree watching Bonny Kate ride away. He joined her and followed her gaze. "Why did Bonny Kate rush off like that?"

"I couldn't tell you," Betsy replied, fully aware of her promise to Bonny Kate.

"Did she seem all right to you?" John asked.

"Oh, she's fine," Betsy replied. "She will be at Daisy Fields the rest of the day if you are interested."

"I wonder why she left so suddenly?"

"You'll have to ask her," Betsy replied.

"That's a curious thing," he concluded. "Say, it's a fine little party, isn't it?"

"Yes, sir," Betsy replied enthusiastically. "I'm having a really great time!"

He looked at her carefully to see if she was sincere and apparently she was. He wondered if she was attending the same party. He was not having a good time at all. There was nothing to be done but make the best of it.

"That's a great group of ladies from powerful families, big land owners," he reasoned. "There would be great social advantages for you and the little ones. A father has to think about such things. Which of the ladies do you like best?"

"The one that just left," Betsy declared emphatically.

John thoughtfully gazed down the road for several seconds. "Me too," he admitted.

"Papa, why don't you court Bonny Kate? She was Mama's best friend, and all of us love her."

John laughed with surprise. "What? Are you giving your old Papa advice about courting now?" Betsy just smiled at him as he admired, with fatherly pride, his eldest daughter. He took the girl in his arms. "My goodness, Betsy, I turn around and suddenly you're all grown up. You shouldered many responsibilities, cooking, cleaning, and tending children. In the process, you've matured into a wise little lady. I'm mighty proud of you, Betsy." She closed her eyes with her head against his chest and listened to the beat of his brave heart. She knew how important it would be for him to listen to that same heart and follow its leading, in divinely inspired directions.

"Papa, I know this has got to be your decision, but I thought you should know how the rest of us feel about her."

John released her, leaned against the old oak, and continued to gaze down the now empty road.

"Which of the ladies would you rather be with right now?" she prompted him again.

"She's made it clear, she won't love me," John said.

Betsy had to clap her hand over her mouth to keep from saying what she was thinking. *Whoa, Papa, where in the world did that idea come from?* Betsy was shocked he would believe that and be so resigned to it. Her promise to Bonny Kate was suddenly a burden almost too heavy to bear. But Betsy absolutely refused to break a promise, so she responded with a universal truth. "A woman can always change her mind."

"Betsy, I can't make you any promises," John said. "It could take a long time to win her love, if that's even possible. Honey, fetch me my hat." John turned and went for his horse, while Betsy sprang to the porch and found her father's hat hanging on a peg beside the door. She waited for him in the yard while he quickly saddled his horse. He rode up to Betsy from the horse barn, and Betsy gave him his hat.

"I'll be gone the rest of the day," he told her. "Please express my regrets to our guests. Tell them a horse-trading deal needed my immediate attention. How do I look?"

Betsy smiled triumphantly. "Handsome as ever, Papa," she answered. "Good luck."

John raced down the lane in pursuit of Bonny Kate. Ruth Brown joined Betsy in the yard, and they celebrated.

"It worked! It worked!" rejoiced Betsy, dancing and prancing like a child. Irma Jenkins, the widows, and the smaller Seviers, came out to see the commotion.

Irma walked over to Ruth. "She left in a huff?"

"Yes, she did!" answered Ruth.

Irma smiled. "I've never seen the huff fail when the man's in love."

Ruth sighed with satisfaction. "And Betsy here played it to perfection."

"And I kept my promise," Betsy added.

"There's power in a man motivated by love," Irma observed. "It takes my breath away to see our colonel, finally, back in the game!"

Chapter 40

Courting Bonny Kate

Sam and Mary Sherrill enjoyed a moment together on the front porch at Daisy Fields. It wasn't often enough that he and Mary could just sit and talk. Bonny Kate had taken Baby Nancy back to Plum Grove that morning, and Mary Jane was up at the Daisy Fields guest cabin cleaning, while little Aquilla was playing nearby. Sam cleaned his rifle with care while Mary shelled a picking of early peas. Bonny Kate rode into the yard, jumped from her horse, tied the animal at the corral, and dashed past them into the house.

"Are those Indians after you again?" Sam called to her.

"No, sir," she replied from the great room. "Colonel Sevier might stop by."

Sam looked over at Mary and winked. "That wouldn't be unusual. Every time she gets a day off from keeping his children, the man comes over here to shop for horses. It wouldn't surprise me one little bit him stopping by."

"But today it's going to be a sign," Bonny Kate predicted.

Sam looked at his wife again and asked, "Do you know what she's talking about?"

"No, dear, but I've been cooking long enough to know when the pot's about to boil."

"It looks more like a boilover to me," Sam declared.

"We'll see directly," Mary said patiently, still working with her mess of peas.

Bonny Kate emerged from the cabin dressed in her best dress, tying her hair back with a wide ribbon.

"Well now, don't you look nice," he observed.

"Thank you, sir. I thought I'd freshen up a bit."

She stepped over to the washbasin at the edge of the porch and poured water into it from a pitcher. She splashed water on her face then patted it dry with a linen towel as she paced up and down the porch nervously.

"My dear Bonny Kate, is there something going on that we need to know about?" her mother asked.

"I don't know," she said, continuing to primp and pace looking up the road frequently.

"You're making me nervous," Sam said. "Sit down, girl."

She obeyed and sat for a few moments in a chair across the porch but couldn't stay there long.

"I thought you went over to the colonel's house this morning," Mary said. Bonny Kate rose again and paced the porch.

"I did, but John . . . I mean, the colonel, was entertaining a whole flock of widows that Irma brought over. They told me to go home."

"Why, the nerve of those women!" Mary exclaimed. "They can't order you about like that."

"No, it wasn't that way at all," Bonny Kate explained. "I was talking to Ruth Brown and saying things I shouldn't have been saying, as you know I am prone to do, when suddenly she proposed this test."

"Well, I'm confused," Sam declared. "Why are we expecting Colonel Sevier if he's entertaining a flock of widows? He'll be charming those ladies with fancy talk all day long. And I bet Irma has lined up the finest-looking and richest ladies in the county. If you wait for him to come here, girl, you'll wait in vain."

"Maybe not," she hoped without any good reason to hope.

"Daughter, I love you. I don't want to see you disappointed again," Sam said gently. At that moment, Bounder, the faithful canine sentinel, perked up to the sound of a rider approaching and gave the warning signal.

"Somebody is coming!" she whispered.

They watched as Colonel John Sevier rode into their yard, carrying a handful of wildflowers he picked along the way to Daisy Fields. He reined in his horse next to Bonny Kate's and dismounted, handling the flowers with great care. He walked toward the Sherrill house slowly and deliberately. Bonny Kate standing behind her parents radiated excitement and wondered what he would say. He stepped up on the porch and removed his hat.

"Good day, Sam, Mrs. Sherrill, Miss Catharine," he began.

"Good day, Colonel," Sam replied.

"I collected this bouquet of wild flowers on my way over and thought it might bring pleasure to the ladies."

Bonny Kate stepped forward to receive them with a smile and curtsy. "Thank you, Colonel Sevier, you are most thoughtful." She admired the colors in the bouquet and missed the admiration he expressed for her in his blue eyes as he studied her face. Sam and Mary did not miss it though.

"Miss Catharine, would you do me the honor of going riding with me this afternoon? I thought we might ride down to the island and do some fishing."

"I'd be delighted," she replied. "I will need a few minutes to get ready. Would you like me to prepare some lunch to carry along?"

"An excellent idea, if it's not too much trouble," he responded politely.

"No trouble at all." Bonny Kate turned and stepped into the cabin.

"I'll help you, dear," Mary offered, following her into the house.

John and Sam stepped off the porch and walked toward the corral. John took a deep breath and exhaled quickly. "She does that to me, Sam, every time I look at her."

"Does what?" Sam inquired.

"Takes my breath away," John replied. "Same thing happened when I was courting Sarah. Look at me, I'm starting to sweat."

"It is the month of August," Sam explained. "We all sweat this time of year. I must admit, I'm surprised to see you today, John. Bonny Kate was telling us you had company at Plum Grove."

"Well, Irma and Ruth and some of their friends came to see me, but we finished earlier than expected."

"The greatest flowers of widowhood were there, I'm told," Sam continued probing.

"She told you that?"

"Aye, but I have a question," Sam stopped to look for answers in John's expressive face. "With a great garden of flowers to choose from, why would a man trouble himself with one little wildflower?"

"I'm very fond of your little wildflower, Sam, and I'd like your permission to court her."

"John, have you thought this through?" Sam decided for the fun of it; he was not going to make it easy for his courageous commander.

"I know it won't be easy," John replied. Sam noted a surprising lack of confidence in his neighbor.

"Easy is not the word for it!" Sam exclaimed. He always thought his beloved daughter was too obvious in her feelings, but she had managed to completely confuse and misdirect one of the greatest strategic military minds in the country, he thought.

"I know there was a man she loved, and he broke her heart, and I know she's still very much devoted to her ideal of true love. I'll have to work hard to win her," John declared.

"Well, if anyone can, it would be you," Sam tried to encourage him.

"But the more time I spend with her, the more I love her. I think about her constantly. I remember how Sarah loved her as a friend and how my children love her. It all adds up to the obvious."

"Maybe she's been too obvious," Sam suggested.

"What do you say, Sam? Do I have your permission?"

"Oh . . . yes. I suppose it's worth a try."

"Do you think I have much of a chance?" John asked.

"John, you are hopeless. But be resolute, never give up in the face of adversity, and never let her get away," Sam advised. "For I believe all things are possible with Divine Providence."

"Thanks, Sam, but don't tell Bonny Kate what we have discussed. Confidences have to be kept until the time is right."

"Of course, John, but be careful with my little girl's heart."

"I will," he promised. "The last thing I'd ever want to do is hurt her. I won't rush this thing. I realize it could take years."

Sam now saw clearly the workings of Divine Providence and envisioned his favorite child's future life. Dear Lord, she was useful, as useful as the man who loved her. Truly, it was a match made in heaven, contrived by one of heaven's angels, who on her deathbed extracted a promise on a cold January night, a promise that would bear the predestined fruit beneath the harvest moon. Yes, August would be a fine month for a wedding.

Bonny Kate and her mother stepped out on the porch. "Try to be back by dark," Mary instructed. "Your father and I were very disturbed that those Indians came so close the other day."

"Yes, ma'am. It disturbed me a little too. How do I look, Mama?"

"The very vision of loveliness," Mary exclaimed. "How could any man look at you and not fall madly in love!"

"Oh, Mama, be serious."

"All right then," Mary said, stepping back and looking her over carefully. "I reckon you'll do."

"Thank you, Mama." Mother and daughter kissed, and Bonny Kate gracefully descended the porch steps with her lunch basket in hand. She walked to the corral where John waited with Sam. Bonny Kate and John mounted their horses and rode away engaged in delightful conversation.

Sam rejoined Mary at the porch after seeing them off. Mary was in a serious mood. "I feel that something is definitely brewing between those two."

Sam smiled. "I'm not supposed to tell Bonny Kate, but the colonel asked my permission to court our daughter."

"Well, well, now we know his intentions," Mary said with satisfaction. "You allowed it, of course, didn't you?"

"Of course," he affirmed.

"How soon will he ask the question?" Mary asked.

"He told me it might take years," Sam told her. Mary broke out laughing, and Sam joined her. Mary Jane came down from cleaning the guesthouse, carrying little Aquilla on her hip.

"What's so funny?" Mary Jane asked.

"Colonel Sevier is courting Bonny Kate." Her mother laughed.

"Well, who in the world never saw that coming?" Mary Jane joined the fun. "I can't imagine what took them so long!"

"He really doesn't know what he's getting into, does he, Sam?" Mary asked.

"No, he hasn't a clue." Sam laughed. "I actually think he's afraid of being rejected. What do you think she's going to say when he asks her?"

"Oh, I'm afraid she's all mixed up too," Mary said. "She's trying too hard to compete with the memory of Sarah. I tried to tell her to just be herself."

Sam's merriment subsided as some serious thoughts entered his mind. "He leads a complicated life with very dangerous enemies. The Tories and Indians are always plotting to kill him."

"And how does a virgin bride suddenly become the mother of ten children?" Mary mused. "I don't know how any woman could manage that. I sure would like to go along today and hear what they say."

"You and me both, my dear," Sam said. "But nothing is going to stop John Sevier once he's made up his mind. This is something that not even Bonny Kate can mess up. He said they were going fishing." Sam started laughing again.

"Like the Good Book says, she's become a fisher of men." Mary laughed.

"She nearly let the bait get too ripe," Mary Jane quipped.

John and Bonny Kate rode their horses into the cool waters of the Nolichucky River and arrived at an island of several acres covered with willows, sycamores, and river grass. They let the horses graze as they made their way to a shady sycamore tree. She spread a blanket on the grass, and they sat facing each other. She served the lunch.

"I'm sorry about this morning," John said. "It was an uncomfortable situation. I had the impression you left because you were upset."

Bonny Kate smiled sweetly and looked directly at him. "I'm not upset."

"Then tell me why you left so suddenly?"

"Woman's business," she replied mysteriously.

"You mean to tell me you left the comforts of Plum Grove, which is equipped for all kinds of woman's business, to ride five miles home without even the courtesy of telling me good-bye?" John challenged her. "My dear Bonny Kate, I know enough about woman's business to think such a trip unnecessary."

"Your knowledge of woman's business seems to be increasing daily, with all the company you keep."

"There now, the answer to my question seems to be coming, slowly but surely," he coaxed her.

"I couldn't see any point in staying there and watching you . . . be uncomfortable," she blurted out.

"So you were concerned about me?" he asked.

"Of course," she answered. "Your well-being is always a concern to your children, and because they are concerned, I am concerned."

"I see," he said thoughtfully.

"And now a question for you, sir," she said. "How were you able to leave so suddenly?"

"I just got on my horse and rode after you," he stated.

"John! You didn't just up and leave your lovely guests, did you?"

"I guess I did," he admitted. He surprised himself when he thought about it that way. He was renowned to be the perfect host, polite, and proper in all situations. But his desire to be with Bonny Kate that day had overcome a lifetime of training and practice in the art of hospitality.

"Oh, John, that's unforgivable!" she exclaimed.

"Yes, ma'am," he agreed. "I feel bad for the ladies, but Irma will see them home. Besides, I didn't think any of them were serious about taking a husband like me, with ten children in the bargain. I'm really in a hopeless situation."

"That feeling of hopelessness has long been a companion to me," she empathized.

"You know our situations are very much alike," he observed. "You are in love with a man who is not free to love you. And I realize I am in love with a woman who is not free to love me."

"Oh, John!" she exclaimed. "You've fallen in love again? With whom?"

John looked into her eyes. "I love you, Catharine Sherrill," he declared with all the conviction he most certainly felt in his heart.

"But, John, how do you know that?"

"When you left my house this morning, the only place I wanted to be was with you," he answered immediately.

"How can you possibly love me? I'm nothing like Sarah."

"That's about as clear as day." He smiled. "But I love to hear you sing 'Amazing Grace.' And I love your laugh and the sound of your voice. I love the way you restored the life of my family."

"That's kind of you to say, John."

"I love how you care for people as a neighbor. I love you for taking care of the sick and comforting the grieving. I love you for listening to me and accepting me as I am. You get along so well with my friends, Isaac Shelby, James Robertson, Landon Carter, and even crazy Will Cocke."

"Friends are rare treasures," she affirmed.

"You understand my politics," he continued. "You share my love for fast horses, good dogs, fine rifles, and footracing. You loved my Sarah, and you love my children. You can't deny it. I see it every day."

"I don't deny it," she declared. Bonny Kate stood up and turned away. She needed to stand and breathe deeply. Her own feelings were surging out of control as she listened to his expressions of love. John remembered Sam's instruction to never let her get away; so he stood, walked to her, reached for her, and gently turned her to face him. Her tear-streamed face was lovely and serene. Her eyes focused on his. He had gone too far this first time courting, he knew he had, and he was hurting her like he promised Sam not to do. But these things were in his soul and had been growing there for months. It just happened, and John knew he had to finish it.

"I know you love your family, and you love the Lord Jesus, but couldn't you find it in your heart to love me too . . . as a woman loves a man?"

"I do, John! Oh, John, I do!" she cried. She rushed into his arms with an embrace as intense as their first meeting at Watauga Fort.

"You do?" he questioned with amazement, surprise, and delight.

"Yes, my dearest! My great love is you! It was always you and only you from the first day!" Her words were a flood of heart feelings she had always hoped to say and to him like a flowing fountain in the desert of sadness.

"My dear Bonny Kate, you could have told me," he said tenderly.

"I had to know you were ready to love again," she explained. "I needed to hear you declare your love for me, your Bonny Kate. I can't be anyone else."

"I will never want anyone else." He kissed her, and she responded passionately. She felt his love all for her, and dear Lord it was real.

Sometime later that afternoon, as they sorted through their thoughts, feelings, and plans for the future, John knelt before her. "Catharine Sherrill, my Bonny Kate, will you honor me by consenting to be my wife, sharing my life, my fortune, and my destiny for all our days?"

"Yes, John, with all my love, I will," she pledged. He rose, and they embraced for another long, passionate kiss.

The people of the frontier could gather as quickly for a wedding celebration as they could an Indian attack, maybe quicker. Within a week, they converged on Daisy Fields for a weeklong wedding celebration like none of them had ever seen. No man was more popular and universally admired than the groom; and no woman was better known for her beauty, domestic skills, athletic abilities, farm management, and strength of character than the bride. Sam and Mary Sherrill were mighty proud of the way their girl had turned out. Betsy Sevier gloried in the victory that she felt she had won in arranging everything and was worthy in every respect to be called her mother's daughter. Sarah Sevier would have been proud to know that Betsy and Bonny Kate had managed to keep the family together.

There was one dissenter to all the happiness, and he declared he would not attend any such wedding. James Sevier, John's sixteen-year-old second son, could not be persuaded to come to Daisy Fields. John went to Plum Grove the morning of the wedding and spent two hours trying to reason with him, but James was stubborn. Perhaps James was offended by the appearance of John marrying too soon after Sarah's death. Perhaps James was disgusted that his father would make such a fool of himself by marrying so young a wife; indeed, Bonny Kate was nearly halfway in age between James and his father. Or perhaps he had always harbored a secret crush on Bonny Kate himself. For whatever reason, he was not there and not a witness to the festivities.

A large gathering of wedding guests waited with the Sherrills and the Seviers, all dressed in their finest. John, in his military uniform, stood with Reverend

Doak, Sam Sherrill, Valentine Sevier Sr., Joseph Sevier, Adam Sherrill, and John Sevier Jr.

Reverend Doak was enthusiastic in his admiration for the bride. "She's a fine Christian lady, Mr. Sherrill. You and Mary have a right to be proud."

"Thank you, Reverend," Sam said. "I know there's none better at spinning and weaving, sewing, cooking, cleaning, child caring, footracing, hunting, riding, and horse breeding. But there's one family skill she ain't never tried. I sure hope her mama taught her something about it."

All the men laughed, thinking how funny it was that the bride's own father would bring that up. Having seen demonstrations of all her other skills, there wasn't a man in the community who hadn't wondered, privately, about Bonny Kate's skills at lovemaking. The only man who would ever know was too nervous a groom to join in the good-humored laughter.

Presently, Esther Doak waved to Sam from the porch, the signal to begin.

"It's time to begin," Reverend Doak said solemnly. He signaled the musicians to play, and the groomsmen took their places. Sam Sherrill and his son Adam walked up to the porch. Adam escorted his mother, Mary Sherrill, down to the front row. John's stepmother, Jemima, was honored in like manner. Then Mary Ann and Rebecca Sevier led the procession as flower girls. Next the bridesmaids, Mary Jane Sherrill and Betsy Sevier, walked down together. Bonny Kate stepped out of the house in a beautiful wedding dress. She took her father's arm and proceeded down to the yard where John and his companions awaited. John and Bonny Kate said their solemn wedding vows and their old lives passed away. They began new lives as one man and one woman, merged into one flesh. That new life together would be abundant and rich in private moments and useful in public service, filled with heroic deeds, personal sacrifices, joys, and sorrows for a great many years. Divine Providence had kept all promises and can always be trusted, throughout the ages.

Epilogue

John Sevier was a pioneer leader, and community builder of the revolutionary period when settlers first crossed the Appalachian Mountains in Virginia and North Carolina. In the United States Capitol building there is a statue of John Sevier representing the state of Tennessee. He served on the national level as a Congressman from Tennessee, as a six-term governor of his state and became a military hero at the Battle of King's Mountain. He was so well-beloved in his time that crowds would turn out and line the roads when people heard he was traveling through their communities. He was nicknamed "Chucky Jack" from his days of living on the Nolichucky River. He was a leader of men, charmingly polite to women, honest as the day is long, and his impulses of generosity towards those in need prevented him from ever becoming truly wealthy.

Visitors to Knoxville, Tennessee can view the monuments to John Sevier and his wife Catharine that stand over their graves on the lawn of the old county courthouse. There is also a monument to the memory of John's first wife Sarah, although her hidden grave is still undisturbed on some lovely hill miles and miles away. Five miles south of Knoxville visitors can tour the buildings and grounds of the Governor John Sevier Home called Marble Springs where some of his worldly goods are still on display.

John Sevier was like a beacon of light in the dark days of the American Revolution, and one of those attracted to his light was Catharine Sherrill. Their romance is quite remarkable if one is to believe her account of it. Did the rescue really happen? Was she really attracted to him from the very beginning? How did John's wife Sarah react and view the situation? What did Catharine do for a period of four years from 1776 until their marriage in 1780? Why didn't she marry at the age when young girls were expected to marry?

The novel *Bonny Kate* was inspired by a chance discovery of a footnote in a history book and developed over the course of seven years. The difficulty in separating history from legend, and fact from fiction was compounded in 1863 when fire destroyed treasure troves of source materials containing diaries, letters and other papers of the Sevier family collected at the home of Tennessee

353

historian Dr. J. G. M. Ramsey. This fictional account is therefore an elaborate hypothesis that incorporates all the history, all the legends, and all the facts that could be collected and treats them all as if they were true. Where there are inconsistencies between fact, legend, and history the author has supplied reasonable explanations that allow for all points of view to persist in their beliefs about what really happened. Many of the events related, and almost all of the conversations had to be fiction, but all support the true historical outcomes that the subjects of the story achieved. The author labored over many histories, traveled over the geography, studied topographic maps, and measured distances both in miles and time required to travel by wagon, foot, or horseback. He studied genealogies and family histories to capture anecdotal information and studied personality types to arrive at realistic motives and emotional context for the characters. As a result of the years of exhaustive research that went into the story the author believes he has done his characters more good than harm to awaken interest in these hardy pioneers. If the work offends anyone in the particulars, please accept the author's sincerest apology, and attribute the offense to ignorance rather than malice. It is a noble thing to appreciate our heroic forbears, and remember with gratitude, their sacrifices and their efforts to win American independence, and build modern commonwealths in the states of Middle America.

Whether you read this book to learn more about the people portrayed in it, or you just love a good historical romance, it is the wish of the author that every reader may be blessed by the same Divine Providence that guided and directed the life of Bonny Kate. The fact that she believed in Providence and often affirmed her faith and trust in it is absolutely true!

Smyrna, Tennessee   M. S.
April, 2007